LEAD ME ASTRAY

LEAD ME
ASTRAY
SONDI WARNER

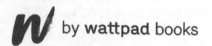 by wattpad books

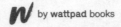 by wattpad books

An imprint of Wattpad WEBTOON Book Group

Published in Canada by Wattpad Books, a division of Wattpad Corp.
36 Wellington Street E., Toronto, ON M5E 1C7

www.wattpad.com

First Wattpad Books edition: March 2022

ISBN 978-1-77729-006-1(Trade Paper original)
ISBN 978-1-77729-007-8 (eBook edition)

Library and Archives Canada Cataloguing in Publication information
is available upon request.

Printed and bound in Canada

1 3 5 7 9 10 8 6 4 2

Cover design by Greg Tabor
Cover image by CoffeeAndMilk

To Evangelyn-Mari, Imi, and Liliana

CHAPTER ONE

—

Aurie

August 9 | Night

No way I was living my best life. Not with my baby sis along.

I side-eyed Haley, the caramel vixen leaning way over the balcony railing for a selfie. In the background, New Orleans traffic lit the night from thirty-five stories below. Shaking my head, I pulled my sister to safety.

"Hey! I was midslay." Haley's almond eyes glittered with amusement. People swore we looked alike, but I didn't see it.

"That Snapchat filter can't *really* make wings sprout from your skinny back," I said.

"This skinny back got us into a VIP party."

"I'm aware." I snorted. "Your cover girl looks will probably get us in trouble by the end of the night."

Trouble was Haley's calling card.

"Don't be such a killjoy," she said with a grin.

My calling card was being a killjoy, also known as being responsible. As much as I yearned for Big Easy excitement, if Mom had known that

I, the college honors student, had allowed the high schooler to crash this upscale shindig, she would have gone apeshit.

"All right, it's almost midnight. Time to go," I said.

"I told you we could get in without being on the guest list. *You* lost the bet."

"Because *you* flashed the doorman. I'm not even sure he spoke English. I could kill you!"

"You owe me," Haley said smugly. She was having a blast.

"Okay, I might've been wrong about the guest list, but look in there. Any of that worth the trouble we'll be in if we get caught?" I waved at the suite beyond the sliding doors. The theme of the décor was luxury and decadence. Drugs everywhere. Sex acts all out in the . . . "On second thought, don't look. Just picture cops raiding the place."

"Girl, you know as well as I do the cops won't raid this party."

Haley was right. Half the guests struck me as celeb types, which meant some of them were probably her followers. She was famous on the 'Gram. This Bougie Meets Trap party was exactly Haley's scene. I was the one hiding outside on the balcony.

Here was a corner of quiet sanity. A wicker sectional with comfy cerulean pillows offered seating. Lush lime-green ferns danced in a late summer breeze. Hidden speakers piped music out to us. Through the sliding patio doors, the four-star hotel room had a rich, dark aesthetic. Like any secret could be kept within its walls.

But I reluctantly followed my sister back inside. We passed three people lounging on an emerald davenport. They clearly manifested fashion as a way of life, while my socks barely matched each other. One of them blinked at me—opaque black contacts covered their entire exposed eyeball—and I shuddered.

"Well, maybe if I weren't babysitting," I said over the music, "I could enjoy the smell of—what is that, vintage malt liquor and designer weed? I prefer being online. It's safer."

"*Safe?* Bruh, if living life to the fullest isn't worth dying for, then what even *is?*"

"Bad, bad philosophy, sis." I laughed. Shrugging, she reached for a drink. I blocked her. We were near the door. "Oh c'mon, Haley. Don't make me drag you out of here."

"Fine. We can go, but like I said . . ." She tipped her chin at someone behind me. "You owe me."

Glancing over my shoulder, I saw a good-looking gentleman ogling us. Golden-brown hair. A face made for movies. I watched the bartender pour him two shots. When he caught me staring, he peeled himself from the bar and sauntered over with the drinks. I shook my head with a disbelieving chuckle.

"Keep it moving. She's only seventeen," I said.

"I wasn't looking at her." He had a resonant Yat accent, very Brooklyn meets Deep South.

Haley nudged me. "He was looking at you," she whispered. "Boom. Enjoy this, my sexually repressed one." I hardly noticed her slipping away. The hot interloper handed me a shot, and I followed the glide of his tongue across his lips.

"I was standing over there, thinking you and I should raise a glass."

"To what, sir, pray tell?" I asked sarcastically.

"To how you successfully crashed my exclusive event."

"Wait. *Your* event?" I choked.

"Mm-hmm, and you probably shouldn't call me sir unless you're asking for a good time."

His grin was seductive. I stammered an apology, but he waved it off and tapped his glass to mine, even as I tried to turn it down.

"My sister and I were just—dammit, where did she go?"

"She's fine. She's under my protection."

Frowning, I followed Haley with my eyes. She was my responsibility, not his. He directed my gaze to three private security types shadowing my little sister. When a bubbly beverage materialized in her hand, our handsome host gestured, and one of his guys confiscated the champagne and replaced it with soda. That made me feel better.

Revelers in pursuit of various kinds of debauchery filed around the stranger and me. I stared longingly at the exit, but I could play nice. *Give this guy two or three more minutes.*

"Cheers?" he said, as if reading the capitulation on my face.

I downed my shot. Whatever was in the glass mellowed me immediately. I wasn't sure I liked that, but I tossed my wavy hair over my shoulder and gave him a winsome smile to get this over with.

"So, you must be some kind of big deal," I probed.

He shrugged modestly. "My name gets around. Places where I don't usually see girls like you. Tell me, what's the girl of my dreams doing here, like a lost sheep amongst wolves?"

I snorted a laugh. "Calling me the girl of your dreams—issa no."

"No?" He lifted a delicate eyebrow.

"Nope. Call me Aurie."

"You like the word *no*, don't you, Aurie?"

My smile froze. "Yeah, sometimes. It's a handy word."

His fingers found my wrist and lingered over my fluttering pulse. I scanned the room again for Haley. His grip tightened almost imperceptibly as his nostrils flared. There she was, talking to her agent.

"I told you, she's safe," he said. Why did his voice both soothe and unnerve me?

It was surprising to see Haley's straitlaced modeling rep, Patricia Gramercy, at a party like this. She probably had Mom on speed dial, too, which meant there would be hell to pay for our bumping into her here. Still, better the devil I knew than the one I didn't. I pulled away from the sweet talker.

"I hate to drink and run, but it looks like my ride is here."

"Your ride? Are you sure?" he asked.

I hurried to the exit as I dug out my phone and texted Haley that I would meet them downstairs. I glanced behind me to see the charming host watching, but not following me. The world tilted once I hit the hotel corridor, and I stumbled into the first elevator I found. Vertigo. I was such a lightweight when it came to hard liquor.

As the elevator descended, I read Haley's text: *Meet who dwnstrs? What r u talkn abt?*

My brow furrowed from a sudden headache. What was *she* talking about? I dialed her. "You and Pat," I said. "I saw you talking to her. Tell her I'll explain everything to Mom."

". . . Been in the bathroom, Aurie. My agent isn't . . ." The signal was patchy. I jerked my head to clear the brain fog, and Haley's voice came in clearer. "Come back up. Back upstairs." The call dropped.

The elevator dinged. Ground floor. Lobby. Unsteady feet. Some of the people . . . looked weird. Double take. Blurry. I kept moving. Through the revolving door, into the night, running from . . . had that been Haley's voice? That mesmerizing command. Made me want to . . . *Come back upstairs.*

Get away from this place.

A concerned face swam in and out of focus, and a lady clasped my shoulders. "You okay, sweetie? Had too much to drink?" It was New Orleans. Everybody always had . . .

"No," I slurred. "I think I've been . . . drugged . . ."

"Jesus. Okay, hun. Gonna get my truck, just—"

"Help me," I pleaded. My vision faded on the woman jogging to a vehicle idling near the hotel entrance. Everything went black. I never saw what hit me.

CHAPTER TWO
—
Mys

August 10 | One a.m.

"I don't even think they *tried* to stop!" The bystander sounded horrified.

A crowd of ten to fifteen people began gathering, streaming out of the hotel doors and from the surrounding parking lot. No Supernaturals in the mix. Just humans and the dead girl. As I watched, she transitioned from translucent to opaque. Within moments, she appeared as real as anyone else.

I tightened my lips around a vape pen and studied the Light behind her. It was fading fast, but Dead Girl wouldn't go near it. She was too hung up on the sight of her own crumpled body. Smallish, curvy. *Bishōjo*. Very beautiful. She would be perfection in a coffin. Poor thing.

At any rate, the hit-and-run wasn't my problem. Mine was not having a john for the night. Bummer, since I had taken off early from the burlesque club to go out. I glanced at the date cancellation on my phone and blew a cloud of vapor in the direction of the hotel. Probably too much traffic for him. Time to bounce.

As I turned to go, Dead Girl locked eyes with me. Shit, shit.

"Is this real?" she asked.

Ignore her. Act natural. Blend in. I tried, but she trailed me. Away from the goddamn Light.

"You can see me, right?"

"Go back, Dead Girl," I mumbled.

"I just walked through a car."

"You've gotta go before the Light fades completely."

She followed me another block through the French Quarter. At one corner, a garishly dressed man in a top hat directed vacationers lining up for ghost tours. I plugged in earpods and ignored being literally haunted. She walked beside me, her feet touching the ground, but not making a hint of noise.

I would stroll aimlessly all night rather than lead the Dead Girl to my place. I had rules about strays of any sort: no feeding them, no bringing them home. My need to fix things tended to remind me that no good deed could go unpunished. Anyway, humanity was beyond redemption. I couldn't help her.

"I . . . I'm dead?" She was on the verge of hysteria. "I don't believe this. I always, always played it safe. There's no way I should be dead at nineteen."

"Oof. That's tragic. My condolences."

"You honestly think I care for sarcasm right now?!"

Grimacing, I half turned. "I'm sorry to sound callous, but yes, you're dead. Crying won't change it. Just catch that Light before it disappears, or you'll be stuck here in Overlay City. Trust me, you'd rather try Heaven."

I spread my arms to indicate our surroundings for emphasis. We had walked off the beaten path, where it wouldn't have been unusual to find monsters or magic in this city. A shimmer of the paranormal glinted wherever the lights of the streetlamps touched. She didn't want to know what was in the shadows.

A nearby drunk hooted, "I want to try Heaven, girlfriend! I want whatever you're on."

I sucked my teeth. To him, it must have looked like I was talking to thin air.

"What's Overlay City?" Dead Girl asked, sniffling up her overflow of emotions.

"A network of ley lines crisscrossing New Orleans where Supernaturals like you can interact with the real world, assuming you haven't missed your ticket out." I squinted at the scene a block back. Ambulance and cop cars, vampires drawn by the scent of blood. Naturally, the Light was gone. "Aaand you've missed your ticket out. Welp, you're stuck here, Dead Girl. Sorry," I muttered.

Drunk Guy tugged my dress. "Hey, what are you?" he asked. I recoiled. I was used to the question, being the Asian Mystery I am, but his breath smelled like the ass end of Bourbon Street. He leered at my face and body. I lowered my head, letting my medium-length black hair hide my expression.

"You're a medium, aren't you?" Dead Girl said, trying to piece things together. "I . . . I must have unfinished business! That's why you're helping me."

"Whoa! Let's dispel that myth. I never said I was helping you, and not all ghosts have unfinished business. Some just don't know when to let go."

"Girl or boy?" Drunk Guy persisted, until his woozy attention was stolen by a commotion in the street.

Two biker gangs were squaring off to fight. To humans, they would appear normal, but I could tell these were Supernaturals. A bruiser with a faint sheen of scales like a trick of the light on his massive biceps viciously shoved a leather-clad menace. That was my cue to leave.

Before I dashed, I glanced at the ghost. She would probably freak once she saw that the brawlers were bona fide fire-and-brimstone demons and dragons. Dead Girl was no longer human, meaning she would recognize the bikers for what they were.

Panic was already radiating off her in waves. Emotions blossomed in my consciousness like blots of watercolor spreading on a page: hers, Drunk Guy's, the bikers'. I squeezed the bridge of my nose, wondering if I could abandon this girl without feeling colossal guilt later.

I was a loner. It kept my Empathy from getting the best of me. On the other hand, I knew what it was like to be lost, hopeless, and afraid in Overlay City. With the shoe on the other foot, I had been "rescued" by a pimp. This was no place for a naïve teenager.

I could take her with me. At least for tonight. Tomorrow, once she came to terms with her untimely demise, she would find her way home. But that was it. The extent of my generosity.

"Come with me, Dead Girl. It's not safe for us out here. FYI, I can't talk to you in front of other people, especially sober people. Only Supers can see you now."

"Supers, as in Supernaturals?" she guessed.

"Exacto. Supernaturals aren't human."

"What about people like you? Mediums, psychics, people who see things others can't?"

I ignored her question and jogged ahead, not in the mood for an interview. She fell in step beside me. She seemed to know the back alleys and side streets. She had to be a local, which made me like her a bit more, curse my bleeding heart.

A labyrinthine series of dark turns later, we strode through a wrought-iron gate to a square dominated by a cathedral. The architectural monstrosity pierced the night sky with three spires, a holy trinity of ugly.

We followed a paved courtyard that curved around the gray brick building. Behind evergreen shrubs drenched in shadows was a hidden door. I said over my shoulder, "You can stay with me tonight, but be ready to find your unfinished business without me tomorrow, all right, Dead—"

"Please don't call me that."

The catch in her voice made me stop and turn. Passing headlights from a car illuminated my face, and she got her first good look at me. I could tell by the way her eyes widened. Dropping my gaze, I bit my bottom lip and waited an eternity for her to stop staring.

"It's Aurie," she said softly. "My name is Aurie. What about you?"

"People call me Mys." I reached out to shake her hand, then realized it would go right through mine. Her attention lingered on the butterfly tattoos on my wrists. Blue monarchs with bodies covered in scars. I hid my arms again.

"Nice to meet you, Mys," she said.

Color suffused my cheeks. I knew what usually came after people saw me in the light. "You can ask," I allowed.

She shifted her weight nervously. "Genderqueer, right?"

Something like that. I nodded. We were silent a beat until she flashed a smile. Then I breathed easier. No judgment. Good. I waved at the door to my basement apartment.

"You live in the church?" she asked in surprise.

Tapping the red brick with the heel of my stiletto, I said, "Hallowed ground. For protection."

"I get the sense you're not talking about protection from urban crime."

"I need to explain some things about Overlay City," I replied, thinking of what lurked in the night. "Let's get inside first."

"I don't know. Maybe I should try to find my way home," Aurie said with sudden jitters.

I huffed in annoyance. "Wander the city if you want, but the thing is, being dead won't protect you here."

CHAPTER THREE
—
Zyr

August 10 | Four a.m.

Who did this to Aurelia Edison? I stared up at the black new moon of another lunatic night, pondering the case. Police tape cordoned off the gruesome stain in front of the Century Luxe Hotel. The Crime Scene Unit was making a clean sweep. Yellow evidence markers followed a scattered trail of vehicle pieces.

My partner and I were interviewing witnesses, but half the spectators had found better things to do. The crime scene was already hours old. The place crawled with reporters. I dodged a videographer and made my way to Detective Tegan Stoney.

The smells of coffee and mouthwash clinging to her bespoke the predawn hour. It was too-early o'clock Saturday morning. I had a keener nose than most, so I picked up on the good time she'd been having before she'd come here. *Not my business.* We both had been called in for this.

"Don't all the cameras make you feel like we're filming *Law & Order*?" I asked.

"Complete with our own sexy leading man," she said.

"Love your sense of humor."

"I was talking about Mayfield." Tegan grinned as she pointed at the barrel-chested former marine crossing the hotel drive toward us. Captain Mayfield's salt-and-pepper buzz cut was as high and as tight as his personality.

"What have we got so far?" the middle-aged Black man called out.

"Hit-and-run," I said. "Nothing that warrants this level of hoopla, normally."

When he reached us, the captain confided quietly, "Yeah, NOPD wants this case closed fast. The victim is the daughter of Emily Leigh Edison of Metairie, better known as—"

"Nannette Baudelaire, Academy Award–winning director of two Best Pictures," said Tegan. She smiled at my surprised demeanor. "And her new movie, *Gracious Fury*, is projected to make that three. It opens next month."

"Well, somebody got cozy with Google when Alexa wasn't looking," I said.

"Actually, I'm a fan of Mrs. Edison's films."

Mayfield asked, "Did you know she summers in New Orleans?"

"Not until now," Tegan admitted. "According to her spokesperson, who I was on the phone with a moment ago, the daughters were raised here, but few people were aware of their link to the director. Mrs. Edison kept her children out of the spotlight."

"All great intel, but I doubt the famous mom was behind the wheel," I quipped.

Mayfield chuckled dryly. "You want to stake your career on jokes, Ravani?"

"C'mon, the perp is an out-of-towner sleeping off a rough night of Hand Grenades somewhere. He'll turn himself in when he sees the body damage to his rental. You could've put anybody on this."

"You're lucky to get anything after that crap you pulled a few months ago. Thanks to your wacky press conference with the psychic, the media thinks you're a nutjob. Take this easy A and solve this thing. Get your reputation back," he said.

I rolled my shoulder free from his condescending back rub. "Get help with one missing person's case, and suddenly you're a nutjob," I said as he left.

"He's fucking with you. You know that." Tegan didn't bother hiding her amusement.

"Yeah, well, I used to get more respect."

The thing with the psychic had pushed the envelope, but I needed an explanation for the leads I followed. Nobody—not even my longtime partner—knew of my network of Supernatural informants. Call it a perk of working for the Council of Overlay Affairs. Whenever unusual crimes spilled into the real world, it was my job to make justice look natural.

Unfortunately, cleaning up paranormal activity was beginning to affect my credibility. I wondered if, as Mayfield implied, I should be grateful for a simple hit-and-run. Nothing out of the ordinary about this one.

I tipped my head toward a surveillance camera at the corner of the hotel. "Whoever did this was kind enough to do it on camera. All I need is a license plate. Let's binge-watch some CCTV."

"Let's go," Tegan replied.

An hour later, we were in the manager's office with the run of the system. There was footage of the victim and her sister taking an elevator, flashing a doorman, and getting into a party on the top floor. But once inside, there was no record. I watched the uptight hotel manager. She smiled.

"Our VIP guests prefer not to be scrutinized, you understand."

"I want the name of whoever booked the floor," I said.

"You'll need a warrant." She smiled more tightly.

I gritted my teeth. Tegan drew my attention to the victim stumbling back into the elevator on screen. "She's drunk," said my partner.

"How much alcohol did they have?"

"Haley Edison blew a breathalyzer result of . . ." Tegan paused and consulted her notes, "less than 0.01, but she couldn't say how much the victim drank. They got separated at the party. CSU will get back to me with the tox report as soon as they have it."

My focus drifted over the girl onscreen. She swept back loose curls and pushed a phone to her ear, and the vision of her gorgeous face stalled me. God, I must need to get laid if I was drooling over a hit-and-run victim. I stared at her plush mouth.

"Who's Pat?" I asked. Tegan skewed her brows. The audio was full of noise, and she couldn't hear what the victim said. "I read her lips," I explained.

"There was a brief call around 11:45 about modeling agent Patricia Gramercy. The sister says the call was spotty, dropped right after she answered."

Nodding, I watched the victim exit the elevator on wobbly legs and trip through the hotel lobby. I zoomed in as a woman stopped her outside the building, but tropical landscaping obscured the view.

Tegan started to say something. I held up a finger and peered intently at the monitor, barely making out the victim saying she thought she had been drugged. Interesting. Toxicology would show what, if anything, was in her system. Now, who would drug her, and why? I squared my jaw, mulling it over.

"What is it?" my partner asked.

"That woman's going for help."

"How do you know? You can't even see her face."

"Call it a hunch. A young, drunk girl stumbling around a four-star hotel? Someone would go for help."

The young woman wandered around the sidewalk in a disoriented state for a few more moments before she stepped into the street. A second later, the SUV hit her with brutal force. Just like that. In a blink. I'd had a feeling it was coming, but it had still been tough to watch.

The stoic hotelier made the sign of the cross, and Tegan stepped away from the desk. I gave her a minute, but forced myself to watch, rewind, watch again. I heard it loud and clear with each replay: a truck idling out of camera range. A clue that the accident hadn't been an accident.

Tegan composed herself. "See a license plate number?"

I shook my head. So, what did we have? A VIP party. A drugged girl. An SUV with illegal tinted windows, no plates. Deliberate hit-and-run. It all added up to one thing: someone had wanted Aurelia Edison dead.

Tegan blew out an exasperated breath. "Okay, we need to find out about famous Mama Edison's enemies."

"I want to know what happened in the penthouse." I was about to say more, but the surveillance video stopped me. A feeling like static crackled along my skin as the image onscreen wavered, and the thin veil separating this world from the next faded before my eyes.

I cocked my head in disbelief as an angel in full wing exited the hotel. Aurie got up. *Is this real?* she asked. The divine entity disappeared into the night, but my jaw dropped as our victim followed someone else out of frame. Suddenly, the crime scene was filled with vampires who were far too interested in the body. I recognized their mien. All well heeled with a swagger of entitlement.

"What in the holy hell?" I whispered, confused.

Tegan gave me a pointed stare, but I couldn't explain. She couldn't see what I saw. "Got another wild hunch?" she asked.

"Let's just say this won't be an ordinary case."

"It never is with you." She laughed.

No, I thought, *it never is*.

CHAPTER FOUR

—
Aurie

August 10 | Two a.m.

I considered discounting all the Supernatural stuff. Angels, demons, vampires? It was too much to accept—especially the part about me being a ghost—but whether I wanted to or not, death was making me a believer.

When I tried opening the ornate hand-carved door, my hand went through it. Would I go through everything I touched?

Entertained, Mys reached around me and turned the latch. I realized as soon as I entered the building that there was something off about the basement studio. For one, New Orleans was below sea level, making a subterranean unit impossible. And yet, the studio was clearly beneath the cathedral, even though there were high windows in the apartment that weren't visible from outside. Magic?

I took in the view with interest. A sleek, modern kitchenette lined the side wall to my left, separated from the rest of the room by a marble island. Only one barstool. Across from the kitchen, there was a comfy leather couch before a bookshelf and a mounted TV. Along the far wall was a full-sized metal bed frame dressed in a white duvet.

It was a fascinating space that revealed a lot about my new friend here. The palette was neutral and the décor minimalist. Somewhat stark, but Zen.

"Make yourself at home," said Mys.

"Easier said than done."

Mys guided me to the couch. "You can't impact the real world—like opening doors or moving objects—but sitting on the couch won't change anything. You can do that without a problem, *Yōkai*."

"In other words, if it shouldn't be moving on its own, I can't move it. Like . . . Newton's second law, but for ghosts?" Mys nodded. "Got it. What's a yoke—"

"Yōkai? It's Japanese for *pesky spirit*."

"Wow. Thanks." I pouted.

Mys flashed a devilish grin that, surprisingly, stirred the butterflies in my tummy. "The *kanji*, or characters, making up the word actually express something like *beguiling* and *ghost*. I hope you don't mind. I tend to give pet names."

"Weird flex, but okay. I like my Japanese pet name."

"Mm-hmm. It also preempts the question of where I'm from. The answer is New Orleans, by the way." Another grin. I smiled back shyly as I sank onto the leather couch.

As the psychic medium pattered around the kitchenette, my gaze wandered over them: tall, thin, dark-haired, dressed in a black lace tunic. Alluring, or whatever.

Mys kept up the small talk in a husky voice that was pleasant background noise. However, my thoughts turned inward and on how to get home. I tried to backtrack from my death, but my mind went blank when I tried to pin down any details. Hadn't I been out with someone? Focusing seemed impossible as my attention drifted again . . .

To the mysterious psychic whose presence was making me feel alive-ish. They brought over coffee. I reached for the mug. We both shied away as it dawned on me: I didn't need to eat or drink anymore, because alive-ish was still very dead.

"You're sleeping the eternal rest, Aurie. Try to adjust sooner rather than later," Mys chided, settling on the couch beside me. "You won't be a ghost forever."

"What do you mean? What else is there?"

"The longer you're here, the more you'll resemble raw energy expelled without rhyme or reason. Like, uh, a poltergeist."

I slumped at the idea that my situation could get worse. "Fan-fucking-tastic. How long do I have?"

"Mm? Time passes weirdly for the dead, since you're untethered," Mys said blithely. "I suggest you get your final good-byes and last hurrahs out of the way. Finish your unfinished business ASAP."

"Right. So, should I just know what my unfinished business is? 'Cause I don't."

My companion drummed their fingers on the armrest of the couch and studied me. "What was your biggest regret in life?"

"Nothing, as far as I can remember." Peering skyward, I still couldn't see my murky past. I met the psychic's skeptical gaze with a lifted eyebrow.

"So, there's nothing you'd go back and change?" Mys asked.

"Nope. I pretty much lived a regrets-free life."

An exaggerated blink. "That's very telling, Aurie. It sounds boring as fuck."

"Hey! If I had known I would die young, I might've taken more chances!"

"Okay, then you regret not living your life to the fullest," said Mx. Glib with a shrug.

"Are you telling me that my unfinished business is to live a little? How am I supposed to do that now that I'm *D-E-D*?" I goofed.

"It's your Afterlife. You work out the specifics, Yōkai. Now"— uncrossing long, sexy legs, Mys rose from the couch—"I'm glad we could wrap up this brainstorming sesh without caffeine, because honestly, I need sleep. Thank me later."

The lovely medium dumped their mug of coffee in the kitchen sink and headed to the shower. I glared at the bathroom door until I had to concede. It made no sense to waste coffee, but other than that, they were right.

I was the only one who could figure out my unfulfilled destiny.

But as I tried recalling my life, I again got only a hazy feeling. Straining to picture my family and friends, I came up short, and a rising panic threatened. This couldn't be normal, could it? It *could* be. I had never been a disembodied soul before—though it did feel a bit like a bad hangover. Maybe memory lapses were par for the course.

I thought about social media. People put everything online. Maybe I had too. Spotting a laptop on the nightstand, I rushed over to search my name, but my hands went straight through the device.

"Oh come on!" I whined.

After several fails, I let out an overdramatic groan and pitched face-first onto the bed. It occurred to me Aurie Edison didn't have tantrums. She was too mature, too dignified, too disciplined . . . and boring as fuck. Deadass.

Mys, the psychic, was semiright. I didn't simply need to live a little. I needed to live a *lot*, and . . . I pressed my face to the blanket and inhaled. Why did the bed smell like the very breath of *gawd*? Forgetting my meltdown for a second, I drank in the scent. What was that? Sex Voodoo Potion No. 69?

"Yes," I exhaled in rapture.

"Should I give you a minute?"

I bolted upright. "Hi!" Fierce heat rushed to my face.

Mys wore a bemused expression and a partially open kimono. The air was thick with assumptions and unasked questions. And steam. From the bathroom, definitely not from the heat wave of my lusty imagination. I scurried to the couch, mortified.

"I hope I'm not interrupting." Mys raised an eyebrow.

"No. I was, um . . . your cologne, er, perfume, it's . . ."

"It's from a place down on Royal Street. Like it?" They spritzed an atomizer, and the room flooded with one part of that heavenly scent. The other part, I realized, was a magical mix of pheromones and chemistry. It was pure Mys.

I held in a moan, and Mys gave me a knowing smile. "I might be able to help with what ails you."

"H-help?" I stammered.

They disappeared behind a decorative silk dressing screen by the bathroom door. "Considering your stay in Overlay City won't last forever and you need help living to the fullest tonight, I'm feeling generous. I might not even charge," they called out.

I snorted at the joke. "Thanks, but I bet you say that to all the girls."

Mys peeked around the screen with a grin. "Nope. My clients are ninety-nine percent male."

"Oh!" Wait. I had met this person outside a ritzy hotel, dressed to the nines, looking for all the world like—

"I'm a high-paid *escort*, and don't pretend outrage. It's a living." They blew vapor in my direction, emerging fully dressed for bed.

I wasn't outraged. Okay, maybe minorly shook by the idea of spending the night with a genderqueer New Orleans sex worker. Somehow, I knew the old Killjoy Me would have said, "Over my dead body."

But I was dead. I gave up trying not to stare. No denying Mys was attractive. The radiant skin, the ever-present sardonic smile. Their brand of sex appeal flipped off conventions. How far could I take things in this mystical new world?

"Actually, there is something you can do for me," I murmured.

CHAPTER FIVE
—
Mys

August 10 | Morning

I had a routine, but it was out the window by the next morning. A schedule didn't stand a chance against the disruption sitting in my favorite chair. Dressed in one of my shirts and smelling like marked territory, Aurie seemed to belong at my place.

I blinked rapidly. No, she didn't belong, and she couldn't stay.

Sitting up, I winced from another kink-free night. (Not that I ever had sex, even as an escort, but that was another story.) Aurie had asked for my laptop, and when she saw me stirring, she pointed at the screen.

"Good, you're awake. Judging by Instagram, I was out with my sister last night."

"Instagram?" I padded to the bathroom.

"I was, um, having trouble remembering."

She caught me standing at the toilet and quickly glanced away. I sensed her curiosity, just as I had sensed her feelings about my cologne. I nudged the door shut, but it stayed partially ajar.

"Is that usual?" I yawned.

"It's not *my* usual. I can't recall anything before I met you."

Fuck. Yay me. I stepped from the bathroom and casually asked, "So, have you figured out where you want me to drop you off?" *Fingers crossed.*

"Yeah, my family's address was the first thing that popped up when I searched my name."

"Yay!" I pumped a fist.

Aurie exhaled. "I'm kidding, asshole. I can't search or anything. I've just been staring at the same split screen you left up for me with my Instagram and Facebook accounts."

"Oh . . ." I considered how much work I was missing out on while I let her use my laptop. I weighed that against how long I wanted my apartment to be haunted. Clapping my hands together, I hunkered down next to her and took the computer. "All right, how can I help you to get out of here?"

"Reverse image search this photo of my sister and me?"

We bonded the rest of the morning as we scoured the internet for personal details that nobody with a fraction of sense should ever post publicly. It was sometime around noon when a knock at the door interrupted us.

"Are you expecting company?" Aurie bit the corner of her lip.

Shushing her, I dug a gun from the sofa and crept over to see who was there. No, I wasn't expecting company. No one knew where I lived. No one should've been able to *find* where I lived, thanks to a powerful spell on the door as ancient as the ground upon which the cathedral stood.

With my Empathy, I felt around and sensed no malice on the other side.

"State your name and purpose," I called out.

"Detective Zyr Ravani. I'm here about a crime you may have witnessed last night."

"I think you've got the wrong place, Detective. This is church storage."

"Hmph . . . I heard the victim ask if you were expecting company."

I gaped at Aurie. "You seem to attract a lot of this," I complained.

"A lot of what? What are you talking about?"

Ignoring her, I opened the door. "Show me your badge."

Detective Ravani wordlessly took out his identification. I sensed my weapon was useless against him. Good thing he wasn't trouble. He was average height, built like his workout of choice was hard labor, and he filled my apartment with ego and wildness when he came in. Against the backdrop of Aurie's cool restraint, his presence blazed.

"He's investigating my case? Ask him about my sister," Aurie insisted.

I stepped aside. "Ask him yourself."

Detective Zyr gave her a slow appraisal that left no question of her visibility to him. Floored, the ghost retreated a step. I knew she felt it too. He wasn't human. After a moment's hesitation, she tried to shake the hand he offered. When her fingers slipped through his, the chemistry was indisputable.

"You can see me?" she asked, pulling her hand back.

"Yes, I can." Detective Zyr breathed with awe. "And I'm staring. My apologies. It's just that you look so . . . alive."

Was he flirting with her? I thumped a mug on the countertop with more force than intended. "Coffee, anyone?" I asked, faking a smile.

"Yes, thank you, ma'am," said the detective. I didn't bother correcting him. I made the coffee and left them talking about Aurie's murder while I showered.

Afterward, I studied the naked boy-girl in the mirror and considered my dilemma. I couldn't do cam work with a law enforcement officer in my apartment. Could I kick him out? Kick *them* out? Would that hurt the investigation? I didn't want to jeopardize Aurie's chance of getting justice.

Brooding, I turned from my reflection. I had to be at Beaucoup de Chair in a few hours. I didn't want to leave her alone with Detective Zyr, although I wasn't sure if I felt protective or possessive of the ghost. Regardless, she had already promised to be gone by the time I returned from my shift.

I vacated the bathroom, deciding to leave early for work while the two of them were wrapping up in my living room. The detective stopped me on my way out the door. "Did you see anything?" he asked.

"Vampires going in and out. Big party. I was there to meet a client, but I guess you could say things got kind of dead after—" I whistled and cut a hand across my throat.

"I meant, did you see the person who did this?"

"Oh. Nope." I pivoted to leave . . .

And saw that Aurie had been crying. *Damn it.* I felt like such a jerk for doing the hand gesture. I grabbed my laptop and hustled out the door.

•••

Blending in with pedestrians, I strolled past a few faeries, some shifters, a couple of chimeras. Mostly humans. Everybody *looked* human to the ordinary eye. But Supers recognized Supers, even if they hid their type.

Empathy gave me an advantage. I could sense the type of every creature attracted here by Overlay City's ley lines. Or any other place where symbiotic paranormal worlds overlapped. There were plenty of Ley-Overs. There weren't many beings like me out there, though.

I avoided my usual Supernatural hangouts and slipped into a normal human café to finally get some coffee. The venue was empty except for a long-haired barista pretentiously reading Faulkner behind the register. I was grateful for the solitude, fewer emotions pestering me.

I finished off an Americano, set up my laptop in a secluded corner, and got to work arranging a date for later.

As an escort and cam queer, I was paid handsomely by clients, and I catered to almost any kink—from feet to furries to fisting. I aimed to please. The caveat? Nothing below the belt could be done to *me*. It was a quirky requirement, but I had regulars. They liked my *je ne sais quoi*.

I had learned long ago that people would pay for fulfillment. Not to be confused with love. Of course not. But often something more fulfilling than sex.

Thus, my thoughts turned to Aurie as I chatted with someone called @Ram4Ram. Necrophilia was not on my list of services, my cheeky offer the night before aside. I had merely sensed that Dead Girl needed to feel like she wasn't alone. We had that in common.

My phone lit up, giving me a reason to ignore the blue funk threatening to descend. My best friend, Kittie Cad.

"Where are you?" I answered, smiling.

"I'm finally out and about," she replied. "A certain politician kept me tied up all night. I see your check-in. Care for company?"

"You're in the area?"

"Ditching my Uber driver now."

A minute later, my best friend strolled into the café as if she owned the place. Wavy bottle-blond hair framed an impeccably made-up matte brown face with highlighted cheeks, vibrant lipstick, and MUA-to-die-for eyes.

"You show no evidence of having missed your beauty sleep. Looking all glowy and stuff," I commented as we hugged.

"Because I lavish my skin with great care, darling!" Kittie Cad whipped off oversized glasses and signaled to the barista to come take her order (not exactly how coffee shops work, and yet he obliged). She peered closely at me upon sitting down. "What is it? Did somebody break your heart? We can roll his ass."

I choked on the last of my Americano, laughing. "I don't have a heart to break, Ms. Cad. I'm bummed about this hit-and-run I witnessed last night in front of Century Luxe. Did you hear about it?"

"I saw it on the news. You were there? Are you okay?"

I scoffed. "It's not like I expected anything better of humanity."

"Don't be like that, darling. You used to believe we could save the world." She reached across the table to pat my hand.

"Kittie, the world's not worth saving." I grinned.

"The minute you fall in love, you'll see things differently."

"Oh?" I raised an eyebrow. "Are you telling me the infamous Ms. Cad has fallen in love and therefore sees the world differently? Who is it, the politician?"

Kittie giggled, accepting a quad espresso macchiato from the barista. "All I'm saying is connecting with others changes how you see the world. Look, I get it, boo boo. I understand why you keep your distance from people, given the stuff with your parents—"

"We don't talk about that, Ms. Cad. And how did this become about the relationships in *my* life?" I tried to keep a light tone.

But Kittie Cad was point-blank. "There aren't any. I don't like how isolated you've become."

"Cut it out. I see people every day. Sometimes several times a day."

"You know what I mean, Mitsuyo. Even if you don't believe in therapy and meds, you need a good support system. You need more friends than the one and only Ms. Cad."

"Why? It's been me and you since back when I only wore dresses and you only wore pants!" My grin dropped to a pout when she smacked my hand away from her coffee.

She signaled the barista again and ordered me another Americano that I could easily have paid for myself. She used a Platinum Card emblazoned with the name Terrance—the last name hidden beneath her manicured thumbnail—with the authority of someone who had permission. The relationship had to be more than casual.

"Thanks!" the clueless barista gushed when my bestie scribbled her name and phone number on the receipt for him. He skipped off, thinking he had hit the novelty jackpot.

"See?" Kittie suggested to me. "It's easy to meet decent people. For my sake, stop complaining about the human condition and put yourself out there. Volunteer or something. Make yourself less of a cynic and make friends in the process. I double dare you."

Kittie knew I couldn't resist a dare. I dipped my head, amused and slightly annoyed at her for being the "mom friend." My good deed for the whole year could be helping Aurie complete her unfinished business. I visualized the ghost as she had been last night, with her face planted in my duvet, swooning.

Surprisingly, I had been comfortable with her, even though her presence had led to that werewolf showing up. That very hot werewolf. I considered keeping the yōkai tucked at home like a secret, since she didn't know where she belonged anyway. I was good at keeping secrets.

All my kind were.

CHAPTER SIX
—
Zyr

August 10 | Late Afternoon

The door to the flat was shielded by some sort of enchantment. My awareness skipped past it each time I tried to inspect it more closely. No one searching for it would find it. If I hadn't tracked the person Aurie had left the hotel with, I wouldn't have found it either.

The woman who opened at my knock was a Supernatural. I didn't bother guessing which type. My gaze went straight to Aurie Edison. Long, curly hair. A face that was mostly gorgeous eyes and plush lips. The crown of her head barely reached my chin; she was petite but shapely. I tried not to be distracted by the fact that she wore no more than an oversized T-shirt, exposing toned, flawless legs.

Something crashed in the kitchen.

"Coffee, anyone?" asked the woman in blue pajamas.

"Yes, thank you, ma'am." I remembered my manners. Not to mention the reason I was here. I led Aurie to the couch. "What can you tell me about last night, Ms. Edison?" I asked, taking notes.

"Please, call me Aurie. I've had memory problems since it happened.

All I can recall is that I was out with my sister. Do you know where she is?"

"Your sister Haley is with your family. We've spoken with her, but I'd like to try filling in the blanks from your perspective. Think a surveillance clip might jog things?" I pressed Play on a video on my phone, and Aurie leaned in to see.

"This is surreal," she said. "I never imagined I'd be helping a Supernatural investigator solve my murder."

"Murder? I'd rather you focus on what you remember, and we'll see where the evidence takes us," I pointed at the screen. "This is how I realized your, erm, Soul was out here. Luckily, Supers can see Overlay City even on surveillance. I used traffic cameras after you left the hotel, and I tracked your companion's scent the rest of the way."

"That's so cool. I low-key wish I could tell Haley about this. She's totally into the occult."

"Is she?" I asked, feeling uncomfortably warm as she scooted closer to me on the couch. Her bare thigh next to mine distracted me with desire. It was the moon wreaking latent havoc with my—

Thump! A coffee mug was plunked in front of me, and Blue Pajamas disappeared into the bathroom with a rustle of silk. I glared after her. What was her problem?

"I remember that!" Aurie said suddenly.

My attention ricocheted back to her. "Remember what?"

"You can't see it from this camera angle, but there was a display placard for the event. It was right outside this door."

"The door to the penthouse suite of Century Luxe."

"Uh-huh. It was in some foreign language. Haley figured swanky internationals wouldn't mind us mixing and mingling. We snuck into the event but, if I'm not mistaken, we spent most of our time there outside on the balcony."

Now, we were getting somewhere. She began describing the night in increasing detail, as if talking about it was unlocking things she had forgotten. "Did you have a drink, perhaps, to loosen up?" I asked.

Aurie curtly tossed her head. "I never drink. I hate hangovers. In fact, that's what being a ghost feels like . . . Wait, I did have *one* shot. This guy said he wanted to drink to us crashing his party. I left right after that, though. Something about him didn't feel right."

"So, one drink. You also told a passerby you might've been drugged?"

Her eyes bugged. "Jeez, I forgot that part. I think I came to that conclusion because . . ." She hesitated, trying to remember. "When I called to get Haley to leave with me, I started seeing and hearing things." Aurie hung her head, twisting the hem of her shirt. "I mean, I watched the bartender pour it up. I thought it was safe," she said in a small voice.

"Don't blame yourself. It's depressingly easy to add something to a drink without anyone noticing," I said quietly.

"Yeah. You know, you try to play it safe, but . . ." The smile she was forcing threatened to collapse, and she swiped her face and turned her head so I wouldn't see the tears falling. She continued in a shaky voice. "I didn't feel drunk. I felt worse than that, if that makes sense."

The bathroom door creaked, giving us a reprieve from the heavy details. We gazed up as the scent of cedarwood and thunderstorms flooded the flat, and I stared openly. The woman who had let me in had transformed into . . . a man?

My body's reaction was hard to control. The hair on my neck stiffened as my wolf nosed to the surface. I struggled to keep it kenneled—a struggle like this only happened when I was in danger or thoroughly aroused. What were the odds this Supernatural was dangerous?

"Did *you* see anything?" I asked as the person prepared to leave.

"Vampires." With that, they walked out the door.

Aurie had composed herself by the time we were alone again. She explained, "Mys is nonbinary, meaning neither male nor female, or like, both. But don't call them 'ma'am.'"

"Got it," I acknowledged, glad the distraction was helping to take her mind off the rough memories. "There's something else I want to show you, if you're up for it. I saw vampires that night, too, and I have surveillance stills. Recognize anyone?" She nodded, and I pulled up the pictures on my phone.

Aurie's face hardened as she pointed at the second image in the lineup. "Him. That's the guy who claimed to be hosting the event."

"Are you sure?" I asked.

She bobbed her head emphatically.

"Cyprian." I spat the name, and an expletive in my mother's native tongue rolled out after it.

"Come again?" Aurie looked puzzled.

"Apologies, I lapse into Punjabi without realizing it sometimes. This is a photo of Darcy Cyprian."

"He's the one who gave me the drink. You're telling me he's a *vampire?*"

I confirmed it. "Not to mention a rich, powerful asshole. Since he's very well-connected in both Overlay City and New Orleans, it'll be difficult convincing Captain Mayfield he had anything to do with this. Mayfield already thinks I'm crazy."

"You don't seem crazy to me," she said, with another forced smile. She was being polite.

"That's nice of you to say, but what do you know?" I couldn't hide a dissolute grin, and she visibly swallowed. "I'm not crazy, Aurie. I'm a werewolf."

"Wow. Ohhkay then."

"We're stronger, faster, and more physically capable than humans. We never suffer from your diseases. We heal abnormally fast, and we live almost double your lifespan, but we're still closer to mankind than the undying. Unlike the vampire, a werewolf's mortality breeds desire to preserve and respect the natural order of things."

"What did he . . . what did he do to me?"

"You truly don't remember anything, do you? I think Darcy Cyprian intended to drug and rape you. Perhaps he realized who you were at the last minute, or was alerted to the fact that your mother is a big-time Hollywood director. I think he followed you to silence you, because an important girl like you could bring a man like him down."

"Oh my God!" She covered her face.

Belatedly, I realized I should have eased her into it. I reached out to console her, but just then, my phone rang. Reluctantly excusing myself, I stepped outside to answer.

"Tell me something good, Stoney."

"We've been on the clock more than twelve hours. Our shift is over, Ravani," my partner said.

I smiled. "Something better than that."

"All right, per the hotel guest list, the floor was booked by the CEO of Corporate Investor Empire, Mr. Darcy Cyprian. I'm guessing it wasn't a company party."

"Imagine that. When I saw him on the surveillance, I was hoping he wasn't mixed up in this."

"Har-de-har. I know you like him for any crime involving a rich pervert, but Cyprian parties with A-listers, not girls like our victim. I'm clocking out after I follow up on this tipster, Paul Jameson. Oh, by the way, I got the expedited tox report. Want me to send you a copy?"

"Absolutely. Shoot it to my phone and I'll send over the tire impressions CSU photographed on the body. It's a wonder we got such clear treads."

"Yep. Mayfield just asked where you were. I told him you were following a lead."

My nose twitched. I lifted my gaze to a man across the street taking photos of the cathedral. He looked like a tourist, but smelled like a vampire. That could mean only one thing. Someone's pet was far too interested in Aurie's hideout. *Shit.* He had to have followed me.

"Are you on a lead?" Tegan pressed.

"You'd have to see it to believe it."

"Damn it, Ravani. Don't have me defending your sanity again."

Funny, how worried she sounded. "I promise, no psychics this time."

"Good. Well, I'm here if you need me."

"Thanks, let me call you back. I'm in the middle of something."

I hit the End Call button and searched for the fake tourist again. There he was, squinting in my direction with a confused frown. Several times, he swept my location but didn't seem to see me. Was it possible the enchanted flat was keeping me hidden as well? Before he could get brave enough for a closer inspection, I veered to the far end of the cathedral alley and pretended to canvass the next street.

I thought of the predawn conversation with my contact in the Council of Overlay Affairs. "Mind what information you share with the girl," my friend had instructed, in her faint Desi British accent. "Darcy's loyalists are invoking the Laws of Fate, saying you can't interfere with life-or-death transitions. Please, whatever you do, solve this case by the book, or forfeit any chance of a conviction."

I couldn't tell Aurie the most important part.

Supernatural politicians were manipulating things to keep her in the dark about what had really happened to her and her sister. It was beyond unethical, and I wanted no part of it. Unfortunately, this was my only shot at taking down Cyprian. He had harmed far more women than Aurie, and would continue his abuse unless I outsmarted him and his allies within the Council. I had to keep whatever secrets were necessary to keep, avoid interfering with Aurie's access to the Light, and get that conviction. There was too much at stake.

Once I was certain that I'd evaded the vampire's pet, I headed to my truck, parked a block from the cathedral. My phone dinged a second time: the tox report. I glanced at it with tired, gritty eyes and stopped in my tracks. Exhausted as I was, what kept me going was the evidence falling into place, evidence that Darcy Cyprian had to be behind this.

What was he planning to do to you, Aurie? No GHB or Rohypnol had been found in her system, but she'd been loaded with Substance Unknown . . . to humans. I recognized the telltale molecular structure as that of Obliviscor, a drug Supernaturals used to get high and forget. No wonder she had memory loss and felt hungover.

It was time the Council of Overlay Affairs saw Cyprian for the criminal he was. Aurelia Edison was the game changer. Because of her relatively high profile, her case necessitated an official investigation into the vampire's activities.

As such, I thought better of driving off before securing my star witness. Could I convince Mys to keep Aurie in protective custody in the enchanted flat until I neutralized the vampire? I needed to talk to the psychic about working together. Breathing deep, I ignored the truck and went on foot in search of the smell of woods and rain. Mys. We also needed to talk about how my wolf had reacted to them.

Because if they weren't a threat, then . . .

CHAPTER SEVEN

—
Aurie

August 10 | Evening

I had been callously run down and killed. How could anyone do that to another human being? I was assailed by the mental picture of my body splayed out in front of the hotel. Like I was sleeping, albeit sleeping the eternal rest, as Mys called it.

After the detective stepped outside, I struggled to pull myself together. Emily Edison's daughter wasn't a victim. She was a doer, and something had to be done.

I gradually noticed my so-called hangover lifting. My mind was growing sharper and clearer by the second. Clear enough to know a guy like Darcy Cyprian might think he was untouchable, but he had messed with the wrong one.

"My life might've been nothing to you, Mr. Cyprian, but it was mine," I growled.

The vampire had taken everything except my determination to see him destroyed. I paced the studio. I would tell Zyr that Haley could pick Darcy out of a lineup. The autopsy would prove he had tampered with my drink. Rich asshole or not, it was an open-and-shut case. Detective Zyr could already see that.

With his mesmerizing amber eyes.

I shook my head at myself as I paced some more. *Now isn't the time to be thirsty, Aurie.* I had just learned the detective was a werewolf. Fawning over a genderqueer human like Mys was uncharacteristic enough, but getting a buzz for someone inhuman? Fail.

"Detective Zyr?" I called out at the door after what felt like ages pacing back and forth. Mys had warned me that time moved weirdly for the dead, but the detective had been gone a while. I called his name again.

No response. I crossed my arms and stared at the doorknob. Maybe his phone call had been an emergency. I considered poking my head through the wall, but it seemed wrong to do that. I waited.

I waited as boredom set in. Then, fear. Darkness. Night crept up beyond the high basement windows, and I couldn't even turn on the lights. I was alone and forgotten as I retraced the same steps over and over.

This must be what it feels like to be dead.

All at once, I faced all the incredible loss that amnesia had, until now, mercifully blocked. I wanted Haley. I wanted Mom. My home in the Garden District. My pink Miata. The stuff that made up my life as a college teen.

I imagined going back as a ghost. It was one thing not to be able to open doors; it was something else entirely not to be able to hug my family. I didn't want to go back like that.

Yet, what else could I do, and where else could I go? Mys had made it clear I needed to vacate the premises by the time they returned from work. I wondered what it would be like not to be seen or heard by anyone. A depressing existence.

Heaven it is, then. "Figure out the specifics of your unfinished business," I said out loud, to keep my nerves from fraying.

I snorted at how Mys had assumed that I'd spent my life purposefully avoiding having a good time. After my dad had passed away, Mom had always been in Los Angeles for work. I'd basically had to raise my sister by myself. It seemed like trying to be a good role model had landed me in this limbo.

My absentminded roaming took me midway through the coffee table. When I saw my legs bisected by wood, I shuddered and hurried back to open floor.

On the bright side, I didn't have to worry about the rebel back home ever ending up with unfinished business. I knew Haley would do everything to the max, my perfect example be damned. My sister had never *needed* me to put my life on hold for her. I should have let her show me how to live it up.

"I wish you were here to help me now," I said out loud.

What did I want? What had gone undone that I could do in this Afterlife? I considered daredevil hijinks like base jumping or doing cocaine, but drugs had never been my thing. For my unfinished to-do list, I needed bullet points I *wanted* to try.

All the same, I had to think outside the box. Which made me remember last night's indecent proposal from Mys. Which made my phantom body start zinging with interest again. Who was I kidding? The zinging had restarted the minute the attractive Detective Zyr Ravani had arrived.

I scratched Supernatural kink from my ideas list, though. How would one engage in "relations" without a body, anyway?

I wondered if I could enjoy traveling by myself. I had always wanted to go places. Except in my present condition, there would be no vacation photos, no exotic food, no fruity drinks with mini umbrellas. Just me, out haunting around. I scratched off travel.

With a groan, I plopped onto the couch, accidentally knocking a lamp off the side table. What else did people put on their bucket lists? Something like . . . love?

Falling in love was a big part of living life to the fullest.

There was this one guy I had been crushing on since freshman year, William J. Varnado. He wasn't your usual leading man, but he was smart and idiosyncratic. I could write to him. Better than that, I could stop by his place on my way home to say good-bye to my family. Although my empathic new friend wanted me gone before they returned from work, maybe I could convince Mys to help me make a side trip, especially if it got me out of here faster.

The more I thought of it, the more it fit. There was nothing else left undone in my life. My planner was an open book in my head now, and my ultraorganized, methodical ass had attended to every other detail. So, my unfinished business must be to confess my feelings.

I tried out the words: "I like you, Willie-Jay."

Tick. The lamp switched on as I picked it up to put it back where it belonged.

Gasping, I shoved the thing onto the side table and sat back with wide eyes. Had I done that? Was it a sign that Dead Girl was onto something with this love letter? My lips shaped into a grin as I rushed to find another light switch. Edged it to the on position, and more illumination—and excited squeals—filled the studio.

Mys had made it seem like I would never again be able to impact the real world, but this changed everything. *This means I can interact with my family*, I thought. I almost walked out the door. I didn't, because I hated the thought of walking through things, and because I remembered the warning about Overlay City.

Mys had explained that Supernatural laws mostly dealt with keeping humans from learning of this hidden world. There were no laws against causing harm, especially not harming other Supers. It could be unsafe for a ghost on her own.

As impatient as I was to be home, it was impolite to leave without thanking my host. No self-respecting Southern girl would ever do that.

Moving to the stylish kitchenette, I popped a grape from the fridge into my mouth to test whether I could eat it. When it went down, I applauded myself for figuring out another Overlay City rule, like the clothes I could wear because they were transmuted by Supernatural contact. I was no longer restricted to a half life. I could eat. I could move things. What else could I do?

My eyes skated to the bathroom door. There was a big, sexy clawfoot tub in there. Could I get a nice, long soak? I tossed off the shirt I had borrowed from Mys and raced to find out.

An hour later, I was floating in water scented with products from that organic cosmetics store where Mys had bought their cologne. A tiny, bittersweet laugh escaped me. It felt like this was my first time living for myself, and that was funny.

Because I was dead.

CHAPTER EIGHT
—
Mys

August 10 | Late Night

Beaucoup de Chair Burlesque stimulated the five senses. Patrons were treated to delicious cuisine: double-battered shrimp with house tartar sauce, spicy boiled crawfish. The music was sensual jazz, rhythm, and blues. Women flashed skin. Whenever the audience broke into applause, we could hear it all the way backstage.

For a lucky few, one-on-ones would be arranged later, but tonight, as Kittie Cad and I made it to work, my mind wasn't on sexual rendezvous. I was anxious to return to Aurie, knowing there was no way she would leave before I got home from work, as I had requested. Where could she go? She needed a guide through Overlay City to complete her unfinished business. That would be my good deed.

"Plus, don't forget the shelter," said Kittie at the dressing room.

"Volunteer at the hospital, the church, and the shelter? You act as if I've committed some heinous crime and need to atone."

"I act like making others happy will make you happy, Mys. Now, lace me up, darling."

I waggled my brows at the red corset. "Is this how your Mister ties you up?"

Kittie swatted me. After I cinched her waist, she adjusted her gaff and reached for her wig. The hairspray and perfume-hazed room was full of girls of all stripes. I was the only dancer slipping into a restroom stall to change into my glittery *Great Gatsby*-era flapper costume.

"Hey, are you scheduled for a date tomorrow night, or can you take a breather?" Kittie asked when I stepped out.

"Got a businessman flying in from the Netherlands. Why?"

She huffed. "Doesn't it get old? I know you're not hurting for money. Don't you want a regular he-only-pays-for-dinner kind of date?"

Wow. I slowly turned away with my makeup bag. Staring at the long mirror framed in glamor lights that we all shared, I dug around in the bag to hide how much that comment had stung, especially coming from my best friend.

Realizing her mistake, Kittie touched my shoulder to apologize, but I shook her off.

"I didn't mean that the way it came out, Mys."

I smiled stiffly at my reflection. No, I sensed what she'd meant to do was to work up to telling me her relationship was getting serious. That our bond would take a hit because of it. Was that why she wanted to set me up with new people? *Gods.* I hoped not.

Kittie Cad knew my abandonment issues—adopted, put out at sixteen—but I had never begrudged her happiness. She had no right to assume I didn't know how to appreciate a he-only-pays-for-dinner kind of date.

What the hell was that, anyway, Kittie? My trembling hands applied makeup. The lipstick fell from my numb fingers as a part of me wondered if she was right. Would I know love when I saw it? I capped the lipstick, putting it in my bag.

"I understand we're not in the same line of work anymore, but don't judge me, Ms. Cad," I said as I strutted off. "Not everyone wants the white picket fence. I'm up next. Don't wait around."

I escaped to the eaves, glad Kittie Cad didn't follow me. I lingered next to the bulletin board, where management had tacked an announcement about Beaucoup de Chair having new owners. By the time my song opened, I was composed. I tucked my vape pen between my breast and the underwire of my bra and sashayed out.

My heels punctuated the stage like exclamation points. At the center, I pivoted to the audience, and my half smile broadened with the building music. I began to dance. Catcalls nearly drowned out Nina Simone's slowed-down cover of "I Put a Spell on You."

I could've performed the jaded seductress for this one. Instead, I played the artless ingenue too deep in love for her own good. That won more applause.

My hands framed my modest chest and slid down my narrow waist to the understated flare of my hips. With a roll of my shoulders, the silver costume revealed my supple spine as I turned and twitched my heart-shaped derriere, to the crowd's amusement.

I tossed the fringe of black hair from my face and gave them eyes. Eyes and emotion. Emotion and vulnerability. Performance. Except burlesque wasn't about choreography. No matter how practiced, it was an improvisation between dancer and onlooker, my forte. I was skilled at sensing what people wanted and giving it to them.

I scanned the audience with Empathy for someone in need of attention. Though I couldn't see past the lights, I felt him as clearly as he saw me. My body carried the music to the throbbing zone of aching desire at the back of the club, and the unseen onlooker's passion built within my consciousness like billowing smoke.

All my life had been such a show. From acting the perfect girl-child to pretending to have the best of both worlds as an adult. It seemed I had even fooled *myself* into thinking my lifelong best friend accepted me. How could she? She barely knew me. I had made sure of that.

After the last fading wail of my dance number petered out, the crowd was rendered mute. It wasn't until my heels plunked the stage in retreat that the club exploded in a standing ovation. People shouted for an encore, but I ignored them. It was some other girl's turn.

I avoided the dressing room and headed to the bar. "The usual, right?" The bartender plunked a lowball glass on the bar top.

"Two fingers of bourbon, please."

A deep voice stirred behind me. "You know, you're not easy to pin down."

"Detective Ravani?" I glanced over my shoulder in surprise. "Are you following me?"

"I'm glad I persisted. That was quite the performance . . . Got someplace private we can talk?" At my speculative eyebrow raise, he flashed a crooked smile. "About Aurie."

"I get off at two. Enjoy the show, and you can walk me home." The upturned gaze and coquettish smile were a smidge more flirtatious than I'd intended, but the detective leaned against the bar and flirted right along.

"Ooh, that's a big ask. You're lucky I left my truck at your place. I guess I can stick around until you're done." He smiled, handing a twenty to the bartender when I reached into my top to pay. I raised my chin quizzically at him, but his eyes were on the butterfly tattoos at my wrists. I hid them on reflex. "I do have one quick question, though," he murmured, his eyes returning to mine.

Something restless and needy stirred beneath his surface, something longstanding that didn't necessarily have anything to do with me, but . . . I wavered as he leaned close enough for his blood orange and spicy cardamom scent to permeate my senses.

"Yes?" I breathed.

"What are you, Mys?"

I gave a wordless smile and withdrew. Detective Zyr observed me until I disappeared behind the dressing room door.

...

Don't let yourself develop some tsundere infatuation. Just don't. I stole glances at the detective as we walked the short distance from the club to my apartment. He was gorgeous. Piercing eyes, wavy black hair, olive skin, manicured beard. He seemed too young to be the lead on the case.

"Twenty-six," he said when I asked.

"Impressive. You must've worked your ass off to get here."

"I love the challenge. Law enforcement helps channel my energy. Otherwise, my frustration builds up." He put a hand at eye level and smiled.

A shiver tickled my insides. I cleared my throat and smoothed a hand over the knee-length linen shift I had changed into after work, a more feminine chic. I ignored the thought that the style change had anything to do with him.

"So, what do you want to know about Aurie?"

"You knew her before?" Zyr asked.

"Fake news. She followed me home last night. Thinks I'm some kind of psychic. Ignores intuition a lot, for a Supernatural."

We shared a laugh, but he sobered. "She might be in danger. A vampire pet was sniffing around your place after you left. Normally, I'd secure paranormal protection for a witness as important as she is, but I can't this round."

I stopped and faced Detective Ravani beneath a streetlamp. We were almost home, but I wanted to prolong the walk. "You think the vampires did this?" I asked.

"My suspect is Darcy Cyprian."

I whistled. "An Overlay City political hotshot. That's a yikes."

"Exactly. I don't want to give him a head's up about where she is, but I can't arrange official protection without him finding out. I need outside assistance. Your place is enchanted. Aurie should stay there until I know for sure he's not searching for her."

"That's a big ask!" I stuck my hands in the pockets of my dress, taking off again. A half smile twitched my lips. "How about a favor for a favor? I've decided to guide Aurie through completing her unfinished business, which I think is to live a little."

"How vague." He lifted an eyebrow.

"She played by the rules her whole life. She probably only needs one superwild and crazy night, and I bet someone like *you* could, um, free her mind, body, and soul. Know what I mean?"

"I'm sure I don't." His twinkling grin said he understood me perfectly.

"Let me spell it out for you: one date with a werewolf." I tugged my laptop bag over my shoulder and nudged him. The idea had come to me on the fly, but it felt legit. It didn't get any edgier than that.

"*Nahin*, no. I hope she comes to see me as family. Anyway, how's that a favor for a favor? What's in it for you?" he asked. We were at the gate to the cathedral, and he glanced over his shoulder, as if hearing something.

"What is it?" I asked.

"I keep feeling like somebody's following us. There's no vampire scent, though."

"Then it sounds like you're trying to change the subject. What do you say to a one-night stand with a haint?"

"I'm serious. They're perhaps two blocks back. I don't want to lead trouble to your doorstep."

As he surveyed our surroundings, I cast my Empathy to see for myself. "I don't sense trouble, but if you want to be on the safe side, come on."

"What are you doing?" he asked in surprise as I dragged him through the gate and into the shadows on the side of the church.

"Try to make this fake PDA look convincing. Nobody ever bothers lovers."

"Wha . . . look convincing?"

He emitted a tense laugh, his lips near mine. My Empathy lit up with his desire to shape-shift to meet the threat, but he fought that urge until a more unexpected craving arose. Suddenly, Detective Ravani was nuzzling my mouth and nipping at my lips, and I helplessly chased the contact, under the influence of his arousal and my own.

As his velvet tongue curled inside my mouth, his question came rushing back. What was in it for me? Why give a kiss like this to a ghost?

Because my parents had taught me that selflessness was the way to eternal happiness. *Damn, damn, damn.* The detective's lips slid and slanted over mine, and I had to get real. It wasn't a completely selfless good deed. My end goal was to usher these people out of my life. No matter how tempting, I couldn't handle complications like this kiss or last night's swoon over my cologne.

I sensed Aurie was the detective's answer to ending a complex rivalry with Darcy Cyprian, and I felt certain Detective Zyr was Aurie's wild ride to Heaven. It was a win-win.

A moan spilled from me when his fiery mouth broke from mine. And what did I need? This. I needed more of this. *No, you don't need to be kissing boys in dark alleys*, I chastised. I needed to be—

"Convinced?" he asked.

Left alone. A remorseful grin flitted across my face as I jerked my chin upward. I wanted every bit of what his firm grasp and hot mouth promised, but one of us had to be sensible.

"I'm convinced you need to know what I am."

CHAPTER NINE
—
Zyr

August 11 | Two a.m.

My impulsiveness was legendary, but I had never blurred the lines like this, not during an investigation. The evening had begun with a fight to keep my hands off the victim. It was ending with those same hands on her friend's captivating body. I couldn't seem to help myself.

We broke apart to breathe beyond the cinders. At least, our lips separated. Mys remained pinned between my body and the church wall. Their small breasts heaved, crushed to my chest, though I tried to avoid our meeting below the waist.

"Convinced?" I asked.

"I'm convinced you need to know what I am."

Slowly, the remarkable creature led my hand over their genitalia. The act nudged me toward erection. *We* were getting erect. My eyes fluttered shut, and my lips parted. Mys had a delicate face that defied categorization by biological sex, but what my hand touched left no doubt.

Maybe I should have walked away. I had never acted on nonhetero urges before. Except this attraction was more complicated than that, and when I dared look again, eye contact held me hostage.

Mys's mesmerizing eyes glowed black in the shadows. At first, I couldn't do anything but bask in the light, unmoving. There was a tightness in my chest, and my mouth was dry. The rising tide of their arousal beat beneath my fingertips.

"Keep going," they said.

The hushed command coaxed my twitching fingers to very slowly stroke downward. Mys repaid me with a seductive moan, repositioning to meet my calloused palm, and my own manhood swelled in response.

I squared my jaw. I realized the heavy breathing amplified by the alley was my own. The man fondling himself through his slacks with his free hand was also me. Even when I let go of myself, I gravitated toward Mys like a dowsing rod. My broad hand cupped their jaw, and our lips collided again.

"Find out the truth," Mys gasped into my hungry mouth.

"Mm-hmm," I hummed. The truth. I pondered that as I grew harder by the second. *Things like this happen, Zyr*, I told myself, *even to straight men*. The button of my slacks unsnapped, and my zipper raced free to discover the truth about both of us, I guessed. "You can't tell anyone about this," I said in a rush.

"Tell anyone?" Mys mumbled through the kiss. Before I lost my nerve, I brought our bodies together. I had a single-minded focus: mutual release.

When the sensual being in my arms responded to my touch like a hair trigger, wildness shot through me. I buried my face in their neck, and my teeth nibbled the line of their shoulder. Mys shrugged into the bite as if begging to be devoured.

Oh, I was doomed.

"You like it," I growled. A breathy *yes* fled the coral lips and feathered over my earlobe. I bit harder, our erotic make-out session tense and promising.

Visions of doing more—I wasn't sure how much more—filled my imagination, but this was all new. The unfamiliar feel of being with someone like Mys was staggering. I backed off the biting and clenched my teeth, used to the soft give of female flesh. Yet, this uncanny fire begged to be extinguished inside the androgynous body keeping it ablaze.

In my head, I was halfway to the condom in my wallet.

"Oh Christ! *Fuck*, Zyr!" Mys shoved me back. To reality. As my feet slid, I was stunned by their strength, but had I misread? No, the other's body jumped, quaking toward mine, and I stared, enthralled at the bulge imprinting their sheer panties.

"What is it?" I was perilously close to pleading to keep going with the bad, bad decisions taking place in this cathedral alley.

"Gods, you're making this impossible. Find out the *truth*," Mys implored. I was dazed with lust, perhaps, and confused about what "the truth" could be, if not their sex. They skittishly returned my hand between their legs, this time guiding me until I felt—

My startled eyes flew to theirs. They nodded, face shuttered. Was that possible? Mys had *both* male and female genitalia, just as Aurie had explained, although I was certain Aurie had had no clue how biologically correct she'd been.

"How?" I blurted in confusion.

Mys tried to wriggle from my embrace. "My Supernatural type is a Japanese *futanari*. So now you get it. This isn't what you want." I hugged them tighter, because their ashamed expression told me they thought I was repulsed. On the contrary.

"Tell me more. Please?" My eyes asked permission to touch. It wasn't mere curiosity. I yearned to know them, a completely foreign emotion. Yearning.

Studying me, Mys gave a timid nod. "Um, Supernaturals like me are . . . rare intersex beings with energy. We have both—oh gods, Zyr." The soul-stirring moan came in response to my gentle exploration below the belt. I managed to keep from licking the sound of my name from their lips.

"Is this good?" I whispered.

"*Mm-hmm.*" A blush arose on the futanari's face.

"Good. Now, what were you saying?" I prompted with mock composure as excitement turned on light in their eyes again.

"With dual-sex energies, we . . ." Mys trailed off in bliss. "Mm . . . Both energies allow us to experience the world on a different frequency that picks—*uhn*—right there!"

I overcame my inhibitions and rubbed my sex against theirs, flinching in ecstasy. *Almost, almost* . . . With the taboo frottage, we careered closer to the edge. Another whine escaped the pink mouth.

I couldn't believe what was happening. It was unethical and unprofessional of me. But there was no stopping it. The wolf within clamored to finish the hunt, and Mys begged to be finished.

I felt the mounting pressure. Their taut thighs quivered, their pelvis pressed for release. I wanted us to get there. Together. Just this once, and only in the dark, where the line between restraint and savagery were permitted to be weak. "Yes, argh!" I went in for the—

"Wow!" someone yelped behind me. Startled, I swore in Punjabi and threw out my arms to shield Mys. When I glanced over my shoulder, Aurie was dashing back into the flat. "I'm so sorry!"

"No, no, no, no, no," I panicked.

"I didn't see anything!" she squeaked from the other side of the door.

Of course, she had seen *everything*. My face burned with embarrassment. I pivoted from Mys and righted my clothes. I hadn't intended for any of this to happen. As I finished tucking in my Oxford shirt, I checked the futanari lounging against the cathedral wall. Unclimaxed. The pretty white dress was back in place, laptop bag over their crotch.

I pointed at the door. "That needs to be explained to her."

"Let it blow over. She doesn't know about me. So, she won't think you're . . . you know."

"I'm not!" I raked a hand through my hair and dragged it down my face. "Look, I got carried away. It won't happen again."

Mys's eyes widened, and a wry expression turned the corners of their lips downward. "No, of course not," they said.

I sighed in relief.

CHAPTER TEN
—
Aurie

August 11 | Three a.m.

"I didn't see anything!" I winced from the other side of the door.

When I'd heard their voices outside in the alley, I had stepped through the door, braving the icky feeling of walking through walls. I don't know why. I was so stoked about gaining the ability to impact the real world. I hadn't expected to find them in a heated make-out session.

They entered the studio, and I hid my face. "I know I'm supposed to be gone," I said.

"No, we're glad you're still here, Aurie." Mys shivered and crossed to the thermostat to adjust the temp. "The detective and I have a proposal for you."

My gaze bounced from Mys to Detective Zyr, rocking on his heels, avoiding eye contact. They were totally normal. Not like two horny goats caught humping in the shadows.

I bit my lip to keep from smiling. "Okay, but I have questions galore." Deadass.

"Questions about your case?" The detective cleared his throat.

"Well, one is about my case. What happened to you? You left me stranded earlier."

Frowning, Mys pointed at the lamp. "Did I leave everything on?"

"Yay, you noticed! I learned a new trick," I said as I dropped to the couch. Every light in the studio was ablaze. The detective scoffed, and I was surprised and amused by his skepticism. "Well, who else could've done it? I spent the day exercising my ability to impact things."

"*That's* why it's freezing in here," Mys commented.

"No way," Detective Zyr insisted. "Transferring energy takes most spirits months, if not years to master. You've been a Soul for what, a day?"

"Why does it take the others so long?" I asked.

"Because the disembodied need time to reconcile being nonmaterial. They have to learn to manipulate the tangible through the intangible. Most never gain the ability before crossing over," he said as he leaned on the marble island. "It's hardly a necessary skill for the dead."

"Says who? And it wasn't that hard to master. I was sitting here thinking about my unfinished business when—voilà!" I switched off the side table lamp by way of demonstration.

"So, you figured out your unfinished business?" Mys asked.

Grinning, I beckoned them to the couch. Mys plopped beside me, but the detective stayed in the kitchenette, probably hiding a boner. I was almost jealous. "After much contemplation, I remembered that I never told William J. Varnado I had a crush on him," I announced, watching expectantly for their reaction to the good news.

Zyr finally cracked a smile.

"That's it? I'm thoroughly unimpressed, Yōkai. How do you expect that to get you to the Light?" Mys poked me.

"What? Haven't you people seen *Ghost*? It's like my mom's favorite movie. You're a medium. You can be my Whoopi Goldberg," I said.

"So meta. First, I'm not a medium. Second, I am not letting you use my body to kiss some college boy. Ew!"

I pulled a face. "If you're not a medium, what do you call it?"

Zyr spoke up. "I think the term is—"

"Your new roommate," Mys said, talking over him. I raised an eyebrow. "That's what we came to suggest to you. Remember my speech last night about Overlay City?"

"Yeah. You said Supernaturals aren't evil, but the bad actors are like criminals with superpowers. Oh, and being dead won't protect me," I recited.

The detective had more to add. "Our suspect is a powerful vampire who thinks he's above the law. Rumors of his predatory behavior have circulated for years, but we've never gotten charges to stick. Be that as it may, I believe you're the key to taking him down."

"Which is why," Mys said uneasily, no doubt reading my expression, "for your protection, we'd like you to stay at my apartment until the detective is certain that Darcy Cyprian doesn't know you're in Overlay City."

My eyebrows clashed. "Dudes, my unfinished business is to go tell my secret crush I'm secretly crushing on him. Besides, I need to see Haley and Mom. There's no way I'm spending my Afterlife here with strangers—no offense."

"It's temporary." Zyr reached a hand out to pat my shoulder. When his fingers didn't pass through me, I was surprised, but it made sense. If I could impact the world now, maybe it could impact me too. He flashed a sheepish grin. Why the hell was that sexy? "While you're here, we'd like to be your Supernatural family."

"I already have a family. Anyway, what if Darcy finds out I'm in Overlay City? Would I have to stay in hiding indefinitely?"

"Nahin. Once the Council opens an official investigation, you're free to move about the city. Cyprian won't be able to do anything while under their scrutiny. If he finds you before that . . ." Zyr trailed off and shrugged. "You're not a protected class like the humans anymore. You're one of us now."

I pictured Darcy getting his hands on my ghost and shuddered. It wasn't like I had a life to rush back to. I slouched on the sofa with a groan. "How long do I have to haunt this cubicle?"

"This cubicle? A while ago you were hauntless." Mys tossed a throw pillow my way.

Giggling, I dodged it and dropped my bad attitude. "Aww, I do appreciate the hospitality. It's just that now I remember my life, I want to go home."

"Let's give it two weeks," said the detective.

"Can I see my family during the day, while the vampires are sleeping?"

Zyr grimaced. "Darcy Cyprian has plenty of humans working for him. Even a brief trip home could be detrimental, since he's sure to have surveillance on your house."

"Wait, does that mean Haley and Mom are in danger because of me?"

"There's no evidence of that," the detective reassured me. "Either way, I had your mom increase her security detail as a precaution, and NOPD is providing extra patrols. You can keep them safe by letting us protect you here for the time being."

Mys squeezed my shoulders. "C'mon, stay with me. We can tell some guy he's your dream zaddy."

"I guess I don't really have a choice. Anyway, I spent all evening working on this stupid love letter. Will you deliver it for me, since I'm stuck in quarantine?" I asked Mys.

"Let me see." The detective lifted it from the coffee table. I let out a yelp and jumped to get it back, but he playfully held it aloft, reading in a teasing voice. "'Dear Willie-Jay, my feelings for you shine in my heart. I wonder if you'll ever see the light. I'm the girl who runs into you accidentally-on-purpose every day—' Okay, no, Aurie, no!"

I crossed my arms indignantly. "*Rough* draft, bruh."

"I knew you could use a Supernatural family, sis," he jested.

I snatched the letter from him and stuck out my tongue. Mys made a show of checking the time on their phone. I inspected it too. "Hmm, nearly three in the morning. Spending the night, *fam*?" I asked the detective with a grin.

He beat a hasty retreat to the door. "It was nice meeting you both. Here's my card, if you need me. I'll . . . probably be a frequent fixture while Aurie's here. You know, to give updates and check on things. Is that okay with you, Mys?"

Mys nodded, their cheeks flushing pink. I hid a grin as I watched the detective exit. Once the door closed, I whispered, "I ship it."

"Don't even." They smiled.

"Was it *business*?" I asked in a scandalized hiss.

Mys turned away and started unbuttoning the collar of the linen dress. A bashful grin curved my lips, and I averted my gaze. It was easy to see why Detective Zyr was hooked at first encounter. Mys was unconventionally captivating. My new roommate stepped behind the dressing screen to finish disrobing. I moseyed off to enjoy fantasies and the faint scent of their cologne.

"Does it matter?" they asked out of sight.

"What? Whether or not it was business? Yeah, I don't want to encroach. I worked hard learning how to transfer energy to take you up on your offer from last night."

Mys poked their head above the screen, saw my mischievous smile, and laughed in relief. "Offer's expired, Willie-Jay's Girl," they said, out of sight again. "Now, if you're asking how ghost sex works, you can fuck other Supernaturals, but your phantom booty can't get it on with non-Supers."

"Aww! Next lifetime for me and you."

"I'm curious. Now that you know I'm not a medium or psychic or some other mumbo jumbo, how do you think I see you, Aurie?" They stepped out wearing the kimono and blue silk pajamas from last night, and that was when it hit me.

I had no idea what they were, but Mys wasn't human.

CHAPTER ELEVEN
—
Mys

August 26 | Early Afternoon

By week three of cohabitation, an exit plan seemed to recede into the distance. "Here are the rules to sharing a living space with me." I smacked my *Attack on Titan*–themed notebook on the marble island in the kitchenette and confronted the root of my malcontent.

Aurie rested her chin on her palms, elbows on the slab. In the background, my apartment was a shambles. Books on the coffee table. My game console on the floor with cords in a haphazard knot. Game discs and vinyl records scattered everywhere.

"How do you clutter up a minimalist apartment, Yōkai? I don't mind you wearing my clothes, but please put them in the hamper," I lectured, picking up a T-shirt from the back of the barstool and handing it to her for cleanup.

"I have a maid at home."

"*Had*, spoiled brat. Gah! I hate dishes in the sink!" Moving to the other side of the island, I slammed bowls on the counter in frustration.

"You should own a dishwasher," Aurie said in a bland voice behind me.

"Why do you even eat and drink? You don't need to! Sometimes I wonder if you're intentionally trying to get under my skin. Like when you leave my phone on Facebook to piss me off. Nobody uses Facebook anymore!" I turned and brandished a serving spoon for emphasis but dropped it with a frown. "Is any of this getting through to you?"

Aurie couldn't have looked less interested. Growling, I stormed past her to get ready for a client. "Yes," she said. "You don't want me here. Call Zyr and take me home."

"You know the Council runs the timetable, but we are *definitely* getting you out of here as soon as possible."

"When, though?"

"Oh gods! As soon as possible, Aurie!"

"Right." She rotated the stool to face me. Her eyes glossed, and she turned back. My bitching and moaning aside, the news of the Council meeting being pushed to the end of September was taking a toll on her.

At the sound of her sniffles, I bit my fist. "Please don't, Yōkai." I sighed.

"I just want to go home!"

"Aurie—"

Thwack! My favorite coffee mug hit the wall and shattered. Aurie covered her mouth, giving me a horrified stare. Yes, it was her fault, but she hadn't touched it. It had flown by itself, which clearly shouldn't have been possible. I studied the broken ceramic shards as she buried her face in her arms and burst into tears.

I disposed of the mess. Then, sweeping loose tendrils of hair from her face, I flashed a soft smile at her to show I wasn't angry, and she squeezed me in a fierce hug. It wasn't easy living together, but if the flying mug was any indication, she needed my help more than ever.

Ensuring the rest of my glassware wouldn't suffer in my absence, I stepped outside to call the detective. "We've got a problem," I said as I paced within the zone of the door's enchantment. "You know when a ghost loses touch with reality, they go haywire?"

"Yeah, I learned that the hard way on a poltergeist case for the Council. Why?"

"Aurie's already exhibiting signs," I said.

"Wait, that takes decades, minimum."

"I know, I know, but premature madness could be a symptom of her anguish at haunting a strange place. You have to admit she's not getting the Afterlife she deserves. I mean, anyone would lose their shit over being stuck in one room for weeks without reprieve."

"It makes me think of her sister," said the detective.

"What about Haley?"

"I . . ." Zyr hesitated, wrestling with something. "There are details the Council doesn't want me to divulge yet. Not to mention, I've got Mayfield up my ass about some stalker kid on Instagram. Meanwhile, Cyprian's lawyers have delivered him an alibi tight as a tick. I swear, that vampire is too many steps ahead of this case for my comfort."

"I can take Aurie to see the crush," I suggested. Zyr expelled a breath, ready to say no. "Detective, there's an unstable ghost in my kitchenette breaking dishes. Unless you're prepared to keep her at your home, you need to let me take her to her unfinished business."

"Damn it," he swore. "I want her to wrap up her business, too, but it's risky taking her out. Let me ask you something. The other night, you said you didn't sense trouble. Your . . . skill . . . tells you when danger is near?"

"More or less. I sense people's intentions. Don't worry. If I feel anything that makes me even remotely spooked, I'll contact you and get out of there."

"Good. I'll put a squad car on standby for you for the next few hours," he said.

"No, not tonight. I have a date tonight. How about tomorrow?"

"A date?" he asked. Too casually.

"Yeah, I'm an escort."

"A sex worker?" He coughed in surprise. "Okay, we'll talk about that later."

No, sir. I smiled. "Nothing to talk about, Detective. Other than Aurie and the case. I'll hit you up in the morning to coordinate her trip."

I ended the call with my boundaries intact. I didn't let myself think that Detective Zyr Ravani felt anything but a passing fancy, nor did I need his intrigue. In the right light, curiosity like his had a way of drying up faster than a puddle on a hot summer's day.

I stepped back inside the untidy apartment. Aurie looked up from washing dishes. "I promise to be a better roommate. I'm much neater than this usually, but it's depressing being dead," she confessed.

I gave an exaggerated pout and marched to her with open arms. "And I'm sorry for the delay in seeing your family. Me being anal about housekeeping isn't helping. How about a trip to see your crush to take your mind off the wait?"

"Are you serious? We're going to see Willie-Jay?" Aurie squealed the question and literally jumped into my arms.

With an astonished laugh, I caught her, but lost my balance. We spun from the kitchenette, the momentum carrying us to the bed. We hit the mattress in a breathless heap. Her weight on top of me was sexy. Her hair fanned my face, and she stopped giggling and stared. For a second, the world slid sideways as my stomach flip-flopped.

When Aurie bowed her head, I held my breath. She wasn't doing this, was she? Her lips brushed mine in a shower of electric sparks. *She is.* The first kiss lit me up like Tokyo. My eyes widened, but I held still. The tip of her tongue parted the seam of my mouth. She whispered my name, and the sound came out muffled and sultry.

I shivered. My eyelids drifted shut. I splayed a hand over her cheek, and my fingers drove through her hair to the nape of her neck to bring her closer. My teeth nipped her lips. I drew the bottom one into my mouth. She gathered my face and sucked my tongue, kissing me deeper. *Sweet lovely fuck, Yōkai.* My palms coasted down her sides to her waist as my hips involuntarily edged upward, but when she rocked her hips in response, I shoved her body back. "Don't!" I whispered. She was one gyration of the pelvis away from learning my secret.

The voice of reason warned me that she hadn't been born Supernatural. She didn't transform like Detective Zyr. Given her past as a normal human, Aurie would never understand my anatomy. What the hell was I even doing?

I flipped her to the mattress and scrambled off the bed. My hair fell over my heated face as I put distance between us, knowing that behind me, she was frozen with confusion and embarrassment. It flooded my Empathy.

"Finish your chores. I've gotta get ready for work," I said gruffly.

Aurie pushed by me with a scowl. "Whatever, bruh," she muttered. I knew I had hurt her feelings, but as with Zyr, whatever this was would pass, and I'd be stuck with the emotional baggage.

She headed for the kitchenette. I disappeared into the bathroom. I stared in the mirror at my mouth, thinking of hers. And his. *Gods.* I wasn't used to this shit. A half hour later, I emerged from a cold shower. I did my hair and makeup and donned a cobalt-blue suit that could trend either masculine or feminine.

Aurie was sitting at the head of my bed with her arms and ankles crossed. "Why do you push everyone away?" she asked.

"Let's not do this. I have to deal with a john in an hour."

"Fine. Go ahead. Ice me out like you do the detective and everyone else who's apparently given up on you."

"She says in a snarky tone without having a whit of an idea what she's talking about," I said irritably. I headed for the door to escape the cramped apartment.

"Oh, I take that back, not everyone," she said. "*Somebody's* been calling for two weeks, but you send them straight to voicemail. I figure it's not a client, because you'd never leave one of them on Read. They're the only people who matter to you."

"Excuse me?" I slammed to a halt, pivoted, and charged at the bed, since she wanted to have this conversation now. "Don't insult me, Aurie Edison! If *they* were the only ones who mattered, *you* wouldn't be here. Trust me."

The hard line of her mouth softened with contrition. "No shade."

"Bullshit!"

"I'm sorry. All I'm saying is I thought us living together would lead to us being friends," she said.

"Why, Yōkai? Because we're roommates? We have nothing in common except proximity. You don't even know what I am!"

"And I like you anyway!" she exclaimed. I pulled back in surprise at the intensity of her admission. She blew out a breath and shoved a hand through her hair, shaking her head. "As a friend. I like you as a friend. Don't you have any of those?"

Rubbing my face, I groaned and dropped to the bed next to her to deal with this complicated mess. The kiss. Her confessing she liked me. Me not walking out the door when I had the chance. "My one and only best friend and I are currently not talking," I replied.

"What happened?"

I sucked my vape pen and shrugged.

"Do they know you're a Supernatural?" she asked.

I shook my head. As my inquisitor grabbed my hand and studied my palm, I tentatively cast Empathy and gathered how she felt for me. Shy attraction. Budding interest. Things I didn't need, but maybe . . . wanted?

"Well, you're not giving me much," she said quietly, "but I advise you to make up with your one and only best friend, and then stop treating people like something you have to endure. I'm not an obstacle course. I'm a woman, Mys."

"I know." I bit my lip.

She whiffled a breath and finally asked, "So, what are you?"

CHAPTER TWELVE
—
Zyr

August 26 | Early Afternoon

Jealous? I stared at the phone after the call ended. Nahin, that feeling wasn't jealousy. Shock at Mys being an escort, perhaps. Tegan breezed by and tossed a stack of papers on my desk, along with something from the vending machine. "What's this?" I griped.

"It's a working lunch before your meeting with Mrs. Edison. Eat and read." She started rubbing my shoulders. Glancing around the station house, I peered at her quizzically, but she waved at the report. "Confirmation that Paul Jameson was Aurie's Instagram stalker, @R1d3rH4rd_2018, and Paulie's got priors eerily similar to our hit-and-run."

"Hmm." I tore open the cellophane wrapper on a chicken club sandwich. At the first bite, my eyes rolled skyward. I wasn't jealous—that feeling was hunger. Or so I told myself. I dusted my fingers and leaned forward from my partner's impromptu massage to study the papers she indicated. "Says here Mr. Jameson found out where his love interest worked and went there to, quote, 'surprise her.'"

"The idiot asshole popped out of a dark alley and gave her the scare of a lifetime. The vic ran right into traffic."

Tegan moved in front of my desk. Her clear, unblemished skin and earnest cornflower eyes made her appear years younger, or her excitement did. She was itching to chase the lead. Her ginger hair caught the sunlight, and a few strands fluttered in the electric charge of her restless energy.

A similar restlessness bustled at every other desk in our department. Cases were being opened and shut. Given the fact we had nothing but dead ends, I should've been the same level of pumped for this lead, but I raised my eyebrows and tossed my head.

"Uncanny."

"Too uncanny," she said.

"But I don't know, Tegan. It doesn't square with what we have," I said, as I pulled up notes on my computer.

Video surveillance and a busted headlight casing had confirmed that the vehicle that hit Aurie Edison was a custom-modified Ford Escape from the late '90s. I turned my screen to show my partner the serial number from a shard of plastic. We had loaded the number into a parts database and, by some stroke of luck, traced it to the person who had ordered the light.

"What about it? The SUV was reported stolen by the owner years ago," Tegan countered. "The guy who used to own it—his alibi checked out. He was in surgery."

"Yeah, he obviously lacked a motive to hurt Aurie," I agreed. "My point is that I don't see Paulie flying into New Orleans that evening, procuring a stolen truck in an unfamiliar city, and using it to hit our victim in the time frame indicated."

"It's not impossible." Tegan shrugged.

"All the same . . ."

"Hey, Jameson already pled guilty to manslaughter for some other girl. Mayfield likes him for this one too. This guy's the poster kid for troubled youth." She tilted her small nose down at me. "Why not see where this goes?"

Paul Jameson was indeed an angst-ridden, disturbed teen. I studied his grayscale mug shot, and a muscle ticked under my orbital socket at the thought of him harassing Aurie. He had come on our radar when he volunteered the info that he was in New Orleans on a lark and hadn't contacted the Edison sisters. The helpful tip had made him appear more suspicious.

Still, I didn't think Paul had anything to do with this. His involvement couldn't explain why Darcy Cyprian had drugged Aurie. My gut told me the vampire was our unsub. I simply had to prove a billionaire corporate investor—and upstanding philanthropist—had committed a horrendous crime.

Otherwise, this semi-innocent kid would take the fall.

Seeing the time, I hurried to my feet and shrugged into my suit coat. "Schedule him for another interrogation, make sure he stays in touch. I have to see Mrs. Edison. I'll check if Haley has anything more to add about Jameson. Wanna come?"

"Ugh, Ravani," Tegan groaned.

I grinned at the look she gave me. Mrs. Edison and I got along famously. Conversely, the director had raised a fuss about Tegan trying to hug her while apologizing profusely for what had happened to Aurie. It didn't help that my partner had slid in an autograph request.

"What's the matter? No longer Nannette Baudelaire's biggest fan?" I joked as she fell in step with me.

"Ha, funny. More like Nannette Baudelaire isn't a fan of me."

"Nah, Mrs. Edison is just focused on putting the person who did this to her daughter behind bars."

"Yeah, but does she know this isn't Hollywood?" Tegan asked. "We don't always get a happy ending."

•••

As we headed down the brightly lit corridor of Bayou General Hospital, Tegan stage-whispered, "I spent my childhood in and out of these places. I was a clumsy dingbat."

"I don't believe it." I smiled and scanned the wall directory.

"Broke an arm, knocked out a tooth." Trailing off, my partner locked her pinky finger with mine like she did whenever she was anxious. We had been friends long enough for the gesture to be meaningless now, but there had been a summer fling years back. Nothing serious.

We took the elevators to the uppermost floor. Emily Leigh Edison met us outside a private room. The door was partially ajar behind her. I caught a glimpse of the teen in the hospital bed.

This was the real reason I didn't want Aurie to see her family. Not until this situation was resolved. I hadn't even told Mys yet. If Aurie learned what was happening here, she would worry herself sick. As evidenced by her recent poltergeist activity, I had to keep her level-headed and focused on crossing over.

"Detectives! Right on time. Let's find somewhere to talk." Mrs. Edison's eyes darted to my hand locked with Tegan's, and I shook it loose.

"Thank you for agreeing to meet us." I smiled.

"Absolutely. I'm anxious for an update."

The attractive middle-aged director walked briskly ahead, and Tegan and I followed her to a secluded waiting area past the nurses' desk. I noticed conspicuous men in suits throughout the hall. Good. She had taken my suggestion to beef up security.

As we settled into surprisingly comfortable hospital chairs, Tegan jumped the gun. "We have evidence Paul Jameson may have been in the area the night of the accident."

Aurie's grieving mother lit up visibly. "My daughter's stalker? Now, we're getting somewhere."

"Uh, let's not get ahead of ourselves." Glaring at my partner, I gave a more realistic assessment. "We're building a case, Mrs. Edison. It could take months to collect and interpret all the evidence, but we'll get justice. As frustrating as it may be, I'm sure Aurie would encourage you to trust the process."

"Sounds like you did your homework. Aurelia was always methodical, all about the process, which is why she went into chemical engineering. She wanted to work for Big Oil, like her late father. Only she wanted to get in and develop more responsible energy solutions."

"I'm sure you were very proud."

She folded her hands in her lap. "I did my homework on you two, as well."

"Oh?" I arched an eyebrow, curious. Mrs. Edison's eggshell-hued power suit and upright posture gave an aura of unflappable self-possession. Gone was the polite but grief-stricken woman I had met earlier. It was clear she was all business this round.

"Captain Mayfield assures me you're his best," said Mrs. Edison. "Interesting enough, my assistant dug up some . . . *footnotes* in your history that call that assessment into question. Detective Stoney, you've been treated for alcoholism?"

I leaned forward in protest, but Tegan stiffened and held up a hand. Her neutral expression curdled into an unamused smile. "My journey to sobriety isn't a secret, but it's hardly a strike against me that I sought treatment for a disease."

"Hm." Mrs. Edison turned her frosty gaze to me. "You were committed to a psychiatric facility in your teen years, is that correct, Detective Ravani? You passed your psych eval when you were hired for law enforcement, but you have been suspended for use of force . . . twice."

"Detective Ravani's personnel file is confidential!" Tegan flew to my defense before I could say anything. "Now, I don't know how you got that information or why you think it's accurate, but—"

"Why would I waste my time with inaccuracies?" Mrs. Edison spread her hands. "I understand you both have personal mental health things happening. I wouldn't want to discriminate on that basis, but would be *crazy* to think I'd just let my daughter become another cold case."

"We would never suggest that," I replied.

"Good, because we don't have months, Detective. Not up to it? I can request someone else take the lead. Otherwise, I expect y'all to treat this case a bit more seriously than just a means to an end."

"I'm sorry, a means to what end?"

Mrs. Edison glowered at my partner putting her fingers on mine again, this time to make me unclench my fists. "You tell me," she said. "I saw a taping of your *famous* press conference with the psychics. I guess you need a fortune teller to convince you to arrest Jameson. Please, don't make a mockery of the Edison family name like that."

So that was what this was about. I stretched out my fingers and exhaled. "Mrs. Edison, this investigation is discreet and running full-speed ahead. I assure you," I said.

"We'll see. Anything else?" She checked the time.

Tegan replied tersely, "Just tell Haley to give us a call when she's available." She handed Mrs. Edison a business card as I stormed off.

I knew the woman was desperate, but I was livid about the threat of being kicked off the case. No one else understood how deadly Darcy Cyprian could be, and this was the perfect crime to bring before the Council. The victim was human, upper class, and important enough to make the front page. Not even Cyprian's djinn lawyers would be able to refute that he had broken Overlay City privacy laws.

Unless Mrs. Edison's impatience jeopardized everything. If she got me taken off the case, the side effects of being a rogue would escalate— the volatile self-control, the labile mood, the deteriorating sanity. I couldn't let that happen. I shot a text to my contact in the Council asking to move up our meeting. No more waiting until the end of September.

As Tegan caught up with me at the elevators, I noticed an angel in the hall behind us. He was a young Black guy with broad shoulders and radiant wings. Probably a guardian for some human here at the hospital.

Squinting, I realized he was the same one from the hotel, and I took a step in his direction. At the same time, the elevator doors opened, and Tegan pulled me inside. I couldn't interrogate the Super in front of her, anyway. I made a mental note to return and question him when I had the chance.

CHAPTER THIRTEEN
—
Aurie

August 27 | Morning

I had always joked that I would sleep when I was dead, but ghosts don't need recharging. I spent the night on pins and needles. At daybreak, I was bouncing with uncontained excitement by the time Mys groggily rolled over in bed. As soon as my slowpoke roommate tossed off the duvet, I skipped to the coffeemaker and popped some bread in the toaster.

"Good morning!" I sang. "Hey, what kind of Supernaturals do you think we'll meet today?"

Mys padded into the kitchen and knuckled sleep from their face. They paused at the fully cleaned studio. I felt a twinge of contrition for my bratty behavior the day before. Everything was in its rightful place now.

I helpfully poured the first cup of joe into a mug I had dug out of the cabinet. It was from the same set as the one I had broken. Accepting the peace offering, Mys flashed a tiny smile, and I braced against the island as they took the barstool.

"I've always wanted to see unicorns," I rambled. "Do they exist? Come to think of it, even if they do, there wouldn't be many in the city, right? Ooh, maybe we'll see fairies!"

At the *ding* I snatched a plate from the cabinet and deposited the fresh toast onto it. Added butter, which melted in salty-sweet rivulets. Plus, there was bacon. Microwavable bacon. I slid the plated food across the marble countertop. Mys saved it from toppling over the edge.

"Glad you're not holding a grudge," they said.

"Oh, I haven't forgotten that you didn't tell me what you are, but I'll pick my battles."

"Which battle do you want to fight today?" Mys asked cheekily.

I leaned over with a conspiratorial wink. "Let's leave early."

"Before we even discuss the game plan? We should probably talk about how not to scare the poor guy to death."

"We can do that while we're out exploring Overlay City! What do you think of this?" I showed off a flirty sky-blue dress from Mys's très chic wardrobe and got a thumbs-up from my roomie. "Too bad he won't be able to see me in this sexy number."

"What's the message?" Mys asked, sipping coffee.

"That my ghost is stuck here because of him," I deadpanned.

"Major creep factor, but continue."

Cackling, I raided the bookshelf for paper and bent over the coffee table with one of Mys's anime journals. I read out loud as I wrote. "*I should've told you how I felt when I had the chance, Willie-Jay. Now, I can't move on until you know how much I like you.*"

Mys gave a dramatic slow clap from the barstool. "Way to make a guy feel like your resting in peace hinges upon him circling yes on your cosmic love note."

"I mean, technically it does. What do you propose, sex guru?" I asked with a grin.

"You could say, 'I desired you with a fire that consumed me 'til my last breath.'"

"Yasss! Poetic. I love that. Is that how you keep men hanging on your every word?" I tossed the *Attack on Titan* notebook onto the couch. Mys slipped off the barstool to put it away where it belonged, and I corrected my error, grabbing it before they could and putting it back myself.

"I don't give away trade secrets, Yōkai. Anyway, I guess we can leave early, since I technically don't have anything else to do with my day."

Smiling, I gave Mys a once-over. Blue-silk pajamas made their body a study in elegance. Mussed black hair framed a well-rested face, sparkling eyes bordered by dark lashes, and pink lips that invited . . . well, wishful thinking.

"I can't believe you don't have a date or three," I joked.

"Are you asking me out?" Mys replied sarcastically.

"Pfft! No."

They left the bathroom door open while they showered. I stole a quick glance, but the opaque curtain hid everything—even my wicked rosy tint as I quietly exhaled and turned away. I lingered outside the threshold to ask more questions about Overlay City. Did centaurs exist? Was there racial animus between the different types? Did all Supernaturals have powers?

"We don't think of it like that," said Mys. "Humans have five senses. We have more. Like, my Empathy allows me to sense what others want, need, and feel. I can't do anything with it, the way you'd expect of a superpower, although it's handy information in a pinch."

Did that mean my roommate could basically read my every lusty imagining? I gulped and made my mind a barren field of G-rated thoughts for all of five seconds before I gave up. To hell with it. We were both adults.

When Mys finished showering, I slipped into the steamy bathroom for a luxurious soak. Just as with eating, drinking, and sleeping, I no longer needed to bathe, but I enjoyed the habit. I left the door open, too, but was mildly surprised when Mys entered to put on makeup. Like I wasn't right there, naked.

"What will you do if this William guy admits he likes you too?" they asked.

I sank deeper into the bubbles. "What can I do? I'm a ghost."

"What if he has the Sight?" Mys glanced at me. Was it me, or was there a hint of desire in those bottomless eyes? "You wouldn't be the first ghost to steal the heart of a living person."

I didn't want to admit how much I liked the idea of an Afterlife relationship. I hadn't had many boyfriends in real life. "I guess we'll cross that bridge when we get there. It's not like I'm irresistible."

"Fishing for compliments?" Mys asked. I stuck out my tongue, and they grinned and left the bathroom as a tinge crept over my face at our unexpected chemistry. There was something to be said for proximity.

•••

Despite the fact Willie-Jay always put plenty deets on social media, online stalking was neither glamorous nor appealing to me ever since I'd had to battle my own internet creep. I knew where my crush lived only because he was in the same building as one of my cousins.

Mys and I strolled into Oak Crest Condominiums, and my heart thundered in my chest at what I was about to do. I took in my surroundings. It was the kind of place I expected a guy like Willie-Jay to call home—classy, sophisticated, with a doorman and a concierge at the front desk. I was weightless with butterflies. Mys tugged my hand, and I realized I was *floating*. I whisper-screamed in panic.

"No one else sees you. Relax," Mys whispered, having a field day.

"What if William *does* have the Sight, and I do some spooky ghostly shit without trying to?"

"He'll be too distracted by how fabulous you look. Now, which floor? I don't want to ask the concierge. He's judging me for talking to myself." Mys giggled.

Burbling with laughter, I gave them the apartment number and tried to keep in touch with gravity. Talk about getting swept off my feet. William was half the excitement; busting out of the studio was the other part of the thrill.

Mys and I had spent the afternoon on a pleasant stroll through Overlay City while we waited for my crush to finish his classes at the university. At first, I contended with people walking through me. Eventually, I learned to dodge the pedestrians. None of the Supernaturals we encountered were much different than humans, but I noticed that I didn't have to sidestep them.

We went past my favorite shops and restaurants, filling up on the smell of Creole cooking. Mys pointed out Supernatural venues I wished we could explore, like a place called Brewtech where hawkers sold magical instruments with all the panache of discount iPhone sellers. We couldn't go everywhere, so I filed away places to visit later if we had the chance.

We paused and watched street performers and talented artists sketching portraits for tourists. We saw tarot readers, fortune tellers, and bullshitters; pickpockets and young boys dancing on the curb. I hadn't realized how much I missed the gleaming black wrought-iron balustrades, or the windows with blue and red shutters, or the unique local syntax.

New Orleans lifted my spirits. In the back of my mind, I knew if all went well, I would be saying good-bye to this place soon. Once I completed my unfinished business, whether Darcy was searching for me or not, I would visit my family one last time and cross over to the Other Side.

•••

Mys and I exited the elevator and walked down a cheery, yellow hall in search of William's door. When my companion started singing quietly in Japanese, I absently commented, "I wish I was bilingual."

"I know basic words and phrases. I'm teaching myself," Mys explained.

"Doesn't your family, er . . . ?" I clamped my lips shut.

Mys shrugged. "I was adopted when I was two. Wonderful folks, but they damn sure didn't speak *my* language, and they never understood my kind . . . Supernaturals."

CHAPTER FOURTEEN
—
Mys

August 27 | Evening

"Yikes for making assumptions." Aurie wrinkled her nose at the awkwardness.

"It's not a big deal." I let my hair fall over my face and gave her a sideways smile, ready to change the subject. The conversation was getting culturally precarious.

"You don't have to talk about being adopted if you don't want to, but I find you fascinating."

"Like a peculiarity?" I teased.

She smirked. "Like an interesting person that I'd like to get to know."

I studied the floor. I rarely talked about my past. There was never any reason to. My best friend Kittie had seen most of it firsthand, and my clients couldn't care less. Aurie's interest felt like a warm flicker within my consciousness.

I struggled to find a safe starting point. There were real traumas in my history, but my memories of growing up secretly Supernatural in a houseful of humans were just basic-level bad.

"The first fifteen years of my life, I had no idea what I was. I thought I was mentally ill. I could feel other people's emotions. When I tried explaining my Empathy to my parents, they said I was making things up."

"What's it like?" Aurie asked.

"Impressions," I murmured, looking at her, "of what you want, what you need. I know exactly how you feel right now." She blushed, and I shrugged and smiled. "I try not to eavesdrop."

"Thank you," she said as she caught my hand. I sighed.

But sometimes I can't stop listening because I find you fascinating too.
"Anyway, I didn't understand why I could see things no one else saw," I murmured. "I remember telling my parents there was a monster outside my window. Later, I found out there were goblins and dragon shifters in my old neighborhood."

"Wow. Why didn't the other Supers help you?"

"I didn't know them, they didn't know me. I had a very sheltered home life. I was even homeschooled."

"Ah, got it. My mom is, um, famous. So, in middle school, my classmates started giving me a hard time about it, and my parents hired private tutors until I graduated."

"Yeah, my parents were fundamentalists. I learned about Overlay City when my best friend Kittie and I were recruited by a pimp who happened to be an elf." I chuckled dryly at the memory of Jasper. "That was after I basically got put out."

"Your parents put you out?" Aurie gasped.

"It's . . . complicated, but that's a story for another day. Ready to go in?" I asked. Our conversation had carried us to William J. Varnado's door. Aurie buzzed with nervousness.

"I hate leaping through walls, but here goes nothing."

"See you on the other side," I said.

I lifted a fist to knock at the door once she went in, but my phone rang. Glancing at the screen, I saw it was Kittie, and Aurie's words came back to me. I had been avoiding my best friend for making a forgivable thoughtless remark, which was wrong of me.

I hurriedly whispered into the receiver, "Can't talk now, except to apologize for behaving like a garbage human being for the past two weeks."

"No, no, it was me!" Kittie Cad insisted. "I wanted you to clear your schedule, but that stupid question came out all wrong. Ugh! Can we put it behind us? Let's start over. Please, hang out with me this weekend, darling."

"Of course, Ms. Cad."

"You're amazing. I'm so relieved to have my bestie back. My boyfriend has been dying to meet you!"

"Okay, uh . . ." A thunderous crash suddenly came from within the apartment. "Can we make plans later? I'm a tad busy at the moment. I'll have to call you back."

I ended the call with Kittie quickly as a visibly upset Aurie opened the door and stormed from Willie-Jay's apartment. I grabbed the ghost and hightailed it before her crush investigated the invisible force wreaking havoc. We ducked into the elevator.

"That bastard," Aurie fumed as she shoved a broken iPad at me.

"What the hell happened?" I asked.

"He was in the middle of uploading revenge porn. I heard him talking about it on the phone to some other guy. That's what took me so long. I don't even know the girl, but, dude!"

"I'm guessing when he saw the tablet fly across the room—"

"Yeah, he realized that was a bad idea." Aurie laughed with rancor. She pushed her hair from her face and paced the elevator on a minor rampage. "Why are men like that?"

"Is it problematic to say 'not all men'?" I joked. She growled and mushed my face, and I caught her hand and held it tenderly. "Come here. I empathize, Yōkai. I literally feel your pain, but don't let one asshole taint your impression of the world." I applauded myself for turning off my inner cynic. Kittie would be proud.

In a whiny huff, Aurie slipped into my arms and snuggled against my chest. I buried my nose in her hair. Was it weird that she smelled like spring? I hadn't interacted with many ghosts, per se, but everything about her felt too alive. Her voluptuous breasts, the gentle flare of her hips, the V of her . . .

Ah, hell. I tried to disengage, but she hugged me tighter, her lithe body flush with mine. My face filled with heat as I stared at the ceiling of the elevator.

"It doesn't bother me," Aurie murmured without looking up.

A fluttery laugh escaped. "I don't think you understand." I willed myself to think of anything else. The shadowy interlude in the alley with Zyr came to mind. *Fuck my life.* Between the two of them, I would drown in an ocean of pent-up . . . something.

"Try to explain it." Aurie coaxed. "And don't say you're not like other guys because I know."

"I'm *not* like other guys." I scoffed.

She leaned back and looked at me. "Why do I make you uncomfortable?"

"I . . ." *I don't sleep with women, but I'm deeply attracted to you?* The elevator landed with a quiet thump and chimed for the lobby. I breathed a sigh of relief. "I'm not uncomfortable with you. This is our floor."

"Liar. But I guess I should be figuring out my own situation instead of putting you on the spot," Aurie groused. "So, what is my unfinished business, if it isn't William Varnado?"

"I have an idea, but I'll need Detective Zyr's help," I said as I led her out of the lobby.

"Watch me turn into a primal scream before I learn what I'm supposed to do with my Afterlife."

"Don't worry," I whispered to her as I opened the door to the Uber. But I shared some doubts. It usually took a while for ghosts to lose touch with reality. It usually took them a long time to gain control of their powers too. Aurie was already proving the exception to the rule.

The Uber returned us to my apartment without incident. I scanned the courtyard one last time before we slipped inside. I hadn't felt a single bad vibe while we were out, and I was confident no one had seen us.

"Call him over," Aurie suggested.

It took me a second to realize who she meant. "The detective? I need to call my friend Kittie and play catch-up. She checked in while we were at Willie's place."

Aurie lit up with smug satisfaction. "I'm glad you two made up. One friendship down, one ship to go."

"Shut it," I giggled.

She settled into my favorite chair, in a better mood. Zyr would be pleased to know our idea had worked. Sort of. Her poltergeist-y jitters were calmed for the moment. I slipped into the kitchenette to whip up two coffees for us. Aurie was a java fiend like me. Then I dialed Kittie Cad and discussed meeting up on Friday night while my roommate planted her nose in a book to give me privacy.

"I promise not to alert the press," I teased through the phone.

"You'd better not! He's the mayor," Kittie confided.

"Me-*ow*, Kittie! So *that's* why everything has been hush-hush."

"You know some people would have a meltdown at him dating a trans woman. Dress casual. It should be a laid-back meeting between friends."

"Understood," I said. It bugged me that we had to pretend, but I truly did understand, as much as I hated it. "Now, let me go, Ms. Cad. Gotta spend time with Aurie before I—"

"Who's Aurie?" Kittie chirped. "A new friend? At *your place*?"

Without lifting her gaze from the page, Aurie turned an ear my way, a knowing smile tickling the corners of her lips. I fumbled for words, inwardly chastising myself for the mistake. Kittie clearly thought Aurie was more than just a friend. How could I explain my new roomie was a ghost?

•••

The pubs in New Orleans were unlike anywhere else. In a city where open containers were the norm—anyone could have an open alcoholic beverage in public—it took a lot more than kitschy décor to keep beer buddies at the bar. The place where I met Kittie and her boyfriend was swamp themed. There was an alligator on the wall and a stuffed possum family in a glass display case by the door.

Aside from strong mixed drinks, the real draw at Pappy's Bootstrap was the live music. As I entered the crowded establishment, the three-man band started up a rousing rendition of "Barton Hollow" by the Civil Wars. I hummed along, standing on tiptoe to peer over the dance floor in search of Kittie Cad and her date.

There she was. Across the pub at a table near the bar, Kittie and Mayor Terrance Rhemus shared loaded eye contact. My best friend was in a millennial-pink pantsuit. She toyed with salon-styled hair as she listened to whatever the mayor was saying. Her sienna face glowed from a touch of highlighter, but mostly from genuine joy.

Leaning over with a grin, she unconsciously arched her body toward her date, and he licked his lips as if he'd like nothing better than to eat her alive. I'd had no idea the mayor was such an attractive man. He had clear brown skin, with a dark manscaped beard over a square jawline. He was a total conservative heartthrob.

This was the real deal, and Kittie deserved it. Grinning, I weaved my way through the pub to greet them. They were so engrossed they didn't even notice me approach. I shyly announced my presence.

"Mitsuyo!" Kittie squealed. "Please meet my friend Terrance. Could you keep him company while I run to the ladies' room?" She hopped up and hugged me, then gestured to her date.

"Um, okay," I said, reaching to shake his hand. "Call me Mys."

"Nice to meet you, Mys. Kristin has told me a lot about you."

As I settled at the table, I happened to glance at the door. To my surprise, there was Detective Zyr with a bombshell clinging to him like she'd never let go. Her body screamed femme fatale. Burnished copper hair accentuated ivory skin. A spray of freckles covered the bridge of her nose. Her bow-shaped lips parted seductively as she stared at the detective.

Who the hell was *she*?

CHAPTER FIFTEEN
—
Zyr

August 30 | Evening

I smelled cedarwood and thunderstorms. I knew that scent. Expectancy and panic warred in me as I looked around for the source, and Mys met my gaze across the crowded establishment.

I hadn't seen Aurie's friend since the interlude in the alley. I wasn't *ready* to see Mys. Flashes of erotic memory exploded in my mind: the taste of their minty kiss. The sound of their moan. The feel of them in my arms. Aurie's visible excitement at catching us. Passion tugged at me.

"Sorry. What?" I glanced at Tegan squeezing my hand.

Her flustered expression softened when she saw she had my attention. "I said I'm glad we picked this place. I miss going out with you."

"Yeah. Wanna sit here?" I pointed out a table. Any table.

As we took our seats, Tegan launched into a conversation I barely heard over the music and my pounding headache—a sign that too long a stretch had passed since my last transformation. I needed to get to my cabin soon or I'd lose control, triggered by seeing Mys on a date, for instance.

And out with the *mayor?*

Seeing them forced me to deal with the amassing complications of this case. Not only did Aurie's mother think I was incompetent and distracted, but the *actual* distraction was away from the task I had been assigned. Mys was supposed to be watching Aurie. I wanted to say something, but it would make me look jealous.

Because I *was* jealous. Aurie was fine at the protected studio. This was simply business as usual for Mys.

I rubbed my face, trying not to stare. A server stopped beside me, and I absently ordered tonic water. My partner asked for the same. Tegan's confession to Mrs. Edison that she had been treated for alcoholism had been news to me, although I vaguely recalled her mentioning AA. I had been preoccupied lately.

Again, my attention shot across the room as the suave mayor leaned toward Mys with a pleasant smile. My restless foot-tapping jostled our table. Tegan slid a hand over my knee. "What's wrong with you, big guy? It's like you're ready for war."

"Nahin. We haven't been out together in a while, that's all. What's up?"

"You don't remember, do you?" Her tone made me suppress my emotions and try to focus—the stiffness of her smile and her wounded eyes told me I *should* remember. I wracked my brain, snapping my fingers as it came to me.

"Wait a minute, it's your birthday, isn't it?"

"Yeah, thirty-two today! Now, tell me I don't look a day over twenty-five."

"You don't."

"Stop lying!" Tegan howled. I shrugged and chuckled. It was the truth. She was fit, and she took great care of her herself. She was undeniably attractive.

"Birthday jitters behind the extraflirty attention lately?" I asked. I crossed my arms on the table and tried to relax. She flushed, erupting in giggles.

"I have not been extraflirty."

"You have," I said lightly. "I don't want people like Mrs. Edison thinking there's chemistry between us."

"Point taken," she conceded as her amused blue eyes met mine. "I guess getting older has me feeling slightly out of sorts. I never thought I'd live to be this age."

"I guess in our line of work—"

"No, it's not that." She snorted a laugh. "Want to know something? I lied about being a clumsy kid. It's embarrassing to admit I was abused growing up. Go figure, I married Reggie. After him, I vowed to never be under anyone else's thumb, but I can't seem to stop making the same mistakes!" She laughed, and it sounded forced.

I nodded, remembering stuff she had told me about her abusive ex-husband. "What about that guy you were dating earlier this year?" I asked offhand.

"Who? The one with the body shop? He was a literal pain in the neck." Tegan flipped her hair over her shoulder and leaned closer to my side of the table.

"Well, that sounds vampiric," I quipped, staring at Mys.

Tegan sighed. "Okay, a *figurative* pain in the neck, grammar king. Anyway, my thirty-two years feel way too heavy. I'd love a fucking drink, but I'm twenty days sober after a hard detox. So, enough with the pity party. Do you wanna be the cure to what ails me tonight?" She bit her lip and grinned at me, adding, "I hear it gets better after thirty. Make me feel my age."

I inhaled and sat back. Any real consideration of her surprise offer of sex was fleeting, but I glanced across the pub. Yep, Mys was watching. Tegan and I probably appeared intimate, especially when my partner grabbed my hand and brought it to her face.

A part of me was glad the futanari had no idea we were merely coworkers, since Mys was clearly out with—

Suddenly a gorgeous blond joined the couple's table, and the facts clarified: Mys was out with friends. It wasn't a date. It was a friendly night on the town, and desire was truly fucking with my head.

Inwardly berating myself, I extricated my hand from Tegan's grasp. "Hey, listen to me. You're smart, vibrant, and sexy. I'm not just blowing smoke up your pretty little ass. You really are. You can do so much better than a one-night stand with a guy like me," I said to her.

"My God! Tell me you're not interested. I can handle it!" Tegan said jovially. My gaze slid to Mys reacting to something her glamorous blond friend was saying, and my heart rate accelerated. Tegan casually peered in the direction I was looking. "Oh, I see," she drawled.

"See what?" I sat straighter.

"You've been staring since we came in. I thought she was an ex, but is she someone current? Why don't you invite her over?"

"No, of course not. There's no, um . . . Would you excuse me?"

I made a mad dash for the men's room, knowing my answers wouldn't hold up to Tegan's skillful interrogation techniques. As I slipped to the walled-off corridor where the restrooms were located, Mys followed. My glare warned them to stay put, but they ignored me. We entered together, and I locked the door behind us.

"What are you doing?" I hissed.

"What do you think I'm doing?"

"I thought you were—" I stopped, unwilling to admit my error.

Mys crossed their arms. "Out playing escort? Yeah, you've battered me with your disapproval since you got here. For your information, I'm—"

"Out with friends. I got it."

"Good . . . And you?" Mys shifted their weight from one foot to the other. I smiled, surprised and pleased that it mattered. I casually swept back my blazer, hands on my hips, as I stood with legs slightly gapped. My eyes roved their captivating face, noting the purple contacts, the straight black hair accentuating the flawless skin.

"She's my partner. There's nothing there," I murmured.

"Oh."

"That's it?" I asked, stepping forward.

Mys backed against the wall. "No, I followed you in here because I sensed what you were feeling."

"You sensed how much I wanted to do this?" My teeth caught the corner of their jaw, and I inhaled their stormy, sexy scent before turning and capturing their trembling lips in a silken kiss. The futanari emitted a moan, and I retreated a half step with a shaky laugh. "You must be psychic, because I wasn't even sure I wanted it."

"That's the irony," Mys whispered. "I usually know what people want before they're sure themselves. For example, I know you want to be in control. You don't want to do anything crazy tonight. Yet, you're all riled up."

"Generalizations. I'm calling your psychic bluff."

"I'm not a psychic. I'm an Empath. There's a difference, and I'm glad I ran into you here, because I sense you're ready for that 'favor for a favor,' Detective. It's for Aurie. She needs you," Mys breathed against my lips, unzipping my pants. I lifted an eyebrow. "The crush wasn't her unfinished business, but you can still give her the release she deserves."

I shook my head and chuckled. "I'm listening," I said as my mouth coasted over theirs again.

CHAPTER SIXTEEN
—
Mys

August 30 | Evening

Zyr's overpowering, raw hunger made me want to be the honey that clung to his lips. I wanted his vigorous tongue to polish me off. However, the heat in this Cajun-themed (and thankfully hygienic) restroom wasn't supposed to be about me.

It was about proving to Detective Zyr Ravani that as much as he wanted Aurie Edison, she *needed* him.

"Give her an Afterlife send-off to remember," I said.

"A one-night stand is Aurie's ticket to Heaven? No way. Besides, what you're suggesting goes against every moral standard I've ever set." Zyr's hands got lost in my hair as his mouth chased mine.

"So you've never broken the rules?" I groaned, kissing him. I touched him the way he had touched me in the cathedral alley. Below the belt. He closed his bliss-glossed eyes as I deftly stroked away his inhibitions.

"Damn it, Mys!" Zyr shuddered, near surrender.

Burying my face in his neck, I soaked in his bergamot, blood orange, and cardamom scent. Did he taste as sweet as he smelled? My tongue glided along his earlobe. *Slay me.* He tasted like fire.

I swallowed a hum. "I know it sounds ludicrous, but trust me. This is her ticket out. It's not just gratuitous sex. Aurie needs to feel something outside her comfort zone, to discover a deeper truth about herself. C'mon, Detective. You understand how . . . transformative real freedom can be, right?"

He emitted a raspy chuckle. "Do I get a say in this?"

"Which part of 'I'm an Empath' doesn't register? I know what you want."

Every part of Detective Zyr Ravani confessed a desire he couldn't renounce, and every fiber of my being sensed his craving. He wanted Aurie and me, both. However, there was no future for any of us. Zyr and I had here and now, a favor for a favor, to get Aurie to her ever after.

I dropped to my knees and gazed up at the detective.

With a shaky laugh, he replied, "Don't do anything you don't want to do."

"Same. You can stop me whenever you want," I countered.

As I skillfully kissed his exposed manhood, he didn't try to stop a damn thing. On the contrary, I stole a glance, and Zyr's intense stare became part of the sex act. I couldn't look away. His naked soul was in the abyss of his eyes. I felt his rapture secondhand, like a kaleidoscope of his emotions blossoming within my consciousness.

"Tell me this is about more than Aurie," he murmured.

"What do you think?" I asked.

"I think you're trying to buy me . . . to pawn me off afterward," Zyr said huskily.

I blinked up at him. "Do you want me to stop?"

"No," he growled after a beat. "You know I don't."

I clutched his hips and resumed control. His body buzzed with fine tremors, his breathing labored. Ecstasy made him angry. My expert fellatio buckled his knees. I excited and perplexed the detective to no end, but he was wrong. This wasn't transactional. I wasn't trying to buy his cooperation. With equal parts fascination and confusion, I felt just as bound to this situation as he did.

Suddenly, Zyr yanked me to my feet. "Mm! Mys!" he gasped. I clutched his face, kissing his lips to muffle the explosive sound of his climax. But when it was over and he pressed his face to mine, I reflexively turned my back to give him space to pull himself together.

"You'll spend a night with her," I said over my shoulder. It was more of a statement than a question. I dropped paper towels over the telltale wet linoleum, using my boot to mop away the evidence of our little interlude.

"So, I *was* being bought and paid for." Zyr blew out a breath.

At the derision in his tone, a twinge of hurt tried to take root. I faced him. "Look, Aurie is helping you complete your life's work by testifying against Cyprian. This is the least you can do for her. Why not give her what she needs?"

"Again, what's in it for you, Mys? What do *you* need?"

I surged with annoyance. "I need you to focus," I said as I threw open the restroom door. "Because the longer you're both in my life, the more it costs me."

"Oh! Pardon me for being bad for business."

"I'm not talking about money, Zyr."

"Then what *are* you talking about?" he hissed as we both stepped from the alcove and into the pub. I suddenly realized I shouldn't have brought up the subject here. Kittie and Terrance looked my way. I tried to give them a reassuring smile, but the detective had my wrist in a vise grip.

"Oh, uh-*uh*!" Kittie Cad threw her napkin down and rose to her feet. At nearly seven feet tall, she towered over most men. My plaintive stare begged her to sit back down, but the mayor rose as well.

"Is there a problem?" he asked.

Zyr seemed to wake up to the fact he was causing a scene. His face flooded with color, and he let me go. I felt humiliated, the center of attention in the crowded pub. Zyr's chagrined gaze darted to his table, but his partner had already left.

I leaned in and whispered curtly, "What do you want me to believe, Detective? That this is leading somewhere? Or that it's never gonna happen again, like you said last time? I don't need your mixed signals. Give that energy to the person who does need you before her time runs out."

Zyr straightened his blazer and dropped his head. "I apologize. Sincerely. I didn't mean to overstep my bounds. I'll go check on Aurie."

I blew out a breath. "Fine. Let me tell Kittie and Terrance I have to go," I muttered.

"Nahin, no, I don't want to ruin your evening. Enjoy the rest of your night."

CHAPTER SEVENTEEN
—
Aurie

August 30 | Night

While Mys was out with their friend, I was daydreaming about our Garden District house with its bold colors and white columns. I saw the oversized hibiscus shrub in the backyard, sheer curtains fluttering at a tall window on the second floor behind it. Beyond the heady blossoms, Haley would be prepping for another iconic Friday night.

Mom might be downstairs in her home office. If she were, she'd be talking a mile a minute on the phone to her assistant. I could see her sharp features unfolding in a smile and hear the bubbly sound of her always unexpected laughter. Or maybe she was back in LA at the chrome and leather condo, drumming up interest in her latest movie.

My funeral wouldn't keep Mom in New Orleans long, but Haley would be waiting for me. I imagined my feet traversing the sidewalk to the porch. I almost felt the front door swing open beneath my touch, and there it was . . . the life I had left behind.

Someone knocking on Mys's door startled me back to reality. "Hey, Aurie? It's me, hun. Let me in," Detective Zyr called out. My lips tightened as the vision receded, reminding me life was for the living. It was going on without me. I brushed away tears I hadn't realized I was crying as I rose from the lounge chair and padded across the room.

"What's up, Detective? The door won't open for anyone but Mys, remember?"

"Oh, you're by yourself? I, um, just stopped by to make sure you were okay. Can you step outside a minute? I don't want it to be a wasted trip."

"Yeah, sure." I was midway through the door when I realized I was hearing Detective Zyr's voice *inside my head*, but it was already too late. Hands grabbed me.

"There you are." Darcy Cyprian smiled with insidious delight at the involuntary whimper that tore from my throat as he lifted me with vampire strength and peered into my face. A shock of golden hair billowed over his deep-set emerald eyes. "It really is you," he whispered, looking awestruck.

I shrank into myself. I had spent hours imagining what I'd do to my killer, given the chance. I came to the disheartening realization that I wouldn't do a damn thing. I was immobilized by fear. I saw no fangs or anything unusual in his unnaturally refined face, but now that I was Supernatural, something within me recognized he was dangerously inhuman.

I looked around for help, but the people in the cars that passed, the group of girlfriends enjoying themselves across the street, they wouldn't hear me if I screamed. No one would know what was happening to the ghost in the shadowy alleyway beside the cathedral.

Come on, think, Aurie! I willed my panicked brain. I wondered what would happen if, instead of focusing my energy on being solid, I did the opposite. I closed my eyes and pictured myself light as a wisp of smoke, and I slipped through the vampire's hands like magic. The door rattled as he struck it with his powerful fists, but I was on the other side, back in the safe haven of Mys's studio.

"Aurelia!" Darcy shouted angrily. I retreated as far as I could, though the enraged voice rang in my head. Finally, he regained control of himself. "Damn it, Aurie. I apologize. You made me lose my temper, but I would never . . . I would never hurt you. Please. Kindly open the door so we can talk like civilized people."

"Never hurt me? You drugged me and God knows what else!" I retorted.

"You believe that? The ones you consider your friends are keeping major secrets from you, pooch." His voice was calmer, but that did nothing to lessen my terror.

I was a different kind of vulnerable now that he knew where I was, and I had no idea how to contact Zyr or Mys. I slammed a hand on the kitchen counter in helpless fury. Why had I gone out? I seemed destined to keep making the same mistakes.

"I'm not your pooch or your pet," I said through clenched teeth.

I heard him chuckle beyond the door. "It's an endearment, not a job offer, and I'm not who you should be worried about. Ask yourself why the detective hasn't let you see your family yet. Why is he keeping you locked up here? Has he even told you what happened to your sister?"

What had happened to Haley? I jerked my head. *Lies.* "I don't know what you're talking about, but if you know the detective, then you know you don't want to be here when he gets back."

"Right," he said. "Clearly, he has you convinced that I'm the bad guy, and the Council's going to put me away. I'm on the Council of Overlay Affairs, Aurie, and I'm fairly influential as Director of Corporate Resources. I'm not going anywhere."

"Claim whatever title you want. I wasn't born yesterday."

"Why would I lie? Detective Zyr has his own agenda, but my agenda is to help you. I have a friend in Hollygrove who can perform your Resurrection. You'll find her card outside the door." He sounded so reasonable.

"Are you for real? Why?" I blurted out the question that had plagued me since I'd woken up dead. Never mind the stuff he was saying about Zyr. It raised numerous red flags, but I would puzzle through that later. Darcy intruded in my head. "I'll be honest with you, as no one else seems to have been since you got to Overlay City. I've been alive so many centuries I've lost count, but you were the greatest surprise in half a lifetime."

"Whatever."

"I'm not lying, Aurelia. You shouldn't have gotten into that party. It was strictly for Supernaturals and their guests, and when I make a mandate, it stands. Yet, all of a sudden, there you were, the girl of my dreams. There's something special about you, and I want you to be mine."

"Don't. I'm not the girl of your dreams, and I'll never be yours."

"Not even if I can help you see your family again?" he asked softly. "Search for the business card when you feel safe to come out. I'll return in a few days once you've seen for yourself that what I promise is real. Until next time, *ma louloute*."

I experienced a sensation like my ears popping. Finally, he was out of my head. My knees gave up. I dropped to the floor. My stomach quaked with nausea. Another phantom feeling in a phantom body. I couldn't vomit, but I dry heaved while the cabinets in the kitchenette banged open and the dishes clattered.

Darcy Cyprian knew where I was hiding now. He had found me. There was nothing to stop him from coming back. It wasn't enough that he had killed me. He was ruining my Afterlife, planting uncertainty where before I'd been sure of things.

Was Detective Zyr hiding something? What had happened to Haley? Why hadn't my friends told me about Resurrection? I didn't know whom to trust. My eyes suddenly welled up, and all four elements on the electric stove glowed hot while the studio lights flickered overhead.

I worried about Haley. There was no way to know how my sister was doing from here. I needed to see her for myself. I got to my feet, but another thought occurred to me, and I stopped at the ornately carved door. What if this was one of Darcy's tricks? If he was waiting for me on the other side, there was no guarantee I'd escape his clutches a third time.

I backed away from the exit and massaged my temples, trying to think. I felt like I was unraveling. Behind me, the dressing screen fell with a loud crash, and the bathroom door banged open. I vaguely registered the showerhead hissing, steam rolling toward the ceiling like clouds seeking the sky.

None of this should've been happening, but it didn't fully register until I saw my body blinking in and out just like the lights overhead. "What is this?" I whimpered, staring at my disappearing hands in horror.

The door burst open as Detective Zyr and Mys rushed into the studio. Their sudden arrival anchored me to reality, but how could I keep a grip when the people who I'd thought I could trust had built a world of secrets and lies, smoke and mirrors? I was becoming a poltergeist. I telepathically slammed the door shut behind them. No one was leaving until I got the truth. My very existence depended on it.

CHAPTER EIGHTEEN
—
Mys

August 30 | Night

"Watch it!" I yanked Detective Zyr from the path of the swinging door before it banged shut.

The minute he'd scented vampires, we'd known something was wrong. A dark energy crackled in the frigid apartment. Aurie swayed on her feet as pandemonium swirled around her. Books flew off the shelves. Framed prints rattled against the walls.

Trillions of invisible pings of emotion played shrilly in my head. The din was underscored by a low rumble—the sound of my big leather couch gaining speed as it rushed toward the detective and me. Zyr caught it at the last second, but his face was a mask of concern as he looked my way for answers.

"What happened, Yōkai?" I asked warily.

"Did you lie to me?" Aurie croaked.

Confused, I shook my head. I held up my hands, taking a cautious step toward the angry ghost as I cast Empathy to figure out what she meant. I sensed her distrust and growing cynicism, but it was the blade of her anguish that cut the deepest.

"You feel alone," I murmured. The sensation felt like the day my parents had dropped me off at my last religious therapy camp when I was sixteen. Right after I'd been released from the hospital. "You feel betrayed," I whispered.

Aurie bit her quivering lip, nodding as tears fell.

"You know, my father once told me, 'If you can't stop acting out, don't come back.'" I held up my butterfly tattoos for her to see. "But you're not acting out. It's just hard to contain what's going on inside, right?"

"You made it out alive," she sniffled. Her focus sharpened on me, and I knew it was progress. I slowly edged another step toward her.

"Yes, I got a second chance, and this Afterlife is yours. To finish your unfinished business. I'm not asking you to turn off your feelings. I'm offering to share the burden if you're willing to tell me what's wrong. We're here for you, Yōkai."

"Darcy Cyprian came." Her tear-streaked face resumed its leaking as she said his name.

"Cyprian, himself, came here?" Zyr growled incredulously.

He turned to charge after the vampire, but I reached out to stop him. Aurie needed us. Incredible savagery raced up my arm and slammed into my chest, and I let him go. Zyr glared at me with fiery yellow eyes, baring his teeth. His claws were out. The previous times when I had thought he was wild paled by comparison.

"You can't go after him alone," I said, trying to reason with the wolf.

"What? You want me to radio in and say, 'Vampires found my enchanted witness protection'? I'm going—"

"You're not going anywhere until you tell me what happened to my sister." Aurie suddenly stood between us, no longer out of sorts. With her growing clarity, the mayhem in my apartment settled. Still, Zyr's eyes widened at her new ability to flicker from one place to another.

"Aurie? How did you astral project?" I asked. My trembling hands hovered at her shoulders to usher her to the couch. "Why don't you lie down a moment until you get your bearings?"

"Answer the question, Detective."

She focused all her attention on Zyr, whom she had by the collar of his shirt. I glanced down. The ghost was levitating to put them on the same level. Her ebony curls floated around her face in a breeze that wasn't of this world, and her clothes rippled in the same chilling current. The cold made my breath condense into fog.

If Aurie was a blizzard of death, the werewolf brought a lethal heat wave. The rings of fire encircling his pupils flamed like solar flares as he balled his fists. I cupped his elbow to hold him back, but neither of them seemed ready to walk away. My concern went up another notch.

"What the hell happened to Haley?" Aurie yelled.

Uneasiness slid over the detective's face. Gods, I wished I hadn't seen it. Was it possible the vampire had gotten inside Aurie's head with a twisted half truth built on something Zyr had omitted? His guilt seared into my consciousness in confirmation.

Aurie's face tightened when she saw his look of contrition. "The sad thing is I low-key liked you," she said brokenly, shoving away from the detective. His amber eyes lost their wildfire, and the fight went out of him. With an apology on the tip of his tongue, he reached for her, but she cut him off. "Don't you dare act like you care how I feel after lying to me!"

"I haven't lied to you, Aurie. You can't trust Darcy," Zyr said feebly.

"No? Then why is he the only one who told me about Resurrection? Neither of *you* ever mentioned it."

I was astounded by her accusatory stare in my direction. "Everything I know about it, I learned in Sunday School," I said as calmly as I could, "but I take it you're not talking about being born again. Wouldn't you like to sit and talk things through?"

Aurie ignored my outstretched hand and continued trudging around the room. I surveyed the carnage of my apartment and kept a concerned eye on her. "You never even told me I would get powers like this," she said.

"Because you're not like other ghosts," said Zyr. "Aurie, I've had scores of dead witnesses, and I've never seen a single Soul like you. Most cross over before getting a whiff of telekinesis. Your ability to impact the real world came astonishingly fast, and your descent into poltergeist-like activity is troublingly premature. There's something . . . *special* about you."

"*Special?*" A near-hysterical laugh erupted from her. She covered her face, and it turned into a sob. When she dropped her hands, her expression was blank. I couldn't bear watching her struggle to hold it together on her own. I pulled her into a hug, expecting her to protest, but she didn't. We sat on the couch. Zyr dejectedly took the barstool across from us.

I studied him as he stared at her. She buried her face in the crook of my neck. While her silky tears wet my skin, his contrition spread scarlet in my consciousness. Whatever secrets he kept, he wasn't unaffected. I sensed he was developing a fondness for Aurie, not merely a physical attraction. After a moment, she dried her face on my shirt and seemed more composed.

"Funny, he said the same thing," she mumbled.

"He talked to you? That's important." The detective dug out his phone to take notes. "Did he say why you were special?" Zyr quizzed her.

"Something about how my sister and I got into that party." Aurie gave a careless shrug. "He said it was an exclusive event for Supernaturals."

"Well, how did you get in?" I asked.

"Like I told the detective, Haley flashed a doorman. What I can't figure out is, how did I get *out* if Darcy wanted me dead? He could easily have killed me in the penthouse. Why let me go downstairs, use Haley's voice to ask me to come back up, all to orchestrate a hit-and-run? None of it makes sense."

"Wait, what do you mean Darcy used Haley's voice?" Zyr interjected.

"He did it again tonight," Aurie explained. "At the party, when I called my sister, I'm certain he projected her voice into my head to tell me to come back upstairs. Tonight, he made me think it was you at the door, Detective. That was the reason I went out."

Zyr set aside his notes, steepled his fingers, and pressed them to his lips. "No, it doesn't make sense. But why would he suppress evidence if not to cover up his misdeeds? Why would he continue to chase after you if he wasn't behind the hit-and-run?"

"I don't know, but whatever his motives," said Aurie, "my sister and I both got into that event. That's why I need to see for myself that she's safe." She vacated my embrace and strode purposefully toward the door, but Detective Zyr rushed to block the exit. "I'm going home to my family. Move."

"Aurie, be reasonable," said Zyr.

"You don't understand! Nobody's keeping you away from the people you love!"

"Wrong," he roared. "The Council exiled me from my pack for choosing to do my job, and right now my job is keeping you safe! So stop acting like you're the only one who's ever lost something."

I hurried across the room to separate them. "Zyr, enough! Aurie, chill! Don't run off half-cocked. Give us a chance to get to the bottom of this. You have to trust us."

"Trust *him*?" She sniffed. "When I first got here and you logged into my Instagram, Haley hadn't made a new post. That wasn't unusual then, but it's been three weeks with no posts. Something is wrong with my sister."

A healthy, popular Instagram model not keeping up with social media? I frowned and turned to Zyr with my arms crossed. He looked miffed, but now I was suspicious too. "What's going on, Zyr? Tell her what she needs to know."

Finally, he pushed a hand through his hair and reached out to me for understanding. "All right, there are details I haven't talked about, because Aurie's not ready to hear them."

"You don't get to decide that. I'm not a child!" she exclaimed.

"You're nineteen," Zyr and I replied.

"Wrong, I'm dead! I think I can handle anything else life fucking throws at me."

I had to admit she had a point.

Detective Zyr blew out a breath and reluctantly confessed: "Your sister's in the hospital."

"Oh my God, did he hurt her?" Aurie asked in distress.

"No, honey. Haley had a psychotic break, but she's under the best care. I haven't been trying to deceive you. I've been trying to keep you focused on the Light. Ask yourself why Cyprian wants you worried about your sister. It's to stop you from crossing over!"

Aurie's eyes drilled into his as if to make sure he was telling the truth. The detective spread his arms like he had nothing left to hide and everything was out in the open.

"Well, Darcy Cyprian definitely succeeded at one thing," said Aurie. "I'm not going anywhere until I know Haley's okay."

Zyr threw up his hands. "That's the worst possible decision you could make. Every second you spend in Overlay City puts you at risk. Listen to me, Aurie."

"Hey! Before we start another war, can we clean up the casualties of the first one?" I suggested, hoping to defuse the situation before things got overblown.

I stooped to pick up the magazines near his foot and noticed a business card on thick black vellum. The words *Spellcaster, Charmer, and Black Magic Woman* were printed in white. I slipped the card into my pocket, intending to find out how Darcy Cyprian expected to make Aurie Edison a modern-day Lazarus.

CHAPTER NINETEEN
—
Zyr

August 31 | Morning

The tires of my pickup truck bit into the coarse gravel of the red dirt road. Driving through tall, stately pines and sprawling oaks, I couldn't get Aurie's questions about Darcy's motives out of my mind. Why would he call her back upstairs? I had a headache from pondering the evidence, but I was no closer to answers.

Of course, it didn't help that there were still some details I couldn't share with Aurie and Mys. I felt certain the three of us together had the brainpower to crack the case, but the Council of Overlay Affairs was adamant about keeping information under wraps. Guilty conscience aside, I needed to win a conviction against Darcy Cyprian. Aurie would understand . . . hopefully.

Another gusty sigh escaped my lips. My good doggo Ajit sensed my mood. The black and white speckled mastiff in the passenger seat lifted his head. "I'm okay, boy," I lied, scratching behind his ear.

In reality, I was worried this case was too much of a guessing game. I thought of the five or six texts from the captain from yesterday.

Reminders that Mrs. Edison needed a callback. Neither Aurie's mother nor Mayfield seemed keen on taking time to solve the hit-and-run the right way.

I had always worked by the book, even if the process was slower. I gripped the steering wheel tightly and frowned. Working by the book meant following the evidence, and I didn't like where the clues were taking me lately. I wanted to trust my instincts.

Was Paulie guilty? He had motive and history; however, that would mean Cyprian's moves that night had been pure happenstance. Of all the impossibilities walking the streets of Overlay City, there was no such creature as Coincidence.

I had decided to spend the weekend figuring out how the pieces fit together—Aurie and Haley Edison, Paul Jameson, Darcy Cyprian—at the one place where I could free my mind.

The sun was higher in the late morning sky as I parked the truck at my destination. I had taken care not to be followed, the way I always did when I came to this place. The rustic cabin was exactly as I had left it a month ago. Standing on a wing and a prayer after having been in the family for several generations.

It was where my younger brothers and I had spent summers with our grandfather. Following Baba Fazil's passing, I had inherited the place and its surrounding one hundred acres. Hazeem and Yazeed had always preferred the fast pace of New Orleans, but this was where I found peace.

"Baba used to say there's buried treasure on these grounds," I said teasingly to Ajit. The dog barked in response, not giving a shit about buried treasure unless it was a good ham bone.

We entered the cool interior of the cabin, and I tossed my keys on the oak table and my duffel bag in a corner. As I moved through the living room area, I shrugged out of my shirt and got rid of my shoes, the belt, the jeans. Bypassing the handcrafted bed, I went out the back door in my boxers to taste the day on the wind. Long, deep inhales carried the smell of freedom. I smiled, relaxing finally.

The wolf within me stirred to life. *Come on out,* I coaxed. Ajit whined some, but he had seen all this before. He scurried to the other side of the porch, waiting for the transformation to be complete.

My canines extended, and I yipped excitedly. Fingers splayed, my nails became sharper than normal claws, and I doubled over in exhilaration as my muscles bulged and reformed. I dropped to my knees with an impatient bark. Finally, I shook out a thick black pelt that shined sleek and healthy in the sunlight, and it was done.

It was almost better than sex. Almost. (Fading man-thoughts of what had transpired in the restroom with Mys crossed my mind—it couldn't quite top that.)

My wolf let out a howl that sent birds flapping through the trees. Shifters like me could change at will, regardless of lunar phases, though full moons wreaked havoc on my emotions. I even retained a hazy awareness of my inner man while I was in wolf shape, but there were perks to abandoning walking upright.

Preternatural senses pricked to attention. Each noise was like a beacon in the thicket. Ajit barked in anticipation, a tame creature by comparison, but a kindred spirit. It had been forever since we'd last hunted. My dog and I took off for the woods. The civilized world was overrated.

•••

Bright and early the next morning, sunlight warmed my face, but that wasn't what woke me. I crooked an arm over my forehead and stretched a leg out from under the blankets. I was caught in a dream of chasing deer under a starry sky. I had earplugs in to help me drown out the noise and sleep. The case had been giving me insomnia.

But there it was again. The sound of someone on my property. Footsteps crunched the driveway gravel out front. I shot up in bed, and the orange foam in my ears plopped out onto the sheets.

My first thought was Cyprian, but he didn't know of this place, and I didn't smell vampires. It was probably a driver who'd made a wrong turn. Bleary-eyed, I felt around for my clothes. Ajit snarled at the sound of knocking.

"It's me, Ravani. Don't shoot."

"Tegan?"

Arching an eyebrow in surprise, I scrambled out of bed and tossed on my jeans. When I opened the door, Ajit dutifully circled my partner, sniffing a few times before returning to his basket and going back to sleep. My curiosity wasn't as quickly satisfied.

"Yeah, your brother told me where to find you," she said with a grin, removing her Ray-Bans. She stared at my bare chest while she hooked one arm of the sunglasses on her T-shirt collar. In casual khaki shorts and trainers, she wasn't dressed like she was on official business.

"What are you doing here?" I asked.

"You're welcome for checking on your ass! I skipped volunteer work at the church job center to come find you. I must've called you a hundred times last night. Nice place, by the way. How come you, uh, never brought me here?" She gave herself a tour of the great room.

I closed the front door and tried to process the fact that one of my siblings had told an unfamiliar person about this place. Hazeem Ravani might have been listed in my file as next of kin, but I hadn't seen or spoken to my brothers in a long time.

The breach of trust was enough to make me reach for my phone, ignoring the Council mandate banning communication between us. It was a big deal because this piece of property wasn't on their books. It was the only place I could call my own ever since turning down the title of Alpha.

Tegan grabbed the cell phone from the table before I could get to it. When she saw the device was powered off, she gave me a look of annoyance and tossed it back.

"I'm sorry you were worried," I stated mildly. "Next time at least let me be missing a full twenty-four hours. I might've been with a friend out here."

"You mean the one *you* ditched *me* for the other night?" Her cheeky grin hid the bite in her tone.

I had forgotten Tegan was there that night. My memory of the pub date centered on the restroom session with Mys and the embarrassing public scene I had caused afterward. "In my defense, you ditched me," I said.

"Eh, I took the hint." She crossed her arms and cocked her hip, grinning. "Anyway, I'm not here merely for your health. Mayfield wants us to move on Paulie. Apparently, Mrs. Edison will no longer take *wait* for an answer."

I swore under my breath. "We don't have anything solid on him. Here, make yourself at home." I showed her to the kitchen table and put on coffee. My bare feet whispered over the planks of the cabin floor as I crossed to open the curtains, then tidied the blankets on my bed.

"The district attorney thinks otherwise," Tegan said behind me. "Paul Jameson has gone from a person of interest to prime suspect. Given his location the night of the accident, which I confirmed via cell tower triangulation, we can charge him with breaking his RO."

"Isn't it our day off?" I complained.

I returned to the kitchen area, filled a dented camp mug, and handed it to my partner. Tegan dropped a hand on my upper arm when I sat next to her. She leaned in with a sympathetic smile. "I'm not any happier about it. It's paperwork. You know how much I hate paperwork."

"We need to stall them. I need more time, Tegan."

"For what?" she asked.

I drummed the table with my fingertips. "One more situation I want to take care of before we make a move," I murmured.

I couldn't let the council members know that Paul Jameson was our prime suspect on the human side. The minute they found out we had someone in custody, they would cancel any thought of an investigation into Darcy Cyprian.

I needed to request an emergency audience to convince them to stay the course. I had half a mind to recruit Tegan to help bolster the case. I also needed to make sure Haley's location was as secure as Aurie's before a wrongful arrest emboldened the vampire further.

"What's wrong?" I asked when I saw my partner's baffled frown.

"You clocked out for a second. I wish I knew what went on in that head of yours. I've put up with your shit all these years, but I still can't figure you out."

I grunted in amusement. "You don't want into my world, Tegan."

"Why not? Could it possibly be any worse than my abusive, alcoholic past?"

Scratching my neck, I casually asked, "Did you hear Haley before the fifty-one-fifty psychiatric hold? She said she saw her dead father that night."

"Yeah, she also said she saw her sister get up and walk away from that hit-and-run. What about it? Haley is schizo," Tegan replied wryly. She met my gaze and raised an eyebrow.

"Schizo because she sees dead people or because she expects people to believe her?" I raised an eyebrow of my own. "We tell supernatural stories all the time as entertaining fictions. What if I told you that I see things other people can't? Things that help me solve cases, like the missing boy a few months ago."

"What, *you're* the psychic?" Tegan said skeptically.

"Not exactly." I ran a hand over my face. She wouldn't be able to help with Darcy. She would never believe vampires existed. "I just—I know what happens to people who perceive things differently. It's not easy to explain, but that doesn't make it any less real. I trust my gut. It's never been wrong for me."

"Ravani, you don't have second sight. You have good instincts. I believe in that," said Tegan, "but don't put too much stock into it. Don't be thinking you know when you have no idea." She chuckled.

And there was the crux. My partner's jive talk got to the root of what had been bothering me throughout the restless night. Did I know for certain Darcy Cyprian had been after Aurie? She said herself that both sisters had gotten into that event the night of the hit-and-run.

What if I had been holding on to the wrong Edison girl? More specifically, had I been holding on to Aurie Edison only because her pretty mouth and dazzling eyes piqued my interest, and I wasn't ready to let her go?

CHAPTER TWENTY

—

Aurie

September 1 | Afternoon

I slid the utility ladder beside the next picture frame as Mys strolled into the studio with grocery bags. "They were out of avocado, but I managed to find the beignet mix you requested. Now, we can eat sweets and binge-watch *My Hero Academia*. What are you doing?"

"Poltergeist-proofing your house. Could you hand me another Command strip?" I asked.

Dropping the bags in the kitchenette, Mys ambled over with the makeshift tool kit I'd left on the coffee table. The damage from the weekend was all but erased. Zyr had helped us clean Saturday morning before he'd left the city. Now I was putting on the finishing touches.

"Cabinet locks? Nonskid furniture pads? Where'd you find this stuff?" Mys asked suspiciously.

"Various and sundry places around your humble abode, duh." I secured the final corner of the frame and hopped down. "What, did you think I hitchhiked to Walmart? And made it back before you did?"

"I can absolutely picture you sending me on a store run so you could sneak out. I can also picture Zyr killing me."

"He'd be fine. You'd just wrap him around your pinky like you do the other boys," I said. Mys playfully shoved me, and I fell to the couch, snickering. I rested on an elbow and peered at them. "I notice you haven't been going out lately. What's up with that?"

"I'm taking a breather. It has nothing to do with him."

"Mm-hmm, only a hit dog hollers." I grinned.

Mys grimaced. "What even is that?"

"Something my grandma used to say. Meaning, I didn't mention Zyr, but you did . . . You keep telling me there's nothing going on between the two of you, but I know something is up. Y'all doing it?"

"Aurie Edison, what does your ass know about doing it?" Mys poked me and sat on my legs. I squealed in feigned pain and made myself disappear, letting my roommate plop to the cushions. The ghostly magic trick was becoming a breeze. As I reappeared in my favorite chair, I stared at the Empath.

"Not as much as you, apparently," I replied in a frisky tone.

"You've probably had more full-on sex than me in your lifetime." Mys scoffed.

I held up a hand and pretended to count. When my roommate parted their lips to say something else, I raised a finger. "Wait a minute. I'm trying to carry the one."

"I'm serious. I don't follow through with clients. I get them off, then I send them on their merry way," Mys said, settling in the corner of the sofa closest to me.

"Okay, but what about in your personal relationships?"

"This might sound pathetic to you, but . . . I avoid relationships and casual sex."

My eyes popped. Dead curious, I leaned forward. "So, what do you do when you . . . get horny?"

"Let's just say I'm glad you're not a roomie that eavesdrops at locked doors. I love myself. A lot." A shy grin materialized.

"Oh my gosh! In the bathroom?" I laughed, filing that away for future reference.

"Anyway, I don't date because I don't have human anatomy." Mys hesitated before adding quietly, "Down there."

I fanned myself, even more intrigued. At their raging blush, I realized it was none of my business what was under their clothes unless they wanted me to know. Moving back to the couch, I grabbed their hand in solidarity. "Who cares about human anatomy? I accept you as you are, and Zyr is your biggest stan. You should ask him out."

Mys pulled a face. "Aurie, no. Zyr is for you and your unfinished business."

"Ha! What on earth does *he* have to do with my unfinished business?"

"What could be more best-life than a wild romp with a werewolf?"

I choked on a laugh. "A wild romp?"

"Yep. I know you want him. I can sense it, but you do this weird thing where you put everybody else's needs first. Your path to the Light is straight-up Selfish Alley, Yōkai," Mys said matter of factly over the sound of me rioting with laughter.

Catching my breath, I managed to get out, "I'm gonna pretend you didn't say you're trying to hook me up with the detective. Whew! Let's circle back to the part where you care about my needs. Mys, I couldn't have asked for a better guide to the Afterlife, but you sincerely have a one-track mind."

"I don't—"

"Forget the unfinished business, babe! Especially if you think it involves a quote, unquote '*wild romp* with a werewolf.'" I giggled. "To me, being there for Haley is more important than living my so-called best life."

"Just don't even think about leaving," Mys fussed.

"I *am* going, but I'll wait for Detective Zyr to take me since he won't even tell me what hospital she's in. I'm not doing my unfinished business. I plan to stick around until I get her out of the woods or until I lose touch with reality—whichever comes first." I pressed my lips in a taut smile.

"It doesn't feel right. You're playing with life and death. What about the case?"

I got up and moved the ladder to the other side of the studio. "What about it? The detective has all the evidence I can give him. Hand me another Command strip, would you?"

"What about me? I feel everything you go through. As you start to lose it and poltergeist out, I'll go through that too."

"You won't feel anything when I leave." I didn't mention Resurrection out loud. I hadn't found the voodoo *loa's* business card, but I had looked up the Supernatural type. A loa was a spirit that interceded with a higher power on mankind's behalf. I didn't really have much faith that she could return me to life. I knew Darcy would be back, though.

Mys's expression was exasperated. Their cell phone rang, delivering me from further what-abouts. "Yeah?" My roommate paused. "Let me put you on speaker."

"Is that the detective?" I hopped from the ladder to move it to the next frame.

Dropping onto the couch, Mys put the phone down on the teak coffee table, and Zyr's voice rang from the device with a sense of urgency. "Guys, we have a problem. Aurie, did you know your internet stalker was near the hotel the night of the hit-and-run?"

"What the hell?" *Paul Jameson.* Last year he had seen my picture on Haley's feed and developed an obsession with us that had led to threats and hate mail when neither of us would go out with him. "Why was he even in New Orleans?"

"According to him, he was on vacation, but Mayfield isn't buying that, so we're bringing charges," Zyr said.

"You mean he's the one who did this?" I asked in confusion.

"I don't believe so. Darcy is trying to get to you for a reason. He'll think the pressure is off once we put someone else behind bars for his crime. The Council won't even consider investigating him if Jameson becomes the fall guy."

"Are you saying Aurie is stuck here in hiding?" Mys lolled on the couch, staring at the ceiling. I was wondering the same thing, but I was also peeved they were basically asking when I was going to leave. On the other hand, when had that stopped being *my* main priority?

I refocused on what Zyr was saying. "I'm doing ninety to get back and fix this with the Council. I need them to keep putting the screws to Cyprian. Here's what I need from you, Aurie. Think back to the night of the party. Did you see who your sister followed into the hotel?"

"You're being hella cryptic. She wasn't following anyone," I said.

"Are you certain? I reviewed her witness statement. She was adamant that you two got into the party *with* this man. But you didn't see him?"

I shrugged at Mys as if my roommate knew any better than I did. "I mean, Haley was always chasing hot guys, but I didn't see her pursuing anyone in particular that night."

"That's what I was worried about. You're not the special one Cyprian was after," the detective said.

Ice went through my veins as his meaning took shape in my brain. I was off the stepladder and halfway to the door without even knowing my destination. "What hospital? Where is she? Hurry up!" I shouted over my shoulder at the phone.

"You have to stay there to avoid putting her at risk, Aurie." His irritating levelheadedness made me want to shake him.

I doubled back to the coffee table. "Zyr, I don't want to see my sister in Overlay City. Now, tell me where she is!" I begged. Mys wrapped me in a confining hug.

"Listen to me, honey," Zyr soothed. "If my theory is right, Haley can protect herself. Not to mention, Cyprian doesn't seem to know she's the one he wants. For the time being, stay put. When I'm done with the Council, I'll head to the hospital to get more answers."

"*Better* answers," Mys emphasized. "The dishes are rattling."

"I'm counting on you to keep it together, Aurie. Focus on your unfinished—"

"Would you both shut the hell up about my unfinished business? I'm here for Haley!"

The detective sighed. "Fine. But I've seen a guardian angel twice while working this case. Should Haley run into anything she can't handle, I'm sure he'll keep her safe, all right? In fact, I'll talk to him while I'm out. See you soon."

"Wait, Zyr!" The call ended, and I turned to Mys in dismay. "No! H-he can't do that. How does he expect me not to worry when he doesn't even know whether Haley is okay? I have to protect her!" I cried.

"I understand that, Yōkai, but we can't fly off the handle."

"I'm not flying off the handle! Fuck!"

At my shout, every single picture that I thought I had just secured to the wall simultaneously hit the floor with a loud crash. Mys flinched. I hitched in a breath, unnerved by the poltergeist activity I couldn't control. The lights brightened to their normal luminosity, and the cabinets stopped trembling.

My roommate studied me with Empathy and more than a modicum of ire. "See?"

"I am so sorry. I didn't mean—"

"How will losing your shit help with Haley? You can't put it off forever. You have to take care of your unfinished business, Aurie."

CHAPTER TWENTY-ONE
—
Mys

September 1 | Evening

Fading daylight illuminated the basement windows by the time Detective Zyr showed up at my place. As I let him in, I peered around the cathedral alley, but I sensed nothing troublesome on his heels. We were taking extra precautions since Darcy's visit.

"Aurie's in the bath," I said. "I sent her off with a God is a Woman bath bomb and some chamomile tea. Judging by the look on your face, she needs her chakras aligned for whatever news you have."

"The Council is reviewing my emergency audience request, moving at the speed of bureaucracy. I'll keep Paul Jameson's pending arrest to myself until I've convinced them to continue investigating Cyprian. In the meantime, our guardian angel wouldn't confirm that he was protecting anyone."

"*Majika-yo?*" I sulked.

"Magic what?" Zyr asked.

"*Majika-yo*—it means *really* or *seriously*. You know what, doesn't matter. My apartment isn't up for another meltdown. Didn't he have anything positive to say?"

He dropped to the couch as if exhausted. "I didn't have the authority to compel him to tell me more, but he commended the center where Haley is held. Said it's top-notch. From what I know, security is taken seriously there, given their upscale clientele. Cameras, lockdown, one-to-one staff to patients."

I sat on the coffee table across from him and curved a foot under myself. "It's better than I thought. Darcy may be a boss, but a system like that would slow down anyone. He can't rush the hospital and kidnap a patient without the authorities getting involved, and he won't risk it."

Zyr nodded noncommittally. *Gods, he's the brooding stoic.* His somberness filled the room, and I could relate. I was more involved in this investigation than I had ever intended to be. I gave in to the impulse to stroke the hair back from his forehead. The move elicited a lingering look from him. "Relax. It sounds like Haley's okay for now," I suggested with a half smile.

He brightened somewhat. "On the plus side, since we're charging Aurie's stalker, Mrs. Edison and I are back on good terms. She'll call me if anything happens at the hospital. Now, we wait to hear back from the Council."

"I hope the bureaucrats hurry."

Aurie stepped from the bathroom draped in my kimono. She was toweling dry her hair. "What's the update?" she asked.

Zyr couldn't stop gawking at her—the smooth, brown legs, the swell of her breasts, the rest of her curves beneath the thin silk—but she was oblivious to the effect she had on him. Her focus was on Haley's well-being. The detective recovered himself and slid his phone to her as she passed by him.

"See for yourself," he said.

She inhaled sharply and cupped the mobile device, staring. Her eyes glimmered as she whispered "Thank you" to Zyr and got in her favorite chair (my favorite chair) with the phone. Over her shoulder, I peered at the image on the screen. Her sister looked very much like her.

In case there was any doubt of her whereabouts, Haley Edison was dressed in blue scrubs with soft slipper socks on her feet, a hospital bracelet on her wrist. She was in bed, displaying a weak smile. An attractive older woman who gave Angela Bassett vibes grinned from a chair next to her. I assumed she was their mother. A man in a black suit with a coiled earpiece was also visible. Security.

"She's been transferred to a private therapy center," Zyr explained. "It's a state-of-the-art facility with unparalleled safety features. According to your mom, Haley's doing much better."

Aurie's relief was palpable, but the respite was brief. "Now, about Paul Jameson. Why didn't you mention sooner that he was a suspect?" she asked.

"Because to me, he's not. We'll get him off the streets for breaking the restraining order, but my primary concern is convincing the Council to open an official investigation into Darcy Cyprian. My source wants an affidavit and video testimony as soon as possible, in case . . ." Zyr trailed off, and he and I shared a look. *In case Aurie couldn't show up herself.* "Just in case," he finished lamely.

"Darcy told me he's on the Council," said Aurie.

Zyr lifted a shoulder. "Didn't I mention he's a rich and powerful asshole?"

"He also implied they won't investigate one of their own." She frowned.

"You underestimate your importance," he replied. "You're the daughter of America's favorite female director. Your mother's moving heaven and hell to get your case solved right now, and the Council will have to take note . . . although Paul Jameson's arrest throws a wrench into things."

I stretched, leaving the coffee table to collect Aurie's mug and wash it in the kitchenette. From the marble island, I asked, "How can we help you get more evidence against Cyprian? Are there police reports? Is there a chance one of the tabloids ran something, since he's such a bigshot in New Orleans?"

"It's possible. I'll find someone else to do the scut work. I need you keeping tabs on Aurie, especially with Cyprian knowing this location."

"And I guess I'll do whatever it takes to keep my shit together," Aurie mumbled.

I paused in surprise. "Are you saying what I think you're saying?" I asked as I dried my hands and moved behind our favorite chair. She peered at me with a comical scowl.

"I'm saying I'll do just enough living my best life to keep the insanity at bay while I stay in Overlay City and watch out for my sister."

"We've been over this, Aurie," said Zyr. "As far as Cyprian knows, you're his target. You don't need to linger in Overlay City." He gestured to me for support, but I directed him to her. He blew out a breath in frustration. "Need I remind you? The game plan is for you to work on your unfinished business so you can wake up on the Other Side where you belong, young lady."

"I'll get there. Eventually. After Haley pulls through and we take out Darcy Cyprian, I can say good-bye to my family and head to the Light."

An idea occurred to me. "What if we test it? The two of you could go out and see if Aurie's displaced energy goes away," I suggested. The detective gave me a pointed eye roll, and Aurie booed, but I was onto something. "What will one date hurt?"

"I see you're determined to live vicariously through me." Aurie giggled.

"One date? That's it?" Zyr asked.

I waggled a hand. "More or less."

He gave a skeptical snort, and his amber eyes skipped over to our companion, who restlessly left the chair and strode to my bed. Aurie fell to the mattress with casual sexiness. The kimono fluttered, hinting at her nudity underneath. My desire flared, and so did Zyr's. It was odd feeling both strains.

Aurie was the first to give in. "I'll do one date, but I'd like to go somewhere a ghost can sample the spirits of the city."

Zyr hooked a finger in his T-shirt collar to loosen it. "Sample the spirits?"

"She means alcohol, and I know a place," I chuckled.

"Then I guess it's a date." He grinned. "For the *three* of us."

CHAPTER TWENTY-TWO
—
Zyr

September 2–7

One date to settle the "displaced energy." I was no stranger to casual hookups, but this took the cake. I had never done anything like it, and the idea preoccupied my every free thought for the rest of the week.

On a countdown to Saturday night, I threw myself into Paul Jameson's fugitive status. He had rather predictably fled the city after Mrs. Edison tweeted that the NOPD was dragging their feet arresting him. A part of me was glad he'd run. Aurie's mom felt guilty enough to back the hell down from the case after that.

Still, there was no time to decompress. Tegan and I had our work cut out for us. I flip-flopped on whether to tell my partner about Overlay City so I could get her help diving into Cyprian's past.

In the end, I conjured up a new case theory set in the world she knew. The CEO of Corporate Investor Empire might have found Haley Edison, the rising social media star, more to his liking. Tegan and I both knew he partied with A-listers.

I suggested to my partner that Darcy Cyprian might have drugged

Aurie to get to Haley. Even if Jameson was responsible for the hit-and-run, Cyprian could have been the reason she was impaired in the first place. Tegan liked the analysis, agreeing to investigate the rumors of him drugging college girls. Be that as it may, we were no closer to fresh evidence by the end of the hectic workweek.

I took a trip to my cabin to clear my head. When I returned home Saturday evening, I had just enough time to get ready for the date. The wildness that I'd tried leaving behind in the woods followed me home in the form of my distracting attraction to the two of them.

Aroused by flashbacks of my interludes with the Empath, my nightly dreams were filled with impressions of the ghost's delectable body. I couldn't outrun my lust for Aurie and Mys, no matter how I tried.

But did I desire both? Or was this all-consuming investigation getting in the way of healthy sexual release and making me eager to bed anything walking? I was a powder keg waiting to blow, and the date night was seeming less and less like a good idea.

Nevertheless, it was an aspect of the job, I told myself. Putting Aurie's Soul in public could tempt Cyprian to do something stupid enough to get the Council's attention.

Ajit greeted me at the door. The dog was my low-maintenance way to avoid coming home to an empty house. Fortunately, I had a great rapport with his walker, a college kid who kept up daily walks and feedings, no matter how erratic my work schedule became. My keys went in the coin tray, and I strolled to the en suite for a shower. I wondered what it would be like not to need a pet simply to avoid being alone.

I told Alexa to play the local radio station, and the device obliged. Whistling the pop song that poured from the speakers, I lathered up and scrubbed my body clean. Admittedly, even if the date was business, I was looking forward to it. I left the shower with a big, fluffy bath sheet wrapped around my hips and stepped to the closet to find something to wear.

I chose a pair of cropped jeans, ditching my usual slacks. A stylish black tee, paired with an unbuttoned gray Oxford, finished the ensemble. From the walk-in came the sound of the music transitioning to advertisements.

"And, if you've got plans for the weekend, you might want to bring an umbrella with you!" the radio announcer cheerfully cut in after the weather jingle. "Let's take a look at the forecast for tonight and tomorrow. Things are going to get wet and blustery, with a tropical storm rolling in from the gulf."

I tuned out the rest. It was that time of year again, but I wasn't worried about a dash of rain. The picture windows in my bedroom overlooked a bright, sunny evening. I stood before the dresser bureau mirror, grooming my hair and beard.

"Not bad, eh, Ajit?" I said to the dog sniffing around in my bedroom closet. He lifted an ear at my ringing phone, and I grabbed it off the dresser. "This is Ravani," I answered.

The person on the other end spoke quickly and quietly. Their terse message was brief, but every word of it darkened my expression until I furiously threw the phone across the bedroom. Ajit barked in confusion when the device hit the wall. Luckily, it didn't break, but that was where my luck ran out.

My meeting with the Council of Overlay Affairs had been canceled.

Impotent rage burned through me. I slammed a fist into the mirror without thinking. It shattered. Staring at my glass-encrusted knuckles, I saw rivulets of blood tracing down my forearm. The Council wouldn't see me. I couldn't believe it. I stormed into the en suite to clean myself up. As the cuts and abrasions began to heal, I stuck my hand beneath the bracing cold water.

How had things taken such a drastic turn? My thoughts raced to piece it all together. I had communicated my findings with a discreet insider. The Council meeting would have been my opportunity to share evidence publicly. It had been called off because of rumors that Mrs. Edison didn't trust my competency.

Cyprian had to be desperate to resort to personal attacks on my reputation. Unfortunately, word was out that Mrs. Edison believed Paul Jameson was the man who had hurt her daughter. The Council members were eager to seize upon that as proof that our Supernatural laws hadn't been broken. It was enough for them, but not for me. Not by a long shot. What would I tell Aurie and Mys?

I marched back into the walk-in closet, Ajit on my heels. I opened a trapdoor beneath a cutaway square of carpet. Within the hidden compartment was an arsenal. I dug out the duffel bag full of weapons. Now, I fervently hoped Darcy Cyprian showed up tonight.

I selected my favorite handgun and switched out the ammo for Holy Water hollow points. I slid a knife into my trainers. Rising, I grabbed the Damascus steel short sword on the top shelf. When I pressed a trigger, it folded into the hilt, perfect for hiding in a back pocket. More than a hint of enchantment was involved.

I turned to my dresser and selected a crucifix ring from the jewelry chest. Where the metal touched my skin gleamed gold. The other side was overlaid with silver laced with Supernatural poison, and I didn't dare touch it. It would leave a mark on the vampire if he showed his pretty face.

I glanced at my sister's photograph tucked in the corner of the broken mirror. A shaky smile crossed my lips, but my expression turned to one of despair as I thought of how many years it had been. I hadn't run with the Ravani pack in four years.

One agonizing event had ignited my meteoric rise as a detective, burning away everything else. It never stopped taking from me, incinerating any chance I had at a normal life. There was no room for family, friends, or—God forbid—a relationship. As long as Darcy Cyprian was free, that fire would drive me to chase him into the depths of hell.

That fire was how I managed to shake my melancholia and get a move on.

I left the townhouse and headed to the cathedral, weaving through traffic on my motorcycle rather than taking my truck. Mys had assured me that the three of us could reach our destination on foot, and Aurie would enjoy the stroll. Belying the tropical storm watch, it was pleasant out.

I arrived at the church, crossed the courtyard, and darted around the side of the building. Mys threw the door open without me having to knock on the brick. When I saw the smile waiting for me, it hit the firewall around my heart, and the enmity simmering beneath the surface instantly cooled. I realized something: I had missed them.

"You felt me coming?" I asked with a small grin.

Mys gave me a "yeah, duh" smile and gave me a quick hug. I could tell by how they pulled back that my feelings, including the carnal ones, were on display to them. I averted my gaze, biting my lip as I made my thoughts blank. It worked, relatively.

"Ready to go?" Mys asked.

"Yep. Keep your senses sharp while we're out," I murmured as I showed the gun tucked in my waistband. Grinning, Mys tugged a silver revolver from a thigh holster hidden in their boot. I smiled approval. In the busiest section of the French Quarter, one couldn't be too prepared.

Aurie slipped out the door, giving a cheerful nod and posing in a skintight purple dress and stilettos. I took in Mys's wide-brimmed black hat, traditionally masculine shirt, provocative black skirt, and thigh boots. The pair of them were imposing. And both seemed uptight. *I'm not the only anxious one.*

"How do you want to do this?" Mys hesitated outside the gate to the courtyard. "Maybe I should linger a step or two behind, so you don't have to be seen with me. I mean, you two are together." Mys cupped their hands.

Aurie chortled amusement. "You are *not* walking behind. Come on. Three's company."

"It's called a *ménage à trois*," I corrected her with a grin. Laughter from both of them floated around me. I extended an arm to each, glad the comment had broken the ice. We took off walking together.

After a few blocks, Mys pointed ahead. "When you get to the door up there, the password is Castor Pollux."

"What door?" Aurie asked.

The "doorman" in black glasses and an earpiece stood before a nondescript section of the side. There was no signage. Not a window or door visible. Aurie glanced at us quizzically but tried out the password anyway, at Mys's insistence. At first, nothing happened.

"Can he see ghosts or not?" Aurie said from the corner of her mouth.

The doorman lowered his glasses to reveal mirthful eyes alight with blue fire. Aurie hitched in a breath, and I grinned. "Your first time?" the djinn asked. Where the wall had been, a shadowy door opened, and Mys disappeared into the portal.

When Aurie balked, I wrapped an arm around her and ushered her forward. "Don't be afraid. I'm with you," I promised.

"What if Darcy finds out we're here?" she stalled.

Smiling, I kept us moving forward. "For once in your Afterlife, stop trying to be the safest, smartest, most responsible person in the room, and enjoy yourself!"

Through the narrow portal was a hallway leading to the thumping music and pulsating lights of an open club. We emerged in the thick of things, and Aurie shouted over the noise: "This feels like déjà vu!"

"You've never experienced anything like this. I'll show you," I shouted back. She responded with melodic laughter.

The Empath was waving at us from the bar with two shot glasses. "From Mexico. Drink up, bitches!" said Mys.

I wasn't into alcohol much, but I needed something to dull my senses tonight. I couldn't stop thinking about the first time I had gone after Darcy Cyprian four years ago. I had just cracked a high-profile case, run the interview circuit, gotten featured on some true crime shows. Everyone was toasting my success.

That success had led me to naïvely believe that a well-respected detective could discuss his sister's rape and be *heard*. Never mind that the bright, young art major had already told everyone loud and clear what had happened to her, yet nobody had listened.

It was my first lesson on how things worked in this world. I learned that money and power outweighed righteousness to some people. No matter how wrong that ethos, those who believed it were usually the loudest in the room.

On the night of Aurie's accident, I had found my bullhorn. Emily Edison's daughter was too high profile a victim to go unnoticed. Darcy Cyprian had been on that surveillance video. His signature was all over the hit-and-run. He had overplayed his hand.

Don't make this personal. Both Mayfield and Tegan had warned me.

My closest coworkers knew the arrogant CEO had already slipped through my fingers once, nearly destroying my career in the process. I had taken on Aurie's case to salvage my reputation and get justice. Now, neither seemed likely. The Council of Overlay Affairs wouldn't even talk to me.

The gloves were off. If I couldn't put Cyprian behind bars, I was ready to settle for putting him in a body bag.

CHAPTER TWENTY-THREE
—
Aurie

September 7 | Night

The clear liquor in the shot glass vibrated ever so slightly as I held it up for inspection. The Overlay City nightclub was lit, but the last time I'd had a drink at a party, I'd wound up dead. However, as I surveyed the scene, the feeling of déjà vu began to fade. No, this was nothing like last time or the hotel.

Less fake and more Supernatural? I smiled and let it sink in that this was a different world entirely. The color scheme of reds, purples, and blues made the place throb with dark passion. The textures were sensual: smooth concrete floors, velvet club chairs, and silk-papered walls.

I didn't feel the same uneasiness as the night of that party either. With Zyr and Mys, I felt safe.

"What is this stuff?" I asked about the drink.

"It's Pox," Mys replied. "It's a Mayan ceremonial liquor believed to link this plane of existence to the spiritual world. Very mystical! I bet this shit will fuck up even a ghost, Yōkai!"

I had never heard of it, but I gave it a try for the sake of doing just enough and all that. I tossed it back and raised the empty glass in salute as the drink filled me with warmth. It had a sweet, smoky richness I liked.

I stared goofily at Mys, who was acting engrossed by their phone while the detective checked us both out. "You look great, by the way," he said directly to me. I knew what this was about. Playing a role, since my roommate wanted to be a matchmaker. Yet, his eyes ate me alive, and I wasn't sure that was for show.

Detective Zyr signaled for another round of drinks. The bartender's stygian skin, strange white irises, and slightly pointed ears took me aback. But I had read about his type, the *dubh sidhe*, in one of Mys's many books about Supernatural beings.

I said thanks in a voice an octave too high before gulping the second shot and thumping the new glass down between us. With a cough and a laugh, I used the back of my hand to wipe my mouth. Zyr smiled—to fucking die for if I wasn't already dead. Facts.

Also, factual: I was the real third wheel.

My roommate could stop being generous and pitch woo if I could find an exit from the love triangle. Then I had an idea. The multi-level entertainment space boasted a spiral staircase to a second floor. "Whew! Being stuck indoors was driving me insane," I said. "I think I'm gonna stretch my legs and explore the upper level. You two stay here and enjoy. I'll be back."

The detective casually dropped a hand on mine and stopped me. "Yeah, if I don't keep my mind stimulated, I go insane too. Unfortunately, it's not safe for you to run off on your own here, sorry."

I chuckled at being seen through. "Why not, Detective? If anything went wrong, couldn't you become a giant wolf like the ones from Mys's favorite movie?" My roommate didn't even look up from the phone at my blatant attempt to bait them into the convo. I pouted. They were doing this on purpose.

Zyr demurred. "Call me Zyr, and it depends on which movie," he said with a grin. "When I shape-shift, I am a slightly larger than normal *Canis lupus.*"

"Not scary big like on *Twilight*?"

"Nahin, not quite as big, but that movie shows a good example of how the gene is passed. I wasn't *turned*. I was born this way. Wolves don't have superpowers like Mys, though."

Still without looking up, Mys said, "I don't have superpowers. I have Empathy. Why are we even talking about me? Shouldn't you two be dancing?"

As if on cue, a DJ with dreadlocks let the beat drop. The club went pitch black until the lights exploded in a pulsating burst of color. We were blasted with a wall of music. It was good stuff. I couldn't help moving to the beat.

Zyr jerked his head at the dance floor. "Wanna go?"

I nodded, but my heart was in my throat. It didn't seem like I could wriggle out of this. I understood what Mys expected of us. Except I had never dated anyone like the detective before. I had always gone for the shy, studious types. Tonight, I was with a whole snack in a place where anything was possible.

I glanced back at the winding staircase past the bar. I had no idea what was up on the second floor, but down here, the club was packed with stylish revelers. The low-lit ambiance gave an air of mystery, and every now and then, party lights sent a disturbance through the darkness.

Zyr guided me past two girls with shimmery black wings tongue-kissing while another dancer with opaque black eyes watched them. It was like every freaky paranormal movie I had ever seen—*The Mortal Instruments, Constantine*, even *Harry Potter*—with one exception. This was real.

When Zyr and I found an opening on the dance floor, I stepped into his arms, though apparently not close enough. As he pulled me closer, a shaky exhale escaped me. My body was a stiff jangle of nerves.

Gradually, the music worked its magic. I wasn't sure if it was the Pox or wishful thinking, but it seemed like sexual tension crackled between us. Zyr controlled the sway of my body, innocently rocking with me. Yet, his fluid moves drummed up X-rated thoughts.

Damn it, Aurie, stop! I drowned out the erotic fantasies and rested my head on his shoulder. Wasn't it odd enough to have a crush on Mys without wanting their secret lover too?

"So, what's up with you and Mys?" Zyr asked casually, as if reading my mind.

I gave him a congenial smirk. "*You* and Mys are what's up. I'm renting you for the night."

"Renting me? Please don't. I already feel a bit pawned off, and *I'm* not the sex worker," he said with a wry twist of the lips.

I leaned back to see his face. "Okay, enough. Time out for being judgmental about sex work. That kind of intolerance doesn't even fit your personality."

"Hey, it's none of my business."

"I'm saying . . . You know Mys likes you, right? My roommate is one of the most understanding, open-minded, ride-or-die, be-there-for-you people I know, and I don't want you to write them off because of what they do for a living."

"Point taken. I can see you care about them quite a bit."

Smiling, I sucked my teeth at his tone. At how we were both feeling each other out. It was the funniest thing. Mys had given their blessing to this match made in limbo. But I couldn't stop thinking of the time we had kissed or the time I had caught the two of them making out.

A hip-hop ballad started, and the detective's proximity during the sexy musical number made my body ache. Or was I aching for the androgynous Supernatural at the bar?

"What about me?" Zyr asked huskily.

"Do I like you? I mean, you're hot or whatever." *I would bathe in your sweat, my dude. Facts.*

He grinned. "I ask because I get the feeling Mys has something more in mind for us than drinks and dancing."

"More like what? The *ménage à trois* you mentioned? Um, letting my hair down and having a few drinks is just enough excitement for me." I laughed.

"Is that right? Well, let's see."

Suddenly, his mouth slanted over mine, and my lips parted in surprise. I clung to him to keep from floating away. Each languid sweep of his tongue made me weaker. As he gathered me closer in a sensual embrace, his rock-hard desire was at my stomach, and I tightened my thighs against the deluge of my own lust. If the kiss lasted a second longer, I would let him take me right there.

The detective let go and stared at me with faintly yellow eyes. "Just enough? Or do you want more?" he asked.

•••

It was after two a.m. when I frolicked into the studio after Mys. Zyr seemed cheerful with our antics, closing the enchanted door behind us. We hadn't run into any trouble on the way home, but I knew Darcy Cyprian was waiting me out. Resurrection had put the ball back in my court. If I could just find that stupid business card.

"You two sloshed?" Zyr asked.

"I'm not sloshed, baby, I'm sparkling," Mys replied. "I've gotta run. Kittie Cad is expecting me." Their high heels clacked on the floor as they grabbed a purse and jetted out the door again.

I made a sound of amusement. It was so obvious, leaving me alone with the hot detective werewolf. "I guess that answers your question. No threesomes tonight," I announced.

Detective Zyr smiled and replied, "That wasn't my most recent question. I asked if you were drunk."

"Pssh! The Poshie-Posh wore off hours ago!" *Okay, possibly tipsy.*

"Good to know. Do you consent?"

"Excuse me?" I arched an eyebrow as he cupped my face. It was hard to hide the tremors, especially when he stepped toward me. Especially when every inch of me screamed, *Consent, consent, consent!*

"Consent," he repeated slowly.

"You have to tell me what I'm consenting to first."

He ran the back of his fingers down my arms to my hands, collected my fingers, and brought them to his lips. "Aurelia, you played it safe your whole life. Don't you trust your instincts? Do you think I'm gonna hurt you?"

"No, but—" Smiling off-kilter, I hesitated. He placed my hands behind his neck as he walked me backward to my roommate's bed. "Is *this* the other thing Mys had in mind for us?" I squeaked.

Zyr heaved an agreeable sigh. "This night is about you learning how to let go of your inhibitions, but I won't do anything you don't want me to do. I need your consent to go any further. Let me know when you're done thinking about it," he said as his lips connected with mine one last time. It was a bruising, throbbing kiss that wiped my mind blank.

When he disengaged and stepped back, I was left standing there, aching.

"Why'd you stop?" I asked in a quivering voice.

CHAPTER TWENTY-FOUR

—

Aurie

September 8 | After Midnight

With the mattress behind my legs, my feet left the floor. Zyr ushered me higher up the bed. My purple dress bunched at the hips, and I reached behind me to unzip it. However, he clutched my face and kissed me so thoroughly that I gave up fighting the dress to give all my attention to what he was doing to my Soul.

The driving plunge of his tongue past my lips made me lose it, which also caused the overhead lights to flicker. "Is that you?" Zyr asked. Nodding, I dragged him back to me, and his growl of enthusiasm raised the hair on my arms. I was making out with a werewolf. *Let that sink in, Aurie.* I knew such intimate contact was only possible because we were both Supernaturals, but it was still surreal.

Zyr ripped off his gray button-down and his black T-shirt. My lace panties were no barrier, nor was my half-removed dress. His five o'clock stubble grazed my neck in descending sweeps of his mouth. As he marked me his, it drove me to madness.

"Shh, shh, shh . . ." He touched a finger to my lips. I curled my tongue around his fingertip, and he grunted in amused pleasure. "Relax. You've already done enough for me. I'm here to satisfy *you*."

I didn't know what that meant, and I didn't care. My eyes raked his muscular torso and the obvious bulge at the front of his jeans. Then I wondered what the hell I was doing.

The situation was so out of character for me, but it felt so right. I had never had a one-night stand. I couldn't even categorize my former sex life as adventurous. My encounters had been mostly functional.

Maybe this time was different because of how much I wanted the detective. Zyr seemed to know it too. Removing my clothes, he swirled his slippery, hot tongue in dizzying circles along my bare skin until I lay gasping and panting.

"You feel incredible," he breathed in awe. "It's hard to believe you're—"

"Dead?" I shivered.

"I was gonna say mine for the night," he chuckled, kissing my belly button.

I stared at the ceiling with eyes glazed by arousal. *His.* The scent of Mys's cologne wafted from the duvet, a veritable aphrodisiac. *Or was I theirs?* My face tightened with yearning. Wanting both Zyr and Mys felt secretly exquisite. Even more titillating, they both wanted me. I pictured the three of us.

Suddenly, Zyr found the spot that needed his hungry mouth. As his face disappeared between my legs, mounting ecstasy unbridled my inhibitions. I moaned louder. I closed my eyes and rode the lightning higher. He murmured deliriously in a foreign language and turned and bit the inner softness of my thigh, and his name flew from my lips like a prayer.

"I wish you were mine for more than a night," he surprised me by saying. I could barely focus on the admission. My pelvis canted forward to take more of his tongue-lashing. "I would show you there's so much more to live for, and I would . . ."

I shuddered uncontrollably as a burst of energy made the sound system power on. Indie pop blared drums and bass. Flashing a wry grin, the detective peered up at me. "I thought this was supposed to help," he chuckled.

Oh my damn. What was he doing to me? Indeed, if no-strings sex was what had been missing from my life, why wasn't it keeping me from poltergeisting out?

"Don't stop!" I gasped.

"You need it? Mm," Zyr moaned.

Pushing my quaking body to eruption, he released a strangled cry from me. "Hahn! Zyr!" I wailed as my arrogant and sexy tormentor finished me off. Like a star collapsing and expanding endlessly, I fell apart. Zyr rose to watch the evidence of my undoing. I tried to cover my face, but he tugged away my hands.

"I want to see you," he whispered. His eyes flamed with lust, cataloging my every move until the last convulsion subsided, and I lay spent. Even that wasn't enough. He finally bowed over my sated body, pressing his lips to mine, and whispered, "With enough time, I would show you a life that leaves no unfinished business. Ask yourself if this is all you want, Aurie. Wake up for me."

What more was there? I drew the pillow over my face, exhaled a groan, and inhaled the scent of Mys. Then I knew what more. I knew what I wanted. I wanted all this to be real.

CHAPTER TWENTY-FIVE
—
Mys

September 8 | After Midnight

I shelved my feelings for Zyr and Aurie as I skated out the door. Everything I had worked toward since meeting the two of them would finally come to fruition tonight, and my good deed would be done. There was no point examining why that made me feel so down.

A block from the cathedral, Kittie Cad waited for me in the mayor's car. I grinned at the champagne Nissan, a step above our normal Uber or Lyft. Brownie points for Terrance Rhemus.

"Thanks for making this run to Madea's with me. I know it's late, but she needs her meds for church tomorrow, and I was her last resort. You look nice! Where were you?" Kittie asked as I hopped in the passenger seat.

"Went out with Aurie tonight." Everyone's favorite Canadian rapper's voice ripped from the speakers. Voguing to the music, I checked my reflection in the visor and hid a smile at Kittie's curious eyebrow. "Don't look at me like that. I was showing her some of the local hot spots."

"So, she's not from here?"

"I didn't say that," I replied as we took off.

Kittie laughed. "You rarely say *anything* about her. When will I get to meet this mystery friend?"

"It depends. Have you ever seen a ghost?"

"Uh-uh! Don't change the subject, Mys!"

"I'm not! It's relevant, Ms. Cad."

Smiling, I stared out the window as we hit the highway. The late-night skyline conveyed the impression of a big metropolis, despite the city's small footprint. New Orleans was a clump of medium-height skyscrapers and the Superdome. All lit up, it promised a good time, but we were leaving the safer enclaves of the tourist districts, headed for the real Big Easy.

Kittie grinned and peered over at me several times before answering, "Okay, yes. One night I was walking home, and I saw a headless man with a headless dog on a leash. Either that was ghostly activity, or it was the 'shrooms." She let out a hoot.

"You believe in the supernatural?" I asked as I sucked my vape pen.

"Boo boo, I'm from this place. Belief in the supernatural runs straight through my bloodlines."

A white cloud of vapor spilled from my parted lips. I prepared to admit the real reason I had jumped at the opportunity to ride along. "First, I need you to do me a huge favor, Kris."

"Ooh." Kittie Cad pursed her lips. "Must be important, if you're pulling out the slave name. What's going on, Mitsuyo?"

"You let me into your world with Terrance. I think I'm ready to let you into mine. Aurie is part of it, but there's more."

"Okay, what's the favor?" Kittie cut to the chase.

I reached into my purse and drew out the card I had found after Darcy Cyprian's visit to my apartment. I handed it to my friend, knowing she wouldn't be able to examine it closely while driving. She saw enough on the black vellum rectangle to make her toss the card into my lap and shake her head.

"*That* is why you wanted to ride with me to Madea's house?"

"Not entirely," I said, fidgeting. "I wanted to hang out with you, but . . . well, this might be my one chance to visit the area. And that might have factored into my decision to come along."

"To visit a voodoo priestess?" Kittie Cad hit me with incredulous side-eye.

"Voodoo loa," I corrected. "And I'm sorry to hijack a ride while you're dropping off meds at your grandmother's, but now I can show you the truth about me. The Supernatural world is real. Ghosts, zombies, vampires, werewolves, angels, demons. They're all real."

Kittie glared at me in disbelief. "What the fuck are you on, Mys?"

I turned down the volume on the radio and faced her. As I further explained Overlay City, my best friend squeezed the steering wheel so tightly her knuckles blanched. Buildings flew by in a blur. I could tell by her expression it was too much to digest, but I had to tell her everything. After all, I had already broken Overlay City law. She wasn't supposed to know any of this.

"I'm not like you. I'm not human. I'm a Supernatural being called a futanari," I explained, "and there are others. Well, not like *me* exactly, but other Supernaturals throughout New Orleans. Except we call it Overlay City. It's a place where ley lines intersect."

Kittie wordlessly accelerated.

I fidgeted with the business card. "You've asked me about my friend Aurie. She's a dead girl I met the night of the hit-and-run in front of Century Luxe. She was the victim, and she needs my help, which is why I need you to take me to this address in Hollygrove."

"Mys, I don't fuck with black magic and voodoo," Kittie Cad replied staunchly.

"I would never insist you do anything you're not comfortable doing, Kittie. But I can't show up in the projects on my own."

Kittie Cad gaped at me. "Oh, you wanted to parlay my familiar face for safe passage? Never mind the sweeping generalizations in your statement, darling! Look at *my* six-foot-seven, black *transgender* ass. Girls like me get killed all the damn time, and not just in the hood!" She shook her head angrily, and I felt two inches tall. This was going all wrong.

"I'm sorry. You're right. I shouldn't have sprung this on you."

"I didn't say no," she snapped back. "I'm considering it, Mitsuyo, but you haven't explained anything. You're a—what now? Like a mutant?"

"A mutant?" I laughed. "No, we're Supernaturals attracted to ley lines. Most of us stay near confluences of power called Ley-Over cities. My type of Super has both sexes in one body, and I can sense what other people feel, want, and need. Gods, it feels good to finally be able to say that out loud to you."

Kittie realized something. "Is *that* how you always knew which johns were trouble?"

"Yes, I kept us safe on the streets before we shut down Jasper the Elf's trafficking ring. You've been with Supers damn near your whole life. You simply didn't register it."

We were off the interstate now, passing shotgun houses. "An elf. Like Keebler," Kittie muttered, shaking her head.

"You don't believe me. Pull over. I'll show you I'm telling the truth." I pointed at a curb where several dudes were standing beneath the yellow light of a street lamp.

Kittie gawked at me. "When I get to Madea's, you can show me whatever you want to show me, but I'm not going in some voodoo trap house."

"I never said you have to go in, Kittie. You can wait for me outside."

"By the way, if your spidey senses didn't tingle at that curb when you asked me to pull over, you might want to get checked. Lord, you're gonna get yourself into some shit you can't get out of."

I glanced in the rearview mirror at the corner in question. The men back there were harmless. My Empathy told me they were plainly hanging out. "Relax, I won't let anything happen to you, Kittie Cad. I never have before, and I don't have a choice in this. I have to do it for Aurie."

"You're in love," Kittie Cad guessed as I turned back to her.

"I care about them both."

"Both?"

"Yeah, didn't I mention the werewolf?" I asked with a dramatic eye roll.

Kittie threw up her hands in good humor. "Okay! Ghosts, werewolves, and I'm taking my fucking futanoonoo friend to see a voodoo loa. Got it."

CHAPTER TWENTY-SIX
—
Zyr

September 8 | After Midnight

Aurie lay in a satisfied heap in bed. I lay next to her, shirtless but still in my jeans. She hardly moved when I padded to the couch and sat down with the sword I half regretted not needing tonight. With a flick of the switch, the curved blade sprang out from the deceptively small hilt. I lifted it for her to see closer when I noticed her gaze brighten with interest.

"Enchanted Damascus steel," I said.

The album from earlier played quietly in the background. Aurie shifted her position in a tangle of white sheets, flashing naked brown skin. Her beauty captivated me. It was a chancy thing. It made me want to climb in bed and go beyond oral sex, but it also made me want to run.

"What makes you sure my sister is who Darcy wants?" Her voice was husky and too trusting. Intimacy had coerced her into letting down her guard.

I considered how to answer. "You said he told you that something special had allowed you to get into his exclusive event . . . Well, Haley was following someone that night, someone who, by all rights, she shouldn't have been able to see."

My reflection in the sword's gleam showed bags under my eyes. It was after three in the morning. I'd gotten a text from my source at the Council asking to meet at my place. I wondered when Mys would return.

"The guardian?" Aurie murmured.

I nodded. "It's possible he gave her safe passage."

She tugged the comforter higher and sat up in bed. "I've been thinking about it. My sister Haley saw things—imaginary friends, monsters in the closet, you name it—but nobody took her seriously. Mom always said she had a vivid imagination. It never hit me she might be a Seer, not even after finding out all this is real."

"They're calling it paranoid schizophrenia now."

"While I'm living it up, she's on lockdown." Aurie shoved her hands through her hair and huffed.

"Hey, come here." Moving to the bed, I pulled her into my lap. She didn't immediately yield to my embrace. *Putting those walls back up.* "I know it's scary, Aurie, but there's nothing wrong with Haley being in a safe place where she can get better."

"I'm doing this for her." She fought dejection as she gestured at her clothes on the floor, the rumpled bedcovers. "Is it in vain? Darcy is on the loose while Haley is a prisoner in her own mind, and I'm dead. Nothing's changed!"

I wanted to say everything would turn out all right, but I couldn't. For Aurie's sake, I couldn't let her get anywhere near Haley. Not even Mys could be trusted with the ins and outs of the Edison situation until the case was resolved. Things could go very wrong, especially since the Council of Overlay Affairs was dragging their heels about opening an official investigation. I shuddered to think about what would happen if Cyprian got his hands on Aurie again.

"I think you should cross over. Hear me out. I know you don't want to abandon your sister, but moving on is best for everyone. In Overlay, you're a target we have to protect, and it's taking resources from putting Cyprian away."

Irritation clouded her expression. "Zyr, I get that you want to solve this thing, and I hate that my presence is a hindrance, but I have a right to be here. I'm helping! I'm not leaving this to the so-called authorities. The last time my family did that, my missing father was found dead. They never got his killer either."

I nodded with sudden understanding. Another cold case. That was why Mrs. Edison was adamant about wrapping things up sooner rather than later. "Did it ever occur to you Haley's psychosis could be driven by her concern for *you*?" I asked.

Aurie crossed her arms and gave me a blank stare.

I tried again. "Perhaps she knows you're here. Once your Soul is . . . off the radar . . . for Cyprian, Haley will gather you're no longer in jeopardy. In fact, I'll make sure she knows you're safe, even if it takes me revealing Overlay City to her."

"Yeah, okay, and Darcy will move on to his next victim, which could be her."

"Aurie, I would protect your family like my own flesh and blood. Cyprian will never hurt anyone else who matters to me!" At my vehemence, Aurie peered at me, and I reined it in. "How much of this is about staying for Haley, and how much is about your fear of what happens when you let go of this world?" I asked gently.

She evaded my gaze and lifted a shoulder. "I've already let go of this world. You said so yourself. Notice the advanced powers and rapid descent into madness? Anyway, we don't even know how to *find* the Light. Mys was so certain this would work, but it didn't."

I gnawed my lip, studying her lost expression. She was right, and the uncertainty was deeply affecting her. It bothered me too. Nothing was going according to plan.

Suddenly, Mys breezed into the flat with the attractive blond from the pub on her heels. Bad timing. I yanked the comforter over Aurie's nakedness. With a tiny yelp and a soft *poof*, the ghost disappeared, leaving us staring at the spot she'd just vacated, where the comforter rustled flat.

"Invasion of privacy much?" Aurie's indignant voice shouted from the bathroom. She slammed the door shut. I covered a grin.

"I take it that was the ghost," Mys's friend said with fascination. "And this is the werewolf? Mitsuyo, you've been holding out."

"Mitsuyo?" I let the name roll around in my mouth. Mys was short for *Mitsuyo*. I liked it.

"I figured the coast was clear. How'd it go?" Obscuring their friend's view with a hand, the Empath pantomimed an apology. I approached with a grin as I finished buttoning my shirt.

"We'll talk about it later, *Mitsuyo*." When I said the name, Mys pulled a face. I paused and tugged the sexy being to my lips. My tongue teased the partition of their mouth, and I imbibed the sweetest sigh from their recesses. Mys turned a faint shade of pink when I let go. "Favor for a favor. We're even now," I whispered.

"Thank you. I w-wanted you to meet—"

"Kittie Cad, *enchanté*." Their friend pushed forward.

I lightly bussed the back of Kittie's hand. "Zyr Ravani, the pleasure is mine. I believe we bumped into each other last weekend under less fortunate circumstances. I can't wait to meet you properly, but you'll have to excuse me tonight. I'm needed elsewhere."

Mys looked at me quizzically. I had questions for them too. I was sure they had a valid reason for bringing a human into the fold, but we would discuss all this some other time. I jogged out the door and hopped on my bike, pulling my cell phone from my pocket.

When the line connected, I asked, "Still up, *Maan*?"

•••

Despite the late hour, my mother—my secret insider on the Council of Overlay Affairs—had let herself into my townhouse. The delectable smell of chicken biryani greeted me when I opened the door. I kicked off my shoes and stealthily padded to the kitchen, where Ajit was watching her cook. The dog barked, giving me away. Of course, my mother the Luna, a born female pack leader, had already detected my presence.

"*Ammi*, you shouldn't have!" I said with a laugh, dropping my keys into the tray.

Farida Ravani turned to me, wielding a wooden spoon. "Ut-ut! Don't *Ammi* me. Where were you? Out all hours of the night!" She scolded in her faint London accent.

I hefted the grand woman in a hug, roaring with mock indignation. She was tall and fit, and it wasn't an easy feat. Mum succumbed to laughter. When I set her down, she pushed her hair out of her youthful face to study me.

She'd had cut it to her shoulders since the last time I had seen her, and her unlined face was radiantly tanned. The only hint of her age was the shimmer in her eyes. I nodded as she suppressed tears to find a smile for me.

"How long has it been?" I whispered.

"Too long. I can tell by how skinny you are." She returned her gaze to the food she was cooking to hide her emotions. Her good standing on the Council required zero contact with me, her erstwhile Alpha-denying son. "Thank goodness I brought food. It's in the fridge and the pantry. I imagined you'd have a woman taking care of you by now. What happened to the pretty girl with the red hair?"

"My partner?" I scrunched my nose.

"Eh, partner. You should've been an engineer," she tsked as she turned off the stove.

Leaning against the peninsula, I cocked my head and grinned. "I know you didn't come over to fuss. How are the boys?"

"Your brothers are prospering. Hazeem's prototype is making waves in the auto industry, and Yazeed was given project lead last month at that big gaming company."

"And my sister?" I asked lightly.

"Much better than a year ago. I speak with her frequently on the phone. She's happier pursuing her MBA in Paris, although she, too, could've been an engineer or—"

"A doctor?" I finished for her with a smile. I was overjoyed at the understated good news. My sister had been so broken by what Cyprian had done to her that, for a while, it seemed she would never recover.

"I was going to say a fine wife, but that would be sexist, right? Especially coming from the first Luna to gain a Council seat since its inception," Mum smiled. "I want to see all of you happy. I want grandchildren."

"All right, all right! Enough with that. How are you, Ammi? How's work?"

The question hung in the space between us until Farida shooed me to the table and brought over a glass of ginger ale along with my plate. I wasn't hungry, but refusing her food would be the ultimate insult. I dug in, discovering I didn't have to fake enthusiasm. I'd missed her cooking.

My mother was my only loyal connection at the Council. She sat across from me, her face in shadow. The dining table, positioned between the open-concept kitchen and living room, was illuminated by the warm glow of the light above the stove. She rubbed my hand lovingly. Because this entire visit was against Council orders, she was risking her political career to meet with me.

"I'm so sorry they turned down your request for an audience," she said. "I came to tell you personally that I did everything I could to get them to change their mind, but . . . it wasn't enough."

"I understand, *Maan*. I don't hold it against you." I looked down.

"I know you don't, but I feel so helpless. Ever since your father left us, you've endured so much. You deserve better than life has given you.

When you're ready to assume your role as Alpha, I'll gladly step away. I like this work, but I prefer leading people who can be shown reason."

"I don't know how you can work with them, especially Cyprian."

"Biding my time, like you."

While she chatted more about her responsibilities as a Council member, my fingertips drummed the table with increasing rapidity until I struck the hardwood with the flat of my hand. My mother placed her warm, smooth hands over mine.

I blew out a breath. "This case should be the final nail in his coffin. But nothing is going as it should."

She leaned back and interlaced our fingers. "Don't worry. The right people are watching the situation. We are all simply cautious. No one wants to make an enemy of Darcy Cyprian."

"I won't let him harm you."

"Hubris will be the death of you," she jested. "As satisfying as it might be to challenge him to an ass-kicking, we need a solution that sticks. Have you gotten video testimony from your ghost? Gathered other witnesses? Notwithstanding the Council's hesitation to meet with you, I could slip someone the tapes."

"I can keep working on it. Are you saying they'll review the evidence without a formal meeting with me?"

"If you can get it to me within the next two weeks, I can guarantee it. After that, I can't be certain. Campaign season begins."

I turned away, thinking of the decisions that would be made in October. New councilors would be chosen for the first time in a hundred years. The person to take control of the Ravani holdings would also be chosen. I knew my mother was thinking about that.

Farida refilled my glass and patted my shoulder as she moved to the window and gazed out. "He knows you're onto him. We have to tread lightly. Despite the risks of meeting tonight, I came to tell you in person that one of his pets works in your precinct," she murmured.

"I figured as much. The other week the surveillance footage from the hotel disappeared. It's highly irregular for evidence to go missing like that, but nobody knows anything about it."

"From now on, keep copies of everything in a safe place away from work. Do you have someone you can trust?"

Her question seemed like subtle confirmation it was time to try telling my partner about Overlay City again. "Tegan has always had my back. I'll tell her what's going on and get her to keep an ear out at the station house."

"I'd like to meet her again someday. She sounds like a wonderful woman for you."

"Maan." I smiled, but my voice held censure.

"Now, I'll go. Don't fret if you can't reach me. I have to keep my head down for a while. I've probably done too much already."

"Yes, Maan. I'll be careful, and you do the same."

I rose and hugged her again, lingering at the door to watch her leave. I hated Darcy for this. Honor bound to pursue him to the ends of the earth, I had turned down the role of Alpha. The Council of Overlay Affairs had broken up Ravani territory, putting our wealth in a trust until a new Ravani pack leader could be elected.

Gone were the years of werewolf turf wars and rivalries, but only so far as the laws were concerned. In reality, instinct couldn't be overridden. Thus, the Council had banned me from interacting with any wolves, even my own family. Nothing drew human attention like agitated shifters.

As a rogue, I was truly alone, thanks to Cyprian. I was also at risk of becoming increasingly uncontrolled. It happened to every werewolf without a pack. The only thing helping my sanity was having a dedicated cause that took all my attention.

I peered out the window and watched my mother stealthily cross the street and disappear into a black Mercedes. I picked up my phone and sent Tegan a text: *I need to talk to you.* It wasn't until after I hit Send that I realized it was five in the morning.

CHAPTER TWENTY-SEVEN
—
Aurie

September 8 | After Midnight

The minute my roommate barged in with a friend in tow, I projected myself into the bathroom and shook off the chilly feeling of teleportation. I couldn't believe it—caught in the buff. I heard Zyr escaping while I tossed on the silk kimono and hastily finger-combed my hair in the mirror to erase any signs of the eventful night. Then I cracked open the bathroom door and peeped out.

"Yōkai, there you are. Get over here and meet Kittie Cad. Kittie, this is Aurie Edison," Mys announced. I crossed to the couch where they were sitting. Extending a hand to Kittie, I was low-key excited to meet someone new. I had spent weeks just interacting with my roommate and the detective.

"I've heard so much about you!" gushed the tall, hawt, and—"Is she here?"—obviously non-Supernatural woman.

"Argh! She can't see me," I groaned.

"Nope," Mys replied with an apologetic smile.

Grabbing a throw pillow, I said, "I guess that's a good thing. I was worried you guys had seen my actual vagina." A wave of the cushion got a startled laugh from Kittie while Mys relayed my comment.

"We didn't see anything, darling. But if we had, it's *au Supernaturale*," chortled Kittie.

I loved her instantly. With Mys as a conduit, we made small talk. Kittie was snarky and lighthearted. I hated to see her leave when she checked the time and realized it was almost dawn.

"Terrance will be expecting his car," she explained.

"Oh, right! Tell him thanks for letting us use it," said Mys.

"Will do. Now, walk me out, Mx. Mys. I don't know how to work your magic door."

"There's nothing to it, Ms. Cad. You just . . ." Their voices trailed off as they exited the studio. I plopped on the couch, wondering what had happened to that pleasant postorgasmic drowsiness. It was gone. *No rest for the wicked*, I thought jokingly.

My gaze fell on the purse on the coffee table. I narrowed my eyes. Was that—? My scalp prickled as I sat forward to examine it closer. A distinguished-looking black business card with raised white ink peeked from the leather folds. I saw the words *voodoo loa*. "No fucking way," I whispered. I lifted the card and tucked it into my pocket before the door reopened for Mys.

"I want details!" my roommate sang, squeezing next to me on the couch.

"What were you and Kittie up to tonight?"

"We can talk about that later. We took a prescription to her grandmother. Didn't you and Zyr . . . ?" The grinning Empath rubbed one finger over the other.

"Well, we didn't go all the way," I hedged. Mys's jaw dropped, and I had to laugh. "We went far enough! Wasn't that the point?"

"Tell me everything." They crossed their legs and sat back with a cocksure smile.

My face was hotter than the tea I was spilling. "He took a page from your book and, shall we say, satisfied me. Oh my gosh! Are you in my head?" I asked when Mys flushed.

"Pfft!" They smirked, not an outright denial. I spun up another memory of Zyr's exquisite mouth, and Mys shoved away from the couch with a lust-fueled chuckle that confirmed it.

"Enough with the telepathic eavesdropping!" I laughed.

"I'm not in your head, I swear. Your emotions leap out at me. The important thing is that it worked." Blushing, they pivoted to face me.

"No, it didn't," I said. "Right smack in the middle of things, the lights started flickering, stuff started flying around the studio. That music you hear playing came on by itself." I pointed at the surround sound system.

"Meta." Mys's eyes sparkled.

"Yeah, apparently, a one-night stand isn't my unfinished business. Who knew?"

"What the hell could it be, then?"

"I have no idea." Meanwhile, the voodoo loa's business card burned through the kimono folds. I rose from the couch and ambled over to the lovely being frowning in the middle of the room. "Regardless, thanks for brokering hot, sexy alone time with a werewolf for me. I honestly couldn't have done it without you." My lips curled in sarcasm. "So, how'd you manage to pull it off?" I asked as I draped my arms over their shoulders.

"Got on my knees and begged for it?" Mys raised an eyebrow.

Mouth agape, I choked on a laugh. "I absolutely believe you!"

Mys laughed too. The shared amusement became a private smile that slowly morphed into a look of worry on their face. Staring into each other's eyes, we swayed to the music. "I'm out of ideas, Yōkai," Mys whispered.

"Well, here's mine. I plan to stay sane for as long as I can, and after that . . ." I shrugged.

"I wish I could figure out what you need." They wrapped me in a fierce hug. Heartbeats and quiet breathing filled the silence as I thought about it. I needed my sister to be released from that hospital, and I needed Darcy Cyprian locked away.

Those things were out of my control. Desire was easier to satisfy, but it was the need that was least useful. Still, the scent of Mys's cologne made bursts of sexual reverie spark. There were undercurrents swirling between us. Wherever our bodies touched, arousal swept in like high tide, and I wondered how obvious mine was.

Could the Empath sense it? Did Mys realize this attraction was underscored by a fear that I was in over my head? Did they know that my attention was split between them and Zyr? I wasn't sure if I could trust either of them. Not only had the detective kept important secrets, but it seemed my roommate was hiding things too.

Yet that didn't stop me from craving them both. Now that the idea was planted, nothing could keep it from taking root. I had no frame of reference for a threesome other than porn; but I pictured the three of us in bed together. Was that what I really wanted? The more I thought of it, the more it—

"Shhh," Mys exhaled.

"I didn't say anything," I murmured against the warm, fragrant skin of their neck. My face rested on their shoulder, our bodies flush. Mys's fingertips skimmed up and down my sides. Lips grazed a faint scar at my temple, migrating in a slow trek to my earlobe.

"Your feelings are so loud that they're almost echoing," Mys whispered as butterflies took flight within me. "You don't want what you think you want. Anatomically, we're not the same. I'm not like either of you. Besides, if tonight didn't fix things, a ménage à trois isn't the answer."

"Why doesn't it occur to you I might want more than sex?" I whispered back.

My roommate stepped from my arms and perched on the corner of the couch. I sat next to them. They weren't getting away from this conversation that easily. "Because you'll be off to the Light soon, and Zyr will be on to his next criminal obsession." Mys frowned.

"You want to know what I think?" I asked as I lifted my chin. "I think you're afraid of the possibilities."

"More like I'm afraid of the physical *im*possibilities."

"Not from what I saw in that alley," I replied.

"Whoa! Fake news," they retorted, blushing adorably and retreating again.

I followed the aimless wanderer around the studio. "Zyr knows your anatomy. We both love you as you are. Anyway, who cares that we eventually have to move on? Doesn't everybody? And isn't it better to have loved and lost than never to have loved at all?" I stopped when Mys stopped in front of the bookshelf.

"No one said anything about love, and only people who haven't lost anything say that about loss." They smiled ruefully as I lolled my head.

"*I'm* saying it, and I've lost everything!" I exclaimed, not meaning to raise my voice, but it was so easy for people with heartbeats to be smug. I squeezed my smarting eyes shut and covered my face.

Mys removed my hands. "Aurie, don't, babe."

"I'm okay. I just need—" I hesitated.

I needed them to remember that my life had passed me by the first time while I was being ultraresponsible and practical. I knew this wasn't love, but the distinction between forever and a day meant very little to me now that I was dead. I wanted to seize my Afterlife.

Without finishing the statement, I dragged Mys to my lips. My stunned roommate drew to full height like the ocean before a tidal wave and—cresting with a sweet, deep moan—they rushed me to the wall. The force of our bodies colliding made books fall from the nearby shelf. My kimono fluttered open. None of that mattered.

I wrapped my legs around Mys with eager wantonness. The Empath surged to meet me, grinding our sexes together. Again, harder. For a woman who had climaxed once for the night, my libido was surprisingly renewable. I wanted more. However, my companion suddenly clasped my erratic hips and pinned me stationary.

"Huhn! Stop, stop!" Mys gasped. It took several seconds for my desire-addled brain to register. My roommate gently shoved me away with a tormented groan. "I'm sorry, but we can't. We're friends."

"Right." I blew out a breath and shot a confused gaze at the floor. It wasn't in my head. I knew the feeling between us was mutual, but. . . "No, I'm sorry I asked for more," I said.

I didn't bother retying the kimono. Mys pretended not to stare at my nakedness. I took the *L*, but I had to grapple with how I felt for them. Who could ignore the fact that I was getting attached? And lust unrequited wasn't a good look.

I marched to the closet and tugged a pair of joggers from the rack, a T-shirt from the shelf. I got dressed and walked through the wall. I never stopped moving.

"Yōkai!" Mys threw open the enchanted door to stare after me.

But I kept going. "I'll be back," I said over my shoulder.

"Aurie, this isn't funny! Get back here! There's a tropical storm warning, and I can't see you."

"I know." It was a new trick, one thing I liked about being dead. I could disappear from view completely when I wanted.

CHAPTER TWENTY-EIGHT
—
Mys

September 8 | Before Daybreak

I smelled rain. Casting another net of Empathy, I waded through impressions of drunken stragglers at last call, but there was no hint of Aurie. Tired electric dance music pumped sluggishly from emptying clubs, and cars zipped by full of people trying to get home. A thin mist blanketed the city.

"Where the hell are you?" I whispered, my chest tight.

I had visions of terrible things happening to her. On the other hand, I told myself that if Darcy Cyprian wanted her, he could've snatched her many times over by now, but he hadn't. She was okay. She had to be.

A light drizzle started to fall. As the cold droplets grew large and came harder and faster, it was time to admit defeat. I returned to my apartment, where I tried calling Detective Zyr. His voicemail greeted me. I left a message about Aurie being missing and tossed the phone on the nightstand with a frustrated sigh.

"Guess I gotta wait you out," I muttered.

Trudging to the bathroom, I showered. My mind wandered through worst-case scenarios while I lathered up. Cool-gray morning sky illuminated the basement windows by the time I finished. Exhausted, I climbed into bed, but instead of the brief nap I'd intended, I was dragged under by deep sleep.

And gauzy dreams of sex. The sheets twisted around me. I was with Zyr. *Irete hoshī* . . . I wanted him inside me. The rough, hungry coupling ached. Then lightning flashed, and Aurie stretched between us. My racing heart echoed the thunder rumbling in the distance.

Fricative anxiety whirred internally like cicadas underscoring the storm. Yet, the nervousness was easy to ignore as her body slowly danced above me. I held her waist, and she rose and fell, riding me to completion.

I gave Aurie a stare from beneath my black lashes. "*Dashite* . . . Uhn! Dashite, come for me," I coaxed her. Abandonment was written on her beautiful face, but it was briefly obstructed by Zyr bowing over me.

"Do you really want to say good-bye to this?" he inquired.

No, of course, not. I smiled languidly as he clenched a fistful of my hair and dragged my mouth to his before I could answer.

With another flash of lightning, the lovers disappeared. "Zyr?" I called out. "Aurie?" My body felt chilled. Somehow, the bedroom of bliss had become a dark hall of nightmares. I dropped to my feet, running past scores of closed rooms. I had the feeling I was chasing something irretrievable that had been truly lost.

At the end of the corridor, there was Aurie. She flickered in and out of existence like the phantom she was. "Where's the sacrifice?" she asked in overlapping voices. Crimson raindrops descended through the high ceilings of the dissolving house. Suddenly, we were outside beneath a blood moon. Zyr howled warnings at the omen. Only it wasn't Zyr howling.

It was a Skype call.

I jerked awake. "Aurie?" I murmured. My gaze flew to my favorite chair, but she wasn't in it. Another clap of thunder rattled the church, and I patted around for my cell phone. Squinting at the screen, I saw that it was eleven a.m.

I fell back and threw off the duvet, stumbling blearily to the laptop, not bothering to answer the client calling me. I pressed Mute and strode to the bathroom. I rushed through my morning ablutions and then put on whatever passed for clothes. On the way out the door, I snatched my purse off the coffee table.

But the clutch slipped from my fingers, and the contents spilled out in a perfect flat-lay composition. I knelt to collect the essentials. Chapstick, sunglasses, identification . . . something was missing. Resting on my heels, panic rose like bile. *No, she couldn't have.*

She had.

I thought back to last night's drive with Kittie Cad. I remembered the sticky Formica table littered with an overflowing ashtray, a single bulb overhead, blue smoke curling from a cigarette hanging from the older woman's lips, a scruffy gray cat scampering underfoot as she cackled at my questions about Resurrection.

"Got the sacrifice?" the old woman had asked.

Aurie had found the voodoo loa's business card. Never mind my plan to explain everything today at daybreak. Now that Aurie had the card, she would go in without knowing the stakes. My hands cramped in a desperate grip on the phone as I redialed Detective Zyr.

I left another message at the tone: "Majika-yo? I need you. Call me back."

As soon as I stepped out the door, a deluge threatened to drown me. Gasping from the icy needles stinging my skin, I didn't notice the Uber waiting curbside until Kittie Cad rolled down the window and shouted my name over the drumming rain.

She shoved open the door. "God, I couldn't find your apartment! Get in."

"What are you doing here?" I dropped into the backseat with her, shivering. Kittie's disheveled blond hair fell over her grief-stricken face, but none of that registered as I snapped my seat belt in place. "You're a lifesaver, Ms. Cad. I needed a ride. I think Aurie has—"

My best friend turned her pleading, ruddy eyes to me and held out her cell phone. "I need you to call Terrance and tell him we went to Hollygrove to see the loa," she interrupted me. I darted a glance at the driver and blinked pointedly at Kittie for talking about Overlay City business in front of him.

"Where to?" he asked in a dull voice.

"Can you wait?" Kittie snapped.

Once she'd stopped glaring at the back of his seat, I whispered, "Hey, you know I can't talk to Terrance about my world. There are laws—"

"Fuck the laws! You broke them before. I need you to break them again for me."

"Kittie, tell me what's going on. Why are you so frantic?"

"Because some *leech* journalist saw his car in what they're calling a drug-related rendezvous in Hollygrove! Can you believe that? They've got pictures, and they're distorting them to fit their narrative! He's destroyed, and I'm mortified this is happening to him because of me."

"I'm sorry, Kris!" I reached out to comfort her, but she blocked my touch.

Her tremulous smile hurt. "Mys, I don't need your apologies. I don't need your pity. I just need you to come out of your antisocial shell for a moment and try to help me fix this," she insisted. "His PR team will devise a way to spin things politically, but that won't save our relationship. Terrance thinks I'm using again. You're the only one I know who can vouch for my character. Convince him I'm not."

Gods. I didn't want to talk to her boyfriend. I caught a glimpse of the dashboard clock. It was almost noon. I calculated how long it might take to convince the mayor Kittie hadn't used heroin in years.

Far too fucking long. Aurie had already been missing more hours than I wanted to count.

Even the driver grunted, "Hey, if you guys don't give me a destination, I'm gonna have to cancel the trip. I ain't got all day."

My best friend narrowed her eyes and slapped the seat in response. The guy got the point and shut up.

"Kittie, I'll talk to him," I conceded, "but I can't tell him the real reason we were there. He'd never believe the truth anyway. It's too nonsensical for hu—" The driver watching in the rearview stopped me short of saying *humans*. "Him," I amended.

"*I* believed you, but say whatever you want. As long as it doesn't involve drugs. Here's the phone," she said as I stole another glance at the clock. "What is it, Mitsuyo?" She bristled.

"Well, ask yourself if he's worth it if he'd jump to such conclusions anyway," I reasoned. Kittie stared at me, dumbfounded. Clearly, it was the wrong thing to say. I opened and shut my mouth several tries before finally getting out, "Look, I don't understand why your boyfriend would take the word of an acquaintance over you, but the vagaries of relationship etiquette are one reason I prefer to be alone."

With an unamused chuckle, Kittie dropped the phone and snatched a cigarette from her purse. She poked it between her lips, and the smell of smoke carried the word *sacrifice*.

"You can't smoke in here, ma'am," said the driver.

Ignoring him, Kittie jabbed a finger at me with the lit cigarette in hand. "You're alone because you would rather believe no one is worth saving than trust someone to care to save you. For as long as we've known each other, I've been trying to prove you wrong and show you I care enough to always be there for you. But you know what? I'm done. Get out."

"What?" Her words slammed me.

"*Get the fuck out of this car, Mitsuyo!*"

I slowly opened the car door to give her time to come to her senses, but that didn't happen. "I never asked anyone to save me," I said as I climbed out. Kittie Cad stared out the other window without another word.

The rain soaked me as the Uber pulled away, and I was left alone. Utterly and completely.

CHAPTER TWENTY-NINE
—
Zyr

September 8 | Morning

I slept through the thunderstorm, replaying memories of Aurie in my arms at the Supernatural nightclub and Mys at the bar flashing smiles that gave away more than intended. Each vision culminated in the explosive sexual interlude afterward.

I tasted Aurie as surely as if she were present in my bed. Her elusive phantom scent filled my nostrils . . . but the smell of breakfast cooking intruded.

Maan? My lips turned down at the corners. No, it couldn't be my mother. She would never return by day. I tried to cling to the sultry dreams until someone nudged my bedroom door open and tiptoed in. Coming fully awake, I rose in surprise.

"Tegan, what the hell? What's up?"

"Should be you. It's almost ten," said my smiling partner. "I didn't get your message until I woke this morning, but I came right over. Sorry to startle you. I thought you heard me let myself in. Does breakfast in bed make up for it?"

I expected Tegan to hand over eggs and toast, but she brandished a plate of savory shrimp and grits. Strong black coffee released steam from one corner of the breakfast tray she had dug out from somewhere in my kitchen. Staying annoyed was impossible. I tugged the comforter over my bare chest, repositioned, and found a drowsy grin for her.

"Thank you," I mumbled.

"My pleasure. Now, what made you text me at the ass crack of dawn?" Tegan gave me a loaded stare.

I eyeballed my plate and wondered if her cooking for me had relationship undertones. Maybe I was reading too much into things. Then I met her gaze, and she tellingly ran a hand over my cheek.

I ducked to shovel a spoonful of grits into my mouth. My intuition was right. My partner wanted more, but that didn't change the fact that I needed someone at the station house I could trust. Tegan Stoney was my best option. Hell, she was my only option.

"I had a meeting with my mother last night," I said, chewing.

Tegan swallowed a slow sip of coffee. "Oh yeah? *That's* why you called me over?"

"Well, she told me I should learn to trust you." At her hopeful glance, I clarified, "With the case, by letting you into my world the way you asked."

"Are you ready to do that?" Tegan's voice was velvet as she gravitated toward me.

Shrugging, I wondered how to talk about Overlay City without sounding like a nutcase. A lifetime of keeping my mouth shut made that difficult, however. I was saved by Tegan's phone ringing in the other room. "You want to catch that first?" I asked. She heaved a sigh at my obvious hedging and hopped from my bed.

As she disappeared out the door, I went to the en suite. A shower would buy me time to figure out what my partner needed to know and didn't. Plus, I wanted to put something more substantial than boxer briefs between us.

Moments later Tegan asked from the bathroom door, "Hey, is your phone powered off?"

"I doubt it. Why?" I shouted over the spray of water.

"Mayfield says he's been trying to reach you all morning. Grab this."

I peeked around the shower curtain to find her covering her eyes and shaking her phone at me. Frowning, I prayed that our superior hadn't heard the bathroom echo and put two and two together. That would have sent the wrong message. I turned off the showerhead.

"This is Ravani," I answered.

"For fuck's sake, I don't know what to say to you," the captain snarled.

"How about you start by telling me who pissed in your cornflakes?" I joked.

I wrapped a towel around my hips. Tegan had already retreated by the time I stepped into my bedroom. I crossed to the nightstand to check my cell phone. The ringer was silenced. As I tried my voicemail, I tripped on a loafer in the process, so I gave up multitasking.

"Things are not *remotely* okay," said Captain Mayfield. "I'm not gonna ask why you're inaccessible. I'm not even gonna ask why Detective Stoney is within yelling distance on a day off. Just get to my office, pronto."

The call ended, and I stared at the device as Tegan returned to the bedroom. "Have we been summoned? We can continue our talk on the drive," she suggested. I grunted something noncommittal. If someone on the job was trying to sabotage me, this weekend call-in probably meant that the chat about having someone to watch my back was already past due.

•••

"Know what this is?" Captain Mayfield slammed the door shut and plunked a Sunday paper in front of me. Ignoring my combative inner wolf, I leaned forward in my chair for a better view. Paul Jameson's old mug shot stared back in grayscale with a headline listing him a fugitive.

"Looks like my reputation restored. As per your request, we used the violation of his RO to charge him. I don't see the problem," I said.

"Oh yeah? Then why is this a thing?" A folder smacked the wood grain next to the newspaper. I rubbed my eyes, bristling. "Go ahead. Look at it," he demanded.

The hulking man braced chestnut knuckles on the desk, standing over me in what I considered a confrontational manner. I suppressed a growl and pulled the new folder close. When I opened it, my mouth went dry.

"Mayfield, I don't think—"

"No, you *don't* think, and you don't listen!" He flumped to his chair. "Those are surveillance frames from two days ago showing Farida Ravani shaking down staff at Century Luxe. Does the name ring a bell?"

"My mother." I sighed.

"You made this personal, which is exactly what I told you not to do!" the captain yelled. "Mrs. Ravani was asking embarrassing questions about Mr. Cyprian. Now, his lawyers have filed an official complaint of harassment."

I shook my head. If my mother had been *shaking down* staff, Cyprian was just trying to neutralize the threat we posed to him. It was a minor hiccup. "Obviously, there's been some misunderstanding. What can we do to make amends?" I asked. I'd kiss up to whoever I had to. There was too much at stake.

Mayfield's brow wrinkled in disbelief. "You don't get it. *Clearly*, your mother isn't authorized to play a role in the investigation. I could stick you with obstruction for this."

"I have no idea why Mum is at that hotel. It's no secret my family and I don't talk. You've known for years that I'm estranged from them. Furthermore," I said as I raised a hand in my defense, "Cyprian's history justifies investigating him. No harassment there. In fact, why are we submitting to his demands instead of letting the legal system work the way it was intended to?"

"Let the system—? Darcy Cyprian isn't some no-account represented by public defenders!" Mayfield sputtered. "I'm sure his legal team will declare prejudicial evidence so fast, your head will spin! You're off this. I should've removed you sooner, but I didn't think you could screw up a simple case of leaving the scene."

"You've gotta be shittin' me," I whispered.

Proving his seriousness, Captain Mayfield held out his hand and beckoned. "You're on paid leave pending an internal investigation. Don't be surprised if you're slapped with a libel suit from Mr. Cyprian, as well. With one of your older cases already under scrutiny, that's the last thing you need, but I can't help you any further, son. I think your career here is done."

My eyes smarted. A muscle ticked in my jaw from how hard I clenched my teeth, but I removed my piece and plunked it on the desk, along with my badge. I thought of Mys and that initial flare of respect in their eyes upon finding out I was a detective the first day we met. How would Mys see me without the shield? More importantly, how would I tell Aurie and Mys I was no longer on the case?

"Mayfield, we both know there are rape kits collecting dust while Darcy Cyprian finds new victims," I hissed, unleashing the truth with a fury I couldn't check.

The captain shoved to his feet again. "No, we know your sister dated him and took the breakup hard. She didn't claim he abused her until after he started seeing other girls, all right? I'm sorry, kid, but it's time to let that go. Yalina Ravani had zero credibility."

"What did you say?" I asked with cold calm. My chair clattered to the floor behind me, and I was on my feet, too, a fraction of a second from attacking Captain Roosevelt S. Mayfield.

The older man retracted warily. "What's g-going on with your eyes?" He pointed.

A knock at the door returned me to my senses enough to realize I was midshift. The fabric of my shirt strained from my bulging muscles. I retracted my claws as Tegan popped her head into the room.

"Everything okay in here?" she asked.

I blew out a breath and backed away. *Thank you. Thank you for sensing trouble.*

"Everything is fine. Detective Ravani was on his way out." Mayfield hardened his voice. I turned to leave, but he wasn't done. "For the record, I blame myself for permitting you to remain too long on this."

"Well, don't. I never needed your permission," I muttered, exiting his office.

I wouldn't need his permission to keep investigating either. Granted, it would be harder. As I climbed into my truck, staring at the rainy day beyond the windshield, I wondered how to navigate this new obstacle. Tegan hopped into the passenger seat and placed cool fingers on my forearm. I withdrew.

"You okay?" she asked. "It'll probably take your mind off things to tell me what you wanted to say earlier."

"It's no longer an issue." I started the truck.

"Fine, I have something to tell you. I know you assumed I rushed over when I got your text this morning out of sheer desperation." Chuckling dryly, she reached in her handbag and removed a thickly packed brown envelope. "The truth is I couldn't wait to show you this. The case files on Darcy Cyprian."

My heart skipped a beat. Had fate closed a door to open a window? I reached for the packet reverently. Gazing at what was inside, I couldn't contain my enthusiasm. "*Dhanwaadji!* Thank you! Tegan, how on earth did you find this?"

She smiled, pleased with herself. "Someone buried this info in the cold case storage room. Don't get too excited, though. No one will believe us when they see how far back these reports go."

"How far?" I asked, curious.

Tegan fidgeted. "I don't want to say. You'll think I'm crazy, but from what I can tell, they go back *fifty* years."

And there was the opening to tell her about my world.

CHAPTER THIRTY
—
Aurie

September 8 | Before Daybreak

I'd left Mys's studio with a mind to stroll a while and return when my temper was in check. Somehow, that aimless wander had turned into a quest to see the voodoo loa, and I realized maybe that had been my subconscious intent all along.

But not even a half hour after finding the place, I shot back through the wall to the corridor and stumbled away from the apartment number that was listed on the business card. It had been a mistake to come. A drunk man sleeping on the landing turned bloodshot eyes toward me. I fled in the opposite direction.

Loud music thumped from one apartment unit despite the pre-dawn hour. Conversations meandered behind closed doors. Arguments festered, and babies cried. This place was alive, but I didn't belong here. A paint-scarred door opened, and a gaggle of teens poured out from another unit, but I ran straight through them. Their jubilant laughter seemed to chase me from the poorly lit hallway.

I squeezed the crumpled business card in my fist as I raced down another flight of stairs. Finally, I spilled into the rainy morning and peered up at the building. I hadn't met the loa. I had met one of her priestesses instead. She had told me I couldn't see anyone without an offering, and I couldn't return to life without a sacrifice.

A *human* sacrifice.

Shaking my head, I took off walking in the downpour. The lightning and thunder didn't bother me. I was beyond it. I trudged through puddles that didn't shift beneath my feet. I hugged myself for warmth I didn't need. Disappointment curled in my stomach. I wouldn't live again. I was dead, and that was final.

The dreary New Orleans scenery passed unnoticed. I tried not to pay attention to the black car that seemed to appear on every street I took, although I did happen to see, loitering near a stop sign, a hooded figure who wolf-whistled when I trudged past. Groaning inwardly at the thought of getting catcalled even in the Afterlife, I ignored him, but he jogged after me.

"Hey, mamas. Got whatever you need. None of that human bullshit. Crack is whack. I got Volupt, got that Obliviscor," he ticked off what I presumed were drug names, since he jiggled a pill bottle at me.

I tucked into myself and walked faster. "I'm not here for that, thanks. I want to be left alone." Ignoring what I said, he fell in step beside me. Out of the corner of my eye, I noticed scales flaring and disappearing on his skin.

"You ain't from 'round here, is you?" he asked.

I stopped to confront him. "Seriously, back all the way the fuck off."

That's when I saw the black car pull curbside just ahead and a driver come around and open the door. I stared warily until Darcy Cyprian leaned his head out and flashed a pleasant smile. He wore sun-shades, in spite of the storm. Also, his chauffer shielded him from the cloud-covered sky with an oversized black umbrella. Otherwise, I think the vampire would have fried.

"Leave," Darcy said to the drug dealer.

My harasser backpedaled so fast that he tripped and fell before sprinting off. I stared icily at my "rescuer." As I strode past the open car door, the nightwalker stepped from the Rolls Royce. Though the car was clearly out of place in the ghetto, the aura emanating from him kept anyone from approaching.

He was dressed in a blue business suit that fit like it was tailor-made. The rainy weather didn't ruffle him any more than it did me. But he took the umbrella and held it over us both after easily catching up with me.

"Isn't it past your curfew?" I snapped.

"Yes. I have to admit, you have me acting out of character. Tell me why you're not happy. Didn't I deliver what you wanted?" When I didn't reply, he added, "Well, I guess we have all day. I'm only risking sunlight."

I stopped and glared at him. "You didn't mention the sacrifice."

"It seemed self-evident." Darcy laughed. "How else did you expect your disembodied Soul to return to the face of the earth? Of course, you need a body."

"I prefer my own, thanks." I took off again.

"We should talk. Give me five minutes of your time." He extended an arm, gesturing toward his vehicle. I glanced up. The sky was getting lighter.

"I don't trust you. You could drive off with me," I said.

"I'll make the driver stand in the rain, poor chap. I promise I won't spirit you away."

I gnawed my lip, knowing I shouldn't go, but he could answer my questions. What he wanted with Haley, for example. I couldn't ask that. According to Zyr, the vampire had no clue he was after my sister.

When the clouds shifted, and a tiny amount of sunlight made him visibly uncomfortable, I hurried back to the car. "Get in," I growled. He folded his tall, muscular frame into the backseat and closed the door behind us. The interior smelled of leather and cognac. The tinted window blotted out the sky. It was fearfully cozy.

"Thank you for your kindness. Rather unexpected, for someone who assumes I murdered them," Darcy said with a smile. The rain came down harder, and I guiltily pictured the driver huddling under an umbrella in the downpour.

"I'm beginning to think nothing in Overlay City is that cut and dried. Now, why do you want me resurrected? Hurry up," I replied.

"Are you ready for more honesty? Because I'll warn you in advance, I tell the unvarnished truth. It isn't pretty."

I crossed my arms. "You want to waste time with a preamble?"

"I did drug you," he admitted.

"Okay, we're done here. You don't have anything new to tell me." I reached for the door, but what Darcy said next stopped me dead in my tracks.

"I drugged you because *you* were supposed to be the sacrifice."

"What are you talking about?" A chill ran down my spine.

"I have a special someone, dear. To be blunt, *they* needed you in order to extend their usefulness to me. In a twist, you enchanted me. This may sound clichéd, but I've only had eyes for you ever since that party."

"Well, I no longer have that body, so?" I tried to play it tough, but my voice was pitchy.

The vampire casually lifted a shoulder. "Bodies are interchangeable. I would know. I get bored with old toys."

"And you switch them out? That's what you were gonna do with me and your special someone?" I couldn't believe what I was hearing.

Darcy gave a closed-lip grin and draped an arm along the back of the seat. "I warned you, I tell the truth. Since your unfortunate accident, watching you in Overlay City has made me certain you're the one I want."

"I'm not something you can own, Mr. Cyprian."

"No, of course not," he said as he touched my hair. "You're not like my pets. I'm offering much more than that." He stared at me with worshipful green eyes, and my skin crawled. He seemed like the type to keep a shrine in his closet. Or, worse, the object of his affections locked away.

Shrinking, I asked, "How did you even find me here?"

"Detective Zyr has a knack for sniffing out the Supernatural. I followed his nose. Of course, I thought he'd be smarter, but werewolves aren't exactly known for their big brains. After all, he took you out last night as bait, as if I wouldn't taste the vampire hunter weaponry on the very air. It was a naked setup." He sneered derisively.

"Underestimate him if you want, but Zyr is smarter than you think. He wants you behind bars, and he'll figure out a way to make that happen."

"No, he wants me punished, dear heart. There's a difference. Don't fall for the cur," Darcy said. "Do you think he cares what happens to you? You're dead to him. Ravani has been after me for years, and you're his perfect pawn. If you choose to be. You have other options."

I squirmed, wishing his words didn't fill me with such unease. Whatever the detective's hang-ups, he was one of the good guys. Be that as it may, the vampire brought up a fair point. If Zyr had suspected someone might be following him—which was the whole reason I was in hiding in the first place—why had he kept coming back to the cathedral? I knew he badly wanted an arrest, but enough to use me?

I jerked my head to clear the thought. "Your five minutes are up, Darcy."

"But, dear heart, I haven't told you the best part about Resurrection."

"What's the best part?" I grimaced.

"What's in it for you."

CHAPTER THIRTY-ONE
—
Mys

September 8 | Noon

In the stinging rain, I squinted after the fading taillights of the Uber and wondered if this was it. Had I lost Kittie Cad for good?

Kris had been my first boyfriend. We'd gone to the same church. When I was fourteen years old, my parents had given their grudging approval for us to start seeing each other. It wasn't that my heart kicked for the gangly kid I had known for ages, but Kris had an Xbox, and her mom didn't mind us playing for hours on end.

At my place, my folks enforced a no video games, no music, no television rule. Above all, I couldn't have boys in my room. They had no idea how different things were at Kris's apartment.

There, I was allowed to ditch my dresses and try on boy jeans. Of course, Kris's mom didn't know she tried on my clothes too. As the Pentecostal church choir director, the woman was homophobic enough to just be happy her son had a friend-girl, rather than worry about what we did behind closed doors.

Now, as I stood in the middle of the sidewalk in the pouring rain,

I remembered our being juniors in high school. Trying on Kris's prom tuxedo, checking my reflection in the mirror while my friend posed in my bra. "Let's get married when we grow up," I had suggested.

"Nah, it's not going down like that," Kris had said, as she smoothed slender hands over a low fade. Her lips were glossy from the Carmex my mother let me keep. "When we get out of this hellhole, you're going to Hollywood, and I'm finding Mr. Right."

Although I had never made it to Hollywood, it seemed Kittie Cad had found her Mister. Now, for the first time, our lives were diverging. Sadness blanketed me at the thought of letting her go, but I had to do it. The mayor's official contact info was online. I would call him and let him know Kittie deserved his love and trust.

After that, I would finish this business with Aurie and Zyr and get back to enjoying my solitude. It occurred to me that I had never truly been alone. But what with Kittie washing her hands of me, I would be, once the ghost and her detective were out of my life. That was what I wanted, right?

Dashing the rain from my face, I went back through the gate and returned to my apartment. The mounting despondency stopped in its tracks and relief washed over me: Aurie was huddled by my door, watching me. Raindrops glistened in her wavy hair and beaded on her clothes and skin like jewels. She lifted and wriggled her fingers, a shaky smile flitting over her lips.

"Don't ever disappear on me like that again!" I rushed over to her and pulled her into a crushing hug.

Aurie laughed. "I told you I'd be back. By the way, to anyone who isn't Supernatural you look like you're hugging the air." She tiptoed to peer over my shoulder as I let her go. "There's Zyr."

I looked too. Sure enough, the Dodge was pulling up across the street. Zyr hopped from the driver's seat, on a call. The voice that poured from the speaker was decidedly feminine. From the conversation, I realized it was his partner. But when Tegan mentioned breakfast in bed, I wondered if she was the reason he hadn't answered my calls all morning.

The detective glanced at the dreary sky and shoved a thick folder under his shirt to protect it from the rain. "I'll meet with you later," he murmured into the phone.

"Come on. Let's get inside," I said to Aurie.

The ghost hiked a thumb in Zyr's direction. "Who do you think he's talking to?"

"She's just his partner."

I wasn't sure I sounded convincing, but then, I wasn't sure I was convinced that was all Tegan was. Zyr rounded the cathedral and slid to a halt at the sight of Aurie already back. I ignored him and opened the door to my apartment. Once inside, my roommate plopped into our favorite chair. It felt so good to see her that I didn't bother telling myself she didn't belong.

The detective slowly closed the door behind us. "Why didn't you call me and let me know she was home safe?" he asked. His black hair was plastered to his forehead by the rain. He kicked off his shoes and wriggled out of his wet shirt, his bare skin glistening.

I looked away with a moody shrug.

Zyr turned to Aurie, but she held up a hand and said, "Chill, bruh."

"Oh, I should chill?" His eyebrows shot skyward. "You ran off and put yourself and everyone else in danger in the middle of a tropical storm."

"I didn't put anyone in danger," she muttered. "I took a stroll, which shouldn't be a problem if I'm not a prisoner."

"No one's treating you like a prisoner, Aurie!" Zyr shouted.

"More like a pawn in your chess match!" Aurie retorted. "You know what, I don't even know why I came back. You both seem to think you can run my Afterlife without me anyway!"

She lurched from the chair and tossed the voodoo loa's crumpled business card onto the coffee table. Staring at it, I slid my vape pen from my pocket and perched on the lone barstool. There was no easy way to explain it. Vapor floated in the uncomfortable silence while she glared at me, and the rain poured steadily in the background. The detective dropped to the sofa, studying me too.

"I was gonna tell you, but you didn't give me the chance," I said finally.

Aurie paced into my line of sight and jabbed a finger at the card. "You kept that from me, knowing it was my one shot at Resurrection."

"Aurie, it's not like that." She pulled away when I reached for her. I threw up my hands. "I had to make sure it was safe, and I was right to be concerned! The priestess told me someone would have to die for you to live again. Is that what you want, Yōkai?" I asked.

"No, of course that's not what I want! I want my own flesh and blood. If I'm resurrected into someone else's body, I basically inherit their life and say good-bye to my own. No more Haley. No house in the Garden District. No Aurie Edison." She raised glistening eyes to mine. "But it was for me to find out, not you, Mys."

Clearing his throat, the detective interjected. "I understand you're upset, honey, but I'd be lying if I said I disagreed with what Mys did. It's not that we think we can run things without you, but it's our job to protect you, even from yourself. More than that, you're our friend, Aurie. We care too much to let anything happen to you."

"I know about caring too much . . . enough to make sacrifices," she whispered, and a frisson of fear shot through me. *What sacrifice?* "I found out Darcy wants a courtesan. In exchange, he'll take care of my friends and family, including the both of you. That's why I have to do this."

"What?" Zyr and I said in conjunction. No way she was serious.

"It's pretty much like being an escort." She crossed her arms and lifted her chin.

"No, there's a reason I did burlesque on the side," I countered. "I took care of myself. No one should get that much authority over your life, Yōkai."

"I have no life, remember? It's over, like your side gig is over. Beaucoup de Chair has been in limbo with new ownership for weeks.

That's the real reason you've been taking a breather, right?"

"How did you—"

"Darcy told me. He has the deed, and the club will be yours the minute I become his," Aurie said without enthusiasm. "He's gonna use his connections to expand my mother's reach in Hollywood, and he'll make sure Haley's career picks back up when she gets out."

Zyr gaped at her. "You told him about Haley?"

"Of course not. He has no idea she's in a psych ward. He thinks she's at Bayou General, injured somehow the night I was killed . . . which is how I know he wasn't behind the hit-and-run." She studied the detective's confused frown. "He told me about your job too. I know you're not as secure in your position as you'd like to be. Darcy can make whatever it is blocking your promotion go away if I agree to this Resurrection.

"Look, I know he's a bad person," she said quietly, "but these are good things. Whatever else happens, the people I love will be better off. He has a body for me, someone who no longer wanted to live and unfortunately suffered lasting brain damage. See?"

Aurie removed a photograph from the back pocket of her jeans and dropped it on the coffee table like we were talking about a potential new car or a piece of furniture, instead of an actual human being.

At the sight of it, Detective Zyr slammed a fist into the table. It smashed into pieces, and Aurie and I jumped back, stunned. A howl of rage tore from his throat. I studied the photo—something in the image had set him off.

"What is it, Zyr?" I gulped.

"I'm fine," he growled, shoulders heaving in a struggle to control himself. "Since we're playing show-and-tell, let me show you how Darcy treats his women." He snatched the envelope from the floor by his wet shirt and tossed it on the shattered coffee table next to Aurie's potential sacrifice. More pictures of Darcy's victims fell out. Dozens of them.

CHAPTER THIRTY-TWO
—
Zyr

September 8 | Night

It was odd seeing hands the size of mine trembling, but they shook as I tore the reports, notes, and photos from the crammed envelope.

Aurie picked up a fuzzy sepia photo of a brunette with swollen eyes, a split lip, and a neck mottled with bruises. She dropped it and rubbed her hands together, as if trying to rub off the ugliness. Her feet danced past scores of other beaten, battered women.

I selected a report and read out: "'Subject, name redacted, states she heard her daughter—age fifteen years—screaming from inside the house. Subject entered the home and found the accused, Mr. Darcy Cyprian, having carnal knowledge of the juvenile without consent.'"

Mys expelled her breath. "That's enough. Don't do this."

"Nahin, I don't think it is enough," I said. "See, *that's* from the '70s. Things were a bit different back then. Hell, they considered domestic abuse like therapy for husbands. Might've colored the report a bit, so let's jump to the present day. How about this?"

Launching to my feet, I smacked another report with the back of my fingers and waved it for them to see. "'Subject: Yalina Ravani.'" My voice cracked, and I swallowed a burning lump in my throat. I didn't need to read the report because I knew it by heart. The words were in my head, whether anchored to this sheet of paper or lost to the cold case files storage room.

I recited from memory, "'Ms. Ravani states the accused hired her as a tutor, but she soon discovered he wasn't a Louisiana State University student. She freely admits they had a consensual relationship for two months. During that time, the accused allegedly became progressively more controlling and abusive.

"'Subject has no police reports, but she produced medical records for lacerations and bites, a broken arm, and sustained concussion from three separate incidences.' Manufactured, no doubt, because she heals as quickly as I do, but that goes to show you how desperate she was to get away from him.

"'The accused, Mr. Cyprian, denies the relationship. Subject presented video evidence of him breaking into her home, for which the police were called. The accused suggested he mistakenly entered the wrong unit after a night of partying with friends. Nothing was stolen and no one was harmed, so Ms. Ravani was persuaded not to press charges.

"'Subject relates that when her family became aware of the toxic relationship, they made arrangements for her to leave the country for her protection. *However*,'" I said, my voice climbing, "'Mr. Cyprian intercepted her at the airport, kidnapped her, held her against her will in an unknown location, and subjected her to repeated sexual assault over the course of several weeks.'"

I took a deep breath. "Yalina Ravani tried to poison herself, something our lycanthropy has trouble repairing. Darcy had no choice but to bring in an experienced Supernatural physician, and Yalina was able to escape. Fortunately, she survived, but there's your suicide victim. He's lying about giving you my sister's body, which he doesn't even have."

The report that had disappeared from official police records years ago fell from my numb fingers and joined the rest littering the coffee table and floor. When I was able to lift my head, I found Mys's face wet with soundless tears. Aurie hugged herself, trembling with emotion. The flat was deathly quiet. All that could be heard were distant rumbles of thunder from the passing storm.

"She was barely your age when he did that to her," I said as I brushed through the pile of papers and found the original photograph Aurie had presented. I handed it to her. "I'm sure Cyprian would like to think that he broke my sister so entirely that she never recovered.

"He had no idea how strong she is," I added with pride, my voice breaking again, "how smart, how determined. She's not brain damaged. She's completing her master's at a university in Europe far beyond his reach."

"From the bottom of my heart, I apologize. I had no idea she was . . ." Aurie trailed off.

"I know. Cyprian was counting on the fact that I never talk about her. He was using you to deliver the message that he can still treat her memory like she's disposable. On the contrary, Yalina isn't just some *body* he can take control of whenever he pleases. I won't let him turn you into that either. No matter what he promises, your Soul is worth more than he can afford, Aurie."

"I'm shook. He told me you were using me as bait, and I believed him," she said with regret.

"Hey, we made mistakes, and he exploited them." Mys shifted from the barstool and put the files back into the envelope. "I, for one, am glad Darcy's finally showing his hand. We know what he's after now, and we know how he intends to get it, although his plan to use a sacrifice he can't access is—"

"A mind game, plain and simple," I said.

"The vampire capitalized on the secrets being kept from me." Aurie agreed. As she assisted in collecting the case file and putting everything away, she studied me. "Of course, it didn't help that Yalina wasn't the only secret you kept."

Chagrined, I looked down. "I guess I'm used to being a lone wolf."

"Same," Mys replied. "I'd hazard a guess Aurie knows the feeling, too, aside from taking care of Haley. But if we want to go up against Darcy, we have to get used to teamwork."

I paced, unable to bring myself to tell them the Council had canceled our meeting. "Cyprian is more formidable than I remember. I had a visit from my insider at the Council last night telling me the vampire had a pet on the inside foiling my investigation. By the time I got up this morning, I was already suspended."

Aurie's eyes widened in fear. "Are you serious? What does this mean for my case? For Haley? This is a big problem, Zyr."

"Don't worry. I'm not gonna stop my investigation, but to be honest I wish I could throttle Mayfield."

"You let your emotions control you too much, *Senpai*. Darcy Cyprian knows it, which is why he sent that photograph to distract you with a side quest. He wants you worrying about Yalina." Mys handed me the loaded envelope and turned to Aurie. "And you."

The Empath continued. "Aurie, he knows you'll martyr yourself to save your friends. Beaucoup de Chair closing isn't my problem. You shouldn't make it yours any more than you should take on Zyr's suspension. I know if you asked your family, they'd tell you they would rather die in obscurity than let you sell yourself to advance their careers."

Aurie didn't respond but her face said Mys was right. She dropped to the couch as her roommate stepped into the bathroom. "This vampire is clever," Mys called through the partially open door. "I wouldn't be surprised if he's been watching us since the night of the hit-and-run. He knows our weaknesses and he's trying to use them against us. That's why we have to stay a step ahead of him."

"By meeting with the Council and getting them to open an official investigation," Aurie acknowledged.

Uh-oh. I stiffened at the mention of the Council of Overlay Affairs. There was no getting around it. It was time to be upfront about the odds we faced.

Mys stepped out of the bathroom in the kimono. "Stop communicating with that creep, Aurie. You don't owe him anything. As for you, Detective, solving this case will require your full attention. I propose we contact these other victims. Their testimonies, along with Aurie's, will give the Council concrete evidence that Darcy Cyprian has been at it for decades."

"We, uh, have a new dilemma." I sighed. "I rushed off last night to meet with my insider. The Council declined to grant us a formal audience. We can no longer publicly present our findings."

Mys groaned. "Let me guess. Darcy got to them?"

I nodded. "They gave us two weeks to come up with unassailable proof of his wrongdoing. As you guys know, due to Darcy's position and his friends on the Council, it will take more than the usual amount of evidence to get him convicted. Therefore, whatever we send has to be top-notch, and we no longer have police resources. I think we'll need more people on this."

"We're all we have," said the Empath.

"Doesn't your friend Kittie Cad know about our world now?" I asked.

"Yeah, but she's not talking to me currently."

"Well, make amends. I told Detective Stoney about Overlay City, too, although I didn't mention our ghost. We'll ease her into that. At any rate, Stoney and Kittie are the only two humans equipped to work this Supernatural investigation while you and I keep a closer watch on Aurie. What do you say?"

"I say . . ." Mys extended a phone to me. "Convince Mayor Rhemus his girlfriend wasn't high when you met her last night, and you've probably got yourself a deal. That's the only way Kittie will speak to me again."

"My dudes?" Aurie squeaked out, raising a finger to get our attention. "One last thing. We don't actually have two weeks. Darcy kind of gave me . . . seventy-two hours to get him an answer."

CHAPTER THIRTY-THREE
—
Aurie

September 8 | Night

The dryer tumbled in the kitchenette, a warm white noise. Lulled by the hum, Zyr and Mys napped on opposite ends of the couch with legs entangled. The studio had become a fading-daylight shade of blue as Sunday unwound. With the downturn, my thoughts shifted back to my eventful journey to see the voodoo loa.

•••

It had started with a tentative knock at the door of unit 15B. While the sounds of the projects thumped and shouted around me, I strained to hear the shuffle of feet on the other side, staring at the peeling flecks of maroon latex around the peephole, afraid to walk through walls.

"Right on time," an old lady had greeted me as the door swung open.

Dressed in a colorful muumuu, she patted a headful of pink foam rollers and waved me toward her kitchen. I took a hesitant step inside and closed the door behind me. The woman had a plump jolliness to her. She looked as though she might sooner trade coupons than hurt me, but I couldn't be too careful.

"Got the sacrifice?" she asked over her shoulder.

"Ma'am?" I squeaked.

Facing me, she shook her head skyward and grinned. "I told that so-and-so you need a sacrifice, gyal." She tapped a cigarette out of a crumpled pack and lit it. I wrinkled my nose, although the smoke didn't burn. She scrutinized me, and I scrutinized her. "Lawd, you scared. I don't bite. You look like your mama," she said with a grin. "Both y'all do, you and your sister."

"You know my mother and my sister?"

She gestured again to one of the folding chairs by the table, and I sat beside an open window that let in the noise of the storm. Weak morning sun illuminated the cluttered kitchen. There were dishes in the sink and a pot of grits on the stove. The place smelled like burnt coffee. I didn't mind any of it. It felt human, and it made me comfortable.

Plopping a battered stack of tarot cards between us, the old woman beckoned for me to shuffle. I did, asking my question again. She had me cut the shuffled deck.

"I got a sense for you. Donno you, but I got a sense for you," she answered as she laid a tarot spread. A scruffy cat hopped on the vacant chair and arched its back in a lazy stretch. Its pink nose sniffed along the edge of the sticky Formica table before losing interest and wriggling in my direction.

"I don't understand," I said to the woman. "What do you sense about me?"

Her eyebrows were threaded with silver. Staring at the cards, she raised them, and wrinkles lined her forehead. When she looked up, I noticed her irises were murky brown, but ringed by an intense cobalt blue. I fidgeted beneath her scrutiny.

"Why you here, baby?" she asked in a smoke-husky voice.

"My friend told me I could meet a voodoo loa here. Are you . . . are you the one?"

"I tend the offerings." She sounded amused. "I say the prayers. I'm Mambo Jolene. They do the interceding on yo' behalf. They do the resurrecting. You do the sacrificing, but you ain't got no offering, and you ain't got no sacrifice. So, what can they do for you?" She paused her rambling speech as she flipped over the first card in my spread, the card in the center. It was upside down. *The Sun.*

She hurried to the upper right corner of the spread, muttering under her breath. *The Hanged Man.* Well, that seemed ominous. *The Hermit* was next. It was in the lower right corner. When the old woman flipped that one over, she pursed her lips and inclined her head. The lower card on the left read *Death.* It was upside down.

I bit my thumbnail as I studied the images being revealed. What on earth could they mean, and did I even believe in the tarot? Glancing at my ghostly hand—as solid as any living person's—I realized I low-key *did* believe all this. If Overlay City had taught me nothing else, it was that impossible things weren't so impossible here.

The old woman flipped over another card, one in the upper left corner. It was the *Wheel of Fortune.* Fortune was always a good sign, right? The final card was *The Tower,* and it was also upside down. I sat back apprehensively.

"What do you see, Mambo Jolene?" I asked.

She cracked her deformed knuckles as she studied me through a haze of smoke. "I see you in the wrong place. You don't know what you want or where to go. You stuck *here*, gyal." She pointed a gnarled finger at me and then the floor.

"You want to see the light, but the lantern don't always light the way, chile," she warned. "Some secrets you must travel into the wild dark to uncover. I get it. You're scared—mm-hmm—you should be. Because if you don't find a way, you die. I mean, die in *reality*.

"Fortunately, you not alone. I'll guide you far as I can. Just bring your offering and a body to sacrifice, and I'll put your Soul in the vessel. Hm?" She lifted an eyebrow and smiled. "If not, you'll suffer. Oh, you'll get free, more or less, but—eh, let's not let it come to that." She laughed as she flapped a hand at a table with candles interspersed amongst bottles of rum and long, fat dry leaves that smelled pungently sweet.

I didn't know why or how I would suffer, but a more pressing question moved to the forefront. "What do you mean by get a body to sacrifice?" I asked.

Mambo Jolene's seamless face broke into a toothy grin. "Are you the Son of Man that you can rise three days later in the same body them crucified you in? You need a human sacrifice." She slid a large knife from a kitchen drawer.

That was when I ran from the room. I didn't want to murder someone to get a second chance at life. I didn't want anyone dying on my behalf.

•••

With an unhappy sigh, I turned from the dryer and tiptoed across Mys's quiet studio to sit on the coffee table and watch my friends sleep. I wished I could do the same. My incorporeal body couldn't rest. It needed nothing but to figure out my unfinished business, and with that, I was back at square one.

Frowning, I realized I was no longer upset at Mys for running hot and cold. After hearing how their parents had reacted in a crisis and seeing how Kittie had given up in frustration, it became clear to me that my roommate was afraid of more than embarrassing anatomy; Mys was hardwired to *expect* abandonment.

I reached across the gulf and tucked a strand of hair out of their serene face. The silk kimono framed their androgynous body like gallery art. I had never confronted my sexuality before dying, but it seemed like affection didn't require a special identity. I simply liked this person, and I wanted them to like me too.

I wanted to promise I'd never abandon them, but that wasn't possible because eventually, I would have to go to that damn Light. I glanced at Zyr. The detective's eyes were open, and I jumped, startled. He grinned sleepily.

"You should join us," he suggested.

"I'm okay. You guys need your rest. We have a busy day tracking down Cyprian's other victims tomorrow." Plus, I didn't think my libido could handle another tease fest with the sexy Empath. Real talk.

"Aurie?" Zyr paused. "You know, you were never bait to me. I admit I hoped your presence would bring Cyprian within reach, but sacrificing you was never the plan. I'll guard you with my life, understand? Always. You can trust that. A wolf's vow isn't made carelessly."

I pondered how to respond. Leaning back on the coffee table, I stretched my legs in the space between us and crossed my ankles. The movement caused Mys to stir, blink awake, and disentangle from Zyr. The detective stared longingly for a second before sitting up too.

"What are we talking about?" Mys asked.

"Trust," I stated. "I want to trust you both, but you guys seem all too willing to keep me in the dark while you figure out what *you* think is best for me. I can't put faith in that."

"You're right," said Zyr, "and I see that now, and I apologize. I'll do my best to keep you in the loop with new information from now on."

I turned to Mys for the same, but my roommate stayed mum. I arched an eyebrow. "Any other big reveals you want to get out the way?" I asked. I wasn't up for another plot twist.

CHAPTER THIRTY-FOUR
—
Mys

September 8 | Night

It occurred to me that Aurie was half-worried I was harboring a back channel to her sister or that I was in cahoots with the enemy. Wrong. The secret I was keeping had nothing to do with the case.

With my back to my companions, I moved from the couch and let the silk kimono slip to the floor. It fell quickly, as if gravity was working double-time. Aurie emitted a startled gasp while Zyr whistled low and slow.

I didn't turn around. I was terrified. I had always felt like a circus attraction; this time I was putting myself on display. But it was in the same way death had forced Aurie to be her most stripped-down self. I also sensed Zyr felt somewhat naked without his badge. We could be vulnerable together.

I squeezed my eyes shut and faced them, and Zyr audibly shifted in his seat. My Empathy lit up with his emotions, but I tried to ignore what I sensed, because it didn't feel like mere curiosity. It felt like something much less temporal. Something that would have to be addressed later.

When I peered at Aurie, her pupils skimmed over me, lingering at my chest, coursing past my abs to the dark thatch of pubic hair. She saw the male genitalia, and her relief flooded me. A part of her had feared I had tentacles or worse. In reality, at first glance, I appeared to be standard-issue. Only at first glance. Biting my lip, I reclined in bed and watched her reaction swiftly change as I revealed *the rest* of me.

"Oh wow!" she yelped in shock. Her gaze flew to Zyr and back to me.

My cheeks burned as I reached for the kimono and rose to my feet. "That's that," I murmured.

"Wait!" she stopped me.

Unable to face her again, I froze as she walked up behind me. My throat swelled, and my ears rang. She wasn't ready to know the truth. She wasn't ready to know. Memory flooded me with the jeers of people who had stumbled upon my secret in the past. Men who had hurt me because I was a freak.

The kimono was a flimsy shield. I wished I could make myself small, invisible. My heart beat painfully in my chest, louder than the thunder and rain. When a hand touched my shoulder, I resisted. But Zyr stepped in front of me and tucked a knuckle beneath my chin to lift my face to his.

"That was very brave of you," he whispered. I closed my eyes as his lips coasted over mine. His stolen kiss briefly replaced the taste of despondency. As I raised my gaze, I saw him glance over my shoulder. "Well, what do you think, Aurie?" he asked.

I tossed my head in a silent bid to be spared. "It's all right. I know it can be a bit disturbing," I tried to sound understanding. I didn't want to feel her dismay again. Yet, I couldn't stop what I sensed, any more than I could stop Zyr from asking.

Aurie stunned me by wrapping her arms around my waist from behind and resting her cheek against my back. "That's not what I think. I think," she said, "you're a gift worth unwrapping."

"What a polite way of saying I'm not what you expected," I allowed with a tiny smile.

"No, you're not!" She giggled, but I sensed her acceptance and something else: her determination to be open-minded. "Now that I know the truth about you, does this mean you'll stop running away every time we kiss?"

"Come again?" Zyr asked, curious and turned on, per my Empathy.

"I never *ran*," I corrected as I shimmied out of the sandwich that they'd made of me.

Aurie playfully caught my hand before I could escape. "Oh really?" she intoned. Her mischievous expression gave me butterflies. I raised a finger and said her name in warning, but she put her arms around my neck and cozied up anyway. I tugged the lapels of the kimono shut just in time. Zyr watched us with interest.

I rallied him. "Would you kindly explain she needs friends more than lovers?"

"Hey, you were the one who suggested otherwise." He laughed. The wolf dropped to the mattress with his hands behind his head. I tried to pretend I wasn't affected, but Aurie sidled even closer, planting desire everywhere she touched.

"Okay, what is this?" I smirked. It seemed she was trying to prove a point. To herself or me, I wasn't sure. Was she trying to see if *the feeling* remained now that she knew I was intersex?

"What is it, you ask? A perfect example of what I was saying earlier. Here you are, mansplaining casual sex like you guys know what's best for me. What about what I want?" She pouted.

Her lips were so close to mine. I was mesmerized, no matter how hard I attempted to look away. Undercurrents of arousal swirled between us. *The feeling* was still there, all right. I started to explain what a bad idea this attraction was. Instead, I found myself wondering exactly what she wanted.

"Well, what do you think is best, Aurie Edison?" I asked.

"We could retry the one-night stand." She raised an eyebrow with a half smile. "All three of us this time," she clarified. Snorting, I retreated a step and shook my head at her, but she was serious. Zyr was as befuddled as me. Aurie parked her hands on her hips between us to show she wasn't backing down.

"We've already established casual sex won't get you to the Light." I scoffed.

"This isn't about the Light. I'm taking Selfish Alley for my own satisfaction, like you told me to do. Remember? No regerts. Yes, I said *regerts*. So, let's do this. Want some candles to set the mood?" she asked, grinning. I stared in amazement. Boldness was crazy sexy on her. Her yearning to explore something different emanated from her in waves. It was hard to tell where her lust ended and mine began.

"No." Zyr's baritone cut through the heightened sexual tension. Aurie's enthusiasm flagged. Maybe I was a little disappointed he'd turned us down too.

"You heard the man," I mumbled. Never mind the desire. I shared the detective's concern that something like this would cross a line that couldn't be uncrossed. To defeat Cyprian, the three of us needed to be distraction-free. And since sex couldn't cure what ailed our dear ghost, it wasn't a risk worth taking.

"Seriously? Neither of you gave it much thought," Aurie pointed out.

"On the contrary. I've been thinking about it longer than I care to admit, but do you know what you're asking, Aurie? Come here." Zyr beckoned as he hit the light switch. She trudged over, and he cupped her girlish face and stared down at her. "We won't be lighting any candles. We have to be adults about this and"—he flashed a teasing smile—"grown-ups do it with the lights on."

Zyr circled the room, powering on more lights. "You deserve to live your best life. You deserve to be loved. And you have a right to bite the shit out of anyone who tries to take that from you." He chuckled.

Listening to him play the showman, I suppressed a tremor. Theatrics aside, could I perform in bed with two close friends, all my insecurities on display? Zyr stepped toward Aurie and lifted her shirt over her head, tossing it aside. Her face glowed with nervous excitement as she followed him with her eyes.

"To be truly free, we give up something. To be free," he continued, "we lose civility to the capricious whims of our most primal selves. You have to be ready for that. You say you want just enough to transcend the mortal coil and get the experiences you missed when you were alive."

"Exactly. I'm ready," she assured him.

"And what are you willing to give up? Are you willing to be uncivilized? Untamed?" he whispered as he gestured for me to get in bed.

I could no longer keep my shivers at bay. With a flick of his fingers, he directed Aurie to climb on top of me. It was like a fever dream. She drove her hands through my hair and pulled me to her lips. Her body followed the back and forth drive of her kiss, and I tried to slow the grinding, but the blood had already rushed south. I was almost dizzy with vulnerability.

Zyr swore in a sexy undertone and settled in bed beside me. Was he touching himself? I peeked when Aurie dipped her head and gave my collarbone an experimental flick of her tongue. Zyr had stripped down to nothing but boxers. My vision dimmed as my eyes rolled back from Aurie's hot mouth closing over my quivering breast.

"Ah, gods." I sighed.

"That's it. Let yourselves go," Zyr coaxed in a husky voice.

Aurie asked softly, "How do you like to be touched?" Her voice was seductive, electric. Her fingers grazed my pelvis. Only a faint reddening of her cheeks gave away her shyness as I guided her. In fact, she tightened her fingers around my tumescence. But when she slid her other hand between my legs to touch my feminine sex, too, I was caught off guard.

"What are you doing?" I said, with heightened excitement.

Zyr cupped the back of my knee in a bid for me to relent to pleasure. "Give it a chance," he whispered.

Smiling, I tried to catch my breath. "Are *you* as willing to try new things?" I asked. I sensed his exhilaration and uncertainty at the question, but he nodded anyway.

"Hell, why not?" he said, so faintly that I wondered if I had heard him right.

I had no clue what had made the self-disciplined law enforcement officer change his mind about our sleeping together. I half sensed that he thought he could pull out whenever he chose, but each of us was bound by weeks of holding back. Now that it was started, it would be completed tonight.

The detective tugged my legs apart and leaned over to kiss me. At the same time, he toyed with Aurie's body in ways that made the ghost switch her hungry lips to his.

Rapture. Any question of performance went out the window. This wasn't a show; having two lovers at once was a helpless but thrilling capitulation. My form quaked, chasing the feeling, arching off the bed.

"Take everything off," I said against Zyr's lips. When he didn't immediately comply, I clutched his throat and turned the tables on control. I felt his quickened pulse when he pulled back, but there was an inferno of passion in his searing gaze. "I said, get naked," I ordered.

With a wolfish grin, he left the bed and returned nude for my devouring eyes. "Satisfied?" he asked. *Not quite yet,* I thought. As if reading my mind, he presented his erection to me, and I kissed him there. But when Aurie mimicked what I was doing on me, it shook heaven and earth for me.

Hitching in a breath, I looked down at her in bliss. "*Gods,*" I whispered. Spasms rippled through my entire frame. I gazed back up at Zyr, continuing the erotic game, ready for it when he gripped a fistful of my hair. Then the eye contact. He was a master at it. I languished deeper in a love affair going nowhere. *Ah, Senpai. Yōkai.* Two aimless crushes.

Suddenly, my undersexed body threatened orgasm. I let Zyr go and clutched Aurie's face to stop her before the party ended too soon. Yet, she languidly locked eyes with me, her lips still pressed my manhood. She was a quick study of Zyr's magical stare. *Oh, you're gonna be impossible to give you up, aren't you?* Temptress wasn't the word.

"I want you," she uttered.

"M-me?" I stammered.

Nodding, Aurie kissed the werewolf, as well. "I want you both," she moaned as she straddled my hips and brought me to her entrance.

"But this isn't my forte," I admitted sheepishly.

"It doesn't have to be. Just make love to me."

After a moment's hesitation, I rolled her to the bed. This was happening. I wanted it. As she squeezed her legs around me, it was like drowning in a fast-moving river of excitement. Zyr allowed me to adjust before easing his way into my current too. With that, the circle was complete, and I was lost. I might've been falling.

I briefly thought of the impersonal performance sex I did for a living. Hotel rooms. Rich men. Emotions tinged with the knowledge that whatever was received wasn't freely given. Here, sounds of genuine ecstasy filled the room from the three of us, and I embraced the unfamiliar: being wanted for desire's sake. I would get nothing in return except memories.

When I couldn't hold back any longer, I sprang from the tangle of bodies. However, Zyr was determined to take me past the point of no return. "Zyr, Zyr—wait!" I clamored as he stroked my member. It was too late. I reached my final destination.

Aurie quickly followed. She dragged me to her lips, emitting a crescendo of moans, and her orgasm exploded in my consciousness brighter than dynamite. At last, Zyr released a primal grunt. Our release was sweeter, more intimate than anything I had ever experienced, all but violent in its intensity.

Gods, why? There was no maybe—I was definitely falling for them. It was like time suspended as we basked in the ambiance of pure passion. Until we collapsed. Three damned souls. One of us already dead.

CHAPTER THIRTY-FIVE
—
Zyr

September 9 | After Midnight

The lights were out, although we had fallen asleep with them on. For a second, I was disoriented, until I heard Mys's quiet snores. It surprised me that I hadn't already left. I wanted to stay. Not least of all because the cozy flat could have been ripped from the pages of a design magazine. It was trendy, immaculate, comfortable.

I tried to move, and my body ached in a friendly reminder of what we had done. I had flashbacks of Aurie and Mys together. Why that had been such a turn-on, I would probably never know.

I tugged the cool white sheet over my naked body and lay there. A drowsy smile touched my lips until reality set in. Darcy Cyprian had given Aurie mere days to decide whether or not she would be his sex slave. He had talked such a good game that she had considered it.

We had to find a safe house he didn't know, and we had to transport her without rousing his suspicions. Cyprian wouldn't take no for an answer. He had already been more patient than I had ever seen him. I didn't want to think of what would happen when that patience ran out.

He doesn't know about the cabin on the North Shore. Pondering that, I turned over and tried to get back to sleep before one worry snowballed into another. But my mother came to mind, and the thought left an empty hole inside. I couldn't think of my family without being reminded that I was alone—alone and destined to destroy myself if Cyprian had his way. I tried to picture how lunacy would affect me. I had struggled to remain sane ever since renouncing the title of Alpha.

Some days had been harder than others. (There was a tightly capped bottle of mood stabilizers back at my townhouse.) But I knew my usual battle with control would be ten times worse as a rogue with an idle mind.

Would I turn on the humans and draw the ire of Hunters? Or would I clash with other werewolves and get sentenced to death by the Council? Perhaps I would roam the forests with the wolves that had never been men.

My greatest fear was hurting someone I cared about. I had kept everyone at arm's length, even my partner. Now? Now, a serious mistake had been made. Regardless of the careless fantasies voiced half in jest, I had never intended to take things this far. Up to the last minute, I had hoped I could avoid sex with Aurie and Mys and play voyeur. *Crazy.*

Pondering this, I sat up in bed and glanced at them, lying in a wonderful jumble. The notion to stay faded. I had to put distance— emotional distance—between us to keep them safe.

My throat tightened, burning as I slipped from the bed and grabbed my jeans. Aurie wasn't asleep. She turned to watch me. Her yawn and stretch managed to trigger my libido, even after the satisfying night we'd had. "What time is it?" she asked.

I caressed her cheek. "It's not morning yet."

She sat up. "Sneaking off?"

"Shh . . ." I pointed my chin at Mys and put a finger to her lips.

Aurie shimmied out of bed. She grabbed a throw, wrapping it around her nubile form, and beckoned me to follow. In the cool, white light of the bathroom, she sat on the edge of the tub while I leaned against the closed door.

"What's the problem?" she asked.

"Nothing. I'm heading home to plan how to move you. I have a cabin—"

"No, I'm done running from Darcy Cyprian," she said as she crossed her arms.

"Humor me. I need to keep busy," I replied.

"You *need* to keep busy?" From her face, I could tell the phrasing meant something to her. "Wait . . . Darcy mentioned rogues deteriorate without work. Was he telling the truth?"

"Depends on what he said," I hedged.

She wrapped the throw tighter around herself and studied me with worried brown eyes. "That it was touch and go for wolves to be on their own, especially without keeping busy. The way he described it, the Council watches rogues so closely because they tend to go feral and . . . kill."

"Hmm. Well, we have a solid team now. I'll coordinate with Kittie and Tegan about talking to the other victims. In the meantime, I want to get you out of the city. If I become a threat to anyone, I'll take myself out of the equation."

Aurie rose from the tub and approached me. "After everything you guys have done to keep me safe and sound, I know we can help you. Don't shut us out," she murmured, lacing our hands together.

"I wish it were that simple, but there's no escaping my nature. Wolves need a pack to stay in check, and unfortunately, I don't have one."

"Mys and I can be your pack."

I couldn't hide the smile that crept to my lips, but I shook my head. "If you run with me as I deteriorate, you'll suffer from my bad decisions. I think I've already messed up by sleeping with you two."

"Are you kidding me?" She yipped with a grin. I covered her mouth and glanced out the door at Mys, undisturbed. Aurie tugged my hand down and rolled her eyes playfully. "What happened between us wasn't a mistake. It was enthusiastically consented-to sex.'"

"I . . . accept that. As long as it doesn't happen again."

She pulled a face. "So, you're sneaking off in the night like a Tinder date gone wrong?"

"I don't want to send the wrong message."

"Which is . . . ?" She arched an eyebrow.

I leaned forward and kissed the tip of her nose. "That I'm a Tinder date gone right. See you in the morning. We'll talk about that cabin in the woods."

Dragging her feet in facetious reluctance, she led me from the bathroom. I finished dressing and headed out of the flat. I knew it was the smart move, despite her disappointment. Lurking in the shadows was someone who reported to Cyprian—I could all but smell them— and the last thing the vampire needed to hear was that I had stayed the night.

CHAPTER THIRTY-SIX
—
Aurie

September 9 | Noon

The weekend storm had passed, and midday sunlight poured through the basement windows. Mys hardly stirred. I had spent the sleepless hours memorizing the details of their beautiful body. The night, including the bittersweet good-bye with Detective Zyr, lingered in the quiet room.

But what had changed? Everything and nothing.

While I busied myself brewing coffee, I tried to ignore the crazy idea that some magical connection had been struck. Mys finally awakened at the bright, aromatic smell of java and the sound of someone knocking at the door. Leaving the bed and knuckling sleep, they let in the detective.

"Hey," Zyr grunted. He breezed to the kitchenette with a crisp new roadmap. It gave a loud crackle as he spread it across the marble island. "I went home last night to keep Darcy's goons from assuming our relationship is anything but business. As I mentioned to Aurie before I left, she may be safer elsewhere: my cabin." He circled a spot on the map with a Sharpie.

Mys groggily leaned in to see and brushed against me in the process, with skin warm from the bedcovers. The brief contact made me feel as weightless as the silk kimono. I fluttered to the barstool. I peered from one friend to the other, experiencing emotions that hadn't been there before—a stirring of something other than desire? A smile touched my lips.

After a blasé glance from the detective, however, I caught myself.

Zyr Ravani was unfazed. Like nothing had happened. *Nothing personal, at least.* "It's in the upper corner of Tangipahoa Parish," he went on gruffly. "About a two-hour drive, barring traffic. If we can get there without Cyprian realizing we're on the move, he won't even know where to begin to search."

"How do you propose we avoid detection?" Mys asked.

"We leave in the middle of the day, take an unfamiliar vehicle." Zyr capped the marker and parked his shoulder against the fridge with his arms and ankles crossed.

A million interpretations for his body language flitted through my head, but I wondered if I was overanalyzing things. My roommate stroked the nape of my neck and handed me coffee. Recognizing the distraction for what it was, I managed a smile.

"His watchers will know something is off," said Mys. "We'll have to shake them somehow."

"So, we're leaving this isolated studio apartment beneath a cathedral for an even more isolated location in the woods," I said. "Can a person die twice? 'Cause y'all are trying to kill me with boredom."

"I'll be there to keep you company, Yōkai." Mys grinned.

"Cool, cool, cool. But, more and more, I'm thinking this isn't the Good Place," I grumbled.

Zyr folded his map and offered his first smile since leaving last night. "Best I can offer is a supply run before we hide you away. Want to go shopping?"

"Oh-ho! Since you asked, I'd *love* to hit a few boutiques, dine in style, walk the boardwalk—"

"And never mind the threat of vampires? You like playing with fire," he modulated.

I held up a finger and reminded him, "I'm normally risk averse, but you two encouraged me to wild out."

He smirked but couldn't hide his amusement. "I was thinking a big-box store."

"Actually, Aurie's onto something," Mys chimed in. "We can lose Darcy's pets if we crisscross the city enough. Besides, I want to show you this gallery on Julia Street. We can do a lunch date afterward."

"A lunch date sounds great," I chirped.

Mys high-fived me and ducked into the bathroom to get ready. Outnumbered, Zyr threw up his hands and plopped on the couch. "Then I guess we'll run the city and do lunch, since clearly, we have all the time in the world."

"We'll make it a working trip. Get Kittie and your partner to meet us out," I suggested. He hunched forward with a wooden expression, popping his knuckles. If ever there was a man who wasn't happy with a decision, it was him.

Sorry to inconvenience you. I channeled nonchalance, but I was hurt. The feeling of empowerment from last night had worn off. Now, I felt mostly confused. From my perch on the barstool, I stole a furtive glance and caught him watching me. He looked away, I looked away. A pensive mood descended. I wrapped my fingers around my mug and stared at the milky coffee.

So, this was that morning-after rude awakening I had heard about—the moment when what had seemed like Enlightenment turned out to be Just Sex. The corners of my lips quirked downward. It wasn't like I had expected much, but had it been naïve to think we could remain friends after falling in bed together?

That was the problem. All at once I hated being in the friend zone.

•••

The outdoor recreation store was beyond the city limits, pleasantly slow paced and uncrowded. Its shelves were lined with athletic equipment and hunting stuff, camping supplies and hiking gear. It wasn't my typical boutique, but I was too happy to be out to complain.

Plus, the detective had promised we could hit the French Market later. We would also have lunch with Kittie Cad and Tegan before we headed to the cabin.

Meandering through the fluorescent-lit aisles behind my friends, I bided my time as our shopping cart filled. A family pack of toilet tissue went in with ready-to-eat meals, cases of bottled water, toiletries. Stuff a dead girl would never need.

Mys slowed to meet my pace and looped an arm through mine. I glanced at the glossy Edge tech magazine they were perusing. I had shelved my complicated reaction to the ménage à trois, but it seemed like Mys and I were tighter than ever. On the other hand, the Empath didn't treat the detective like he should be any cozier.

"Hey, what do you think of this?" Zyr held up a fancy-looking first-aid kit.

I watched them debate the merits of getting it, not a hint of chemistry evident. I wasn't as good an actress, but I'd be damned if I played the salty one while Zyr and Mys were over it.

"The woods are hazardous," I spoke up. "I mean, obviously, I have no use for first aid, but even if one of you senses trouble and the other heals superfast, someone might get an agonizing splinter or something."

It was a try-hard joke, but it garnered a laugh. I had to suppress a wistful simper as Zyr's resonant baritone chuckle rolled through me. Mys gave my hand an affectionate squeeze. Discreetly. It reminded me that my mood was on full display to them, and my cheeks flushed.

Tossing the kit in with the other items, I hopped on the end of the shopping cart to be pushed to the next aisle. Only then did I notice the woman next to us staring in alarm. To her, the huge first-aid kit had flown into the buggy on its own.

I mumbled an apology to the glowering detective as the woman scurried by. Mys covered a giggle with a cough, and our disgruntled companion eventually cracked a smile. At that, the rhythm of my phantom heart misfired.

This is trouble, everything in me seemed to say. Well, it couldn't be called trouble, exactly. Just a situation-ship. Even *that* was probably too official a title. It was nothing. I made myself remember why I had engaged in this trifle in the first place: I was running out of time. I could feel it.

Deep down, I knew stopping Darcy Cyprian was my real unfinished business. The case file gave us the leverage we needed to ensure the vampire never hurt another soul. Tegan and Kittie Cad would make short work of convincing his former victims to come forward for justice, now that we knew who they were.

Which meant that I didn't have months left, possibly not weeks either. Last night had been about indulging in a fantasy. Today was about getting my affairs in order. At no point was I supposed to catch feelings. I would be crossing over soon.

The thought of leaving pushed other concerns from my head and made me anxious for my sister again. On the drive to the store, Zyr had been adamant that visiting the mental health center was off-limits, but he had put my mother on speaker to let me get an update on Haley.

"She's doing better than expected, Detective Ravani. Sleeping peacefully," my mom had relayed. Zyr shifted the phone closer to me.

"I miss you guys," I said, tears collecting on my lashes. I dashed them away, knowing that neither Mom nor Haley could hear me. And then . . . a weak voice in the background groaned my name. My eyes flew to Zyr's in surprise.

Mom interrupted all my unasked questions. "She's been calling for her sister a lot lately, but I can't bring myself to tell her that Aurie's—"

"I'm right here," I wanted to shout.

I heard my sister reply faintly, "Aurie, I told Jack . . . don't worry."

"Jack? Who's Jack?" the detective asked. I raised an eyebrow and shrugged.

"I don't know. Probably a figment of her imagination. She's incoherent at times," my mom apologized. "Anyway, Haley needs her rest, and I'm afraid this chat is disrupting her sleep. Was there anything else you needed?"

"No, no. I'm glad to hear she's progressing. Please . . . contact me immediately in the event of unexpected visitors or anything of that nature," Zyr requested. I tipped my head in mute appreciation for the brief conversation. It had to be enough to hear their voices.

"Will do, Detective," Mom vowed as she ended the call. "By the way, thanks for being as hands-on as you are—I underestimated you—but don't worry so much. She's gonna make it out of this, okay?"

Emily Edison was right, as usual. Haley would survive and recover from this brush with devastation. I no longer needed to keep a vigil. Using her as an excuse to stick around wouldn't work anymore. There was only one thing left for me to do now, something I had been putting off since discovering I was dead.

•••

"Are you hot natured or cold natured?" Zyr asked.

I snapped to the present and dodged a customer who nearly walked into me. Mys answered for me: "I love that you're being extraconsiderate, Senpai, but our girl doesn't feel discomfort anymore."

Zyr stared at the blanket as if suddenly realizing how ridiculous it was, but I was touched. "Watch it," I teased. "A shopping trip, phone privileges, and now this? I might start thinking you care." Swearing, he thrust the fleece back on the shelf with such force that several bundles fell as he stormed off. "Hey, what the hell is wrong with you?" I called after him with a frown.

He spun to face me and hissed, "I *care*, honey. That's the fucking problem! In a case like this, that's a goddamn liability."

"Dude, seriously, I get it." I was talking to his back again.

"Nahin, I don't think you do."

An angry scowl stitched my brow. With arms wide, I receded at the same pace as him. "You don't think I do? Oh, that's right. I need you to think for me!" I retorted.

"Oh, gimme a break, Aurie! You know that's not fair!" Zyr pivoted and snarled.

"Exactly, it *isn't* fair!" I shouted back.

"Guys, I feel every sting in every word," Mys said quietly in the growing chasm between us.

Zyr clenched his teeth and glared at the floor. I jerked away to hide my face. Throwing a tantrum was so twenty years ago, but the aftermath of our threesome was doing terrible things to my pride. Not to mention the other shoppers who were watching the detective argue with the air. Through a blur of vexed tears, I noticed a man squinting at us—or rather at Zyr and Mys—but I was too frazzled to think much of it. People often stared when we were in public.

As badly as I wanted privacy to lick my wounds, it wasn't safe to wander off. I trailed my companions and pulled myself together. I wondered why I was letting infatuation get the best of me. How much did it matter that Zyr had admitted his feelings? And was it my imagination, or was his temper flare a sign of his increasing instability?

The three of us migrated to the front of the store to check out. That was when I realized that the watcher remained suspiciously attentive. I managed a closer inspection. Black slacks and a white tank accentuated bulging arms covered in tattoos. He could be a cheap extra in a mafia flick.

"I think I see a pet," I muttered.

"I don't smell anything." The detective's skeptical gaze followed my line of sight, and he swore under his breath. Half a big-box store separated us from the goon. Unfortunately, a similar-looking thug exited an aisle on the opposite side of the building. "Shit. Let's go," Zyr growled.

"What? Why? We knew we'd be followed." I threw up my hands in protest.

"He's right. We should leave," said Mys as the men zeroed in on us. "There's a weird vibe coming off these guys."

"So, we're going straight to the cabin?" I asked incredulously. The thought sent a surge of fury through me, and the shopping cart slammed to a halt as Zyr tried to push it forward.

"What the hell, Aurie? Now isn't the time for this!" he exclaimed. I lowered my gaze, but I had no control over the poltergeist activity. It made me more determined than ever to complete what I had planned for my last day free.

"I *need* to see my grave before we go," I said.

"I'm not taking you to a fucking cemetery! I never promised that!"

"Can you two keep your shit together for like five seconds? Let's get out of here!" Mys commanded. I choked up, unable to argue with the goose bumps racing up my arms, telling me that peril was closing in. The shopping cart jerked from my telepathic grip as I fled the store with Mys.

Once in the parking lot, we gained speed. We flew past onlookers who stared in concern. A few people shot off running or walking faster on reflex. When one frightened voice asked if there was an active shooter, general panic rippled through the crowd at the suggestion.

It was too much. Mys whined in obvious distress, and the small sound pierced me. I could imagine the disorienting emotions coming from every direction. "I got you, babe. This way!" I said as I wrapped an arm around the Empath's waist and maneuvered us to the truck. From there, I looked for Zyr. I saw him back in the store scattering merchandise and carts in our wake to give us a fighting chance at a clean getaway. His good name would be in shreds after this.

All because of me. I swallowed the burning lump in my throat.

Zyr sprinted out of the store and blew through the parking lot, gesturing for me to get in the truck. "Go, go, go!" he shouted. Mys pushed me into the backseat, but I wedged the door open.

"I don't want to do this anymore. Let me out!" I said.

The detective shook his head. "I swear I'll find a way to make today up to you, but let me get you to safety, Aurie, please!" His voice cracked with desperation.

"You can't make it up to me! What could you possibly give me that outlasts the grave? Don't you get it? I'm telling you to let me go so that helping me doesn't ruin your lives too!"

Zyr's hand shot into the cab. He grabbed my face, bringing us eye to eye. Static crackled between us. The fierceness of his expression woud've warned another woman off, but not me. We were both a little wild and crazy in that moment. A sob broke from my chest as I stared into the yellow fire in his amber orbs.

With a heavy exhale, he eased his grip. "Honey, life is full of things that outlast the grave, like loyalty and honor." His voice softened. "I'm not letting you sacrifice yourself for everyone else. We're in this together."

"Why? Why would you two risk everything for me?" I asked.

"Don't make me spell it out for you," Zyr whispered.

My eyes widened. *Spell it out for me? Please, do . . .*

CHAPTER THIRTY-SEVEN
—
Mys

September 9 | Early Afternoon

Clutching Senpai's shoulders, I dragged him from the quad cab and shoved him toward the driver's side. "We should leave now. I feel them getting closer," I urged as I hopped in the passenger seat and slammed the door.

The items we had spent a leisurely forty-five minutes shopping for had been left behind, except for the first-aid kit. I had grabbed it on the way out without thinking. Now Zyr threw it back to Aurie. I tried to guess what charges we would face when this all hit the fan.

He peeled from the parking lot on two wheels, and the speedy reverse jostled us like bobbleheads. Aurie let out a squeaky yelp while I hugged myself, struggling not to puke. Pedestrians were a hairsbreadth from being flattened. Commendably, the detective navigated the human obstacle course like a pro.

We sped toward the road. A shimmer hovered over the blacktop, and sunlight glinted off other vehicles. The beads of sweat rolling down my face had little to do with the late-summer heat wave, however.

Empathy was destroying me. There were too many people. Too many impressions. Panting, I squeezed my eyes shut.

"Can you sense how many are following us?" Zyr asked, switching on the AC.

His voice was calmer than he felt. I knew. He buzzed with yellow and orange agitation, and his need to morph was a painful throb in my head—his head. His fight or flight reflex had only one setting: a bright-red impulse to battle hard. Oddly enough, deep-purple desire twisted in his gut at the same time.

"I'm not sure. I think no more than the two we saw, but they don't *read* like the usual vampire pets," I breathed.

"They're not pets. They're mercenaries, hired guns. The vampire scent wasn't on them. I bet Cyprian never even met them in person. That's why I didn't smell them." As Zyr spoke, he studied the rearview mirror to see if they were coming up behind us.

I processed the news while I tried to let the cold blast from the vents soothe me. Fists unclenching, I stretched my fingers. I took a few deep breaths and squinted to view the oversaturated cerulean sky, my blurred vision growing accustomed to the noon sun.

"Is that why my Empathy didn't work until the last minute?" I looked over at the detective.

"My guess is they weren't sure of their targets. Probably working with photographs."

"Top shelf. Gotta hand it to Cyprian. He's clever, but those same weaknesses can't be exploited again, now that we know his game," I said.

I glanced at Aurie in the backseat. Her face was devoid of emotion, but she was a tangle of feelings. Sad about not seeing her final resting place, confused by Zyr's noncommittal push and pull, depressed by the constant threat Darcy posed.

I reached between the seats and interlocked fingers with her. Some of her tension unfurled. A tenuous sort of resignation took its place, and she locked our hands together tighter.

"Why did he send mercenaries?" she asked as she stroked my thumb with hers.

"To keep an eye on us." Zyr met her gaze in the rearview mirror. "By now Cyprian realizes you don't plan to give him what he wants. We have to shake these men, or they'll follow us to the cabin. There's no hope if he learns our destination."

"But why send killers for a dead girl?"

"They're not here for you," Zyr muttered.

Aurie went quiet.

My attention returned to the chase. As quickly as the feeling of being hunted had subsided, it came rushing back. I had never dealt with malice like what radiated from the hired guns in the SUV. They weren't after a paying gig. They relished killing. They preferred inflicting pain.

I caught a glimpse of Zyr with the steering wheel in a white-knuckled grip, and in the fabric of my consciousness, he didn't feel like himself—too volatile, too close to skipping his marbles.

"You okay?" I asked him.

"Yeah, hold on."

A sharp jerk, and the Dodge swerved into the right lane. Gasping, I dropped Aurie's hand to grip the door for dear life. *Duhnnnnn!* A horn blared from a car we passed dangerously. A child waved. I shakily waved back, since the kiddo didn't appear scared by the erratic maneuvering his parents took to avoid hitting us.

"Gods! Be careful, Zyr," I said.

The truck increased speed with a yowl of the engine. Behind me, Aurie yanked her seat belt on. My apprehension rose like heartburn as the same vehicle we had just passed swerved up beside us. Road rage or racing? I couldn't tell.

The same kid in the backseat beamed, his eyes sparkling with excitement. He held up a Matchbox race car. *Racing.* There was no way the detective saw him. Zyr reached into the center console and pulled out a black and silver Glock, his attention on the SUV speeding to catch us. "I've had it with these motherfuckers," he complained.

"Are you crazy? You can't fire that on a busy interstate!" I yelled. I turned to the child, who was so thrilled by the idea we were racing that he hadn't noticed the weapon. The kid gave another gleeful wave, but I didn't have the energy to respond in kind.

My terror was mounting. I realized Zyr had split his attention between the road and the men chasing us. The Dodge truck seemed to have a mind of its own. It moved seamlessly with the flow of traffic at eighty to ninety miles an hour, while its driver extended his gun arm past me, tapping the passenger window with the gleaming barrel.

Our pursuers drew level with us. The two burly mercenaries grinned from ear to ear, and the detective's lips twisted in a disturbing facsimile of a smile to match theirs. His bloodlust would have been fascinating if not for how real shit was getting.

I'm gonna die. I scrunched lower in my seat. *We're all gonna die*.

My gaze flew to the chipper kid in the sedan nosing ahead in the other lane. That kid could grow up to be the next eSports racer. I pictured the devastation a stray bullet could cause, and I stopped cringing and straightened.

"Zyr, put the fucking gun away!" I shouted.

Aurie reached from the backseat and snatched the firearm from his hand. I did a double take, stunned. Zyr glowered at her in the rearview, but she tucked the gleaming steel beneath her body and crossed her arms. "Focus on driving," she directed. Her bold moves seemed to bring the detective to his senses. He clamped his hands on the steering wheel.

I faced forward to see the young race car enthusiast's family take an exit ramp. Thank the gods. One crisis averted. Even so, killers were still in hot pursuit.

Heart in my throat, I peered over at the SUV, but the vehicle had fallen behind ours. The men within shared dumbfounded looks, pointing in fear at our truck. I realized they had seen the gun flying into the backseat. *Oof.* It would seem like bad juju to them, especially since they weren't familiar with our world. I smiled in relief.

"Let's go before they decide we need an exorcism," I said.

Zyr shifted gears. The truck let out a rumbling roar and screamed down the interstate. The drive was doubly terrifying because the road we traveled stretched over bayou. The trees we flew past blended with sky and river.

We skipped from one opening in traffic to another, eating up the miles. Finally, I checked the side mirror, and the SUV was gone. The high-speed chase was done. Still, we continued at a swift cruise.

Silence filled the quad cab as our mood settled. The blinker ticked at the next exit. Another long expanse of bridge with less traffic. Looking out over the glassy water and stoic trees, I squinted at the glaring sun. The day was too gorgeous for death scares.

Zyr peeped at me and grinned as I touched my chest and arms. "I know you weren't nervous," he joked. "Relax."

I snorted a laugh. Sobering, I studied him in profile. "What happened back there?" I asked. Sunlight hit his eyes and turned them topaz. His tan skin soaked up the golden rays. He squared his jaw with a bob of his Adam's apple.

"I'll get you two settled at the cabin. After that you might not see me for a while, but I'll make sure you have everything you need."

"That doesn't answer my question," I said.

Aurie sat forward to rest her head on my shoulder. "It's because he's a rogue," she replied.

Zyr's face tightened as he wordlessly stared ahead.

I admitted I didn't know much about rogues. He'd given me a crash course. Idle, isolated wolves became progressively more savage to the point of being a danger to others. It was a bizarre coincidence to deal with two deteriorating Supernaturals at once. Aurie and Zyr couldn't have met each other at a worse time.

"Seems like it would be the other way around, like being with a pack would make you more canine, and being around people would make you more humanlike," I mumbled at the passing scenery. I almost suggested that the case should be enough to keep him focused and sane. I was learning to trust other people's instincts about themselves, however. I had been dead wrong about Aurie.

"You have to understand our nature," Zyr stated. I swung my gaze to him. "Every shifter has an animal spirit that's separate from us but one with us. There's a constant battle for supremacy between the civilized and the untamed sides. Usually, self-discipline keeps the wolf in line.

"But, in isolation, the wildness speaks so loudly that it's all we hear. Unless we have something else keeping our attention, it takes over, especially around the full moon," he went on. "Why do you think humans have werewolf stories in the first place? Fear the lunatic."

"Wait a second, I thought you said you were born that way. The old stories about werewolves are real? You can infect others?" Aurie asked with interest.

"Infect? We can *turn* humans. It just isn't done. The Council disapproves," he said.

As I listened to them discuss the pros and cons of creating more werewolves, I fumbled for my vape pen. Concern for Zyr's well-being struck a ripe blue note within me. I reached into the backseat and laid a hand on Aurie's knee. A sense of peace emanated from her, taking away some of my stress.

I sensed that the mellow vibe corresponded to her acceptance of the inevitable. Death was no longer a threat to her. It made her feel invincible. She wasn't worried about Zyr because he had given his word that we'd be with her in her final hour. But it would take more than confidence to find a breakthrough to help him the way we were helping her.

I peered at the man who had stolen my stone heart with that first kiss in the shadow of the cathedral. He had learned the truth about me and kissed me again anyway. And Aurie had insisted on loving me, regardless of who or what I was. Somehow, she had managed to make me, the loner, not want to lose her.

None of us wanted to lose. The irony of being an Empath was realizing how they felt before they knew it themselves. Something was growing between us like a green shoot forcing its way up through rocky, inhospitable soil. Yet, how long could a fragile flower nurtured by darkness and death survive?

CHAPTER THIRTY-EIGHT
—
Zyr

September 9 | Late Afternoon

The red dirt road wound through pine trees and oaks. Sunlight hung in the woods, turning dust motes and pollen to gold flecks, the sight of which soothed my frazzled nerves. Deer pranced away at the sound of the four-wheel drive. The trail dead-ended in a vibrant glade, where my cabin was located. There was one way in, one way out. Long-eared hares played hide-and-seek in the tall grass, and birds chittered in protest as my Dodge came to a stop.

I wanted to kiss the ground.

Somehow, we had reached our destination without anyone taking a bullet. I stared with relief at the faded walls of the lodge, the aluminum roof dulled by time, the yard that was more wildflower field than lawn. Inside the cabin, there was a great room, an updated bathroom, and a loft. Aurie and Mys would be comfortable here.

As I killed the engine, Mys slowly awoke from a catnap, and Aurie stretched, taking in our new setting. I could almost hear her brain working up a plan to sneak off. Not for the first time, I regretted keeping her in isolation. At least here she could leave the house. No sneaking necessary.

"Nothing for miles except nature and God," I mentioned.

"Are you staying with us tonight?" Mys nudged my hand. Without thinking, I laced our fingers together atop the center console. It hit me that I was encouraging intimacy, and I disengaged. Inky black hair fell over Mys's pink-tinged cheeks. The flicker of emotion was so brief, it was easy to miss.

"I need to do a perimeter check," I muttered. "Take the keys, and you two get settled inside. I'll be back." I stepped from the truck and inhaled the rich, loamy odor of the forest. The smells were intoxicating, hyperreal. Courtesy of my wolf.

I called it forth as I unbuttoned my shirt, ignoring my friends, ready to shift. I had my reasons for doing it in plain view this time. I needed to make sure no one had followed us, and man-shape wasn't ideal for reconnaissance. I also wanted to remind Aurie and Mys of the more savage aspects of my nature. They needed to see the rogue, the creature that would bite the hand that fed it.

Mys had overplayed the experienced jade this morning. Aurie had given me a look of yearning that knew no bounds. All because of a drunken Sunday-night dare. We never should've landed in bed together. Yet, they were the only two beings who had ever made me want to throw caution to the wind.

I knew that a relationship, especially an unconventional polyamorous one, was off-limits. The wildness of going full rogue had taken root, and there was no alternate happy ending. Walls had to be built. Feelings had to be hurt. Last night had to remain purely about sex. When an inward voice quizzed me, *Was it, though?* I reminded myself of my own lunacy. Enough said.

I tugged off my shirt and dropped it on top of the shoes I had kicked away. The sun spilled over my shoulders like a weightless massage, but my fracturing psyche couldn't appreciate it. When I caught Aurie and

Mys staring, a rueful smile touched my lips, but this wasn't a striptease. It was more serious.

Naked, I stretched to my full height. I let the muscles that had bunched up on the drive unfold. Wildness rushed up like a forest fire. It was intense enough to make me latch a hand on the truck for balance.

I heard a gasp as claws extended from my nail beds and dug into the fiberglass. A raw groan of elation and a guttural growl flew from my lips. At first, I was cognizant enough to be embarrassed by the uncontrolled display. The cognizance was brief. Sensibility went dark.

I staggered and—though one of my friends sympathetically tried to catch me before I fell, the other wisely held them back while I writhed and thrashed on the ground. I made it to my hands and knees as the last of the transformation reached a crescendo.

Arousal and virility pumped in my veins. It throbbed in my loins. My heaving chest housed a freight train ready to jump the tracks. Suddenly, I was too primal to know the difference between a good meal, a good fight, and a good fuck. One moment, I was Detective Zyr Ravani; the next, I was the black wolf running for the woods. Howling mad.

Even as I crashed through the underbrush, I heard Aurie's racing heartbeat and giddy, excited laughter as she watched me go. Mys whined with exaggerated angst, "Maji-ka. Really, Senpai? *Really?*"

As a man, I might've smiled wolfishly at how their reactions diverged from what I'd expected.

Instead, with my rogue tendencies growing stronger, I focused on the ground, which felt warm and welcoming beneath my paws. The sky was bright and forever. The birds were such teases, the hares such distractions. The world was mine, and the sweet, dark woods were full of possibilities. Like the possibility of a coming threat that might be chased down, hunted.

Destroyed.

•••

It was night by the time I limped back to the cabin barefoot and clearheaded. My blue jeans, which I had discovered folded neatly on the hood of my truck, now hung from my hips, covering my nudity. Aurie and Mys looked up expectantly when I opened the door, but I hesitated at the threshold. The whir of cicadas swelled in the awkward silence. I closed the door behind me and muttered, "I lost track of time."

It was a feeble excuse, but it had taken a while to check the dozen or so motion-sensor cameras studded throughout the forest. My gaze flicked to the laptop on the table, on which I could monitor anyone who got within a quarter mile of us.

"Feeling better?" Aurie asked in a skittish tone. Beside her, Mys had a wary stare. That was my fault. But where was the middle ground between being friends and leading them on?

I forced a smile as I braced an elbow on a support beam and took in the scene. Someone had found the flannel bedding. The old full-size bed was made. Mys lounged on my pillows. Aurie leaned against the headboard with her knees up, arms hugging her legs. Music played from a mobile device lying between them. The bedside lamp cast a soft glow on the cozy setup.

"I see you've carved out a niche for yourselves," I mused aloud.

"Hope you don't mind," Mys drawled and brandished a lowball glass. "I helped myself to the medicinal whiskey."

There was a secret I needed to reveal to the Empath—and preparations that had to be made to ensure Aurie's safety once the inevitable happened and I went feral—but the delicate conversation had to be held in private. Staring at the simple smock and cowboy boots that Mys wore, I wasn't sure I could trust myself alone with them.

Aurie was no less tempting. Her curly hair was pulled in a puff atop her head, and her delicate earlobes and wonderful jawline begged to be kissed. "You missed a few phone calls." She held up my phone, springing me back to reality. I started forward.

"Don't worry. We didn't snoop," Mys added. "We brought in your things and locked the truck when you didn't come back. Also, we borrowed your gun in case the big bad wolf got you."

"I *am* the big bad wolf," I quipped.

Breaking into a grin, Mys reached across Aurie and handed me the firearm. At the brush of her warm, pale fingers, I ached to climb in bed with the two of them, postrun sweat and all. But thoughts like that would lead to folly. I drummed up the mental picture of an ex and channeled the feeling of disinterest. I watched the Empath's smile and eyes go flat. It cut me to the quick, but I hid that too.

Aurie patted the mattress. "Care to join us?"

"He's busy," Mys grumbled.

Double gut punch. "Because your stay here is a *business* arrangement," I replied.

"Whoa! Dial down the rudeness," Aurie asserted.

I focused on my phone. Tegan had been trying to reach me. I had forgotten the lunch meeting. *Shit.* I redialed her, ignoring the unfamiliar number in the Missed Calls list. "Please, don't tell me you're waiting for me with Kittie Cad," I begged when the line connected.

"Oh, you mean the girl you were supposed to introduce to me that I had to find on my own?" Tegan retorted. "Of course we're not waiting around at Deanie's *hours* past our scheduled meeting. I sent her home. Where the hell are you, Ravani? I think I just saw your face on the evening news."

"At the outdoor recreation store?" I stepped to the back porch to get away from the distraction of Aurie and Mys. The one piece of good news was that Kittie had actually shown up to meet my partner. That meant she had accepted Mys's apology and was satisfied with the good word I had put in with the mayor.

Tegan squealed, reminding me that was the *only* good news. "Holy fuck! That really was you? What's going on, Zyr?"

"Long story. We had to move a witness to my hunting camp,

and Cyprian's people came after us. I had to take evasive action. Misdemeanor disorderly conduct, tops," I tried to joke.

My partner's uneasy laughter morphed into a groan. "I'm gonna regret this, but what can I do to help?" she offered. My eyebrows shot upward in surprise. I glanced around the shadowy backyard, thinking I could use someone with her capabilities on this detail. However, I shook my head as I tallied the risks.

"I'll cover my end. I need you to track down Cyprian's victims. Think you can secure video testimonies for the Council of Overlay Affairs within the next forty-eight hours?"

"Forget that case! I meant is there anything I can do to help *you*. Zyr, your erratic behavior has people believing you're a danger to yourself and others. Do you know what that means?" Tegan asked.

Of course. It meant a comfy stay in a padded room. Still, the public meltdown at the store could work in my favor, allowing Mys to return to life as normal and Aurie to go on to fulfill her destiny while investigators focused on me.

The line beeped, saving me from Tegan's pointed questions. "Look, there's another call I have to take," I said as I glanced at the caller ID. It was the unfamiliar number from earlier. Over Tegan's protests, I switched lines, and an unmistakable voice greeted me. I was stunned to hear my younger brother.

"Ammi told me to call you if things went awry," said Yazeed. "Mother's under house arrest."

"What do you mean, she's under house arrest?" I exclaimed.

"It's Cyprian! He convinced the Council she's colluding with you to tamper with the election results. Where are you? We need to get you out of Overlay and beyond the Council's reach so we can help Ammi," he said in a rush.

I squeezed my eyes shut, trying to think as the blood pounded in my temples. My first instinct was to drop everything and run to my mother's aid. Then, I looked through the open cabin door at Mys and Aurie.

"Yah, I can't do that." I sighed. "I have obligations here. The Ravani name will be cleared as soon as Darcy Cyprian's arrested. Otherwise, he'll simply come after our family again."

"Other obligations?" My brother scoffed. "Bullshit. Tell me where you are. I'm coming for you."

"I'm at Baba's cabin, but don't put yourself at risk by coming here. Get with Hazeem. You guys take a flight to Yalina's and lie low so the Council doesn't implicate you too. You have my word I'll take care of Ammi."

"Zyr, things are already in motion. Things that can't be undone. I'm on my way to you. I'll . . ." The signal cut out for a moment, then his voice returned with an odd echo. "I'll find you."

I'll find you . . . There was a soft click as the line went dead. Why would Yazeed say he'd *find* the cabin? My brothers knew the way here as well as I did. Like the backs of our hands.

The cell phone slipped from my numb fingers as it hit me.

CHAPTER THIRTY-NINE
—
Aurie

September 9 | Night

My attention darted to the porch, where Zyr picked up the phone he had dropped and placed a new call. The steady stream of conversation Mys had kept up since our arrival went mute as the detective glanced over his shoulder at us and purposefully shut the back door. All the same, Mys and I clearly heard him tell someone, "Change of plans. I need you."

What the hell was that? I wondered. With a toss of silky black hair, Mys lifted an elegant shoulder as if caring less. I tried to be as unaffected. What right did I have to be upset at Zyr seeing someone real? Especially if Mys wasn't bothered.

"So, what happened?" my intuitive roommate changed the subject.

"With what?" I tabbed to something else on the playlist, and a gravelly tenor voice erupted from the cell phone. Rhythm and blues music accompanied lyrics begging for mercy from love unrequited. Groaning, I blotted out my feelings and let the song play.

"With you. Seems like you have better control of your glitchy poltergeist freak-out moments now. Was it the ménage?" Mys probed.

I pulled a face and laughed. "No, asshole, and I wasn't *glitchy*. I think getting rid of Darcy is doing it for me. I mean, that's the best I can offer Haley. After Count Jerkula is officially canceled, my sister can make it on her own, which makes me think the investigation was the real—"

"Unfinished business," Mys finished for me. "Ten out of ten for my predictive skills. Oof."

I smiled with my eyes closed. Warm fingers skimmed my arm, whispered over my palm, and brought my hand up to even warmer lips. Butterflies lifted and settled in my core. When my eyelids lifted a fraction, I was captivated by the pink mouth curved into a hammock of a smile. I wanted to lie on those lips and fall asleep, safe and sound forever.

But I couldn't. This wasn't a forever thing. Unexpected emotion welled to the surface. It was impossible to hide. Concern sketched Mys's brow. "What's wrong?" they whispered. I shook my head.

"Nothing. I just wonder how?" I hesitated before blurting out, "How do you do it? Client after client, night after night, love after love?"

Mys sat up and cupped my face. "I don't. Work is work, but this . . ." Our lips clashed in a kiss that stole my breath. I flowed into their lap, as desire surged, but the kiss was comfort, not seduction. Mys gentled it to a languid exploration that was interrupted by Zyr reentering the cabin.

The detective made it a point to slam the door. I gripped the base of Mys's neck, moaning as we kept going. "My, uh . . ." Zyr cleared his throat. "My partner will be here in a few hours."

Mys broke the kiss to give him a disapproving glower. "Why is *she* coming?" asked the Empath.

"Because we're short on supplies," Zyr muttered. Our unrelenting stare made him shift his weight and admit, "I got a call from my younger brother, but I have reason to believe it wasn't really Yazeed."

"Did you give him our location?" I asked in alarm.

He nodded grimly. "I could be wrong, but I'd rather have Tegan here for reinforcement if Cyprian's trying to find us. Besides, there's nowhere else to run, and this isolated stretch is probably the best place for a showdown. I know these woods better than anyone. We have the advantage."

"How will we defend ourselves?" Mys asked.

Zyr opened a closet and brought out a rifle. "We've got this and the Glock in my truck. Tegan will stop by my place to grab more weapons and ammo, including the holy water hollow points I keep on hand for Overlay City business. I've got motion-activated cameras throughout the woods. We'll keep watch so we don't waste bullets on wildlife."

"What can I do to help?" I asked. Both of them gave me a quizzical look. I rolled my eyes. "I'm an asset. My dad made sure my sister and I learned everything we could about wilderness survival. He truly believed Louisiana is the sportsman's paradise."

"You're telling me you know how to shoot?" Zyr raised a skeptical brow.

"Well, I *am* a girl raised in the South." I grinned.

Zyr grunted and thrust the shotgun into my hands. "Let's see."

"Bet," I bragged as I followed him out the back door. The night seemed to close around the three of us, save for the fireflies winking in the trees. I let out a surprised yelp when a huge barn owl swooped across the yard.

"Be careful with that." Zyr chided as he eyed the gun. I chuckled nervously.

He directed my attention to his fire pit. "Need some light?"

"Are you sure you want a kumbaya campfire in the middle of this *business* arrangement?" I retorted. He ignored my jibe and grabbed a cord of wood from a neatly stacked pile beside the cabin. Mys joined the mercurial werewolf carrying bundles to the stone pit, while I explored the nightscape.

I overheard Zyr speaking softly to my roommate. "If things go south, I want you guys to go with Tegan. Help her get to the Humanity Ambassador. You'll all be given asylum since her life is at risk by association. "

"What about Kittie?" Mys whispered.

"She'll be safe there too. Someone at the embassy can draft a formal request for Aurie to get an audience with the Council. Present whatever evidence Kittie and Tegan manage to collect and give your official testimony. When you and I get the chance, there are some other things I need to go over with you so you can be ready for what's to come . . . but I think we have a little more time before I go feral . . ." he trailed off.

I hugged myself and turned back to my companions. "Do you think he'll find us?" I asked.

As he lit the kindling, Zyr looked uncertain. "Cyprian? We'll be ready either way," he muttered.

Mys pointed at a line of soda bottles on a crooked fence illuminated by the growing campfire. "See if you can hit one of those," my roommate suggested. Shaking off my fear for the detective, I grabbed the shotgun and squared off to make my late father proud. After all the losses I had suffered in life, I didn't know how much longer I would get with these two, and experience had taught me not to take a single shot for granted.

•••

"She's here." Mys glanced up from the magazine we were scanning together.

"Mm-hmm," Zyr grunted. He was freshly showered, and his citrus and cardamom scent blended with the rich, woodsy musk of the cabin. He had spent the bulk of the night staring at surveillance footage from the surrounding woods, giving me a chance to gossip with Mys.

"What does she feel like?" I asked.

The Empath stared at a glossy advertisement a few seconds before responding, "Like . . . high school."

"What the hell does that mean?" I giggled.

"She has a crush on the detective."

"Ohhh," I intoned, wrinkling my nose. "That's why you don't like her."

After flipping to another page, my roommate didn't say anything. I gave them a nudge. "I don't *dis*like her. She just feels overeager, but that's probably good for us, right? She'll do anything for the detective." Mys flaunted a smile that didn't reach the eyes.

She can't be that bad. I turned to greet the new arrival. Tegan entered the cabin like a wake-up call, talking way too loudly and with far more enthusiasm than anyone should've been able to muster at this time of night.

The sight of her stopped me in my tracks. Her hourglass figure was poured into designer jeans and a formfitting T-shirt that showed off every curve. Features cut to perfection were symmetrically aligned for maximum attractiveness. Mys visibly shuddered. Was it jealousy? Were we jealous?

"Where's Ajit?" She asked as she flipped waist-length red hair over her shoulder and flashed a vibrant smile.

"At home. I have an arrangement with the dog walker. He's a college kid I basically keep on a retainer since I work such crazy hours. Anyway, come meet everyone," Zyr invited. His smoldering partner surveyed the room with a baffled look, seeing only Mys. Zyr gave a crimped smile and added, "I might've left out a detail or two when we discussed Overlay City. Now, I think it's time you know everything. This is Mys, my—"

"No, yeah, I get it!" Tegan supplied. "*You're* the pretty little thing from the pub!"

Mys said coolly, "I'm his friend."

Tegan arched a delicate brow that stood out against her blemish-free ivory skin. "Well, Zyr has always been full of surprises. It's nice to meet you. I hope we can be friends too."

"And this is . . . Aurelia Edison," Zyr said, gesturing at me.

"Beg your pardon?" Tegan blinked at what surely looked like open air.

I put my hands on my hips and walked around her, reveling in being invisible. "I certainly see the appeal. I mean, she's hot. I'd bang her."

Zyr hummed in reproach. "Don't do that."

"Don't do what?" Tegan asked with a bewildered grin. "All right, you're making me uncomfortable, buddy. We both know where Aurelia Edison is."

"Yeah, Zyr." I slammed the door and rammed the hand-carved table against it for good measure. "She doesn't believe in ghosts."

CHAPTER FORTY
—
Mys

September 9 | Late Night

Aurie said, "That was probably childish of me."

I covered a smile as Zyr's partner pointed at the table with her mouth agape, fumbling for words. Tegan finally managed, "How did you do that?"

The detective glared at our friendly ghost. "I didn't. I think you'd better sit down, Tegan. We need to talk," he said.

Our guest sat next to him on the couch for the quick rundown of how Aurie had come to be with us. Meanwhile, I sprawled on the floor with my back against the wall and Aurie's head in my lap. I stroked her hair, not caring that it looked weird to the normie.

"You know none of this makes sense, right?" Tegan said for the umpteenth time.

"Yeah, I know, Tegan." Zyr sighed.

"You know why, right? Because—"

He cut her off, saying, "If you believe in Overlay City, a disembodied

Soul isn't much of a stretch. I need you on standby to get Mys and Aurie out of here if trouble shows up tomorrow. From there, we play it by ear. Can you commit to that?"

"Sure, sure! I've got some time off to spare, but Mys should be in charge of keeping up with . . . Aurie . . . since I can't see her."

"Thank you." Zyr visibly relaxed. "Were you able to find everything at my place?"

"Yep. Brought the duffel bag from under that trapdoor in your closet, and I grabbed the box with everything we have on the Cyprian case. Everything's in the car. It's a burner car, and I also bought burner phones. Take the battery out of yours now."

"Perfect! You've thought of everything. I'll bring in your bags in a moment. Let me show you the loft. It's not the Ritz, but there's a bed up there. Want to take a walk-through?" he asked.

Zyr led his partner up the stairs. Behind his back, the redhead gave him an adoring look. My Empathy picked up on the history he tried to pretend didn't exist. The detective was over her, but Tegan was nowhere near done with him. Such an outstanding amount of yearning poured off her. It was almost like she was obsessed.

"Are they together?" Aurie asked. I shook my head as my eyes followed them into the loft. "What are her intentions?"

"To be of service," I murmured.

"But she wants him. She's so pretty. Ugh! I've never been insecure in my life. What the hell is going on with me? My unfinished business doesn't need this," she groaned.

"You're falling for him," I deduced. Moments later Zyr and Tegan descended the stairs and exited the cabin, chatting with the synergy of two people who had known each other a long time. They ignored us, which was fine by me. Almost. I blew out a breath and admitted, "We both are."

Aurie looked up at me. "What are we gonna do about it?" she asked.

"Make the most of whatever time we have left."

I felt her deflate. The energy seeped right out of her. The sense of peace she had exuded earlier was less settled now. She was right. Her feelings for Zyr were affecting her unfinished business. I drove my fingers through her hair and soothingly scratched her scalp.

"Do you believe in reincarnation, Mys?" she asked, eyes closed.

I stared at her wistful expression for a beat. "I don't know. I'd like to think if we miss the opportunity to do things in one lifetime, we get a second chance in the next."

She sat up with me, shoulder to shoulder. "I'm not sure if I'd want a second chance. This Afterlife has been hell." She laughed.

Zyr returned with several suitcases and Tegan on his heels. "There's hot and cold water in the bathroom," he said over his shoulder. "You're welcome to whatever's in the kitchen too. Perhaps tomorrow one of us can make a store run while the other starts on the case file."

"Sounds like a plan. I can make preliminary contact with the victims over the phone to limit who sees us coming and going," said Tegan. "Are you sure no one else knows about this place?"

"No one aside from my brothers," he answered.

"Let's keep it that way," she replied.

"What about Kittie?" I piped up.

"Do you think it's smart to risk her coming here?" asked the redhead. Without waiting for my response, the two of them disappeared to the loft again, and I heard her say she was exhausted. She asked Zyr where he would sleep. He said the sofa was a foldout. I bit the inside of my cheek.

"If I had to live another lifetime," I exhaled and picked up the conversation where Aurie and I had left off, "I'd want to meet you and Zyr sooner . . . before it was too late."

•••

It was the dead of the night, but I couldn't sleep in the unfamiliar bed. I sat on the back step, watching Aurie dance around the banked fire.

She didn't need rest. I thought of Zyr on the cozy foldout and Tegan in the loft—probably with one eye open to make sure we stayed in our proper places.

I had sensed her envy when she called me the "pretty little thing from the pub." After that, it had been nothing but projected cravings for sex, sex, sex with Zyr. I rolled my eyes so hard my head ached.

Aurie smiled at me. Her attention shifted to someone behind me, and her expression turned wry. I glanced back to see Zyr in the open doorway, shirtless, his pajama bottoms barely clinging to his hips, as if eager to be removed. My body responded. *Damn.* I turned away.

"What are you doing up?" His husky voice was heavy with sleep, and he absently sifted his fingers through my hair. At his touch, full-body chills wracked me. I moaned his name in admonishment. "Don't," he huffed.

"Don't what?"

"Say my name like that."

"Pfft! I'm sure your partner will keep you on the straight and narrow." I snorted.

Aurie's tantalizing bare thigh flashed beneath the kimono as she moved closer to the porch to join the conversation. Zyr stared. "What," she challenged. "Am I underdressed? Some of us didn't pack enough for a three-week stay."

He blew out an exasperated breath. "All right, what's up with the Tegan-hate?"

"Who's hating?" we asked at the same time.

"Look, she's on our side. I need you guys to keep our team together, because I can't do it on my own. I haven't had the best self-discipline lately."

"Aww, sorry to hear that," Aurie said without a hint of remorse.

"Is this a game to you? Do you want to see me lose control?" he snapped.

Desire cut through me. I couldn't tell if it was his or hers or mine or some combination of all three. I shifted to ease the ache of lust, and I noticed Zyr's burning eyes. In the dark, the yellow fire was brighter than ever. Yes, I wanted him to lose control, but this wasn't a game. Nor was it business as usual. Aurie had asked how I got over the feelings. Truth was, I had never felt this way, and I was beginning to think there was no getting over it.

"Go back to bed, Detective," I muttered.

He threw up his hands. "You know what. Come with me."

"What about Tegan?" I asked drolly.

"What about the truck?"

"What about it?" I rebuffed.

"Grab some blankets and meet me there."

Aurie scrunched her nose as if contemplating the offer. "Much as I'd love to weakly succumb like some dick-whipped heroine, no. Tonight, I realized I don't even know if you're single, and I really like to know more about the people I sleep with. You and Mys have this unmistakable connection, but where do I fit? Maybe I need more than a climax."

"Since we're keeping it one hundred, what more do we have to offer each other, Aurie?" Zyr stepped off the porch and met her unwavering stare.

"You were the one who said there are things that outlast the grave," she retorted.

"Yeah, like heartache."

She hugged herself, shaking her head. "Or like respect. Just because I'm dead doesn't mean I want to be treated like your cheap thrill, Detective."

"You're not. I respect you enough not to make promises I can't keep when I'm falling apart bit by bit."

"Falling apart? So am I!" Aurie wailed.

"Then you of all people," he said through gritted teeth, "understand why I can't give you more."

"No, I don't, Zyr. Because I'm offering you my broken pieces too," she said. My jaw dropped at her impromptu admission. When I glanced at the detective, however, I felt a heaviness in the pit of my stomach.

"I never asked for that from either of you," he replied.

CHAPTER FORTY-ONE
—
Zyr

September 10 | Two a.m.

Aurie looked down. Her bottom lip trembled as she nodded slowly, processing what I had blurted out in the heat of the moment. A rough growl rumbled in my throat, and I shoved my fingers through my hair. How had things gotten so off-kilter?

"Regroup," Mys ordered, dragging us both to the back step and making us take a seat on either side. Aurie placed her head on the Empath's shoulder. Mys wrapped her in a hug. No such warm embrace was extended to me. I was the bad guy.

I crossed my arms and hunched forward to stare at the ground. Night sounds crept into the silence that descended. Underscoring that was the faint electronic hum of motion sensor cameras, another reminder we weren't on a romantic getaway.

"I mean, what do you both expect? That we come out of this smelling like roses, happily ever after?" I argued. "We trashed a store and went on a high-speed chase. I almost shot someone. It made the evening news.

Don't you understand? It's not only pointless, it's dangerous to start with dramatic outpourings of devotion now!"

Devotion. I scoffed. I had devoted my life to chasing a madman, and the madness was catching. Aurie was on the same path. Our futures were inexorably tied to Darcy Cyprian's. His house of cards would collapse, but so would ours.

The difference was Aurie would find herself right where she needed to be, and I would descend deeper into this hell.

I squeezed my eyes shut, releasing a sigh. The sound became an anguished expletive when wetness seeped through my lashes. I shook my head in dismay, scrubbing at the tears. It seemed like the more feral I became, the less control I had over my emotions. I had a burning lump in my throat, a bitter pill of things I couldn't say.

"I'm sorry. I didn't mean to push it. I—" Aurie broke off, chagrined at my embarrassment.

Mys finally wrapped an arm around me and brought our heads together. "Please, admit that last night left the three of us with unresolved issues. I'm tired of trying to put out this dumpster fire of hidden emotions," said the Empath.

Aurie tossed her hair from her face to confront me. "I know it's nuts to wish for anything, but when you're on borrowed time like I am, you say what needs saying, even if no one wants to hear."

I had to admit, "You're right. If I'm honest, being with you is the stuff of magic to me too. I never imagined finding companionship like this, but you and I don't have much longer on this plane. And how do you think it will turn out for Mys when we reach that eventuality?"

"Don't worry about me," said Mys. The Empath kissed my temple as I pressed my palms to my eye sockets and took a shuddering breath. I pictured Tegan waking up and coming outside, finding us together. It surprised me how little I cared. My gut told me my partner needed to see I was well and truly off-limits to her.

Tegan Stoney was gunning for a rekindling of our flame. Yet she had been the one to make our brief relationship nonexclusive. Even though we returned to being friends—no harm, no foul—I couldn't be with someone who had cheated on me.

Under different circumstances, I could see myself with Aurie and Mys, but I was devolving into a monster with every passing second. We had no future. There was nothing left but the wild dark to come.

"If you think about it, we're all existing on borrowed time," Mys pointed out. "Maybe instead of trying to make up for our pasts or planning for our futures, we should just be right here in this space, in the now. What do you say?"

Giving in, Aurie draped her arm across my neck and closed the group hug. My mouth captured hers. I couldn't help it. I dragged them both to my lips in a three-way kiss. Mys broke free with a moan and lurched from the porch step to face us, breathless and unsteady. I was fighting the same unsteadiness.

"Before we get lost in lust, we need clarity on this," Mys censured.

Aurie grew introspective. "I'm willing to take things one day at a time, but it's really up to you, Mys. The detective has rightfully pointed out that you're the one with the most at stake. So, what memories do you want to hold on to when this is over? Sex or something more?"

Perturbed, Mys let a curtain of hair fall over their face before throwing it back and pasting on a nervous smile. "I'm the least qualified to call it. I have no experience whatsoever with being in an exclusive relationship."

"Wait, does that mean you want to keep things open to see other people?" I asked in surprise.

Mys smirked. "No, Detective. It means I guess no-strings sex is fine with me since commitment isn't your favorite word."

"Not that I have much experience with dating, either, but there has to be some middle ground between commitment and cheap thrills," Aurie said as she gave me side-eye.

"All right, hypothetically speaking, what if I want an exclusive relationship?" I rose to my feet and slid a hand inside Mys's blue silk pajama top and ran my fingertips down their side.

Mys swayed in my arms. "Ideally? I would love a he-only-pays-for-dinner kind of date."

Indeed, they both deserved a less transactional affair, but I put up fingers to count each strike against us. "We're on the run," I said. "Someone is trying to kill us. Two of us are mentally unstable. And this pansexual threesome is breaking all the rules. How exactly are we to cram a relationship into the equation?"

"You want the truth? I've seen weirder hookups on an average Saturday night at Fusions gay bar," Mys deadpanned.

I barked a laugh and turned to Aurie. "What about you? How do you see this working out?" I asked her.

"I mean, sure, we're fighting Supernatural evil while trying to get to know each other, but how is that much different from your regular day on the internet?" She tilted her head and asked, "What does your gut tell you, Zyr?"

"It says . . . to give you all of me."

With a triumphant grin at my answer, Aurie dashed over, fitting between Mys and me like she was made for us two. The moon illuminated the Empath's dark, uncertain stare over Aurie's shoulder. "Are you sure?" Mys checked. "We're not friends with benefits, but *together* together?"

I nodded as my heart gave a funny kick. This felt right. Temporary, but right. We were still on the run with the odds stacked against us. We still had to acquire the evidence to convince the Council to prosecute Cyprian. I was still a rogue wolf destined to lose my mind before everything was said and done. Yet, perhaps for the first time since renouncing my Alpha birthright, I didn't feel alone.

"We're *together* together," I confirmed.

Mys said playfully, "Now, about that offer to do it in the truck."

"Issa no for me!" Aurie cracked.

"What happened to living life to the fullest?" Mys nibbled her earlobe teasingly.

"That's not my unfinished business, and sex in a truck sounds hella cramped. Thank you, no," she said, tickled pink.

"I was talking about the truck *bed*, but okay," I clarified to another round of laughter.

My heightened sense of hearing registered Tegan stirring in the loft. I gently disengaged from Aurie and Mys and suggested we hit the sack. It was late, and I could tell Mys, at least, was exhausted. As we reentered the cabin, Mitsuyo's eyes dimmed at the foldout. *Fuck it*, I thought as I dropped into bed with the two of them. We were together now, right?

Nothing left to hide.

CHAPTER FORTY-TWO
—
Aurie

September 10 | Morning

I had lain awake through the night, watching the fog roll in and blanket the forest beyond the window. When the pale dawn tried to illuminate what the mist hid, a hush cloaked the cabin, punctuated by the old air conditioner's hum and my companions' quiet snores. While Mys and Zyr slept, I left the bed to settle on the sofa. From there, I watched Tegan slip downstairs and tiptoe into the kitchen.

She couldn't see me, but I studied her. She rose on the balls of her feet and peered into a cabinet, fumbling out the whiskey bottle and lifting it to her lips with trembling hands. Before the room temperature liquor sloshed into her mouth, however, she thrust the bottle away.

"One month," I heard her whisper. "You made it a whole month. Don't ruin it."

I quirked an eyebrow. At the same time, Zyr stirred, and I realized the werewolf had probably heard her all along—superior senses and whatnot. He made a point of turning his back as his partner hurriedly returned the bottle to the cabinet and scurried to the loft again.

The fog was lifting outside when he finally sat up with a dramatic yawn. It wasn't lost on me that he had conveniently given Tegan enough time to resettle upstairs, but my attention was no longer on her. It was on him. Tired circles ringed his eyes. The tight line of his mouth was unhappy. I unfolded from the couch and ambled toward him.

"You look like shit," I said.

He issued a good-natured laugh. "Is that any way to greet your dear lover, Ms. Edison?"

"Let's say you've made an honest woman of me, Mr. Ravani." I smiled.

"Well, Dear Lover and Honest Woman," Mys groused from a cocoon of bedding, "keep it down. I'm trying to sleep."

The two of us early birds shared a grin. I framed Zyr's face with my hands and stared into his amber eyes, where the yellow glow of fire was a constant now. It was a wonder that Tegan Stoney hadn't noticed it. My gaze slid to Zyr's twitching fingers, which he balled into fists and tucked beneath his crossed arms.

"How are you holding up?" I whispered. He shrugged.

"Head's not in the right place."

"What can I do to help?" I asked.

"The busier I am, the better. We should stash supplies throughout the woods in case you three are forced to make a run for it. I'll get Tegan to park her car near the main highway where she can get you guys out fast if necessary."

"I think your partner has her end of things covered. I asked what you need," I said gently.

His scruffy face mustered a smile. "I need you to try to be nicer to her. You can trust Tegan. I'm worried about leaving you and Mys alone once I'm—"

I placed a finger over his lips. There had to be a way to reverse the process of going feral. I didn't want to think otherwise. "Don't worry about us. I'll . . . do my best with Tegan. Anything else?" I asked.

"Yeah," Zyr murmured as he stroked my cheek. "I want you to have a happy birthday today."

"You got the date from my case file?" Pleased, I kissed his soft, warm mouth as he nodded. "But shouldn't I focus on my death day from now on?"

"You're too vibrantly alive for that. I wish I could spend many more birthdays with you, getting to know you."

"Nice thought, but I'm pretty sure this is my last one." I sighed.

"Aurie, I need you to know—"

The sound of Tegan getting out of bed made me pull away. It would look strange if she caught us in a heated embrace. For her, Zyr would appear to be kissing thin air. He gave me a rueful smile as I resumed my position on the couch. "We'll talk later," I promised. "She's not comfortable with disembodied spirits yet."

I turned away, wondering how I had fallen for not one but two people in such a dramatic leap. My whole life, I had played things safe . . . until last night's agreement to be exclusive in a polyamorous relationship. A part of me realized I wasn't being as revolutionary as I wanted to believe. I was dead. If I were alive, would I still boldly embrace this pansexual love affair? In front of family and friends? My heart thundered at the possibility that I might not be brave enough.

Mys plopped on the sofa next to me and banished the unsettling thoughts. A smile materialized on my lips. "Good morning, sleepyhead."

"Ready to kick some ass?" my roommate asked.

We both seemed to reflexively glance across the cabin at the detectives discussing the case over breakfast. It was obvious where Zyr's focus lay, even to Tegan. A rosy blush spread over Mys's face as the werewolf's luminous eyes made contact for the umpteenth time.

"I do believe Zyr Ravani is smitten with you," I teased.

Chuckling, Mys replied, "Judging by his unchecked emotions, I'd say he's taken with you too. His feelings are all over the place when it comes to everything else, though."

"Do you sense him losing grip?" I asked.

"It's hard to tell," Mys whispered. "I'd love to use my cell phone to do a search on feral wolves, but Tegan made it clear we're not to turn them on." The Empath's dark gaze flew to the other woman. I knew she was simply trying to help, but she had clipped our wings without realizing it.

"How long does it take for the full transformation?" I asked.

"The Council keeps things like that hush-hush."

"Then we'll see what Zyr knows. Maybe something in werewolf lore can provide a clue. I'm not giving up on him," I said. Mys nodded, but there was more doubt in their shimmering eyes than I cared to see.

As the morning wore on, Zyr found time between taking stock and scribbling a list of supplies to give us the heart-tugging rundown of his partner's troubled past. We sat around the laptop at the kitchen table. Each display on the screen showed a different corner of the surrounding woods. Nothing stirred, but Zyr was still on edge.

"I'm perhaps the only person in Tegan's life who hasn't used and abused her," he murmured. "For that, she's loyal to a fault."

I glanced at the bathroom door, where the sound of her showering drowned out our conversation about her. "What's her deal with sneaking into the liquor cabinet this morning?" I wanted to know.

"She's a recovering alcoholic. Don't fret. I took the bottle and hid it in my truck."

Mys shifted in the chair. "She's determined to do whatever you need, but does that loyalty extend to us?" my roommate asked.

"She's here, isn't she?" Zyr countered. "Hey, I know experience hasn't given you much reason to see the best in people, but you have to sense how much I care for you. If I thought Tegan was a problem, I never would've invited her. Besides, she can't hide her intentions from you. You're an Empath."

Mys looked at me. I shrugged and gave an encouraging nod. We dropped the subject when the gorgeous redhead emerged from the bathroom. She was dressed to kill in formfitting jeans, leaving no doubt whose head she wanted to turn. *Trust her?* Mys and I wore matching smirks.

•••

Around noon, Zyr invited me on the supply run. It was a thinly veiled ploy to continue talking up his partner. By the time we arrived at a decrepit gas station forty minutes later, I was sick of discussing Tegan, but I had a grudging respect for her. Most people who went from abusive parents to destructive spouses didn't turn out so great.

I studied the cracks in the concrete lot that sprouted patchy grass. The pumps looked to be about a hundred years old. "Is this place even open?" A beat-up truck found a parking spot beside us. "That answers that," I mumbled.

"Coming in?" the detective asked. I slid *through* the door, and he grinned. "Good job. Remember not to touch anything. Keep a low profile."

I nodded as he covered half his face with a camouflage hunting balaclava. When he hopped out of Tegan's burner car, nobody blinked twice. Louisiana was the sportsman's paradise. Long as he wore the requisite camo, he was like any other weary traveler.

Inside the musty store, the battered shelves carried dented, overpriced canned goods and stale loaves of bread. There were jugs of milk in the cooler, more than likely expired. Zyr cleaned the shelves and dumped the food and other staples at the register.

"Let me guess. Y'all out gator hunting?" the friendly cashier asked as she rang him up. Her grin showed off a missing front tooth. "Must have a camp close by."

Zyr sped her along. "Yeah, and the wife's waiting," he fibbed with a vague hike of his thumb behind him. I swallowed my amusement. Grabbing the bags, we ducked out the door and headed to the car. We were almost there when he stiffened and snarled. His canines gleamed sharper than I remembered.

I followed his line of sight to a cute bunny in the field across from the store. "Oh no," I whispered. I shoved him toward the vehicle. He dropped into the driver's seat, and I tore open a pack of beef jerky. "I don't think you should skip any meals while you're like this."

"I'm fine," he snapped, but he took the food and pulled off the balaclava to eat. That was when we noticed the cashier watching him through the store window. I groaned. Given Zyr's face on the news the day prior, we didn't need anyone recognizing him. It was too late to hide again, however. He started the car. "I'm okay," he repeated shakily.

Silence wedged between us, and I struggled for something to say to break the tension of the long drive. "Um, what was it you wanted to tell me before Tegan came down for breakfast this morning?" I asked.

"I'm not sure how much time I have left. When I phase out, Tegan will . . ."

"I get it, Zyr. Tegan will pick up where you leave off. I'll find a way to convince Mys to give her a break." I smiled. Too brightly. "We'll make her feel welcome until she leaves tomorrow."

"She'll let you know everything you need to know after that," he said tiredly.

We pulled up to the cabin, where Tegan was waiting on the porch. Soon as Zyr killed the engine, his partner dug in the trunk and brought out a toolbox. She whipped her hair in a ponytail to squat behind the car with a screwdriver.

"What's going on?" Zyr asked.

"Taking a page from that hit-and-run driver," she grunted and popped off the license plate. "I don't need trouble traced back to me."

"I'll keep you out of trouble. How'd you come by the car anyway?"

"Friends in low places." Tegan chuckled.

"Or an ex with a chop shop?" Zyr quizzed her with a grin. The briefest uneasiness flitted over his partner's face. I watched her from the front step. "Relax. Your secret is safe with me," he said as he removed the bags from the car. He took the goods inside while Tegan finished scrubbing any identifying marks.

"Speaking of secrets." She glanced his way. "She doesn't know, does she?"

I raised an eyebrow. "Who doesn't know what?"

Zyr rubbed my shoulders and said in my ear, "I'll explain later. Why don't you go help Mys find someplace to hide the first-aid kit and other gear, and I'll come find you two in a minute."

His words were seductive as his warm breath feathered over my earlobe. I wasn't comfortable with him using sex appeal to potentially hide something from me. I wanted to ask more questions, but Tegan's brow furrowed at the whispered exchange. I pictured how wonky the interplay looked to her, and I stepped away.

"You know how I feel about secrets," I said over my shoulder to Zyr.

CHAPTER FORTY-THREE
—
Mys

September 10 | Late Afternoon

"He wants us to hide the first-aid kit," Aurie announced, marching into the cabin.

I looked up from the map I was studying. On the off chance it was left to me to get us to safety, I wanted to know the roads. Outside, I saw Tegan and Zyr engaged in a heated conversation, and I zeroed in on Aurie's simmering anger as I refolded the map. "Everything okay?" I touched her arm.

She waved me off with a smile. "I'm fine. Let's get this over with," she replied. We checked the kit to make sure it was adequately stocked. I stuck my cell phone and battery inside for good measure as Aurie filled a beach bag with a blanket. At my quizzical look, she waggled her eyebrows. "Zyr's gonna meet us in the woods."

"Nice, but you were bothered by the prospect of getting busy in a truck?" I laughed.

"Ha-ha," she deadpanned in amusement. "Apparently he has something to tell us. This might be our last shot at privacy while Tegan is here."

I nodded, understanding. "Speaking of which, while you were out, I called Kittie to really patch things up and talk about her role in the investigation, and Tegan was all ears. It was annoying, but at least I know Ms. Cad is no longer pissed with me." Finding out Kittie had reconciled with her lover, Mayor Rhemus, had been a huge relief too.

Loaded down with supplies, Aurie and I cut through the treeline behind the cabin, headed in the direction of the main road. There was no path, but the deeper we went, the less foliage was underfoot. It was easy to keep a brisk pace with the help of a compass. We made our way over a carpet of pine needles, and the canopy of trees overhead blunted the sun.

I looked up after we had trekked for what felt like close to an hour. Perspiration beaded my forehead. "RIP my inner outdoorsman," I huffed.

"At least you're an avid dancer. The living Aurie would be a crawling river of sweat by now," my companion acknowledged. "Perks of being a dead girl."

"That was a mile, right? I think this is far enough. Take note of the landmarks." I annotated the location on the map. Pointing out a decomposing tree stump, I suggested we hide the supplies inside.

"Tegan will have to park somewhere near here. She's not half bad, by the way," Aurie stated.

"If you say so. I've never met anyone quite so obsessed with one person." I covered our stash with dead leaves and debris, and Aurie spread the blanket for whatever romantic rendezvous she had planned.

She stood up and dusted her hands on her jeans, confronting me with a shy smile. "Eh, you'll see worse in the comment section of any BTS video. Anyway, Zyr wants us to play nice, and I don't think that's such a bad idea. You'll need friends when we're gone."

"Now you sound like Kittie Cad," I said as she stepped into my arms and kissed me. "I don't need people, Yōkai. They just clutter up my headspace . . . My mom used to say people will only love you if it's convenient for them."

Aurie's eyebrows knit in dismay. "Harsh."

"No, honest. Think about it. Even grade-school kids don't want to be friends with someone they consider unlucky. Researchers did a study once, and it turns out people gravitate to those who have it easy. Hence, the popular kids are usually the prettiest, the smartest, the richest. Well, I've never been that person."

"I'm glad you're not that person. If you were like that, you never would've taken me in," Aurie said. She studied me with soft brown eyes. "You know what I think? I think love itself is inconvenient. And those who have had it hardest in life know how to love hardest because they don't mind the struggle."

I looked down with a laugh. "Sometimes it takes great loss to hold tighter to whatever we have left."

"Good point. Maybe I was one of the popular kids once," she said, "but dying taught me that nothing worth holding on to is easy. Today is my birthday, and I want you to make a birthday promise to me."

"That we'll have cake for dinner? Because I can make that happen, although you should've told me earlier. Zyr's pantry is woefully inadequate. Nothing but protein in there. He's like a caveman or something. Or a werewolf."

Aurie giggled. "Promise me that no matter how much of an inconvenience you think you are, you'll try for me."

"Try what, Yōkai?" I blew out a breath.

She draped her arms around my neck and tilted her head. "Try harder with people. You may have felt you lacked a support system in the past, but Zyr and I don't want to leave you alone, Mys," she said around the shape of sudden unshed tears. I felt them like a lump in my own throat. I reached up to take her hand.

"Aurie," I whispered, clasping her hand to my lips.

"No, you have to learn to trust people. I know it's difficult experiencing others' emotions, but I'm not asking you to surround yourself with a crowd. I'm just asking you to open yourself up to one person. You can start with Tegan . . . and when you're ready, I want you to try to meet someone new."

I shook my head. She collected my hands and kissed each butterfly tattoo before pushing the hair from my face and looking me in the eyes. "I want you to fall in love," she murmured.

"Again?" I clarified. Her lashes swept her cheek while I tried to find the words to tell her the lightning had already struck twice. I didn't think it could happen again.

We were interrupted by the sound of someone crashing through the forest toward us. Tegan erupted from the trees with a shout. "Hey! Zyr asked me to find you."

"What's going on?" I asked.

Aurie grabbed the picnic blanket and thrust it into the beach bag. Tegan heeded the invisible shape uneasily. "There's a hurricane watch," she informed us. "We've gotta get back to the cabin. Now."

•••

Tegan, Aurie, and I stared at the weather radio while Zyr paced and frowned. I glanced out the window at a sky that was as blue as ever. The digitized voice of the National Weather Service announced current location, expected directional track, barometric pressure, and a host of other data that made no sense to me. I got the gist. We might or might not be experiencing a hurricane soon.

"That settles it, Tegan. Get back to the city tonight," Zyr stated.

"Don't jump the gun. The storm track isn't set in stone," said Tegan. "We all know it's that time of year. Tropical depressions and even hurricanes churn up from the Gulf unexpectedly, but there's no need to panic until we know for sure where it's headed."

Aurie raised a hand. "I thought she was already leaving."

"She was but . . ." Zyr cleared his throat as my face dropped. "We decided she should stay and work on the case as long as she can. Keep in mind the Council gave us two weeks. If Darcy hasn't found us by tomorrow, I don't want to throw in the towel early."

"The worst part is," he went on, "if the weather gets bad, my cameras will likely go offline. We'll be fighting blindfolded when or if he attacks."

"At the moment," I said, "I'm more concerned with riding it out in a log cabin in the middle of a pine forest. Do we know whether or not this building will hold up, Senpai?"

Tegan bristled at my use of an endearment. I felt it like nails raking down a chalkboard. I peered at her curiously, and my thoughts exploded with her ardent longing for Zyr. I swallowed, turning my attention back to the detective. He looked jittery about the integrity of the cabin as he dropped into the chair next to me.

"This place has held up for decades without issue. I wish we had a cellar, but we don't. We have a bathroom and mattresses." Hesitating, he clasped my hand and brought my fingers to his mouth as our eyes met. "Beloved, you should get out of here too," he said quietly.

Beloved? I smiled as warmth suffused me, but I tried not to let the term go to my head. I knew what he was thinking. He could heal from any injury, and Aurie was already a ghost. Tegan and I were the only ones in real danger if the storm came this way. Except there wasn't a chance I'd leave them.

"We agreed we're in this together," I replied.

Tegan held up her phone. "I can't get a bar of service out here. Tell you what. Let's sleep on it. Tomorrow, I'll ride to that store where you got supplies, Ravani. I'll see what I can find out about the hurricane track. If it's bad, we might all need to find a hotel out of state and hunker down."

Zyr didn't reiterate that we weren't leaving the cabin, but it was written on his face. Tegan stood up and squared her shoulders, as if used to battling him. He shrugged noncommittally with a dry laugh. "All right, sleep on it, Tegan. We'll talk about it again tomorrow," he said.

She grinned and dashed up to the loft. No doubt she would shower, change into more skimpy pajamas, and be ready for a family game night or some other *Leave It to Beaver* activity before the sun set.

Aurie foraged in the kitchen for something to cook while our guest was out of fright range. Zyr stretched in the door frame, studying the sky. "What are you hungry for?" she asked him. So casual. Like this was our normal. Like we could do this the rest of our lifetimes. He gave a response I didn't hear, and they settled into a rhythm as he helped her cook.

It was late in the evening, but the day had been jam-packed with preparations for a possible showdown with Darcy Cyprian. One I suspected (hoped) we might never see. We were all tired. I pulled the box containing the case file notes closer and studied the photographs and police reports that Aurie had neatly organized for us earlier.

Once we got video testimonies, everything we needed to force the Council to open an investigation would be right here. Never mind the police wanted Zyr for questioning, and Darcy Cyprian might or might not be closing in on the cabin. Not to mention there was a Category 3 hurricane barreling toward us.

We just had to survive.

CHAPTER FORTY-FOUR
—
Zyr

September 11 | Morning

"Once you get back from the convenience store, park on the side of the road here to be in line with where Aurie and Mys hid the supplies. Think you can follow the map to the cabin on foot?" I asked from the passenger seat.

Tegan flashed a thumbs-up and pulled over the burner car. "I won't be gone long," she said. "I want a clear idea of when and where this storm is gonna hit. I'm sure somebody at the store can fill me in on what the local news is saying."

I put her copy of the map in the center console and hopped out of the car. As I turned to point my partner down the road, the late morning sunlight cut across her face, and her lips parted in a tense smile. "Don't tell me the unshakable Tegan Stoney is nervous," I teased with a grin. Strolling to her side of the car, I leaned in the open window.

Tegan let out a strained giggle. "I was just thinking we should run away from everyone and everything," she replied. Her poignant stare belied her playful tone. I lifted an eyebrow in surprise, and she laughed again. "All right, your little friend can come."

I pulled away from the car. "You and I are not the type to run from our problems. The store is a straight shot ahead, southeast. You can't miss it. See you when you get back."

"Wait a second." Tegan grabbed my hand, suddenly serious. "I think you owe it to our friendship to stop playing whatever this game is and be up front with me. Why did you call me to the cabin?"

I paused, wondering what she was getting at. "Because I needed my partner, Detective Stoney."

"Are you sure? Or is it because you knew I'd come at the drop of a dime and do whatever you ask?" She flipped her hair over her shoulder and confronted me with clear blue eyes.

My jaw flexed. "I would never think to use you like that. I wanted you here because you know the case. You and Kittie Cad have already gotten further by phone than I have in a month of canvassing."

"I don't get it. The thing with Mys. Are you gay? Is that what you've been trying to tell me all along? What about us? Have you always been—"

"Nahin, Tegan, I'm not gay. Please." I clenched my teeth and inhaled. Pressing my steepled fingers to my lips, I released the breath and tried to explain. "When you and I were together, we had a genuine connection, but you know why that ended."

"Right. Because I was tangled in another manipulative relationship, and I didn't know how to turn him down that *one* night he called." She clasped my belt buckle, confronting me with those earnest blues.

I braced a hand on the car and met her gaze. "I consider you my closest friend, Tegan. Hurting you has never been my intention. I thought we were on the same page. We agreed it never would've worked out for us."

She angrily dashed away a tear. "Forgive me for thinking you might've changed your mind after all these years of proving myself. At every turn, I've tried to show you I'm in love with you, Zyr. But that's my luck. Always picking the wrong guy, huh?"

"Tegan," I murmured with regret. I didn't want to say what needed to be said, but I had no choice. "If being here makes you uncomfortable, please don't think you have to stick around for my sake . . . I won't hold it against you if you don't come back."

She tightened her lips and drew her hand back into the car, facing toward the road. "I know where the store is. I saw it on the drive up," she said, clutching the steering wheel. The Ford shot off before I could say anything more. As it faded to a speck in the distance, I realized she hadn't told me whether she'd return.

"Damn it, Tegan," I whispered.

I headed home through the woods, troubled by the conversation. I knew the terrain well, but my heightened olfactory sense made the trek much easier. It struck me that the restraints keeping my wolf in check were thinner than ever.

When I entered the cabin, there was Aurie, curled on the couch with a book. Her tiny smile lifted me up. Mys was still asleep in my bed, cedarwood cologne drenching my pillows. Padding to the couch, I leaned over it to hug Aurie from behind. Her soft, voluptuous body filled my arms.

"I've missed you guys," I whispered in her ear.

"We've been here the whole time," she replied, smiling.

I squeezed her tighter. "No," I murmured as I kissed her neck. "I've missed you guys."

I needed an escape that only my lovers could provide.

•••

The wildness was already stirring. I felt it beating in my loins as I stood behind the couch and hugged her. I let my hands slowly trace down her body to the crease of her thighs, and I spread her legs for me. With my free hand, I tilted her head to nibble at her neck.

Her tiny whimpers excited me. I dragged her head back and let the hot trail of kisses find the hills of her breasts. When I couldn't take the provocative rise and fall of her chest anymore, I moved around the couch and knelt before her.

Aurie flowed into my arms, joining me on the floor. As I thrust into her body, it was as if she was born to dance in my fires. The erotic roll of her hips ushered me deeper. Her sounds of ecstasy sent me higher. She stared at where we connected, and the quickening in her body thrummed in vibrations that matched mine.

We were right there. Ready. Harder and faster and right there. I felt my control almost slip as I pushed Aurie over the edge to climax. A sudden gasp of pleasure from across the room made me realize Mys was awake and sharing the experience.

"Wait for me, baby. Wait," I moaned.

I couldn't help myself. I couldn't *stop* myself. And it happened so fast, everything a blur. I joined Mys in the bed, kissing the nape of their neck, the quivering spine, the supple buttocks. I slipped deep into the only fantasy I had denied myself.

"Yes!" Mys whined in ecstasy.

Aurie slipped between the sheets with us and caressed the lithe, lovely body too. I couldn't quit. I was theirs, begging for more, for all they had. Like a dying man searching for air, and the two of them were my survival. With a shuddering moan, I broke through the ceiling of the universe and found the ultimate release.

Finally, finally . . . my raw, wild hunger was sated.

But now I'd never get enough. I was irrevocably both of theirs, and come hell or high water, I'd die before I'd let anything happen to them.

CHAPTER FORTY-FIVE
—
Aurie

September 11 | Late Afternoon

I was an aching, yearning pile of ectoplasm, I guess, lying in bed next to Mys as Zyr dragged himself up between us. *Oh, but we aren't done*, his eyes seemed to say. My lips parted in anticipation. Tegan's absence gave us room to unleash the fear and passion building between us.

We blissfully tore the cabin apart as the puddles of sunlight stretched from pale morning slivers to late noon slants through the dusty windows. After hours had passed, the bedcovers were scattered. The chairs at the kitchen table were thrown aside.

The laptop on the table flashed different angles of the surrounding woods, where nothing untoward stirred, and the weather radio stood silent sentinel, waiting to warn of the next hurricane update. But nothing else had been left as it should be.

When we finally came to ourselves, I stared at claw marks that raked the log cabin wall as Mys held up a sofa cushion that had been rendered a tattered piece of foam. We both laughed until my roommate looked at me closer and bolted upright on the couch.

"Wow, Yōkai. If you were living, that would leave a scar." They pointed.

I inspected myself. "Holy shit!" I exclaimed. Zyr lifted his head from the floor where he had collapsed midway between the bed and the sofa. He swore in Punjabi and got to his feet to stumble over where I lay sprawled on the mattress.

"Let me see. Let me, Aurie," he demanded as I tried to wave him off. His brow crinkled with concern. Somehow, he had managed to leave wicked claw marks down my side, from the bottom of my rib cage to the top of my hip.

"Don't worry about it. Pain feels like next to nothing as a ghost." I scoffed.

"You don't understand! I'm going feral. I should've known better," Zyr said in a tremulous voice. He retreated a few steps.

"I told you, I'm okay! Chill." I tried to smile, but the puzzled expression on my roommate's face gave me pause. Mys came closer to examine the marks. I lifted my arm and twisted to see for myself. *How, though?* I wondered. *How could a ghost be injured?*

"This isn't natural," Mys intoned.

The detective's Adam's apple bobbed. "No, it's not. Because Aurie isn't your average, run-of-the-mill ghost, as I've tried to explain from day one," he said thickly.

The half smile froze on my lips. "Then what am I?" I asked. I hugged myself as I sat up. I felt sick. This was what Tegan had asked about. One last secret between us, despite Zyr giving his word there would be no more.

He shoved his hands through his hair, his tortured face contorting with raw emotion. "If I tell you, you could crack up worse than me right now," he breathed.

I made a sound of disbelief.

Mys raised both hands in a mollifying act. "All right, let's keep calm and . . . and sort this out. Zyr, pull yourself together. You're on the verge of a shift. That's the last thing we need at the moment. I'm, uh, gonna get cleaned up, and we'll have a nice chat. Is that fine with the two of you?" My roommate slipped off to the bathroom before I could reply. The sound of the shower quickly filled the cabin.

"This is insane," I whispered.

Restless, I slid from the bed and started returning the cabin to rights while Zyr burned a hole in the floor with his pacing. I stared when he slammed a fist into the wall, but I didn't know how I was supposed to feel—concerned? For him or for myself? What was he hiding?

He dragged his jeans on without facing me. With a plaintive groan, he threw his head back and scowled at the ceiling. My numb fingers hesitated upon lifting the last chair, and I watched him. "You need to tell me what's going on," I managed.

"I don't want the same thing to happen to you that happened to Haley. Wallace said that you could—"

"Wallace?" I asked, confused. Zyr jerked his head toward the cabin door. I was startled by his abrupt movement, but I couldn't pass up the opportunity to get answers. "And what happened to Haley? You've been vague about my sister from the very beginning. This time I want the truth!"

Zyr shushed me as he hurried to the laptop to see the surveillance. It dawned on me that the werewolf had heard something I hadn't. It wasn't Tegan coming back from the far-off convenience store. Someone else was speeding along the main highway. Over his shoulder, I saw the jeep on the laptop screen. He threw on the rest of his clothes.

"Who is it, Zyr?" I sighed, at the end of my rope.

"I don't know."

I parked my hands on my hips. "Is it Darcy?" I tried again.

"Aurie, I don't *know*. Get Mys and be ready to run on my signal. Wait, one other thing."

"What?" I snapped.

He dropped his gaze. "Tegan. She . . . We had a disagreement. She may not return."

"You mean she may not return *in time*."

"No, Aurie, at all. She left midmorning. She should be back by now. It's after two."

I blinked in shock. The multitude of speeches about trusting her. Shaking my head, I marched to the bathroom and banged on the door. When I glanced back, Zyr was already out of the cabin. Mys exited the bath, toweling dry. I shoved the backpack with the rest of our belongings at them.

"What is it? What's wrong?" Mys asked as they struggled into black sweats and a matching hoodie.

"We might have to go."

Snatching the kimono from a hook on the wall, I covered my nudity and sprinted to the partially open door to eavesdrop. Zyr was in the front yard with a gun in hand. He was staring toward the red dirt road, and I faintly heard what had forced him outside—a car stereo at top volume getting louder as the vehicle drew nearer.

"Do you sense anything?" I hissed at Mys.

The Empath hovered behind me. "For one, Zyr isn't as worried as he was when he first walked out, but I'm not sure about the new arrival."

A red Jeep Cherokee emerged from the trees, bouncing over the deeply rutted lane and coming to a stop in front of Zyr. The driver turned the volume down a negligible amount before standing up in the open truck and grinning as he made the touchdown sign with his hands.

"Have you missed me?" he shouted at Zyr.

My eyes bounced from one man to the other, and I saw the resemblance. This was the younger brother Zyr had told us about. The one from the phone call that had left us scrambling to prepare for one of Darcy Cyprian's tricks. Mys strained closer as the younger Ravani hopped from the vehicle.

The guy was less tanned but had the same black wavy hair and amber gaze as his brother. He had a gorgeous baby face, and rangy muscles tightened beneath his T-shirt as he reached into the backseat and pulled out a heavy-looking duffel.

"I told you not to come, Yazeed," the detective said over the music.

"No choice," his brother replied. "I had to get you to come with me so we can take care of Ammi."

"That's what I'm doing, Yah. Taking care of our mother." Zyr spread his arms. His younger brother approached and opened the duffel bag. He held up bundles of cash. My eyes popped, though the detective looked less impressed. He snorted a laugh and shook his head. "You're wasting your time and whoever's money you're trying to bribe me with."

"This isn't a bribe. It's a way out! C'mon, use your head, all right?" Yazeed stepped up in desperation. The interaction was almost drowned out by the obnoxious music. "Sooner or later, the Council will find you, bro. They don't give a damn about whatever case you're building. You're a fugitive to them now! But if you come with me, there won't be any trouble."

"I told you I—" Zyr growled, clutching his skull. "Goddammit! Turn the fucking radio down so I can think!"

Yazeed took a step back. "You're going feral," he gasped. When the detective didn't reply, his face crumbled. "This is crazy, Zyr. We have to go. You know you don't have much time left."

"I have everything under control," Zyr mustered. "I'm gonna put that bastard Cyprian away for good. Going on the run will make me appear to be guilty, and the Ravanis haven't done anything wrong."

There was a pregnant pause as they stared each other down. Yazeed was the first to look away. "What if I told you the Council is willing to let Mum go if they get you?" he asked quietly. I felt Mys turn to stone. Suddenly, I was airborne as my roommate hauled me toward the back door and escape.

The last thing I heard was Zyr. "You wouldn't," he said hoarsely.

Mys threw me to my feet in the backyard, and we sprinted toward the forest. As we ran, the kimono fluttered behind me like wings. Mys thrust a revolver into my hand.

"Please, tell me what the hell is going on," I panicked.

"Yazeed betrayed him," Mys stated. Branches swatted our faces as we scrambled over anything in our path. My companion fumbled the compass out of the backpack still in hand and directed us toward our hidden stash of supplies. The location was at least a half hour away. "We have to get our stuff and find Tegan."

"She's the wrong person to put our faith in. She might not be coming back. Zyr said they had an argument."

"Fuck all! I have to get you out of here before they find us."

"They who?" I asked. That was when I heard what Yazeed's loud music had been masking. The swelling sound of chopper blades drawing closer. "Who?" I repeated frantically.

"The Council of Overlay Affairs Security Force. The minute they realize Zyr is feral, they'll order euthanasia. It's a crime, and if they find us, they'll consider us accessories."

"Oh my God! We have to go back!" I pivoted, but my roommate clutched my shoulders and shook me hard enough to make my teeth clack.

"Listen to me! Then the whole case against Cyprian would go up in flames while we tried to defend our innocence. We have to do what Zyr told us to. Do you understand?" Mys was fighting tears. I nodded as I clamped my lips together to keep from wailing. I understood. We were on our own.

CHAPTER FORTY-SIX
—
Mys

September 11 | Late Afternoon

It felt like we had been running for over an hour, but the map showed there was yet another mile to the main road. My legs burned, reminding me I wasn't really the superagent I played in video games. Aurie and I had gathered the first-aid kit and other supplies. They weighed me down. My shirt was plastered to my back.

A raven flapped out of the bushes, and it seemed like a bad omen. One for sorrow. I was scared shitless.

I tried to move faster as I dug out the burner phone. "Come on, Tegan, come on!" I groaned. She wouldn't answer my calls. Arms pumping, I fired off a premade text: *The cabin is compromised.* She knew to meet us at the rendezvous point farther down the road. If she didn't show up by the time Aurie and I made it there, we would have to accept that she had abandoned us.

"Slow down. I think we're far enough," Aurie said at the sight of me flailing.

"No, we have to keep going, Yōkai. From what we witnessed back at the cabin, the Council of Overlay Affairs thinks Zyr committed a crime. They won't stop until they get him."

"Mys, you can't keep pushing yourself like this. We have to take a break, babe." Aurie gripped my arm.

Halting, I locked my hands behind my head and took deep breaths. "They could have drones," I said. As I struggled for air, I shook sweat-soaked hair from my face and blinked up at the sky, which was getting more overcast by the minute. It had to be after four o'clock, but it seemed later because of the storm. My stomach pitched from overexertion, but I took off walking again. We were nearing the main road.

"Do you see or hear any drones? Because I don't." Aurie had no choice but to fall in step, but she gestured back the way we had come. "You know what? Maybe I should let them find me. My testimony against Darcy Cyprian could clear Zyr's name," she suggested.

Stopping again, I cupped her cheeks and locked us in an all-consuming staring contest to be sure she was listening. "Darcy Cyprian is behind this. He's trying to use the Council to get you defenseless. As long as he's a member, we can't trust them. You saw how they used Zyr's brother against him."

I squeezed my eyes shut. They had dangled before him the powerful lure of freeing Yazeed's mother. I knew how he must've felt. I covered my face and took a moment to process what was happening to us. It hurt. It hurt, it hurt, and I felt like I should go back for Zyr. Only, I couldn't. I had to get Aurie to safety.

My ears pricked at the sound of a car engine idling somewhere close. Grabbing Aurie, I jerked her into a crouching position. Aurie and I backtracked deeper into the woods for our safety, but I stopped at a familiar voice. "It's Tegan," I mouthed. Aurie nodded as we lay pressed to the ground, my nose in a damp clump of pine needles. We both listened.

"I haven't had a drink. Would you stop? God!" she exclaimed. There was a pause. My eyes met my companion's. It sounded like Tegan was on the phone. "I'm doing everything I'm supposed to be doing . . . Yeah, you explain how it works then, jerk! No, I'm sorry . . . I didn't mean that. My nerves are just shot!"

Wrinkling my nose, I felt a sneeze coming on. I tried to suppress it. There was no use. The involuntary reflex erupted in a quiet snort. Aurie's eyes widened as we registered that Tegan was no longer talking. A car door slammed. I raised a fist to signal to prepare to make a break for it if we had to.

"Mys? Is that you?" the woman called out. I didn't dare respond, because a new thought occurred to me. It *sounded* like Tegan, but Cyprian kept nasty tricks up his sleeves. I cautioned Aurie not to say anything. I needed to see to believe.

"Please, tell me it's you." The woman's voice quavered. Whoever it was, she had left the road and was struggling through the thicket. Worried, I fondled my gun as I cast a net of Empathy. "I, uh, got your text when I was halfway to the cabin, and I turned around . . . So, if it's not you . . ."

My consciousness brushed up against the telltale walking lust machine that was Tegan Stoney. Chafing inwardly, I rose to my feet. She whipped in my direction with her gun drawn, her eyes saucers in her pale, freckled face.

"Relax, it's us!" I shouted.

"Oh!" Tegan gasped, laughing as she quickly lowered the weapon. "My gosh! I almost shot you. Why'd you take so long to respond?

"We had to make sure it was you," I replied.

"Of course it's me. Is Aurie with you? What happened at the cabin?" she asked.

"I'll explain everything on the road. We have to go." I grabbed Aurie's hand and tried to head toward Tegan's hidden car, but the redhead dug in her heels.

"Where's Zyr?" Tegan demanded to know.

I looked down, in pain. "They've got him," I said. When I lifted my gaze, her blue orbs had dimmed at the realization that not all of us had escaped. "We're not giving up on him. We'll implement Plan B and appeal to the Humanity Embassy for asylum, where Aurie can get an audience with the Council to try to free him. She'll need the ambassador's help, otherwise she could be arrested for accessory."

"Accessory to what? None of this makes any sense."

"Aurie's one of us, Tegan. She's a ghost, which means she and I can be charged for concealing the fact that Zyr is going feral. Her only protection is the embassy for crimes against her when she was human," I explained anxiously, eyeing the direction to the cabin. "We can't stay here. We have to keep moving."

"All right, I'll get you out of here, but there's one thing that's been plaguing me ever since my arrival. How does one become a ghost, Mys?" The detective lifted her chin as if she wouldn't budge without a crash course in Supernatural lore and laws.

I stared at her in disbelief. "You die, Tegan. Some people have unfinished business, or they die horrific deaths that leave a confused soul stuck between the real world and the next, but it's not rocket science. You expire."

"That's what I thought." Tegan's expression smoothed. She reached in her pocket, and I stiffened until she brought out an old medicine bottle made of blue-green glass that matched her eyes. "I found this at the gas station," she said, popping the cork.

I had no clue what the bottle could do for us. It was as if the thought of Zyr being taken was too much for her lovelorn brain to process. "I don't want to be callous," I replied, "but there are OA security forces on our tail. We can talk souvenirs later. Shall we go?" I hiked a thumb at the road.

"How do I know you're not trying to trick me to save your own ass?" Tegan queried.

Aurie glared at her. "Is she delusional?" she asked.

"Do you need to return to the cabin and see them arresting Zyr for yourself, Tegan?" I snapped.

"No, I believe you about the detective, but how do I know Aurie is with us? I have to be certain, because I made a promise to Zyr." Tegan scanned the clearing where we stood, and she held up the bottle. "Ms. Edison, if you're present, will you take this bottle and hold it like this?" She made a fist around the bottle with her thumb where the cork should be.

Aurie muttered under her breath at how bizarre the request was. I crossed my arms, resisting the urge to throttle Zyr's partner. Grief did strange things to people, and Tegan was grieving. I sensed it. It was the only other emotion I sensed beneath the cloying miasma of her love and lust for Zyr.

"Go ahead, Yōkai." I nodded. Aurie accepted the glass bottle exactly as Tegan requested. "Yep. Like that," I said. At my response, Tegan swiped out a hand and came away with the glass, and suddenly Aurie was gone. Snap. Poof. *Gone*. I turned stone with horror. "What did you do!" I yelled.

Tegan held up the recorked vessel. "I put her away for safekeeping."

"N-not possible," I stammered. The shades and hues of Aurie's trapped Soul grazed my consciousness, and my Empathy screamed. Tegan was telling the truth.

"Oh, it's quite possible to catch a ghost," she explained in a soft-spoken, treacherous voice. "It's an old folk custom passed down by slaves. The trick is to throw the needle when your haint is over the lip of the bottle. The point stabs right through and drags them down. Isn't that fascinating?"

"Let her out, Tegan!" I surged toward her.

Yanking back, the madwoman grinned. "You gave me the cue for when to trap her. 'Go ahead, Yōkai. Yep. Like that.' So helpful. I have to admit I didn't think it would work, but I can tell by your reaction that I shouldn't have worried. Same as when I heard you could sense emotions. You were easy to fool. A few well-placed sexual fantasies, and you were out of my head."

I suddenly realized my mistake. My mistake. *Oof.* I had been such a fool. No one was so enthralled that they thought of one person every waking hour. No one! Her obsession with Zyr had been a screen to hide her real motivations. I lifted my gun, and she smiled a knowing smile.

"Remember who brought the supplies, now," Tegan said in that New Orleans drawl. In horror, I checked the chamber and realized there were no bullets. I trembled with rage as I lowered my useless weapon. Meanwhile, Tegan lifted Zyr's silver and black Glock. At the last minute, she inclined her head with a touch of regret. "I wish I could tell you this isn't personal, but we both know better."

"Fuck you, Tegan!" I launched the full force of my wrath at her. Then the world went black.

CHAPTER FORTY-SEVEN
—
Zyr

September 11 | Late Afternoon

"You wouldn't," I choked out.

Only, I knew he would do anything for Mum, even something as misguided as this. I glowered at Yazeed with barely checked fury, squinting as pine needles and debris flew past my face. I vaguely heard the screen door slam around back and registered that Aurie and Mys were fleeing the cabin. Good. We had planned meticulously for every worst-case scenario. They knew what to do. Even without help from Tegan.

"You led them here!" I accused Yazeed.

My brother dropped his head. "Believe me, it was the only way."

The sky darkened, and the wind picked up, but it wasn't the coming storm. It was a helicopter emblazoned with the gold crest of Overlay Affairs Security buzzing over the clearing. Violent gusts whipped by the blades battered the tall, spindly trees. Combined with the noise of Yazeed's blasting radio, the din made my ears ring.

Flashes of insanity snatched at me. I twisted my neck to shake it off. Now wasn't the time to lose my grip. Nonetheless, excitement and

SONDI WARNER

adrenaline pumped through my veins for a showdown. Not against the vampire, but against my own flesh and blood. Yah looked like fresh prey, and my claws came out of their own accord, but I forced them to retract. My brother wasn't the enemy. He was being used.

Somehow Cyprian had convinced the Council of Overlay Affairs that I was the real threat. For the first time, I considered the possibility this wasn't about my sister, Yalina Ravani. Perhaps it had never been about her. Was Darcy Cyprian trying to destroy my whole family? My deteriorating thoughts congealed around one crazy revelation: if he was, I was the reason he had gotten this far.

Cyprian had used my instincts against me. Though my mother had warned me not to be blinded by hubris, I realized too late the things I had missed. I had dropped the Alpha title and weakened the pack, pursuing revenge. I hadn't recognized the vampire's mercenaries because I'd expected to smell his henchmen coming. I had even let down my guard upon seeing Yazeed in the jeep.

Every step of the way, I had played into Darcy Cyprian's hands.

From the helicopter, someone with a loudspeaker ordered me to drop my weapon. I let the gun fall from numb fingers and clenched my teeth as I held up my hands, but surrender was the furthest thing from my mind.

Yazeed waved at the chopper. "Please, give me time to bring him in," he shouted.

Shaking my head in wry amusement, I figured the poor kid honestly believed he was here to talk me into turning myself in. "They played you," I growled. "They're not taking me without a fight. Worse, you led them to the one piece of Ravani property they didn't already know about. Now this place will be dispersed to whoever earns the title of Alpha during the October elections, along with the rest of the family holdings."

"You think a patch of *land* matters more to me than you or Mum?" Yazeed reached an open hand to me. "I don't want anything to happen to you. Please!"

"I'm not going with them," I said.

Distress twisted his face, and he balled his fists. "Don't make me have to use force, brother!"

"I don't want to hurt you, Yah!" I baited him.

"Think of what you're doing to our family!" he shouted.

I spread my arms, feeling the muscles bulge as my body bulked for transformation. "I am," I muttered. I was finally thinking more clearly than I had in years, and I knew what I had to do.

A yellow fire burned around my irises, matching my brother's. He hunched forward as I doubled over, and we circled one another while the shift worked its magic beneath the surface. We had done this hundreds of times in our youth, but this battle wasn't for play.

I stumbled to a knee when Yazeed lunged at me. His claws sliced through my forearm. I backed off as ribbons of blood flew through the air. Jerking away from his painful clutch, I sank my teeth into his shoulder and yanked him off his feet. It hurt me to the core when my baby brother let out an agonized yowl, but I dragged him to the ground.

Stay down, I said in his thoughts. As wolves we could communicate better. The helicopter hovered above, unable to land in the densely packed forest. Snarling, I nipped at Yazeed's narrow legs and thick haunches to give the security forces a good show. He returned the attack with a swat to my nose.

At the same time, I sent a flood of information into his head—the pertinent details of the case and how this might be our last shot at saving our pack. The thoughts were delivered in sensations, rather than words. It was the preferred method of communication between werewolves because I didn't have to explain anything. Yazeed saw what I had seen, and now he knew what I knew. I had only needed him to shift in order to make him understand.

Tumbling in a rough-looking grip, though inflicting minimal actual damage, he asked in my head, *What about our mother?* I showed him the ace up my sleeve, and he bared his teeth in a wolfish grin. Darcy Cyprian wasn't the only one with a clever plan.

Peripherally, I glimpsed a fext soldier leaning out of the chopper with a tranquilizer gun. Scope to his face, he aimed at me, but I rolled the smaller, less developed wolf to where I had been standing, and the dart cut through the air and impaled him in the neck.

Yazeed took on a blank stare. *Damn, that ached*, he channeled to me. His fading consciousness signaled he was fading out for the count.

I am so sorry, Yah, I said via telepathy. I took off racing into the woods. Three soldiers who'd just rappelled to the ground gave chase, but I knew the forest better than I knew my own name. I had the advantage. Leaping over a low-hanging branch and scrambling under bushes riddled with thorns, I heard the crash and thrash of man-shaped objects hurtling after me.

Fext soldiers were an army of undead, instinct-driven zombies. However, they weren't invincible. An arduous chase would try anyone's patience. I scurried into a hollow tree as my pursuers followed me far off the beaten path. Hours passed. The woods grew darker, and I knew they would give up soon.

As soon as I heard my pursuers pass my hiding place, I dashed out and took a northerly route to draw them away from Aurie and Mys. My four legs ate up the mile, until suddenly a drone zipped overhead. Another one joined it minutes later. Growling at the devices, I focused on disorienting their pilots with a zigzag track.

My friends needed time to reach the rendezvous point where Tegan was supposed to meet them. And if my partner chose not to return? Aurie and Mys were resourceful enough to get to the embassy, as planned. But I had to believe Tegan Stoney wouldn't bail on us.

Even if Tegan harbored a secret desire to restart our failed relationship, we both realized her feelings were largely nostalgic. We were a team. She had my back, and I protected her. That was the way it worked. In fact, after this was over, I would take the fall to keep her out of trouble.

I would also try to find time—somewhere between now and going feral—to convince Tegan that she deserved better than the losers she dated on the regular. Like the guy who owned the chop shop where she had gotten the burner car.

I slammed to a halt. *The chop shop.* Illegal tint, no plates. I struggled to retain a man's mindset, but the fuzzy picture taking shape grew clearer due to wolf instinct, not logic and reason. Details of memories, passing thoughts coalesced.

Buzzing overhead drew my attention. The drones whirred behind me where the fext soldiers hadn't been able to keep up. Chomping at the air, my four paws splashed through a muddy stream to a burrow on the other side. Once I'd shaken the drones, I was able to think.

At the chop shop, Tegan could get *any* burner car, such as the Ford that had hit Aurie Edison. I remembered the Century Luxe Hotel surveillance footage of Darcy Cyprian entering the penthouse suite had disappeared from the evidence locker on Tegan's watch. Paul Jameson's cell phone triangulation had been completed by her. She had been the one to place him near the party, though Jameson swore up and down he was only in New Orleans on vacation.

Tegan had warned me off Darcy Cyprian. She had searched the cold case storage room for the vampire's older criminal record and claimed the reports were nowhere to be found. Yet, she had come up with the case files the day I was suspended. Such convenient timing.

I had missed so much, but this seemed too far-fetched to be believed. My trusted friend and partner couldn't be one of Darcy Cyprian's pets, could she? I suddenly remembered Tegan's profuse apology to Mrs. Edison for what had happened to Aurie. In retrospect, her emotional outburst wasn't the misguided reaction of an enthusiastic fan. It was guilt.

But why deliver the very evidence I needed to take Cyprian down? Why put the cold case file in my hands in the end?

Because the two of them were ushering me to a location off the grid.

Tegan knew about my cabin. Cyprian had pressured Aurie with a tight seventy-two-hour schedule, knowing I would try to get her away from him. We had been corralled into the woods, and I had invited a snake into camp. Now, my friends were running straight into a trap.

I had to get to them. I bounded out of hiding and galloped back toward the cabin. I came up short as a drone descended right in front of me.

CHAPTER FORTY-EIGHT
—
Aurie

September 11 | Evening

Unraveling, I slammed against walls of blue-green glass. I threw myself at the barrier harder and harder, but every attempt to pass through or teleport out failed. Suddenly, I looked down at myself and discovered I couldn't even see my body! I was nonexistent.

A startled outcry burst from my lungs. I couldn't hear it. I had no voice. I clamped a hand over my throat in horror and realized I didn't feel the touch. Savage. I backed away in confusion—more an impression of movement than me actually taking a step. What the hell was happening to me?

There was no time to freak out. It was more important to know what was happening on the other side of the glass. I saw Mys wearing a stunned expression that morphed into one of jarring epiphany and then simmering fury. I strained to hear what was being said.

"I wish I could tell you this isn't personal, but we both know better," Tegan sneered.

My God. Zyr's partner was betraying us. I couldn't understand how she had deceived him—and an *Empath*—so thoroughly. In a flash, Mys dropped to their knees. The doe-like eyes blinked once and stared, fixed. Then the gamine body hit the pine needles and didn't move again.

A choked whimper rattled me inside out. I froze in utter disbelief, every part of me cold except the burning where my eyes should be. I screamed Mys's name. Banging and striking the walls of the prison that encased me, I screamed so much my phantom throat should have been raw. It was no use. I couldn't do anything to help. I slid to my knees like the invisible tears rolling down my absent face.

Tegan, the traitorous monster, didn't linger over the scene of her gruesome crime. She took off through the woods with the bottle imprisoning me.

Mired in stunned despair, I realized we'd reached her car only when I heard the door slam. We were off, but the drive was a blur. All I could think about was Zyr and Mys. Tegan had taken one of them from me. I didn't know what had happened to the other, but I was certain I would never see my lovers again. It was like dying twice.

I went numb. I didn't notice it was getting dark outside until we stopped at the old convenience store. Through my glass prison, I saw the cashier that Zyr and I had met the day before. She was smoking a cigarette near the double doors. The thought of Zyr's efforts yesterday to get me to like his undeserving partner replayed in my head, and I forgot about the store attendant.

Tegan held the bottle near her face. "I don't know what you are," she murmured, "but I know you're not Aurelia Edison. Even though you've managed to convince Zyr otherwise. I had to get you away from him . . . I just wish there'd been a better way." Her lips tightened as if she sincerely felt remorse. I wondered what the hell she was talking about, but the question faded when I saw who she was there to meet.

Tegan, what did you do? I tried to ask.

Beneath a darkening sky studded with the first specks of stars,

Darcy Cyprian stepped out of his familiar black Rolls Royce. He was in his usual dapper suit, with perfectly coiffed blond hair, as if he had stepped straight out of a photo shoot for *GQ* magazine. Aside from his polished appearance, the vampire was fully in his element against the backdrop of shadowy wilderness.

He caught the attention of the cashier. The woman seemed rattled by his presence, and she didn't even know *what* he was. She hurried into the store, locking the door behind her.

It took so much effort for me not to descend into panic when Tegan handed the bottle with me in it to Darcy. His icy fingers wrapped around the glass and seemed to caress me in ways I didn't want to be touched. I cowered as he removed the cork.

"Ma louloute?" he purred.

I had no choice. My Soul came spilling from the vessel like a genie. Sucking in air, I prepared to flee—by teleportation or some other disappearing act—but Darcy jerked my hand over the bottle, and I was back in the glass prison faster than I could say, "It's Aurie, you bloodsucking motherfucker!"

"There you are. No running from me tonight." He grinned as his gaze shifted to Tegan. "Thank you for your service, Detective Stoney. What about the cold case files?"

"Destroyed," she said. "I got rid of everything this morning when your nosy ghost was having a lazy soak in the tub. Not something I'd imagine a ghost doing, but I thought you might like that detail. I know how much you enjoy naked, vulnerable young things." Her tone was derisive. Darcy wasn't amused.

"Have a care, my pet. You're not talking to one of your piece-of-shit love interests," he said, with quiet menace and a saccharine smile.

"I'm sure you think I should feel insulted, but I deeply approve of you staying the fuck out of my love life. Now, I've held up my end of the bargain. Do your part," she fired back.

"What about the tranny? I can't have anyone knowing about this."

Tegan flipped her hair in obvious annoyance. "*She* is on a wild goose chase hunting down a list of victims I made up. I never gave *her* the actual case files. So, you don't have to worry about *her.*"

"And Zyr's little psychic friend?"

"I took care of Mys too . . . permanently. Are we done here? Call them off."

Darcy Cyprian gestured to his driver. The chauffeur stepped away to place a phone call I couldn't hear. At the end of it, he nodded to Darcy, who spread his hands obsequiously for Tegan. "Your esteemed partner is no longer a fugitive," the vampire promised. "In your world or mine. It'll take a few hours for the paperwork to go through, but that's only to keep him preoccupied while we make our getaway."

"We?" Tegan arched an eyebrow.

"Yes, step lively, Detective Stoney. We're not returning to New Orleans tonight. I extend to you my hospitality and bid you enjoy my country estate in Ponchatoula while I wrap up some business. I'm gonna see a man about a dog." He pointed for Tegan to get in his car, but she balked.

"That wasn't part of our agreement. I only did this to get Zyr out of your clutches. I'm going home."

"Come, now." Darcy wriggled his fingers playfully, reaching for the woman bending away from him. He got a firm grasp of her shoulder and shoved her into the vehicle. "We both know that's not the *only* reason you came here," he said as the car door slammed. "You came to clear *your* name."

Tegan threw herself at the opposite door. I knew how she felt. She couldn't get out. Unlike me, she couldn't even see past the opaque windows of her new prison. She whipped around to face Darcy. He gave her a cool stare as he poured himself a cocktail.

"I've done my penance, all right? I made sure the boy they were trying to charge—the stalker—will only get stuck with the crime he committed, breaking the RO. I even started volunteering," her voice quavered. "But what happened to Aurie that night was a terrible accident that wouldn't have occurred if you hadn't drugged her. I've kept your secret, Mr. Cyprian. Let me go."

As he stared at the ceiling of the car, he sipped his drink and shrugged. "That's not the way I see it. The way I see it, none of this would have happened if you hadn't been drinking and driving in front of Century Luxe that night, Detective."

I shuddered in dismay. *That* was why Tegan's face had seemed familiar to me? Zyr's partner had lied, schemed, and apparently, *killed me*. However, I didn't wish Darcy on anyone. As the Rolls Royce took off, Tegan whimpered and tried the door again. It wouldn't open. She squeezed her neat frame into the corner of the car and faced the vampire, who I now realized was blackmailing her.

"Mr. Cyprian, I stopped drinking," she reminded him.

"And I am so proud of you." He casually dropped a hand on her knee.

The detective pulled her firearm. Two rapid retorts. The blasts were deafening. The leather and cognac interior of the car burned with the acrid smell of gunpowder.

When the smoke faded, Tegan emitted a horrified scream as she backpedaled against the seat. Her eyes were fixed on the black, smoking holes in Darcy Cyprian's chest. The wounds sealed inward, the last puff of smoke getting swallowed into the holes, no evidence remaining except the rents in his shirt.

"Zyr was telling the truth. You're really—I need to go home! Please, I want to go home!" Tegan pleaded.

Darcy shook his head, bemused, as he dusted his crisp black shirt. "That was unnecessary, but I'm glad we got it out of the way. Your skepticism is a thing of wonder. What did you expect when you heard you were dealing with a vampire, my pet?

"I prefer no one know my involvement in this. Unfortunately, you're someone, Detective Stoney," he went on. "I'm willing to keep you alive if you stay in line, but try another stunt, and you'll be dinner." He picked his teeth with a long fingernail. He was exactly as cringeworthy as a B-movie villain, and so much more disturbing—because he was believable.

"I'm a law enforcement officer." Tegan sniffled and scrubbed her face. She sat up straighter, her expression hardening. "I knew the moment you got me in this car, my chances of survival would plummet."

"*Au contraire*. Aurie can vouch for my honesty. You have my word that tomorrow you can go back to busting bad guys with an unblemished record. I've already made the car you were driving disappear. After this, no one will know you were at the hotel that night, drinking because you spied your worthless ex going in with a coed. Most importantly, no one will find out that you killed Aurie Edison."

"You don't understand. You don't know what really happened that night," Tegan managed.

"No, no, no! Of course not," Darcy condescended, patting her knee again.

Tegan sank into miserable silence.

I tried to piece together everything I had learned. Tegan had been at the hotel the night of my death, spying on her crush. That sounded exactly like her. Deadass. Ironically, she had been the one drinking when she'd assumed I had had too much. Upon telling her I had been drugged, the woman I'd thought was my savior had asked me to wait while she got her car. Somehow in my disoriented state, I had stumbled into the street.

And just like that . . .

Tegan Stoney had been responsible for my hit-and-run. So, what was she doing, delivering me into Darcy Cyprian's hands?

CHAPTER FORTY-NINE

Mys

September 11 | Night

Surrounded by darkness, I reached for the only source of light: the bright, searing stars of pain exploding at my temples. I blinked awake. The first thing I noticed was the stark absence of other people's emotions. That convinced me I was in bed at my apartment, the one place where the outside world couldn't intrude.

But that wasn't right. I smelled the rich odor of dirt, dead leaves, moss, pine straw. There was thunder in the distance, and raindrops broke through the haze of my awareness. Something slithered across my forearm. I yelped several times and shook off a centipede as I sat up. I wasn't in my home but the woods.

"Aurie?" I called out shakily.

Moisture trickled down my face. Touching it, I stared at the dark smudge on my fingertips. There wasn't enough illumination for me to see what it was, but I knew. When I placed my fingers near my nostrils, the whiff of blood was overpowering.

Injured and dazed, I felt around the soft earth for the first-aid kit, calling louder for Aurie. A gnawing sense of dread ate at me, but even if I'd had the strength to search the surrounding forest for her, the swelling laceration at the side of my forehead required triple antibiotic ointment and at least a butterfly closure strip until I could get real medical care.

I battled confusion. Flashbacks of what happened unfurled bit by bit as I tended the wound. Tegan. She had struck me with the butt of Zyr's gun, hard enough to knock me out. I knew that shit took serious force. Wincing, I found my useless revolver beneath my ankle. Tegan had done a number on us.

Us? Aurie was gone. The realization knifed through me. Tegan had captured her in a magic glass bottle. I couldn't process it. It was too surreal. I patted my pockets for my vape pen and took a long hit. A temporary sense of calm flooded me as clouds of vapor floated past my lips. Just as swiftly, my distress returned. I didn't know what to do.

I rifled through the supplies for my personal cell phone, salvaged from Tegan's thieving hands. The battery slid into place, and it lit up, but I had no service whatsoever. I suppressed a powerless scream and took off toward the main road. I didn't dare use the mobile flashlight. Fext soldiers could be raking the forest. Shadows made every step a pitfall. Yet, somehow I managed to find the highway.

By the time my feet touched the asphalt, I felt like I was moving just for the sake of motion. For a second, the weight of grief rendered me too weak to continue.

I stood in the hushed rain as more than raindrops coursed down my cheeks. Images of Aurie's face the night I'd met her swam before my eyes, and I remembered why I had taken her in. She had reminded me so much of myself—afraid, confused, alone, but brave enough not to lie down and die. When Zyr had stepped into our world, I knew I was doomed. He was fierce and gentle, and he made me feel safe outside the walls of my home.

I had never desired to get this involved.

I had spent a considerable portion of my life pushing people away. I had used cynicism to block the painful emotions that made life ugly and unbearable. In the process, I had also blocked out love. Zyr and Aurie had blown my wall of ambivalence to hell and back, making it impossible not to fall for them.

Now the broken beat of my heart needed to learn the rhythm of farewell. I wasn't ready to say good-bye. I had steeled myself for that eventuality, but it wasn't time yet. Aurie hadn't crossed over, and Zyr hadn't totally lost his damn mind, so I couldn't let them go without a fight.

Away from the canopy of trees, I jerked the phone from my pocket in desperation and tried it again. Seeing a signal, I could've sobbed with joy. I swiftly scrolled through my contact list. My lips trembled around each name, client after client.

The spike of elation plummeted. No one in my directory would drop everything and come, not even Kittie. She was probably cozied up with her significant other. I didn't have a family to call, a mom who would miss me, a dad who would wire money in times of need. I squeezed the cell phone in a balled fist and trudged forward, running out of options.

There wasn't any point in contacting emergency services. I wouldn't be able to answer their questions, like what I was doing all the way out in the middle of nowhere. Besides, I had an innate disdain for physicians. My body was a medical curiosity which made for a less than pleasant patient experience.

Despair gripped me. I prided myself on knowing when to fold. But this was different. I couldn't give up. Aurie's words came back to me: *Try harder with people.* The lump in my throat wouldn't go away. I steeled myself for rejection as I lifted the phone and hit Kittie's name. If she didn't answer, I was on my own.

The phone rang twice. Hearing the line connect and her voice on the other end made me erupt in tearful laughter out of shock. "I can't believe you're not tied up with Terrance!" I exclaimed.

"Of course I am, darling. What's wrong?" Kittie picked up on my distress.

I shooed the mental image of the lovers knotted in *Kinbaku-bi*. "I hate to intrude on you guys, but I'm in a bind, no pun intended. Something happened, Kittie. I need to find Aurie. Unfortunately, I don't have a ride, and I'm currently at . . . the north end of Tangipahoa Parish." I grimaced, knowing I was asking a lot. "If you can't make it, I totally understand. I'll figure something—"

"I'm on my way."

"—out. I can try to find an Uber driver to get me to a car rental agency—"

"I said I'm on my way, Mitsuyo. I take it this is related to you-know-what, and you don't want too many you-know-whos involved. We're in luck. Terrance says we can use his car."

I blinked, registering the fact that my prayers had been answered. My eyes stung with fresh wetness. "You don't know how much this means to me," I whispered with emotion. I heard her sigh on the other end and could tell it was tinged with a smile.

"I told you, you're worth saving, darling. I'll be there in a jiff," she said.

Relief surged through me as I told Kittie Cad how to find me, then ended the call. I shouldered the first-aid kit, my bag of clothes, and the rucksack full of supplies. The trek through the storm was becoming more exhausting, but I had oomph in my step now that Kittie was meeting me at the old convenience store.

We would grab the cold case files from the cabin and present our evidence to the Humanity Embassy. Without testimony from Darcy's other victims, I wasn't sure it would be enough. Yet, I held on to a tenuous hope that the Council of Overlay Affairs would at least reevaluate Zyr's case and see that Cyprian had caused his feral state. They couldn't euthanize him knowing that, could they?

I put two and two together about Tegan. She had to be a consort of the vampire, meaning she'd likely delivered Aurie to *him*. I just couldn't figure out Darcy's deal. He had expended a crazy amount of resources to get Aurie. I speculated this couldn't be a simple case of silencing a witness. Everything circled back to his reason for drugging her at the party.

"She's special," I muttered to myself. Both Zyr and Darcy had called Aurie that, but it didn't seem like a motive.

As I wrestled with the mystery, something slinked from the trees and paused in the middle of the road. There was no way. Absolutely no way. Petrified, I cast a net of Empathy. It didn't work on animals, only I wasn't sure this shadowy wolf was all beast.

"Zyr?" I called out with a heart full of hope and a head full of fear that I could be wrong. The black wolf shuddered and shifted until a naked man took its place. "Zyr!" I ran to him. He caught me in a hug and spun me like in movies. I was too overcome with emotion to think it was corny. I squeezed him tighter as his lips crushed mine. Fighting sobs, I kissed him back.

"I thought I had lost you," he groaned.

"Big mood!" I giggled through tears.

"I went back to the cabin. It's destroyed. Where's Aurie?" Zyr asked. My enthusiasm paled, and I squirmed to the ground. His glowing amber eyes traced over my face. "What did Tegan do?" he whispered hoarsely.

From the duffel bag of supplies, I handed him clothes to change into while I explained how his partner had turned on us. His face blanched at the description of Aurie disappearing into the bottle. "What made you realize Tegan was involved, and what do you mean, the cabin is destroyed?" I asked. "I was gonna grab the evidence once Kittie gets here to pick me up. I thought I was on my own. Come to think of it, how did you escape?"

"I hid, but someone must've called off the fext. They would've never stopped searching for me otherwise. Before they left, however, they burned down the cabin and destroyed my truck," he stewed. "It occurred to me Tegan had access to a burner car similar to the one that hit Aurie, and all the forensics pointing away from Darcy Cyprian came from her. I don't know why it took me so long to figure everything out, but there it is. My instincts were wrong."

"Not wrong, but certainly manipulated, same as mine. She kept her intentions hidden behind a cloak of rampant sexual desire for you. Maybe my jealousy helped," I admitted.

He chuckled dryly before sobering. "Regardless, with the time that's passed since the raid, there's no telling where Tegan is now or what she did with Aurie."

"We'll search every corner of Overlay City if we have to," I said forcefully.

I saw a flash of teeth as Zyr grinned, stopping in the road and dragging me into another soul-stirring kiss. "Of course, we're not giving up on her. I have something Darcy Cyprian knows nothing about, and it gives us the edge. Kittie is on the way?" He collected the heavy supplies from me.

Nodding, I held up my phone. "She's meeting me at the convenience store."

"Smart move, keeping yours. Tegan baited me with the burner and took mine. Come on, we have to hurry if we don't want to leave Kittie waiting. The store is almost an hour's drive from here. God knows how long it'll take on foot." We picked up our pace, with lightning crackling above us and thunder giving chase.

"I get that Haley has the Sight," I said over the sound of rain, "but even if Darcy thinks Aurie is the one who has it, there's nothing particularly special about Seers. You could throw a stone into a roomful of people in New Orleans and probably hit at least two. What gives? Why is he dead set on getting Aurie?"

"There's more to it than just having the Sight, which Cyprian discovered when he hexed the party at Century Luxe. I got a glimpse of the placard the girls couldn't read outside the penthouse that night. It was marked with sigils designed to keep out humans." Zyr gave me a pointed look.

"Sigils? Like my door? Then it must have been faulty. A well-cast spell is damn near impenetrable."

"So I thought. Until I learned Haley was following their guardian angel that night. She recognized him as Wallace Edison . . . their father."

I stopped in my tracks. "Wait, what?"

"It gets more bizarre." He stopped in the middle of the road as the storm raged around us. "There was nothing wrong with the sign. Only magic could've gotten past the barrier. I didn't want to believe it, but Haley is a witch. A powerful one. At some point, she'll perhaps be strong enough to go up against Cyprian. Ever since that night, however, she's been too fragile, and I doubt she even understood her powers before then."

My eyes widened at the flurry of coincidences that had lined up for this to happen. "You're telling me the guardian angel protected Aurie and Haley from Darcy that night, and now Darcy's after the wrong sister while the angel—their father—is guarding Haley at the hospital?"

"Not quite. Wallace isn't at the hospital for Haley."

"You've lost me," I admitted.

"I'm sorry it's all so convoluted. I'd thought keeping things to myself was the only way forward. The Council was prepared to toss the case if I leaked certain details, but there's no time left for secrets. You have to know everything now. There's more."

CHAPTER FIFTY
—
Zyr

September 11 | Late Night

Ignoring the intensifying storm, Mys studied me a full twenty seconds before asking, "So, what's the ace up your sleeve?"

I shook my head. "You know how you say it's easier to show than tell? This is one of those moments. I was trying to explain before the security forces dropped in on us, but perhaps it's better to reveal things when we get back to New Orleans. Did Kittie give you an ETA?"

"She left thirty minutes ago."

"Shit. We won't make it to the convenience store in time." I strained to hear a car in the distance. Nothing but silence. "No luck hitchhiking either. How do you feel about being carried?" I raised an eyebrow.

"You're serious?" Mys giggled.

"Yeah, I'm serious. Otherwise, what's the use of having greater-than-average strength?"

A shy Mitsuyo draped themselves over my back. My mind and body felt like I had been in a blender for the past few hours, but the gentle touch of their slender fingers clutching my shoulders and their arms sliding around my neck soothed me. Their scent was intoxicating.

"How badly did she hurt you?" I murmured, my nostrils stinging from the faint smell of blood.

"It's superficial. I'm okay."

I turned and kissed their lips. "I wish I could take away the pain."

"You just did." Mys stared into my eyes.

Blushing at the frank display of affection, I turned away and took off at a brisk pace. Perspiration beaded my skin, and endorphins rushed through me. My lungs expanded with air as my feet pounded the pavement. I ran as fast as I could through the night while the clouds overhead raced across the face of the moon. The dappled light plunged us in and out of shadows.

I hardly saw the otherworldly beauty of our surroundings. The only thing on my mind was Aurie. Whether I took down Darcy Cyprian, I had to tell her the truth before we were out of time. Things had gotten way out of hand. From the day I had met Aurie and Mys, I had imagined coming clean once I felt they were ready to know the most important details of her case. I hadn't factored in Cyprian ruining my career and leaving me feral.

The worst part was that no one ever talked about how long it took to go completely wild. It seemed that in evading the fext soldiers, I had remained a wolf longer than I should have. The tantalizing call of madness tickled the frayed edges of my consciousness.

I kept thinking of the savage ease of being the animal. How I had tricked the drones into anticlimactic crashes into trees. They were glorified toys. I had terrorized the lost soldiers, watching them bumble through the woods until their superiors airlifted them.

When the hunt was called off, I heard it on their radios and circled back to my property to ensure Yazeed was okay. After I saw them load him into the helicopter and leave, I briefly shifted to man-shape to investigate the burning cabin. I could have remained a man. Instead, I had shifted back into a wolf until I stumbled across Mys. I couldn't tell my lover how right things had felt in animal form and how wrong it now felt to be on two feet.

The high-spirited sprint to the store took an hour. I jogged onto the grass-studded, cracked, and crumbling car park with Mys on my back as the cashier was locking the doors. I fell to my knees at the edge of the property, and Mys slid from my back and leaned over me.

"Are you okay?" my lover whispered empathetically.

Chest heaving, I inclined my head in the affirmative. The trip had been rigorous, but I was fine. Better than fine, even. The physical activity had pushed the most undisciplined parts of me to the background. The feral thoughts crept back into my head as I rose to my feet. I seemed to hear every prey animal in the night.

The cashier smoking a cigarette got my attention. "Y'all need some help?" she asked. She was turning the key in the double doors. I remembered her scent from the day Aurie and I had gotten supplies. It took a second to remember that that had been only yesterday. It felt like lifetimes ago.

"No, we're, uh . . ." I headed toward her.

"Looking for your wife?" she supplied.

I stopped and cocked my head. "Have you . . . seen her?"

The woman with the missing tooth cast a worried glance over her shoulder before rushing to meet me by the pumps. "I don't want no trouble, okay? I seen the redhead girl hand her over to a man in a black car."

"Are you sure it was Aurie?" I described her, and my informant nodded emphatically. Mys migrated closer, realizing the woman had something important to say.

"I know who you're talking about," said the cashier. "Your wife, the one I seen with you the other day you came in. Thought I was seeing things—sometimes I do, you know—but tonight I seen the *three* of them get in that black car and take off: the redhead, your wife, and the man. Said something about goin' to see a man about a dog in Ponch'toula," she stated.

"I'm Detective Zyr Ravani, ma'am. Can I get your name?"

"Kathleen," she said, sucking the cigarette fretfully and gazing around again.

"Kathleen, you're a Seer, aren't you? Can you tell me what the man was like?" I asked.

She fondled a dime on a string around her neck as her gaze vacillated between me and Mys. "Something like you, *Rougarou*, but you don't scare me like he did."

I pulled back at the Cajun word for werewolf. "I promise you have nothing to worry about from me. Did he say where in Ponchatoula he was going?" I tried.

"His country house, that's all I know. Now, won't y'all wait over there off the store grounds. I don't rightly feel comfortable with you this close, being . . . you know."

I nodded, retreating with Mys. "Thank you for your time," I said in parting.

The Empath whispered, "What was that about?"

"She realized I wasn't human."

From an overgrown open field across from the store we watched the lights of the establishment flicker out one by one. The woman anxiously emptied rubbish into the garbage bin and made sure the doors were locked. Then she climbed into a dusty yellow Volkswagen and hightailed it.

"Humans are weird," Mys uttered.

"I think I know where Darcy is," I whispered. "As far as I know, he doesn't have a country house. He owns a luxury condo in the city, but his lawyers have a place just outside Ponchatoula. My money is on it."

I heard the telltale crunch of tires on concrete signaling Kittie Cad's imminent arrival. Her timing was impeccable. Mys beamed as the champagne Nissan skidded past the convenience store, which was harder to see with the lights out. Kittie braked, rolling down a window.

"Mitsuyo?" she squawked.

"Over here!" Mys called out as we ran to the car.

"All right, what the hell is going on, Detective? What did you do?" Kittie hopped out and came at me with a high heel.

Rejoicing at the sight of her, I wrapped her in a hug, and the shoe dangled ineffectively. "You have no idea how happy I am to see you," I professed.

"This isn't about a broken heart?" She side-eyed me as she stepped out of my embrace.

"Cut it out, Ms. Cad," Mys called her off. "I just got him back. Don't hurt him."

"Mm-hmm. I hear you. I'm still keeping my eye on him, boo boo."

Laughing, we climbed into the car. It felt good to laugh after the harrowing day. I instructed Kittie to take the fastest route to Bayou General. But with each mile, my anxiety escalated. When Mys bubbled with more questions, I shook my head. I couldn't say anything. I was too on edge. It was an agonizing two-hour drive that Kittie Cad managed to shave down to an hour and a half.

The Nissan swerved into the hospital car park on two wheels. The building was a square block of concrete and glass nestled in a well-lit corner of the city. A navy-blue-black sky provided a stark backdrop. Kittie's car was barely in park when Mys pointed in surprise at a young teenager pacing in front of the entrance to the hospital.

"Zyr, isn't that—"

"Haley," I finished the question as my eyebrows shot up. The seventeen-year-old had traded in psych ward scrubs for a floral smock, but she was definitely the girl from the picture I'd shown them earlier in the week. The young witch appeared to be waiting for us. I hopped from the Nissan and trotted toward her.

"What are you doing here?" I asked. Mys and Kittie Cad were on my heels. Haley yanked me toward the automatic doors of the hospital.

"We have to hurry," she urged. "By now, Mom has been notified I ditched the therapy center. We don't have much time before they come for me."

"How did you find out?" I asked, at a loss for words.

She flashed a wry grin. "Mom tried her best to keep it from me, but I knew my dreams had to mean *something*. All the signs led me here . . . now."

Mys and Kittie Cad matched her long-legged stride, wearing matching perplexed expressions. Upon our speedy approach, the elevator doors dinged open like magic. A tall, unassuming man in a gray suit beamed at us as we crowded the lift.

"Wallace?" I greeted him in surprise.

"Right on time," the guardian angel said in a deep bass.

"I've never seen you more than a few feet away from the hospital room. Uh, Kittie and Mys, this is Haley and Aurie's late father, Wallace Edison," I introduced.

"L-late for what?" Kittie asked.

"Nice to meet you, erm, Mr. Edison," Mys commented.

Wallace grinned. "I can tell you're wondering why my presence isn't alarming the locals. People only see what they need to see. As for my family, sadly, I don't remember my time on earth, but it's been exciting getting reacquainted with my daughters, even if the circumstances haven't been ideal."

Haley's smile held a twinge of sadness when she turned to me and changed the subject, "I managed to draw the storm inland to give you cover."

"That storm is *your* doing? I'm . . . deeply impressed and scared of you," I said in awe.

"Please, the storm was easy. A simple chat with the ancestors already whirling off the savannah. I can see pieces of the future and work basic spells, but what we're about to do is the *real* tough stuff. Facts."

The elevator doors opened on our floor, and the five of us filed from the carriage. Under brighter lights, Aurie's sister did a double take of Mys. "Damn. Hella lucky, sis," she whispered in compliment. I smiled in agreement as the Empath blushed. "Anyway, the visions took forever to figure out, but I think I finally got it. Detective, you know what you have to do?"

"I'm pretty sure," I answered uneasily.

Mys raised a hand, vaping. "I wish I knew what was going on here," they said, a wisp of white clouds surrounding their beautiful face. Kittie nodded in agreement, equally confused.

"Mages and witches aren't quite Supernaturals," I whispered, "but they have an understanding of magic that surpasses human knowledge, which gives them insight into our world. In some ways, you might say they're more powerful than our kind. That makes them an asset to someone like Darcy."

"And a threat," Haley added.

Signaling for quiet, we snuck past nurses and security guards, and I opened the door on the private room where I had met with Mrs. Edison along with Tegan weeks before. I wondered how much my partner had known at that point. As we rushed inside the room and closed the door behind us, Wallace further expounded on Mys's question.

"You asked what's going on here?" the angel rumbled. "Darcy Cyprian doesn't have Aurie. I never would've let that happen . . . Aurie's been right here from the start."

CHAPTER FIFTY-ONE

—

Aurie

September 12 | After Midnight

"Come forth," Darcy called to me. I spilled feetfirst to the floor, unfurling with all the enthusiasm of a woman marching to the guillotine. I slowly rose from a kneeling position and clutched the silk kimono, hiding my vulnerability.

The room in which I found myself was illuminated by a gilt chandelier. Vivid silence permeated the elegant space. My downcast eyes studied rich mahogany floors. I tried to make sense of two lines of white to either side of me, almost like a path starting at the front door and disappearing up the stairs. I tried to teleport out, but it was no use.

"Don't exhaust me with an escape attempt. You'll be unable to cross the salt, Aurelia," the vampire revealed. "There's a bit of sodium chlorate in the mix, highly volatile. Your companion can't assist you in getting rid of it either. The slightest wrong move could lead to a fire that creates its own oxygen and sustains itself. Don't trust me? See for yourself. Sweep it aside, Detective."

Tegan's wide eyes took in his face, and she shook her head. I vaguely remembered reading something in one of Mys's books about table salt keeping spirits in or out of a designated area, but Darcy had taken it to extremes. As a chemistry major, I knew sodium chlorate could be as dangerous as he claimed under the right conditions.

"Where the hell are we?" My voice echoed with more bravado than I felt. Darcy gestured at a silver platter of libations on an entryway table. I lifted my chin a fraction higher in defiance. "No, thank you. The last time I accepted your hospitality, I wound up dead," I said through clenched teeth.

"We're home. Be amicable," he suggested.

"I told you, I don't drink anymore," said Tegan, hugging herself.

We were in the foyer of a great house. With the front door still open behind us, winds whipped in from the night. Tegan evaluated the antebellum plantation with dilated pupils that confessed her terror. The setting seemed ripe for dire expectations, least of all the coming hurricane.

I turned away from the storm. Majestic baroque balustrades traced a wide staircase to a second level and then a third. There was a woman with white-blond hair studying us. She retreated into the shadows when she saw me watching.

Another stood at the foot of the stairs. She appeared a few years older than me, tall and statuesque. The storm made tendrils of long wine-dark hair dance across her eyes, but she swept the locks behind her fair-complexioned ear to glare at the vampire. Her stern, handsome face was uncompromising.

"You know you should not have brought them here." The timbre of her voice sent shivers through me. Power emanated from her, and I wondered what type of Supernatural she was.

Darcy flashed an indolent smile. "I don't expect the three of you to be privy to this, Mal. You and your sisters should have the night to yourselves."

The dark-haired woman gathered the folds of a sumptuous gold and black brocade skirt and fled the house, calling over her shoulder, "Ava! Cherie!" Two rare birds flew down the stairs and flitted after her into the dreary night. I hardly saw what they looked like. Upon their exit, the heavy doors slammed shut, and the chandelier candles guttered but stayed alight.

Now, I was alone with them—my murderer and the rapist who had drugged me the night I was killed. This didn't bode well.

"Master Cyprian," a male voice said from the stairs.

So, we weren't entirely alone. Good.

I regarded the second landing and discovered a young man dressed in black and white livery. He could have stepped out of the nineteenth century. In fact, the whole house had the feeling of time standing still. The servant wore a blank expression and held a thick leash. I sucked in a breath at the large black-gray wolf nosing at his feet.

"The room for the sacrifice is prepared," he announced.

Darcy cupped an arm around Tegan and me and whispered conspiratorially, "Are you sure you don't want that drink now?"

•••

The artwork on the bedroom walls had to be worth a fortune. The Persian rug under my bare feet was probably worth double that. Everything in the elite country estate screamed grandeur. I sat on the satin-covered high canopy bed, watching Tegan gnaw her fingernails and frantically pace.

"It doesn't make sense. None of this makes sense," she whimpered.

"It does if you accept Overlay City is real, but you never accepted that, did you? You honestly thought Zyr was a little fucked-up in the head." I sighed, knowing she couldn't hear me. "And you thought Darcy was indulging him in some way."

"Vampires!" She grunted a laugh. "Oh God, help me. I've gotta get out of here."

"But you knew I was haunting the cabin. I showed you!"

She looped back to the window and stared out at trees battered and thrashed by the storm. I was right next to her, and she had no idea. Groaning, I fell backward to the mattress and thumped the pillows in frustration. Tegan jumped and stared at the bed.

"Aurie?" she stuttered.

I sat up. "No shit, Sherlock."

"Aurie, if that's you, give me some sort of sign."

I marched over to the delicate white Chantilly lace dress hanging on the chifforobe. Darcy had asked me to wear it to dinner, which would be served within the hour. Given I had only the kimono to cover me, I was happy to oblige. Tegan had already changed into a long pink chiffon wrap courtesy of the vampire.

I lifted the hanger and turned to her. "Is this enough of a sign?" I asked as I tore it off the hanger and started dressing. Once the fabric settled over my skin, it disappeared. Because it was transmuted by contact with Supernaturals, it conformed to my type, and since I was invisible to her, the dress became invisible.

Tegan backpedaled, covering her mouth. "No. No! I'm losing it. I have to be."

I rolled my eyes. We didn't have time for this. If there was some way out, she could find it. The pathways of salt that crisscrossed the house kept me bound to where Darcy wanted me, but not her. She just couldn't disturb it violently. Although he had locked the front door from the inside and secreted away the key, the detective had the freedom to snoop for other exits.

I searched the escritoire and came up with a pen, but no paper. Swiveling, I saw a novel on the table by the bed. Perfect! I grabbed the pen and dashed across the room to grab the book. With each movement, Tegan visibly wilted as realization dawned.

"I only half believed Zyr's explanation about Overlay City," she whispered, "but whoever you are, you can't be the ghost of Aurie Edison."

Exasperated, I turned to a blank page at the back of the book. *Why not??* I wrote, scratching two lines beneath the word for emphasis. I turned the writing toward her.

"Because I didn't kill her," she said emphatically. "If you're her, if you're dead, tell me something only Aurie would know."

I smirked, scribbling down, *When I was fourteen, I fell off a skateboard and blacked out for two days. That's how I got the scar on my forehead.*

She read that and shook her head. "Even if Aurie has a scar, anyone with access to social media probably knows it, and there's no telling how she got it."

I have a birthmark on my inner thigh. Few people know that besides Zyr and Mys because we're lovers. I wrote, desperate to get through to her. *I can promise you your partner will never forgive you for harming us. If you truly care about Zyr, work with me. Otherwise, I'll soon see you on the other side because Darcy Cyprian absolutely can't be trusted!*

After Tegan read the missive, she started pacing again. I wasn't sure she believed me, but at least she was listening. "Why does Cyprian want us here? I mean, for all he knows, you're not. You're in some hospital bed across town. But why does he want *me* here?" she asked the room at large.

I sat on the edge of the bed, pondering that. Of course, Darcy knew I was present. He could plainly see me. Tegan was blind to the truth because she wasn't a Supernatural. So, her question was valid. Why did the vampire want her?

Before I could formulate a response, there was a knock at the door, and a servant entered. The young maid addressed the mauve, silk-papered wall. "Dinner is served, *mam'selles.*"

I waited for her to leave to write another note to Tegan. "Whatever he wants, it can't be good," I whispered as I jotted it down: *Darcy has killed before, and he'll kill again. Take this dinner opportunity to find an escape.*

"What about you?" she had the decency to ask. There was another knock at the door.

My hand trembled as I wrote instructions as fast as I could: *Get to the embassy and talk to the Council of Overlay Affairs. Tell them Darcy kidnapped you. Free Zyr. He's our only hope.*

•••

The dining room was as impressive as the rest of the house, rendered in dark woods and warm tones. Yellow lamplight turned the cream damask walls golden. An oversized gold mirror above the unused fireplace magnified the space.

I hesitated at the threshold, feeling underdressed without shoes. I had attended my share of sophisticated dinner parties with Mom and Haley, but I was out of my element in this museum. The place couldn't be called a home without irony.

Rather than a chandelier, an odd contraption swung over the eight-person dining table. I suddenly realized it was a fan. It stirred the rain-laden air blowing in from floor-to-ceiling windows open along one wall. Dinnertime would include a serenade by the storm, apparently.

Darcy rose from the head of the table and clapped at the sight of us. "You both are magnificent, ladies. I can sometimes be sentimental. Thank you for indulging me," he said.

"Would you indulge *me?*" I asked, taking a seat. Darcy came around and pushed in my chair. His fingers grazed my shoulders, and I wanted to shun him. It took everything in me to remain still.

"What would you like, ma louloute?"

"Explain to me what's going on here."

"We have business to attend to later, but right now we're simply enjoying an intimate dinner between friends. Ms. Stoney, is your seat to your liking?" He raised an eyebrow at the detective. She cast around like a lost child on the first day of school, but she managed a nod. "Splendid, my pet. Eat up."

The longboard was spread with a light repast of country ham, mashed potatoes, and boiled corn on the cob. Tegan served herself and ate at a distracted pace. Whenever the vampire gave all his attention to me, her shrewd cornflower eyes scanned the room, and it dawned on me the damsel in distress act was exactly that. An act.

"You know that's not what I meant," I tried again.

"What did you mean, Aurie? We seem to get lost in translation. For example," he said, "when I asked if you would be my mistress, I thought it was understood to be a rhetorical question. The answer was an obvious, 'Of course, my dear.'"

The vampire whistled for the servant with the wolf. As the animal trotted into the elegant dining room on its leash, Darcy grabbed fork and knife and stood at the longboard, carving ham for the beast. The vampire's plate remained empty. Naturally. I wondered if he drank blood from a wineglass or preferred it straight from the source. Had I been hungry, the very thought would have been enough to turn my stomach.

"Why are you keeping Tegan hostage if you have me?" I asked.

"Tegan, you are an honored guest," said Darcy, laying a hand over hers. "I apologize for your inability to join in our conversation, but Aurie was asking why you remain. The simple answer is I couldn't wait to begin my union with you, Aurie, and I need a witness to ensure all things are right and proper. Now, both of you enjoy the meal. We have a long day ahead of us."

Not only was the thought of us being united repulsive, but I had a sneaking suspicion the vampire was lying about Tegan's role here. A servant had already announced that a room had been prepared for *the sacrifice*. Although Tegan had no clue what that meant, I did. Aside from the staff—who I was certain Darcy didn't see as equals—she was the only other person here. She had to be the vessel.

I could neither forget what she had done to me nor forgive her for what she had done to Mys. However, I sure as hell didn't want Zyr's partner killed so her body could house my Soul.

"I'm dead, Darcy. I no longer need food," I muttered as I put away my fork with disinterest.

He threw down his napkin and grimaced but recovered his composure before losing his temper. "Would you like to tour the gardens instead? In our condition, the weather isn't a deterrent. I relish a stormy night's stroll."

I brightened. Tegan could make a getaway. "Your home is beautiful. I'd love a tour of the entire estate and grounds!"

"Splendid!" Darcy held up the glass medicine bottle and made a sound of enjoyment when my smile wavered. "It's the only way I can trust you, my sweet puppy. On a leash until you're housebroken."

I casually shrugged, though I wanted to crawl the length of the table and jam a steak knife into his eye socket. Deadass. I dialed down my attitude. Whatever it took for Tegan to find Zyr before this deranged monster made the two of us share one skin. Peeping over at Tegan, I remembered Mys saying she wanted to be of service. This was her chance.

Darcy's fingers clasped mine as we headed out of the dining room. His eyes swept my body in the Chantilly dress, and I wanted to disappear. He hesitated in the archway, giving instructions for his personnel to keep the detective comfortable. While he was talking, the maid rushed in and whispered something in his ear.

There was a book in her hand. I held my breath. So did Detective Stoney. I saw her freeze in my periphery as Darcy flipped open the book and read. He clicked his tongue. "I thought we were better than this, ladies." Holding up the copy of Lewis Carroll's *Through the Looking-Glass*, he said, "This was a first edition."

"It's not what it looks like," Tegan whispered.

The vampire left my side and curtly approached her. "Is it ever with you?"

"Wait! I'd like my new body unmarked. Please, Darcy!" I shouted from the door.

"This?" Looking at me, he pointed at Tegan in perplexed amusement. "This isn't yours. It's dinner. I knew she wouldn't last the night. Women like her never do."

No! I squeezed my eyes shut as he fed off the last person who could've saved me. If Tegan wasn't the sacrificial lamb, then who was?

CHAPTER FIFTY-TWO

—

Mys

September 12 | After Midnight

Visiting hours were long over, but Haley's magic had ensured that no one saw us sneak into the private hospital room. At the sight of the girl in the bed, I felt like I was in the topsy-turviest manga ever. I stared into the unmistakable face of Aurie Edison. She was alive. Her eyes were closed. Her head was thickly bandaged, and her wrist was in a splint. One leg was elevated in a cast. Where the other should have been, there was nothing but empty space below the knee. Yet, her chest was slowly rising and falling. Definitely alive.

"It's worse than I imagined," Haley murmured with a studied frown.

"She's been here all along?" I was almost afraid to ask. As if asking would break the spell, and I would wake up again in the woods with everyone I loved gone. I glanced at Zyr, who stepped up beside me.

"Yes," he replied, "which is why Tegan thought Aurie couldn't be a ghost. Aurie never died. Wallace confirmed what I suspected: crossing over might've led to her waking from the coma."

"You knew how to help her all along?" I felt destroyed.

Zyr spread his hands plaintively. "Don't you think I tried? That was why I was willing to do anything to help Aurie complete her unfinished business—to help her wake up."

"Regardless, she's beautiful, Mys!" Kittie Cad interjected as she read the room. "It's a miracle she survived the accident."

Wallace spoke up behind us, "Aurie was hit with such force that she had bleeding on the brain, several broken bones, and a compression injury that led to losing her leg. Keeping her alive was my doing."

My best friend peered at the guardian. "How did you manage?" she asked. He unfolded radiant wings, and Kittie's jaw dropped. "Uh-uh, I don't think I'll ever get used to your world, Mitsuyo."

I tried to laugh, but the mood in the room was somber for such a happy reunion. Zyr had his eyes glued to the clock. Haley leaned against the bay window, the cityscape a backdrop to her worried frown. I was assailed by their uncertainty, a flurry of agitated emotions keeping us all uneasy. Underscoring it was my own pain.

I turned to the detective. "Why didn't you tell us, Senpai?"

"Fear, hubris, misguidance? So many reasons." He frowned. "None of them seem valid now. It started with the Council trying to ensure Cyprian had enough loopholes to evade a conviction, so they wrote new legislation to toss high-profile cases if certain information was leaked. I couldn't risk that. Long as the vampire's on the loose, all of us are in grave danger.

"And given how tenuous Aurie's hold on reality got over time, I started to wonder if hearing she was in a coma that she might or might not come out of would shatter her psyche beyond repair . . ." He trailed off with a shrug.

"You have no idea how scary it is when you think your mind is against you," Haley murmured quietly.

"You said you would be more transparent after we . . ." I bit my lip and looked down.

Zyr tucked a knuckle beneath my chin to lift my gaze. "Everything I learned after that, I shared with you and Aurie. Sure, I worried Cyprian would use his voice tricks to coerce one of you into revealing something crucial, but I shared anyway. I've been tormented by the things I couldn't say from the very night of that penthouse party."

"That fateful night." Haley sighed. "You know, I think I made it out of the hotel just as she got up and followed you, Mys."

Kittie Cad nodded at me, surely remembering the day I'd told her about the accident. Forever ago. I glanced at Aurie in the hospital bed. "She thought I could help with her unfinished business, but I had no idea what to do. I still don't know. What's next?" I shrugged in confusion.

"Next? I hope it involves you forgiving me," Zyr murmured.

His glistening eyes begged for reprieve as mine dropped to the floor again. The old me would've written him off, but this lovelorn version couldn't. Maybe part of Aurie's suggestion that I try harder was not reerecting walls around my heart. It felt pointless to pretend I could stay mad at him.

"For the record," I cleared the lump from my throat and swiped away a tear, "I can't handle any more fine print. Understand?"

Zyr pulled me into a hug, breathing a tremulous sigh of relief into my hair. As his lips grazed my forehead, he agreed. "No more fine print. Everything—past and present—is in all caps from here on out."

"Awww!" Haley pushed away from the window to join the hug. "After everything Aurie has been through, I'm just glad you guys took care of her, and I'm glad you taught me the truth about Overlay City, Zyr."

"I felt you needed a crash course." He reexamined the wall clock. "At the start of this investigation, it was a simple leaving the scene with a victim in critical condition. Finding Aurie's Soul wandering the city was a shocker for me."

"Actually, I believe she's done something like this before," Wallace reflected.

Haley scrunched her face at her late father. "What do you mean?" she asked.

"According to my charge file, Aurie had a skateboard accident and was out for two days. While unconscious in the hospital, she thought she was at your grandmother's house the whole time."

"Just like now," Haley gasped.

He tapped his forehead and pointed at her. "As a guardian, there's only so much I'm permitted to tell you. But think about it."

"What if her Soul really was at Grandma's?" she pieced together.

I said, "That would be pretty damn unique—"

"Pretty damn *special!*" Zyr said simultaneously. "That's what got Darcy's attention! If that's the case, it would mean that you're both . . ."

From her side of the hospital bed, Haley arched an eyebrow. "Witches? So, it runs in the family? I see things that aren't there, and she goes places she shouldn't be."

"And if Cyprian has an inkling of that fact, he's trying to use Aurie to cement his standing within the Council of Overlay Affairs. Witches tend to be autonomous, above the laws and norms of our Supernatural realms *and* their real world. Historically, those who have chosen to mingle in our affairs were well-received. Revered, more like," said Zyr.

Haley and Aurie were both witches. My gaze shot to Wallace for confirmation, but his attention was on the TV mounted in a corner of the room. He had found The Weather Channel and settled in an armchair beside the hospital bed.

Kittie joined me at the foot of the bed, watching the green, yellow, orange, and red radar splotches on the television screen. We were under a hurricane warning, with the storm slated to make landfall along the coast within hours.

As the meteorologist covered the swift-moving weather system, the screen filled with an image of the cyclone's large, swirling clouds. Its footprint covered three states. I was glad Haley had assured us it would be a glorified wind event when all was said and done.

"We're running out of time for Aurie to heal without my intervention." Zyr sighed.

Wallace nodded in agreement. "As I said, there are limitations to what I can do. For example, I can't mend her body and Soul. We have to rely on less conventional methods. I know you've been trying to avoid this, Detective, but I think it's time you change her."

"Change her?" Kittie repeated with a touch of fear.

"You don't mean what I think you mean, do you?" I asked.

Haley crossed her arms and inclined her head. "He does," she acknowledged. "For the past few weeks, I've dreamed of wolves. I knew it would come to this, but like you, Detective, I was hoping we had other options. She's not healed enough to wake from the coma on her own."

"As a wolf, she'll heal faster," Zyr murmured as he stroked Aurie's face. "Best-case scenario, she wakes from her coma with her Soul out of Darcy's clutches."

"Okay, I can't take up for you anymore, Detective. Why didn't you try to fix this sooner?" Kittie sputtered.

"Because," I said as the blood drained from my face. "She could die from the bite . . . or Zyr could lose control and . . ." I couldn't bring myself to admit Aurie could become his prey. I didn't want to think of how close to feral Zyr already was.

He shuddered at the thought too. "That's the worst-case scenario, but we're in a hospital. If anything goes wrong, she can get immediate medical treatment."

"And will she be . . . whole?" I asked. Zyr grimaced and shrugged as I swallowed thickly. "You can't mess up, Senpai." All the weeks of thinking there was no future for us receded into memory. The three of us had a fighting chance, but not if things went wrong tonight.

"Can someone keep an eye on the nurses' station?" Haley requested.

"I'll go," Kittie Cad volunteered. She slipped out of the hospital room, leaving the rest of us with the patient.

Zyr eased the blanket from Aurie's unmoving form. Her hospital gown was loose enough to reveal the smooth brown skin of her torso, and we both stared at three slash marks. They were fresh. I met his gaze as he realized the wounds were from our morning sex session. I squared my jaw. Another wave of doubt assailed me.

Haley seemed to sense my reticence. "I can't say my visions show me everything, but I know this is our path, and I know the time is now," she murmured, placing a hand on mine. I tried to feel reassured.

Zyr hastily removed Aurie's sensors and unhooked the intravenous line. I noticed Haley staring at the monitors, using her magic to keep them bleeping and blurping so as not to alarm the nurses. The teenager edged closer to the door with me and gave the werewolf a wide berth.

It was Wallace who used the remote to raise the hospital bed in a semireclined position. He threw open the curtain. The moon might have been full, but it was covered by thick clouds.

Zyr's gaze swept over the three of us. "Could you guys turn away?" he asked with awkward hesitance. I was more than happy to avert my gaze; so was Haley.

Wallace, on the other hand, remained unmoved. "I'd rather keep watch if it's all the same with you. Protecting her is kind of my job." He raised eyebrows for Zyr to carry on. My partner's apprehension trickled like ice water through my veins. Zyr wasn't sure he could do it.

"Think of the alternative," I murmured without facing him. "As you said, last-ditch effort. We have no idea what Darcy might be doing to her right now. Would you rather she suffer the fleeting pain of transformation, or whatever he has in store for her?" It was a nice pep talk, but I was petrified too. I sipped from the vape pen.

I winced at the dramatic grunt and gasp of the werewolf shedding his man-shape in favor of the animal. I didn't dare look after his plaintive yelp. I heard a shuffle and pictured the canine nosing around the bed. Then there was the deeper rumble of a growl, followed by what could only be the crunch of teeth sinking into flesh.

I shrank into myself, and Haley groaned in discomfort. Yet, I tamped down on my fear, filling my head with memories of the sensual love bites Zyr regularly dispensed during sex. It was such a freakish juxtaposition.

"Haley, I think we need you," Wallace murmured.

From my periphery, I witnessed Aurie's sister turn and raise her hand. Glowering at the sky, her fingers blurred with energy, and a spill of moonlight astonishingly washed over the hospital room. Drawing in a sharp breath, Haley dropped her hand after bringing the light nearer.

I caught her as she pivoted away from the strange optics of Aurie's transformation. There was the rattle of metal, the whisper of blankets and sheets being disturbed. Almost like someone forcefully shaking the bed. The disruptive noises grew louder. I heeded the door, hoping no one outside heard. At another bark from Zyr, there was an answering bay that sounded different than the first.

"Is it done?" I chanced a peek. My eyes widened at the sorrel-colored wolf on the hospital bed. Zyr crouched on the other side, reaching a hand toward the pile of clothes that had withered from his frame when he shape-shifted.

"It's finished," he breathed.

But the guardian shook his head. "I think there's been some mistake."

Zyr and I both regarded him. "What are you talking about? She's alert, healed. It went better than I had hoped," the detective said. Haley stepped toward Aurie, and the four-legged creature pawing the sheets snarled. Haley stiffened.

"No, Aurie isn't in there," the guardian insisted. He gestured at the female wolf with helpless open hands. I felt the blood drain from my face as I realized his meaning.

"Oh gods," I whispered in dismay. We had Aurie's body, but Darcy Cyprian still had her Soul.

CHAPTER FIFTY-THREE
—
Zyr

September 12 | Before Daybreak

I had done this. I had turned Aurie Edison—in contempt of the law,
undeterred by my lover's protestations, against my own best instincts—
although the latter was least reliable. I was rapidly losing my mind, and
I wondered if the change had seemed like a good idea only because I
was going insane.

The she-wolf paced the length of the semireclined hospital bed and
whimpered. Her tawny fur was sorrel and cocoa, and her eyes were
terra-cotta. She had all four legs. She was a beautiful specimen, but
an aberration. She circled the narrow cot with growing disquiet, her
foreclaws tearing at the bedding.

When she barked in distress, each sound caused Mys to flinch and glare
at the hospital room door. I hurriedly donned my clothes, worried too.
Through the privacy window, I spotted our accomplice inconspicuously
flirting up a nurse, even though it was well past visiting hours.

Kittie would signal if anyone headed our way, but we couldn't very
well carry a wolf out. I skipped to the window overlooking the city.

Jackpot. The bay window wasn't sealed. I got it wide enough for an oversized wolf to squeeze out. We could feasibly scale the building together.

However, the buffeting winds tried gamely to yank the window latch from my clutch. We were on the uppermost floor of the modest-height hospital. I fought the gusts until I had to accept we couldn't go outside in this weather.

Blinking against the rain, the smell of the storm made me crave expanses where I could run wild and free. As I receded into the private hospital room, closing the window behind me, I dug two fingers into my temples and rubbed at my pounding headache. I was deteriorating, but this wasn't about me.

My gaze flew to Haley. "Can you call it off?" I asked brusquely.

The teen shook her head. "The bad weather is to keep humans from seeing what we do tonight. When you explained the Overlay laws, I thought a storm could cloak our getaway. Now the hurricane is too close; it'll take hours to move it."

"Not to mention," Wallace said quietly, "she's too agitated to climb down." The dauntless angel approached the feral wolf on the bed. A menacing growl rumbled through the room, but he petted the canine, and his touch seemed to have a curative effect. The wolf hopped down and settled at his feet.

Mys pleaded with me, "You have to fix this."

"If I'm wrong about Cyprian being at his lawyers' estate in Ponchatoula, I don't know whether I can." The words dropped from my mouth like lead. I hated to admit it. Inside every shifter was an animal spirit that was separate from us, but one with us. I had apparently freed the animal within Aurie while the woman was still without.

I jerked my head to fend off another flash of savagery that clawed and scraped in my skull. Aurie was a feral husk of what she should have been—just like I was becoming. The flaky, briny redness drying on my lips was like a lover's kiss, and the call of the hunt was almost too loud to ignore. It had taken Herculean effort to refrain from biting her more than once.

Soothing fingers traced my spine, but dervishes of foreboding swirled inside me. "Are you okay?" Mys whispered.

I pressed a hand to my head. "Nahin, I should've realized sooner that my partner was covering for Cyprian. God, I wish I knew how deep Tegan's involvement is. So many unanswered questions. I've never trusted my instincts less."

"She was behind the wheel," said Wallace, giving the she-wolf a vigorous scratch.

"Come again?" I wasn't sure I had heard him correctly.

The guardian angel looked at me. "You asked the depth of your partner's involvement. Detective Tegan Stoney was behind the wheel that night, trying to get help for Aurie. She saw Aurie disoriented and scared outside Century Luxe. Unfortunately, Tegan was too impaired herself to manage the big SUV she'd borrowed from her ex."

I choked, remembering the scent of coffee, mouthwash, and something else on her that night . . . liquor. When Tegan and I had arrived on the scene, I'd told myself what she did on the weekend was none of my business, but I had known she'd been drinking.

"Are you saying Detective Stoney hit my sister? By *accident*?" Haley broke our stunned silence.

The angel tipped his head.

"Ho-ly shit," Mys uttered in disbelief.

"Why didn't you tell me sooner? You could've saved Aurie from falling into Cyprian's hands!" I almost shouted. Mys grabbed me and shushed me. The truth hit me, and I sobered. "You couldn't say anything that would affect her destiny."

"That's no longer an issue," Wallace said with a nod.

"How did Tegan get involved with Cyprian?" I drilled him.

"He sent his security guards after Aurelia, but they made it to street level too late to save her. One of his men saw Tegan leaving the scene."

"But, of course, the vampires fled Century Luxe before the ambulance and police arrived." I filled in the blanks.

"I protected Aurie as best I could. Her mother unwittingly picked up the slack by keeping information about the family from leaking to the press. Later, Cyprian used his knowledge of what Tegan had done to blackmail your partner into disrupting the investigation," Wallace explained.

Shaking my head, I pushed my hands through my hair, then let my head fall back. My eyes stung, and my throat burned.

"Everything she did tonight, she did for you," he added. "There was no malicious intent. Tegan didn't believe she was delivering Aurie's actual ghost to an actual vampire. She knew Aurie was right here at the hospital. Tegan thought whoever or whatever she was delivering to Darcy was an imposter."

Haley tore at her thumbnail, mumbling to herself, "Yeah, well, whatever Tegan was thinking doesn't matter. We've gotta get this wolf outta here."

I considered mentally flooding the she-wolf with the awareness we needed to get her downstairs without fanfare.

Wolves like me—raised with an understanding of the flimsy barrier separating man-thoughts and the wildness waiting in our heads—had no trouble understanding the complex mental language. But this fledgling had never been trained. Her mind would struggle to retain the slippery concepts I tried to slide inside.

"Conjure a leash. We'll have to lead her," I said to Haley.

"Hand me the IV line. It's easier to work with something tangible than to create it out of thin air. The only question is . . . how do we get past the nurses' station with a wolf on a leash?" She blinked at me as Wallace tore the line from the drip and handed it to her. Running the plastic tubing through nimble, graceful fingers, Haley began to flatten it and transfigure it into a leather strap. With a few more strokes of her hand, she dropped the leash and collar into my palm.

"Haley, change into Aurie's hospital gown," Mys blurted.

My eyes lit up at what the Empath had in mind. "It could work," I said as Haley darted to the en suite to change.

Mys held up fresh scrubs from the wardrobe and peered at me for my opinion. "I could be a nurse?"

"Absolutely. Staff here have seen my face enough to know me. They won't stop Detective Zyr Ravani and *Dr.* Wallace Edison from transporting a sensitive patient."

"I'll use a glamor to appear bandaged and beat-up. One more thing." Haley brushed her father's shoulder's in passing, and the guardian's unassuming business suit was covered by a white coat. "But the wolf?" she asked, hopping onto the hospital bed to play her part.

"An oversized police dog," I suggested.

"The divine comfort I've provided should last the duration of our descent, but try not to rile her," Wallace replied.

"What's Plan B?" Mys asked. Even out of the all-black joggers and hoodie, the pallor of their skin was impossible to miss. I raided the drawer for bandages and changed the dirty butterfly tape at their temple, wishing I had never gotten them into this. I blamed myself. Cyprian was my problem.

"Plan B is we don't fuck up Plan A," I said wryly. Mys flashed a smile and pulled me into a kiss.

Opening the door of the private hospital room, the group of us filed out again—completely transformed from how we had entered. Mys pushed the hospital bed, and Haley lay immobile as I led the "police dog." Wallace strolled ahead of us to the elevators with the aloof gait of a busy physician. Kittie Cad looked up from flirting and grinned in surprise. Quickly excusing herself, she darted into the lift with us.

The good doctor blocked the elevator camera by holding up the patient's file until we reached the ground floor. No one seemed to notice when we ditched the props in the parking garage and sprinted across the car park to Kittie's Nissan, disappearing into the tempestuous night.

CHAPTER FIFTY-FOUR
—
Aurie

September 12 | Before Daybreak

I couldn't watch him kill her. I didn't want to hear what was happening. I shoved aside the maid who had betrayed us and ran from the gilded dining room, nausea cramping my insides. There was no way out of the house. The lines of salt kept me confined to one path. So, my bare feet slid on the hardwood in a mad dash to the guest room.

I raced up the stairs to the room we had been appointed. Slamming the chamber door behind me, I gulped air. I was at his mercy. Darcy had coerced Tegan to come with us, giving her false hope she'd make it out alive, all the while knowing he would kill her. He was a deranged psychopath, and I was at his mercy.

I gave up thinking help would come. I dropped to my knees and skittered along the perimeter of salt in search of an opening. With mounting desperation, I shoved aside furniture, squinted under the chifforobe, tore at the bedcovers.

Everywhere I turned, the line of salt was unbroken. I couldn't sweep it away. Sodium chlorate was volatile on its own. But if Darcy had added anything to the mixture—as he claimed—the salt could go up in flames at the slightest disturbance.

I just needed a glass of water to render the $NaClO_3$ harmless. Yet, Darcy had made sure the bathrooms were out of reach to me. My brief surge of adrenaline petered to hopelessness.

Tears soaked my face as my nose ran, and harsh sobs punctuated my hyperventilating. I backed up to the bed and gave the room one last terrified survey. There was even salt covering the windows.

"Why the fuck did you choose me?" I screamed.

The outburst shattered the mirror above the bureau. Whatever remained of my sanity felt broken in as many pieces. As I cried out again in frustration, the expensive art on the walls crashed to the hardwood floor. I whirled in an arc, letting the mad energy spiral out of control, and the fabric clothing the four-poster canopy whipped in the wind that spun from my body.

I begged to become a full-blown poltergeist. I flickered in and out, but my Soul clung stubbornly to this plane. Sobbing, I threw myself to the bed.

"She was warned she'd become dinner if she offended me," Darcy Cyprian said from the door. I sat up abruptly and stared daggers at him. He extended a glass of absinthe, but I refused it. As he sat on the bed, I crawled to the other side of the mattress. "I'm brutally honest, Aurelia."

"You're a literal fucking monster, that's what you are," I sneered in contempt.

"Enough with the histrionics," he chastened in a dulcet voice. His serene expression was illuminated by saffron light from the bedside lamp. This gentle persona he put on for my sake was more disturbing than if he had come in ranting and raving.

Darcy reached across the chasm to cleanse my face with his handkerchief. I recoiled, and he snatched my chin hard enough for his nails to pierce my phantom flesh. I hitched in a breath. Yes, there was the menacing behavior I expected. His eyes, the color of the absinthe in the glass, bore into mine, and his chiseled mouth became a constricted pout.

"There now." He smiled finally. "Your lovely face is dry. You should thank me."

"Th-thank you," I forced myself to say.

He gave a blasé chuckle. "I know there's no love lost between you and Tegan. She killed you, after all. Take the drink. I added Volupt to settle your nerves."

Trembling, I took it because I had no choice. "Why are you doing this?" I whispered.

"You're really going to have to work on your listening skills," he murmured. "I told you. We're embarking on an extended lifetime together."

"Because you want me as your sexual partner?"

Humming, he raked his fingers through my hair and used a knuckle to catch an errant teardrop from my lashes. Under his touch, I gagged inside, but I knew better than to respond with open revulsion. His frigid gaze said he would be unforgiving.

"The vessel I've chosen for you is top of the line," he said, changing the subject.

"Where is she?" I rasped. I wanted to understand. If Tegan wasn't the vessel, then who was?

"You'll meet her soon. A powerful girl like you—combined with her pedigree—will make a truly one-of-a-kind Supernatural. Beauty, aptitude, wealth, immortality."

"I never asked for any of that." I wiped another tear as my face fell.

"Did you know the ancient Greeks were said to have a drug of forgetfulness?" Putting a finger to my lips, he scooted closer. "They called it Nepenthe. Homer's *Odyssey* says that it banished all grief and sorrows. Modern scholars can't quite agree on whether it was a fictional medicine or, indeed, opium, but here in Overlay we have an equivalent: Obliviscor.

"I gave it to you that night in the penthouse to wipe your memories and plant a new life story. Because you were living a sorrowful existence, Aurelia. So much suppression of natural talent hidden in that anal-retentive head of yours."

I stared at the ripples in the absinthe glass made by my quaking hands. "So you lied. You weren't trying to replace her. You meant to do away with me from the very beginning."

He tilted his head. "No, no, no, no. You misunderstand. From the moment I met you, only you would do, but the devil is in the details. I needed you to believe you were greater than the sum of your history. It was . . . regrettable that Detective Stoney's indiscretion derailed me. I almost had you convinced a family friend was handling your sister."

"Patricia," I surmised.

"I wouldn't know. I simply coaxed you to think of someone you trusted. Incidentally, we'll have to work on your mental defenses. Especially if I'm to make you the wife of the soon-to-be highest member of the Council."

"*Wife*? You're insane. I'd rather be dead than married to you."

"Yet, you were willing to share my bed?" He laughed. "Interesting. You're a witch, Aurie. A sorceress, a mage, a powerful enchantress. Did you know that? I'm guessing you didn't."

What the hell? My eyes widened. It dawned on me he must mean Haley, but I didn't correct him. I shrank into myself as he cozied closer.

"You're worth more to me as my betrothed than as a bedmate, Mrs. Darcy Cyprian, my immortal wife," he gloated. "And now that you've been in my world, I'm sure you realize the merits of such an elevation in status without me resorting to drugging you and planting false memories, am I right?"

I set the glass of absinthe on the bedside table and faced him. "What happens if I don't agree to this?" It was swagger, but what was the use of continuing to cower? He already intended to have his way, whether I went like a lamb to the slaughter or kicking and howling the whole ride.

He tightened his mouth, picking at invisible lint on his dinner jacket. "Your Soul will be transferred as soon as the loa arrives. I suggest you prepare for a new way of life."

"What about my old life?" I countered.

"You weren't happy with your old life!" Darcy flared with controlled rage. "You were too afraid to lose it. Even now, with every moment you've felt alive, you've feared life's temporality! Your safe bubble is an illusion. No matter how you've held fast to your calculations of risk and reward, you've erred, Aurelia. Escape this irony of man's condition. Overcome your terror of death by embracing eternal life."

A helpless wave of anguish washed over me because he was right on many levels—especially about the existential angst—and yet he was wrong in his final assessment. I suddenly understood why I had felt whole and fully alive with Zyr and Mys. Not because I'd imagined my feelings for them might somehow transcend time, but because the fear that love couldn't last forever hadn't conquered the fear of never having loved them at all.

It was, I had discovered, better to have loved. It was better to have risked, failed, suffered, lived my best flawed life, than not. And in my final act, I intended to prove that to Darcy Cyprian.

"You're making a big mistake," I said flatly. He had no idea Haley was the powerful witch he wanted, but I would gladly take her place. I couldn't let my sister suffer the eternal hell of being married to him.

"Try to defy me, and everyone you love will suffer. Trust me. Contrary to what you may believe . . ." He walked around to my side of the bed and leaned into my face. "I never lie."

•••

I didn't drink the Volupt-laced absinthe. After Darcy left the room, I flipped back the covers and poured the liquid beneath one of the pillows on the opulent bed. The Supernatural drug might've soothed my troubled thoughts, but I didn't want to be placated. I paced my metaphorical gilded cage, mindful of the servants, mindful of the bumps and thumps in the dark and scary house, mindful of the coming Resurrection.

At the same time, my joyless thoughts searched for a silver lining. If I became the vampire's wife, my mother could retire in greater luxury. Haley would become the show-stopping supermodel she had always wanted to be. Would the position lend me the clout to save Zyr from whatever Yazeed had cooked up with the other council members? I could be my remaining lover's last hope. This would be the reward I extracted from this Faustian bargain.

Noticing the pallor of the morning sun behind the storm, I rushed to the window. My fingers accidentally brushed the line of salt on the windowsill, and I choked on a strangled scream. It burned savagely, though I suspected that was a Supernatural effect rather than a physical one. With more care, I stared through the glass, finding the rain and wind fiercer than ever. Still, an old-model Lincoln Town Car was making its way toward the house along the long plantation drive.

As I squinted at the car, the maid who had ratted out Tegan and I knocked to announce Master Darcy wanted me in the music room. I unclenched my teeth and followed her down the stairs to the great hall, through another corridor lined with exquisite art and décor, into a modest room plunged in shadows.

Heavy drapes extended from a high ceiling, covering the windows and blocking all sunlight. By the soft glow of candles, I made out the shape of a grand piano and a tall harp near the fireplace. Other than that, a huge rug had been rolled back. Furniture had been moved to make space in the center of the room.

The hardwood was as dark as Darcy's transgressions and made the lines of salt appear to glow. Shapes and patterns blossomed from the path I walked. A chill ran down my spine. My eyes traced a heart pierced with a trident, surrounded by asterisks or stars. Other symbols I couldn't understand marked the ritual space. It was scarily beautiful.

As my vision adjusted to the darkness, I honed in on Darcy Cyprian hugging the wall, sipping cognac and observing. But my attention was stolen by the new arrivals.

"This the motherfucker, eh?" A beautiful young woman pivoted from the fireplace. She surprised me with a thick Irish brogue. Frizzy strawberry-blond curls rioted around her rosy face as she jerked her chin in my direction and grinned. "What say ye, Sam?"

"That's *tifi*, Maman Brigit," said a handsome player with a Haitian accent. He stood by an altar set with nine candles, bottles of rum, and what looked like large tobacco leaves.

The two of them circled me, and I studied them just as they studied me. *Voodoo loas.* They weren't of my world, and it showed in the way they flaunted conventions.

The shapely woman wore a pastel green and purple dress that hugged her ample bosom. Her wardrobe struck me as both dated and timeless. The man wore black sunshades resting up over his brow. He held a top hat that simply didn't belong in the twenty-first century, especially against the fresh fade trimming his angular ebony face.

"Don't be scared, gyal. I'm Samedi, and this is my wife, Brigit. Maman, position the *sèvis ofrann bèt*, the sacrifice," Sam beckoned.

Me. I gulped. The woman smiled benevolently and placed me in the center of a ritual shape that resembled a cross bracketed by two coffins. She closed the salt barrier after me so I couldn't leave the spot.

"Now for the vessel," Sam requested, gazing at Darcy.

The vampire pursed his lips and whistled, and the servant from last night entered the dark music room with the wolf on the leash. I wasn't sure why until Brigit led the large animal to the other circle.

The female loa suddenly broke out in a keening requiem that made me writhe on the inside. Her voice was exquisite, but the wailing death song caused the lines of salt to incandesce in the dark room. A sensation like hundreds of hands began tugging and pulling at me as her chanting vibrated around me.

"What is she doing?" I wheezed.

"Maman Brigit is guiding you through the darkness." Samedi held up a votive candle that made his face leap with shadows and light. "Getting you to the Other Side."

This was my Resurrection, but . . . My wild eyes flew to Darcy, and the vampire grinned. What was happening was obscene. My Soul was being placed into a wolf.

"It's all coming together, isn't it?" Darcy murmured to me. "You see, her name is Loulou. I saved her from certain death at the hands of the Council. That's what they do to feral werewolves."

I hitched in a breath, because my first thought was what would happen to Zyr.

"Sadly, she can no longer shift into anything resembling a human without the proper enchantment," he said as it slowly dawned on me that this was my fate. "But, on the bright side, I've found that wives are so much easier to control when they're on a tight leash. Don't you agree, ma louloute? Or should I say, Loulou?"

CHAPTER FIFTY-FIVE
—
Mys

September 12 | Morning

Kittie Cad gripped the steering wheel with both hands as the cramped Nissan flew down the highway at breakneck speed. "Yea, though I walk through the valley of the shadow of death," Kittie shrieked, "Lord, please don't let Terrance kill me if anything happens to his car!"

I gripped the door handle, reminded of the high-speed chase to the cabin. We were following the same route, except this time no one was in hot pursuit. The hurricane had cleared the roads of any but the savviest and bravest of drivers. And big trucks. One flew past with a loud blast of the horn.

We were gliding through torrents of rain that obscured our view. The windshield had become a waterfall, and gusts shoved the car along like a toy. In the backseat, Zyr and Wallace bracketed Haley and the wolf. I huddled in the passenger seat. We were almost to Ponchatoula, Louisiana. The GPS gave instructions to take the next exit.

Meanwhile, my Empathy flurried with anticipation, my own and everyone else's. I anxiously fondled Zyr's Damascus steel sword.

The blade was the only weapon Tegan hadn't sabotaged at the cabin. Now Zyr had given it to me. Small comfort.

Sighing, I wondered how I had gone from my superchill, I-hate-everybody life to trying to save the city from a raving vampire. Raised in a fundamentalist Christian human family as an intersex futanari Supernatural, I couldn't have felt more detached from others. Yet, as the Nissan sped down the off-ramp, I had the distinct impression that any sense of isolation I felt from the rest of the world was smoke and mirrors.

None of us was alone. Our foils and triumphs were tiny pixels in the big picture of the universe. It felt like everyone in the car was supposed to be there. Each of us had a purpose, and the outcome depended on our ability to conceive that an insignificant detail could be the whole point. Maybe my brain was just regurgitating some Tumblr guru nonsense, but . . .

Aurie had played things safe in life, which led to her having mostly positive experiences, which had allowed her to trust a perfect stranger at precisely the right moment. Maybe I had always felt like a loner because someday she was going to need a hidden, enchanted apartment. Maybe Zyr's obsession with Darcy Cyprian was in preparation for what we were about to do now, and maybe the case was a pretext for the evidence the three of us needed to make our lives make sense.

I had blanked out, philosophizing, when Kittie suddenly lost control of the car. "Oh shit!" she yelled. I snapped free of reverie as a collective scream went up. The vehicle fishtailed and banged the guardrail. Sparks flew, quickly extinguished by the downpour.

"Kittie, watch out!" I grabbed the wheel, pointing at the trees we were about to impact. Kittie yanked the wheel back in the nick of time, but it was too much. Too much noise and activity.

With a tortured growl, Zyr slammed his head against the back window. The vicious smack silenced our noisy panic. I gasped at the sickening smear of blood on the glass. A dark bruise appeared at the detective's temple, and a line of red trickled from his lip, but the injury would heal itself. I was more concerned with his unnerving mental regression bleeding through my consciousness.

A visibly shaken Haley righted the car with a flick of her fingers. Zyr remained in distress, though. The she-wolf in the backseat bayed in mutual discontent, but she had Wallace to calm her. Zyr had no one. He braced himself to strike his head again.

"Don't!" I begged.

"I can't . . . control it," he labored to say as he clutched his head.

Snatching off my seat belt, I fought through the crawl space to the backseat and into his lap. I gathered his face and probed the vacant amber orbs. At first, my Empathy folded around nothing but savagery. It took longer than I felt comfortable with for Zyr to return to his senses.

"Please, focus on Aurie, and hold on for me. Please, Senpai," I whispered. I pressed my forehead to his. After a beat, his arms snaked around me. He nodded and flashed a tormented grimace that was supposed to be a smile.

"Is he all right?" Kittie whispered. I didn't know how to answer. How to explain we were saving one friend while losing another? She reached between the front seats to rub my back. "We're at the town limits. We're gonna get through this, okay, guys?"

No one said anything. I floundered in a tidal wave of emotions, sadness and grief, which linked me to the others in the car.

I barely knew Haley or Wallace. Still, it seemed like my life had hurtled toward this moment with the getaway driver, the psychic witch, the guardian angel, the ghost, the werewolf, the people I loved. Seconds before the car had swerved, I'd been close to understanding my destiny. But if this was it, then was I destined to lose my soul mates within months of finding them?

The champagne Nissan crested a hill. It dragged into Ponchatoula doing forty-five miles an hour. At daybreak in the picturesque small town, nothing stirred. The storm-ravaged sky was a lighter shade of dark gray, since we were farther north of the hurricane. Only the outer rain bands had reached the area.

Haley gestured ahead. "Pull in at that gas station so we can take stock."

Kittie found a parking spot beneath the flickering sign of a convenience store chain, and the rest of them piled out of the car. I didn't want to leave Zyr's lap, but when I raised my head from his shoulder, I realized he had fallen asleep. Unfolding from his embrace, I decided to jet inside to use the facilities.

I needed to regroup. The restroom stall door closed behind me and, standing over the urinal, I heaved a sigh. Falling in love had been easier than expected. That night at the cabin when the three of us had slapped a label on our intimacy, I'd thought I could handle it. Prepping myself to accept the loss to come was proving harder.

I lingered over the sink and shook my head at my teary-eyed reflection. Sniffling, I exited the restroom, past Kittie raiding the coffee machine. Haley was shoplifting. Wallace was stretching his legs outside. I paused next to him beneath the store overhang. He was talking quietly to the obedient wolf at his feet. A few early birds stopping in for gas greeted the docile animal too. I jerked a chin at one of them.

"So, how does it work?" I asked, thinking of the wife that Wallace no longer knew. Thinking of Zyr no longer knowing us when the time came. "What if someone from your past life runs into you?"

The guardian smiled. "I won't know them, but truthfully, they won't know me either. People see what they want to see: the good doctor, the insurance man, the homeless person."

"But not Haley."

"Haley was the exception," he chuckled. "I went into that hotel the night of the hit-and-run trying to evade a teenage girl who shouldn't have recognized me."

"Was it fate, or did she somehow defy . . . destiny, or . . . " I trailed off. Wallace touched the side of his nose and winked. I puzzled over his nonanswer, my lips around the vape pen. It sizzled, empty. I glared at the useless device. "I'll be back," I muttered as I darted into the store for another pack of cartridges.

The guardian angel and the wolf were nowhere to be seen by the time I returned. Glancing around, I trudged to the car to fill the tank for Kittie. There was a miniature TV embedded in the gas pump. The local news mentioned the missing daughters of a famous Hollywood director, but the coverage was overtaken by talk of the bizarre hurricane that was behaving in ways weather shouldn't.

"Good job, Haley," I whispered. I peered in the backseat to find Zyr awake. I opened the door and felt his forehead. He was feverish. "How are you feeling?"

"Like we shouldn't linger." He smiled wanly.

"Yeah, same." I studied the ground. "Look, there's something we should talk about before we reach the Ashivant place. It's Tegan. Her role in this seems accidental at best and misguided at the very worst."

"I want to rip Tegan to shreds," he growled. I squeezed his hand, and the sharpness in his tone eased with a solemn exhale. "But I know she's not responsible for this, and I made a vow to protect her. She'll have to answer to the Council."

He glanced past me at our returning crew. Wallace guided the wolf into the backseat, and Haley beamed as she showed off a pocket full of candy. She handed chips to Zyr. Kittie Cad handed me a coffee. I returned to the front seat to give them space in the back.

"You guys ready to kick some ass?" Kittie Cad rallied. "So, what's the game plan?"

Several pairs of eyes shifted to the detective. Clearing my throat, I answered for him. "Haley and I will locate Aurie's Soul while Zyr finds the vampire. Wallace, you keep track of Aurie's wolf, and Kittie, if you can stick by the car for a speedy getaway, that would be great."

"Darling, fast is my normal setting," Kittie preened.

We hit the road again. I observed Zyr through the side mirror. My consciousness occasionally flared with bursts of primal unrestraint. Yet, he wasn't hurting himself anymore. He had wrestled the last of his self-control into working order. It allowed me to breathe easier.

The main strip of Ponchatoula was lined with quaint antique shops and boutiques. It was a blink-and-you'll-miss-it kind of place. As we crossed a set of train tracks, the sleepy town quickly receded. The Nissan headed off the beaten path to the Law Offices of Ashivant, Ashivant & Claiborne.

I wondered how corrupt Darcy's attorneys had to be to let the vampire get away with committing his atrocities on their grounds. That is, if he was there.

Lightning arced across the sky. I worried my bottom lip with my teeth as we turned onto a dirt road, and I noticed prominent *No Trespassing* signs. I imagined all the ways this trip could go wrong. Louisiana had stand-your-ground laws, meaning that if we got shot, it would be our fault. We were the trespassers.

Swallowing fear, I squinted ahead. The trees making the country lane feel claustrophobic gave way to bucolic fields on either side. Another burst of lightning traced electric outlines along the maelstrom of clouds. I caught sight of the house at the top of a hill, a stately manor that hearkened back to times when—

Crack! The appalling sound of shattering glass. Zyr was slamming his head against the window again. I jerked around to face him. His eyes were all fire. My cry for him to stop went ignored. He flailed. Haley fought him off when his convulsions violently overtook the backseat. Attempts to physically restrain him were futile.

The detective was shifting, changing right before our eyes, with no control over it.

"Zyr! Oh gods, stop the car! Kittie, stop the car!" I pitched.

My best friend slammed on the brakes. "Watch out, Wallace!" Kittie stared in the rearview. Zyr snarled and snipped at the angel, at anyone and anything within reach. Haley fended him away with magic.

I hopped out of the car, falling in my frenzied rush to his door. The rain had made the dirt road a sloppy mess. When I managed to fumble the handle open, the untamed black wolf shot past me, disappearing into the dense underbrush of the woods behind us.

"Zyr!" I yelled in horror.

"No, don't! Darcy will hear you," Haley cried.

"Get in the car, Mys," Kittie urged.

I fell to my knees, spasmodic with tears. Without warning, the she-wolf tore from the leash and shot off after Zyr. "No, don't!" I tried to grab the leather strap, but it ripped through my hands, leaving a painful tear.

My ears rang, and the world stopped. This couldn't be happening. I screamed, though I didn't hear it over the ringing. I screamed until my lungs compressed and I had nothing left within me but suffering. Now I was hysterical. Now there was no consoling me.

CHAPTER FIFTY-SIX

—

Aurie

September 12 | Morning

Ma louloute. The feral werewolf, Loulou. Darcy's meaning became clear. I wouldn't get the chance to help Zyr, my family, or anyone else. I would be locked in the wolf's body until he needed me. Indeed, his docile, well-kept pet.

"You bastard!" I spat through clenched teeth.

Darcy wheezed a laugh around a sip of cognac. "I've been called worse."

My face contorted as I felt myself snatched, and my body folded backward at the waist. My mouth gaped in a soundless scream. The music that was pulling me yanked harder. The wolf in the other ritual space let out a chilling howl and jerked against the leash, but she could no more escape than I could.

The loa Samedi paced the space between us. The tall, stately Black man cast a glance at Brigit, and she sang louder, making the power rip me sideways toward the canine, warping my face. I bawled in fury and agony. I begged for them to stop.

"You said . . . it wouldn't . . . hurt," I wept.

Darcy shrugged. "Ignorance isn't dishonesty."

"*Mwen pa renmen*," Sam mumbled to himself. "I don't like it. I think we got a problem."

"What do you mean?" Darcy arched an eyebrow at him, covering his mouth with his kerchief as he continued watching my body be ravaged by the loas' undisputed power. His look of disgust told me the sight was as disturbing as it felt.

Brigit unexpectedly went slack and stopped singing. The invisible hands tugging me dispersed as soon as the silence descended, and I fell to my knees with a drained whimper. "What in the five fucks of Lucifer! What's with her, lovey?" she asked Samedi.

Darcy rushed forward. "No breaks. This is time sensitive. I have another appointment, Baron Samedi. I want the job completed."

Fanning her florid face, Brigit snorted. "Oh, eat it, Nightwalker."

"Watch your mouth, Maman." Sam grinned. "My apologies, Monsieur Cyprian. We can't resurrect her. She's . . . not my province."

"What? Do what we agreed, Sam!" Darcy sputtered. I stared between the two men from my position huddled at their feet. I didn't understand what was happening.

Samedi spread his arms and backed away. "My province is the dead. Keep the offering for another rainy day, Monsieur. Come along, Maman." He bowed low to Darcy, somehow managing to make a mockery of the gesture.

"Goddamn you, Samedi!" the vampire roared, pointing a shaking finger at him around the glass of cognac. "You better not set one foot off these grounds! We will discuss this in my office!" He slammed the tumbler on a side table and stormed from the room.

"If you insist, Monsieur." Sam chuckled, but the sound was laced with ire. His gaze met Brigit's. I cowered on the floor as they stepped over me and followed Darcy. I had no doubt the vampire would find a way to convince them to do his bidding. He was persuasive like that.

I traced the meandering path that had brought me to this altar—from Darcy's stupid business card for the loas, to his promise of Resurrection, to the visit with the voodoo priestess. At the thought of the old woman in the projects, I remembered her cryptic advice: *The lantern don't always light the way, chile. Some secrets you must travel into the wild dark to uncover.*

Apparently, Brigit was the lantern, but she couldn't take me to the Other Side. How did one "travel into the wild dark"? I was in so much pain—and after weeks of experiencing little to no physical discomfort in the Afterlife—that I couldn't think straight. I felt like even if there was an escape plan tucked in the words, I was too blitzed to figure it out.

I locked eyes with the baleful black and gray wolf. When a servant scurried in to take her away, the canine made a whimpering sound. I worried about what would happen to her, but I almost cried when she glanced over her shoulder, looking as if she felt sorry for *me*.

I was shocked out of self-pity by the sound of someone whispering my name. My eyes doubled in size as a woman made a crouching run into the room. "Tegan?" I gasped.

"I'm gonna get you out of here," she hissed, blindly reaching toward me.

She couldn't see or hear me, but it didn't matter. "Oh my God! I've never been happier to see you!" Shuffling to a sitting position, I realized what the loas had unwittingly done when they stepped over me. The line of salt closing the ritual space was disrupted enough for me to get out! I clamped a hand over my mouth to hush my excited breathing.

"They're right in the next room," Tegan whispered. "We'll have to be careful. Follow me."

I crept after her. Both of us surveyed the creepy corridor to the foyer. I didn't know what I expected to see when we rounded the corner. Definitely not the front door wide open. With a gasp, Tegan and I leapt behind a tapestry as the women of the house entered the foyer and looked around. Rain poured through the open door, soaking the hardwood.

"Are you done, *Master* Cyprian?" the dark-haired one snarked.

Darcy stuck his head out of his office. "Something has come up. I'll need another hour."

"What? No, I don't think that can be arranged. We have business."

"Another hour, Mal!" he shouted.

She pulled herself to her full height. Either she gave him side-eye, or she saw us. I shrank deeper into the shadows as the woman gave a nonchalant shrug. "It's your call," she grumbled. Mal and her sisters dispersed throughout the house, but they left the front door as it was. Open. I had a suspicion it was done intentionally, if only to spite their charismatic leader. It was our way out.

We stepped from our hiding place. "If the barrier still prevents you from leaving, don't worry," Tegan said over her shoulder. "Keep out of sight. I'll get in touch with the Council, like we discussed, and I'll bring Zyr to save you as fast as I can."

"Don't be ridiculous, Detective Stoney." Darcy Cyprian disengaged from the shadows of the great hall, and we stumbled to a halt. Believing his lawyers were trying to help us had been wishful thinking. Chances were, Mal had looked in our direction to signal him. The vampire's beautiful face radiated ebbing patience. "I made it clear Aurie Edison isn't going anywhere, and neither are you."

He stalked toward us. Behind him, Baron Samedi and Maman Brigit played audience to the game of cat and mouse, wearing matching expressions of disinterest. Darcy avoided the patch of floor bathed in the weak light of the storm. At his hesitation, I nudged Tegan. However, my hand went through her body.

No, not now, I thought. As I mustered the energy to regain my powers of touch, a movement on the staircase drew my startled attention. One of the Ashivant sisters—the blond ingenue—descended sedately with Loulou on a leash. She looked about my age, or barely older, but something in her expression held childlike wonder. She paused when she saw the group of us.

"Cherie? Where are you going?" Darcy snapped in annoyance.

"I'm taking her for a walk," she said.

"In a hurricane?" Samedi asked with a blithe smile.

Brigit chuckled, swatting his arm. "Leave at it, Sam."

While they were distracted, I willed Tegan to make a run for it. Unfortunately, Darcy seemed to read my mind. His attention whipped back to us, and he forgot Cherie. "You." He pointed at me with contempt. "Aurie, I'm beginning to think you're more trouble than you're worth. Did you honestly think you could get away with it? That I wouldn't find out?"

My whole body went slack. *God, no.* He had figured out I wasn't the witch. I stammered for something to say to keep him from connecting the dots and realizing it was Haley he wanted. Darcy took another menacing step toward me, but Tegan braved his wrath and stepped between us.

"Leave her alone," she demanded. He glared at her with enough malice to kill.

A shrill scream from the blond shattered the silent standoff. Even Darcy jumped. Cherie stumbled backward into the foyer. When she turned to face us, her maple eyes bore delight instead of distress. "More wolves!" She gleefully pointed toward the door. The leash trailed from her delicate fingers. Loulou was free.

"What do you expect me to do about it, *ma petite?*" Darcy blew an exasperated breath.

When I peered outside—where the vampire didn't dare approach—sure enough, there were several wolves frolicking in the rain. One blacker than night, and the other a ruddy shade of brown. The gray and black Loulou had joined them, and the three seemed to take to each other like a ready-made pack. I squinted . . .

"Go get them for me," Cherie pouted.

"We've been over this, pretty one. You can't have every pet you lay eyes on. Besides, it's daylight, and I don't have time for this. If you're going with Loulou, get the mongrel and get out," Darcy ordered. His gorgeous but vacant companion seemed to give up on the idea. She turned away from the door and started to head back upstairs. "Cherie!" he called after her in annoyance.

She gave a penitent smile and returned to close the door, but suddenly the wolves were at the threshold. One of them bayed, and the others answered with hair-raising growls. Darcy appeared unnerved as he flapped a hand at Cherie to hurry. Instead, she ran back up the stairs.

Tegan backed into me in retreat as the wolves advanced. I was almost afraid, but my head filled with words from what felt like a past life. *I am the big bad wolf*, Zyr had said after shifting into a big, black *Canis lupus* remarkably like the one growling at Darcy Cyprian right now.

"Shut the door for me, Sam," Darcy bid anxiously.

The cocky loa put his hands on his hips. "You may be the master of this house, Monsieur, but not of me."

CHAPTER FIFTY-SEVEN
—
Mys

September 12 | Morning

Air whistled through my parched throat, and I collapsed to the wet ground. Cold, muddy water soaked through the knees of my pants, but I didn't feel it. I didn't feel anything except the excruciating spasms of a broken heart.

Kittie dashed from the idling car and grabbed me. I saw her lips moving, but I couldn't hear a word she said. My defeated cries blotted out everything else. I was pulled to my feet. My numb body was shoved into the car.

My vacant stare registered Haley crying and pointing straight ahead, Wallace scanning the woods for the she-wolf from the backseat. Kittie Cad threw up her hands in frustration and jerked the gearshift, and the car shot off with a splatter of mud.

Without my seat belt, I slid, unmoored, into the dash, but I righted myself and leaned my aching head on the cool glass of the passenger window, still wracked by sobs. When my best friend tried to rub my shoulder in comfort, I shrugged Kittie off. There was nothing she could say or do. Nothing anyone could say or do.

My tingling hand fell upon the hilt of the enchanted Damascus sword, and the ringing in my ears faded to a buzz. It thrummed deep in my bones. I throbbed with the fury that morphed from despair. Chest heaving, I cast a murderous glance at the plantation where the root of all my heartache was supposed to be.

"Change of plans. Find Aurie. Leave Darcy to me," I spat through clenched teeth. "Drive faster." Kittie Cad met my gaze and wordlessly accelerated. The speedometer needle kissed the redline as we closed the distance to the enemy.

My enemy. Darcy Cyprian was mine now. I knew he had destroyed everyone and everything that had come up against him, but I had nothing left to lose. Justice no longer mattered. I wanted restitution for what he had taken from me, and he could only pay with his life.

The yowl of the engine blended with the din of the storm. Faster and faster, we flew along the narrow dirt lane, the house enlarging by the second. Just when it seemed the Nissan would crash into the marble columns, Kittie slammed on the brakes. The vehicle whirled in a 180-degree arc, tires spraying rain in a beautiful monochrome rainbow.

Haley threw open the car door midspin—as if the whiplashing action was in slow motion. Wallace, Kittie Cad, and I stared after the teen in awe as she launched from the moving vehicle and nailed her landing on the front steps of the house. Looming bigger than life, the vivacious teenager became something else in the hurricane gales.

She gathered an energy as ancient as time. The rain lashed her, but it didn't faze her. The gusts turned her hair into a black banner of defiance. Her balled fists at her sides emanated power. The gloves were off for all of us.

"Looks like someone's expecting us," said Wallace as he squinted at the open front door.

Kittie was skeptical. "Is it a trap?"

"It doesn't matter. Cyprian is in there. I can sense it." I leered at the house as I hit the switchblade of the Damascus short sword and found my place beside Haley. The steel gleamed in a flash of lightning.

Haley and I charged into the dark portal. She raised both hands, and a blast of wind preceded us as lightning illuminated the foyer. Swirls of damp white sand spiraled up from the wet hardwood. Salt, I realized when I wiped my lips.

"Aurie!" Haley's voice boomed over the thunderstorm. No more trying not to alert Darcy to our presence. I looked for him. Surveying the dimly lit interior, I tightened my grip on the short sword when I spotted Tegan Stoney hugging the wall near the front door. I tried not to resent her involvement in this fiasco, but I wasn't happy to see her.

"Where is she?" I snapped.

"W-we were nearly out the door when Darcy caught us," Tegan replied, her face devoid of color and eyes wild with fear. She was no longer the overconfident detective I had met. The vibrant corona of her hair danced in the wind and made her appear unhinged in her distress. "I'm so sorry, Mys. I tried to help her escape, but it was too late."

She pointed across the great hall at Aurie flanked by a man in a top hat and a woman in a purple and green dress. These were the voodoo loas, I realized. At that precise moment, Aurie saw me, and her face lit up. I braced myself to battle black magic if I had to just get to her, but the loas made no move to stop her as she ran to me.

"Yōkai!" I whispered in relief as I held her trembling Soul.

Aurie clung to my lips in a searing kiss before caressing my injury. "I thought she'd killed you," she whimpered. Shaking my head, I buried my face in her neck and breathed her in. Over her shoulder, I met Tegan's gaze. The detective appeared to feel genuine remorse, but my attention was dragged back by the kaleidoscoping colors of Aurie's emotions in my Empathy. Gods, I had missed her.

"All right, all right. Enough before they're forced to rate it *R*," Haley quipped behind us. Aurie jerked from my embrace and gaped in astonishment at her sister as Haley shoved me aside and threw open her arms for a hug of her own. "Remember me?" She laughed.

"What are you doing here? It's not safe for you!" Aurie exclaimed through tears of joy. She ushered us deeper into the shadows, where she clutched Haley's shoulders and gave her a quick once-over and another fierce hug. "We have to go. Darcy thinks I'm some powerful witch. The thing is, he's got me mixed up with you."

"Girl, there's so much I need to tell you about that," Haley said with a grin.

Tegan interjected, "Yeah, you two should catch up later. The clock is ticking." She reached for Aurie's hand, but her fingers went through her.

I pulled up short. "Wait, you can see Aurie?" I asked in surprise. She hadn't fumbled around for her blindly. She had reached for the ghost directly. That meant . . .

Tegan nodded slowly, and Aurie untucked from her sister's arms with a frown. "You can see me?" she repeated. As if in explanation, Tegan lifted her hair and displayed her unblemished ivory neck. Aurie inhaled sharply. "What happened to the bite marks? I saw him bite you. He . . ."

"He killed her," I whispered in dismay, recognizing Tegan's Supernatural type. I had been too preoccupied to notice at first, but it was clear. She was no longer a living human being.

At Aurie's concerned groan, Tegan's eyes clouded. "Don't feel sorry for me, okay? I've been given a chance to fix this mess, and that's what I intend to do. Now, get your family and go! While the wolves have Darcy distracted."

"What wolves?" My heart skipped a beat.

Aurie and Tegan directed my gaze down the hall, and there he was. Darcy Cyprian. The vampire was struggling to evade three ferocious wolves. Against the backdrop of the majestic house, Darcy moved like the howling winds outside, but the wolves were almost as swift and just as determined. Antique furniture and décor flew around them in the turbulence.

The sorrel-red she-wolf took a bite out of the air where Darcy had been a moment before. He materialized at the top of the gilded staircase on the second landing. With preternatural speed, the gray wolf tore after him. The oversized black wolf jumped over the balustrade and landed a crushing blow before the vampire could flee again. Pinning Darcy to the floor, the feral canines ripped at his clothes and flesh, and he oozed stagnant blood.

"My God!" Tegan grimaced at the savagery.

We watched, enthralled. Until Darcy escaped. He backpedaled faster than the eye could detect. The wolves were briefly disoriented, but my Empathy lit up with icy white impressions of his vampire sprint. I sensed him zip across the ceiling toward the front door. "Wallace!" I shouted. The angel slid into the house just as Darcy slammed the door shut to block out the daylight.

"No!" Tegan wilted in disbelief. "How do we get out now?"

"I didn't plan on leaving without his head," I replied with a bitter half smile.

I brandished the enchanted sword as Haley's hands began to glow in preparation for our last stand. Yet, Aurie didn't move; she was frozen to the spot. I followed her line of sight to the guardian angel, who had spread massive white wings.

"Dad?" Aurie breathed.

Haley cracked a grin. "I told you, we have lots to talk about, sis. *After* I kick this vampire's ass."

CHAPTER FIFTY-EIGHT
—
Aurie

September 12 | Morning

I whipped around, not sure which way to look first. At Mys and Haley, running to join the fight against Darcy; at Tegan, who was now a ghost like me; or at my dead father. A younger version of Wallace Edison stood in front of the heavy oak doors. He spread wings so white they lit up the foyer, spanning at least his height.

"Dad," I whispered again. My heart raced as the angel approached me with a benevolent smile, but his eyes weren't the same as my father's. I hesitated before hugging him.

"No, I'm not the man you remember," he admitted. "Nothing of my prior existence is known to me. It happens that way so guardian angels can focus on protecting their future charges instead of holding on to the past, but . . . by some miracle . . . my charge is you."

"I can't believe it. How many years have I prayed just to see your face?" An errant teardrop fell, and he swept it away. "I worked so hard to take care of Haley and make you proud, Daddy."

"You did well. I've been watching over you, sweetheart." He gently chucked my chin. "I'm beyond proud to be your guardian. That's why it's time for you to wake and live again so I can continue to do my job."

"We . . . tried." I shrugged, unable to explain what had gone wrong with the Resurrection. I glanced over my shoulder at Baron Samedi.

"*Mais oui*," Sam replied as he ambled toward us. "Unfortunately, we were misled about the state of mademoiselle's readiness, and so we have overstayed our usefulness, right, Maman?"

"So ye claim." The saucy Maman Brigit smiled furtively. She planted a fist on her hip, watching the skirmish raging along the second-floor landing, in no hurry to go.

I was captivated by the fight. Dressed head to toe in black, Mys maneuvered with the prowess of a dancer. Or a ninja. Their lithe body demanded attention. The glint of the sword flashed in a blur. There was something infinitely appealing about the way their muscular form wielded it in defiance of physics. Darcy moved too fast for me to see with my naked eye, but the Empath seemed to sense the vampire's every move.

My jaw dropped as wide swaths of light emanated from Haley's fingers and lit up the battle scene. Whenever Darcy would materialize, she'd singe him with the glowing beams, and the wolves would continue to strike. The black Alpha led the attacks with a relentlessness that left the vampire unable to heal as quickly as his wounds were reopened.

For the first time since being dragged into this house of horrors, I felt a twinge of hope. I pivoted to the elegant top-hatted loa, who was studying the locked front door with interest. "Baron Samedi, wait. I want to thank you for not transferring my Soul into Darcy's wolf, but can I . . . can I ask another favor of you?"

"As you please." A half smile played on his lips as he bowed to me.

"Resurrect my friend." I wrapped an arm around Tegan.

"What are you talking about?" She blinked, stunned. I knew it was crazy. She had been my rival in ways I hadn't even realized until it was too late. Yet, she had also come back for me, and Zyr's words replayed in my head. *Loyal to a fault.* He would've wanted this for his partner.

"If Tegan's body has only been d-dead a few hours"—I winced over the word—"is it still usable?"

Sam cocked his head. "Depends. Got payment?" he asked in an eerie throwback to my meeting with the voodoo priestess. I chewed my lip, pondering. Stealing from Darcy's altar was out, I guessed.

I conferred with Tegan and my father. "Apparently we need to pay for this service."

"Aurie, you can't be serious," Tegan whispered.

"Yes, I'm serious. Enough with the skepticism. Any ideas on what we can offer?"

"Whiskey or tobacco is preferred," Samedi mentioned.

Eyes widening, Tegan rocked on her heels in sudden epiphany. She shot off down the corridor, and I hurried after her. Wallace followed on my heels. The four of us skidded to a halt at the entrance to the dining room. Tegan's dead body was still slumped at the table. I covered my mouth and spun away.

"Sorry," she muttered. "There's, uh, a flask in the pocket of my jeans. I'll grab it."

Gulping, I recovered. "No, I'll get it. You can't quite manipulate the real world as a ghost."

She sighed glumly. "Of course. How could I forget."

"And we'll need the body," I murmured.

Nodding, the guardian angel moved with me to where Tegan's red hair splayed across her plate of half-eaten food. I gently cleaned her face with a napkin. Averting my gaze from her ashen pallor and lividity, I patted around her pockets for the flask. I returned to where her ghost waited in the hall after I found it. Wallace emerged, carrying the dead woman's body.

The loas were waiting for us in the music room. As Haley and Mys dealt with the vampire upstairs, I led the rest of our ensemble back to the site of the ritual. Wallace placed Tegan's body where Brigit indicated. Samedi came to me with an open hand, and I smacked the flask into his palm. He opened it, sniffing. He tossed the bottle to Maman Brigit.

"Good stuff," she said with a dimpled grin. I smiled until she added, "Good, but not enough."

"Wait, what?" I frowned.

Samedi studied his well-groomed fingernails. "This is no simple transfer of a Soul into another body. You're asking to reanimate a corpse. It will take more than a sip of whiskey to do that."

"I-I don't have anything else," I argued. "I'll get you anything you want when we get out of this place, but this isn't even my house. I don't know where—"

Wallace pressed something into my hand. "I believe this might be of interest."

I stared in confusion at the mini square of plastic until it dawned on me what it was. Gasping, I shoved the vape pen refill at the loas. "Tobacco. I mean, it's *like* tobacco. It's a New Age way to get nicotine," I promised.

Samedi turned it over a few times, studying the pod. Finally, he nodded, and I breathed a sigh of relief. Sam gestured for the priestess to place Tegan in the ritual space. I squeezed Tegan's hand, knowing she was afraid.

"It'll be okay," I whispered.

"But why are you doing this for me, Aurie?"

Lifting a shoulder, I answered, "You were actually trying to help me the night of the hit-and-run. Not only that, but you came back from the dead to free me today. You may be an arrogant skeptic with a teeny tiny crush on the man I love, but you have your redemptive qualities, Detective Stoney."

She smiled and shook her head as I backed away to let the loas do their thing. When Brigit began her dirge this time, it didn't look nearly as painful as when I had been on the chopping block. Exhaling, I hugged myself. Wallace appeared beside me.

"Why do you think you couldn't be resurrected?" he asked softly. I had no idea, although I had a feeling he knew why. "Samedi couldn't resurrect you because you're still alive, Aurie. You've been in a coma for over a month."

"That . . . that's not possible." I shook my head, remembering the way my body had lain, broken beyond repair in front of Century Luxe Hotel that night.

"Yes, you suffered greatly . . . in ways you may never recover from . . . but you didn't die, sweetheart. I made sure of that. Your body rested while your Soul did what it needed to do in Overlay City. Now, Aurie," he repeated more firmly, "you have to wake up."

An avalanche of dizziness crushed me, and it took all my strength to remain standing. I clutched my head in confusion. Maybe it was Brigit's amplified keening—or the swell of power in the room that I felt prickling along my skin like electricity—but I had to get away to think. I covered my ears and ran from the music room.

The blind sprint sent me colliding with the dark-haired woman of the house. She towered over me. "Are you the reason for all this ruckus?" Her sultry voice radiated power. My jaw dropped at the golden shimmer of her skin. Definitely not human.

Wallace caught me when I tried to run again. "I'm sorry, but there's no escaping this, Aurie. Your friends need you," he said.

Quaking in panic, I felt myself unravel, similar to my experience in the glass bottle. My hands began to fade. I was unable to feel the floor beneath my feet. A silent moan of uneasiness swelled in my throat, and I tried to hold on to reality, but I couldn't.

"Dad, help me!" I screamed as I was suddenly flung backward into a dark void. Memories of my Afterlife swirled around me, a tunnel of moving pictures. Vague impressions of my mother's voice merged with the antiseptic smell of a hospital room. The images sharpened. My mind punched through medical tests and procedures back to the harrowing ambulance ride. I slammed into the concrete ground in front of Century Luxe.

Finally, I was staring into Tegan's glazed eyes as she gripped the wheel, heading straight toward me. The clock ticked forward to the moment of impact. I didn't want to experience it again. I didn't want to be dead. I squeezed my eyes shut and heard wolves.

When I opened my eyes, it was me. I was the red wolf snarling down at Darcy Cyprian, and this was war.

CHAPTER FIFTY-NINE
—
Mys

September 12 | Morning

The sorrel wolf let out a howl that cut through the din of battle, attacking with renewed strength. Her foaming mouth clamped around the vampire's delicate wrist, and she snatched, fileting skin. Once the other wolves got him in their teeth, they yanked him farther down the corridor.

Darcy scrambled free yet again. I sensed the effort it took for him to keep evading us, but his voice whispered in my head: "Go on, wear yourselves out."

I shuddered in revulsion. "You first," I spat as I jerked the drapes from a nearby window. The vampire's arrogant laughter strangled into a roar of pain as he fled deeper into the shadows. But Haley's power vibrated the air around her, and a concentrated blast of sunlight shot from her hands after the nightwalker. The heat scored the floorboards, leaving charred, smoking gashes.

"Where'd he go?" she asked when he disappeared.

"Down there!" I pointed.

Exhausted, I raised my aching sword arm and flew downstairs after him. The bruised and battered wolves ran with me, but I didn't know how much longer we could keep this up. It seemed no matter what we did, no matter how prescient my Empathy, Darcy Cyprian stayed one step ahead.

I dropped to my knees out of breath when I reached the ground floor. A shadow unexpectedly stretched over me, and I stared up into the striking face of a woman with dark hair. "Ms. Ashivant, I presume," I grunted, rising to full height. My Empathy folded around her and felt nothing, and I recoiled. That had never happened to me before.

"Indeed," she replied, "and you're not welcome in my home."

"But that *monster* is?" I gestured with the sword to where Haley and the wolves still battled Darcy. His lawyer gave me a bored stare. I wondered what she was, half-afraid to find out.

Pausing, she murmured, "You have no idea what's happening as we speak, and you're just in the way. I have an important meeting with the Council of Overlay Affairs here soon. I suggest you and your friends pick your battles."

Good. If the Council was coming, they'd bear witness to Darcy's unfolding crimes—namely kidnapping and killing a human detective whose murder could bring scrutiny to our world.

The lawyer whistled, and the gray and black wolf peeled away from the snarling pack with a whimper. "Loulou, go to Cherie!" she snapped.

For a split second, Darcy had the upper hand. He fended off the other two wolves easily. I stared in dread as he gripped Haley by the throat and lifted her in the air. My stride ate up the distance between us, but I couldn't strike fast enough. Haley struggled as he squeezed the life out of her.

"You picked the wrong cause to champion," the vampire chuckled darkly. I feinted toward him with the Damascus steel sword, but Haley's dangling form shielded him. "It's not like you imagined, is it? Your moral high ground, your strong convictions, your *righteous* indignation—none of that can save you in real life."

"Let her go!" I shouted. The wolves paced restlessly around him.

"In real life, winning is arbitrary. Pure luck and happenstance," said Darcy. "For instance, you were lucky I chose Aurie instead of you, little teenage witch. Unfortunately, you had to interject yourself into my plans, and the more I think of it . . ." He hesitated.

I bared my teeth as I raised the sword higher. Darcy smiled at me over Haley's shoulder, his arm snaking around her waist to hold her closer. "The more I think of it," he whispered, "maybe I picked the wrong Edison sister after all."

With unbridled rage, the red wolf pounced from behind. Darcy cried out in shock. He was torn from his feet and hit the stairs, and Haley spun out of his grasp. I leapt on top of him before he could sprint away, and I pressed the hilt of the short sword to his throat. His fangs dripped venom. Eyes redder than hot embers burned with malice. I pushed the hilt harder, but he only laughed.

"Don't you understand? You can't kill me," he hissed. "Stop extending the inevitable."

"You want to know what's inevitable?" I sneered.

"Your demise," he choked out, "when I'm head of the Council!"

Haley leaned over him. "You deluded son of a bitch, let's see how your plans hold up to the light of day." Manacles shaped of glowing power wrapped around Darcy's wrists. He was chained to the stairs, unable to escape Haley's magic. Every time he tried, Zyr and Aurie in wolf form rained wildness and fury upon him faster than the vampire could heal.

As I watched him get ripped apart, I didn't feel my usual Empathy. I planted the blade at the neck of the mass of evil writhing in chains of sunlight.

My gaze flicked to the woman in the high-backed chair. Her glimmering skin caught the candlelight, and she looked like a work of art. A cold, impassionate masterpiece. Still, she didn't lift a finger to help her client.

Wallace and Tegan ran into the foyer. The newly resurrected woman looked pallid but very much returned to life. I couldn't wait to collect my friends and get out of this nightmare house. "Finish it," I said to Haley. I readied myself to bring the Damascus sword sweeping down to cut off Darcy's head. She threw open the door and . . . I faltered.

There was a group of people waiting in the drenching rain. They stared in confusion at what was happening inside. "My word! What's the meaning of this?" Someone gasped. Behind them, a line of luxury cars were parked in the driveway, and one had an official seal. The Council of Overlay Affairs. They were finally here.

Suddenly, a flurry of blackbirds exploded from the staircase. The wolves gave chase, but the birds flew en masse out the door. Where the vampire had been, only dissipating wisps of smoke remained. "No!" I cried in panic.

I pushed through the bewildered crowd of council members. Haley, Wallace, and Tegan met me in the driveway, and Kittie stepped from the car to see what was happening. Dismayed, we stared at the birds disappearing into the turmoil of the stormy sky. But Darcy couldn't have escaped. He couldn't survive the sun, not even with it hiding behind the black-gray clouds of a hurricane.

I pivoted to his lawyer standing in the doorway. "Where is he?" I asked.

She glowered at me. A portly, balding man from the Council approached, and she lifted a hand in apology. "I'm afraid we will have to postpone our meeting, Mr. Distefano." She sighed. "My client is indisposed."

"You called *us* here, Mal," he huffed.

Ms. Ashivant's response was interrupted by the red wolf's violent quake. I hitched in a breath in wonder as a nude Aurie Edison unfolded from wolf form. "You were called here because of me," Aurie announced. Then she hit the wet ground with a start.

"Yōkai!" I ran toward her.

Immediately, we realized what Zyr's last-ditch effort to save her hadn't been able to fix. The rain drummed in silence as Aurie grappled with being changed beyond repair. "What happened to me?" she asked, clutching the leg that had been amputated below the knee.

I knelt beside her. "The accident. Zyr thought he could heal you, but . . ."

"But he couldn't?" Her chest heaved as her eyes filled with swift tears.

I shook my head in regret. Richter Distefano, the head of the Council, snapped his fingers, and one of the council members hurried forward with a coat. I draped it over her shoulders. Holding her, I felt such anger and despair. I could almost hear her inner thoughts: *I played it safe, and now this.*

But when Aurie dried her tears, she appeared more determined than before. "You were called here because of me," she repeated calmly. "Darcy Cyprian wanted the Council to meet his new bride." I helped her stand, noticing that Mal didn't contradict her, but the lawyer didn't look happy about the news either.

"*You* are Mrs. Darcy Cyprian?" Mr. Distefano asked.

"No, I'm not because Mr. Cyprian's plans were foiled yet again. He drugged me, kidnapped me, and planned to put me in the body of a feral wolf so he could keep me under his command. He said a powerful witch would be an asset to getting elected. The problem with that is . . . I'm not a witch. I'm Aurelia Edison, and I'm sure you've heard of me."

"From Detective Zyr Ravani," I stated. "We're equally sure he informed the Council that Aurie isn't the only human Darcy has harmed. You know we were gathering evidence to petition you to initiate an official investigation." There was no way they could ignore us now. Kittie Cad joined us at the foot of the stairs, and we faced the Council down.

"Well, where's the evidence?" Mr. Distefano asked in clear annoyance.

I didn't know if his irritation was because he really didn't want to know what Darcy was up to or because we weren't taking the proper channels to get the information to him. Either way, we didn't have the evidence anymore. As I struggled for words to explain how the raid they had sanctioned had left us without the means to challenge the vampire, Tegan pushed forward, waving something.

"It's right here. All on a jump drive. Detective Ravani asked me to make a backup for safekeeping," she replied, and my jaw dropped in astonishment. She had come through for us after all. Tegan added with pride, "No matter how things appeared, there was never a question of my loyalty to Zyr, even when it meant deceiving that wily vampire."

CHAPTER SIXTY

—

Aurie

September 12 | Happily Ever After

Baron Samedi raised his top hat and spoke up in his melodic Haitian patois. "If I may add," he said, "Monsieur Cyprian hired me to resurrect tifi with intentions exactly as she describes."

Mal cut eyes at him, but Brigit shoved the slender woman aside and descended the steps to the head council's level. "Not to mention, he wanted for us to kill the wee lassie when we begged off just now in the music room!" she fumed. All tea, all shade.

"And it's not only Aurie Edison," Tegan went on. "We have evidence spanning over fifty years for crimes ranging from carnal knowledge of a juvenile to sexual assault. It's all there."

I leaned heavily on Mys for support while Mr. Distefano held up the jump drive and smirked at Darcy's attorney. "Do you have anything to say for your client, Ms. Ashivant?" the man asked.

Mal lifted a shoulder blithely. "I haven't seen the evidence, nor do I have personal knowledge of any of this. As far as I'm concerned, it's hearsay and defamation of character."

"I beg your pardon!" The head of the council stiffened. "Need I remind you the accusers are standing here talking about what happened in *your* music room?"

My gaze ping-ponged to Mal Ashivant.

"I'm sure Mr. Cyprian welcomes an investigation exonerating him of all wrongdoing." She crossed her arms, and I shuddered. She sounded like a woman who was used to winning.

"You understand the magnitude of the allegations against him?" Mr. Distefano pressed.

"I don't discuss allegations. I defend against prosecution. Let me know when you're ready."

"We will do that, Ms. Ashivant. Also, please inform your client that until this matter is resolved, he should refrain from submitting a Declaration of Candidacy."

At this, Mal seemed perturbed, but she said nothing else. Instead, she disappeared deeper within the house. Mr. Distefano glanced at the eleven other individual members of the Council of Overlay Affairs and their security personnel standing in the gusty rain. He twirled a finger in the air, signaling they should wrap it up and leave. "Waste of my damn time," someone muttered.

A straggling council member stepped forward. A wide umbrella shielded her elegantly coiffed hair and face from the storm. "Detective Tegan Stoney?" She looked up.

"Yes?" Tegan greeted her.

"I'm Farida Ravani. Thank you for your loyalty to my son," she replied in a clipped British accent. I lifted an eyebrow in surprise. Zyr's mother could easily pass for someone half her age. Tegan gawked as she shook hands with her. "I've heard such great things about you, Detective."

"I wish I could say the same, Mrs. Ravani, but Zyr has always been secretive about his family."

"I'm sure, in these trying times, there was only so much he could say.

But I know you're the reason his position was reinstated, and the internal investigation dropped on the human side," said Mrs. Ravani. "I also know I owe you a debt of gratitude for getting me released from house arrest."

"I wasn't sure Cyprian would keep his word," Tegan demurred. "Especially after he found out I'd handed over a Soul he couldn't resurrect."

"Well, it doesn't matter what that rat says to the Council now, no one will believe him. Thanks to each of you." Mrs. Ravani's grateful smile encompassed every one of us. "Please give this to Zyr for me when you have the chance." She pushed something into Tegan's hands and hurried to a black Mercedes to join the rest of the vehicles leaving the grounds.

I glanced around for Zyr, and a subtle voice whispered primal thoughts in my head. I knew it was her. The red wolf. My life would never be the same, not just because I was a shape-shifter now. I kneaded my amputated stump as phantom limb pains bothered me. Seeing this, Mys wrapped me in a tighter embrace. Haley dropped a hand on my shoulder and gave it a squeeze, and I braved a smile.

Darcy had called me special, but no amount of magic had been able to save my leg. A part of me cried out for what was lost. Mostly, I relished being alive. It was like waking up from a sad dream and realizing the worst of it wasn't real.

I wasn't dead. Mys wasn't rotting in a pine forest somewhere. Zyr wasn't languishing in some Overlay prison. We had actually succeeded, and Darcy Cyprian would pay. Even if our berserk attack on the vampire hadn't killed him, his political aspirations in Overlay City were done.

Tegan faced Mys. "And I owe you an apology." She sighed.

"Eh, you redeemed yourself when you delivered the evidence." Mys shrugged it off.

"I tried to do what I thought was right. It took me a minute to figure out the best thing for Zyr is you. The both of you." Tegan smiled tiredly as she stared in the distance. "I guess there's no point in calling for backup."

"Not unless they're ready to deal with whatever that is in the house." Mys chuckled and hiked a thumb back at the mansion.

"Our resident witch can take on those lawyers," I teased.

"What about you, coven sister?" Haley quipped. "Don't you realize what happened? *You* are the reason your Soul traveled to Overlay City, because *you* are also a powerful witch, exactly as Darcy suspected."

I blinked in amusement until Wallace confirmed it with a nod, but before I could get more answers, a car pulled around from the side of the house for Baron Samedi and Maman Brigit. The top-hatted voodoo loa smiled and waved good-bye to me.

"Thanks for everything," I called after them.

"You know how to find us if you need us," he winked. They drove away in their Lincoln Town Car like regular people with slightly eccentric fashion sense. I wondered if I would ever see them again. I knew I wouldn't scoff at *vodoun* anymore. Some things were real, whether one believed or not. Like the fact that I might be a witch.

Lightning cracked, thunder rumbled, and Haley yelped. Kittie Cad hopped in the Nissan, shouting, "Get in, y'all! That's our cue to go."

"Wait, where's Zyr?" I asked.

"Here." Wallace guided the big black wolf that I knew to be my lover to the car. Tegan held up the red gift box Mrs. Ravani had asked her to deliver. She looked around, confused, since she didn't know he was a werewolf, but it dawned on me why he hadn't yet shifted to man-shape. My heart slammed in my chest.

"He's gone," Mys said with difficulty. Haley caught me before I fell, weak with grief, and Mys opened the back door of the Nissan to help me inside. "He went feral. We're lucky the Council didn't realize it, or they would've taken him."

"This . . . is Zyr?" Tegan asked in shock.

Nodding, I beckoned for the wolf, and the guardian brought him forward. The gift box fell from Tegan's numb fingers, spilling open to reveal a thick gold chain. My sobs arrested in my chest. The chain was similar to the ornate collar worn around Loulou's neck. A vague memory of Darcy boasting about controlling her shifts whispered in my mind.

"Give it to me, quickly, Tegan!" I sniffed. My trembling fingers fumbled with the clasp of the chain until Mys took it and did what had to be done. It went around the black wolf's neck, and . . .

There he was. Zyr Ravani was back.

Mys gasped. A fresh wave of tears crested my eyelids. Zyr surged into my arms, and the Empath clung to us too. Wallace quietly materialized something to cover the werewolf's nudity. Once his privacy was restored, the rest of our friends stared, dumbfounded, at Zyr's miraculous recovery.

"How did you know?" Haley asked in awe.

I wordlessly shook my head because I *hadn't* known for sure. I had gone with my gut and taken a chance. Everything that had occurred in Overlay City had transformed me. In some ways, I felt broken. I averted my gaze from the empty space where my leg used to be and peered at the shadowy plantation behind us. In other ways, I was stronger than ever.

I was still in the dark about our destiny, but one thing was certain: I couldn't go back to being the girl who played it safe, the girl with unfinished business. I was a witch, and I would fight for Mys and Zyr no matter what it took. None of us would stop until Darcy Cyprian was put away for good. It had taken losing everything to learn to live my best life. But I had no doubt: this was it.

ACKNOWLEDGMENTS

—

All my love goes to those who helped bring this book to life. As an author, I carry the story within me, but it can only be unlocked with the patience and understanding of my family. The gratitude I feel for my inner circle knows no bounds. When others might have warned me to be realistic, my loving partner encouraged me to pursue my wildest dreams, my teenagers made sure that I, an '80s baby, could authentically connect with Gen Z on the page, and the littlest one of the family picked a fine time to grow up and be a big girl so I could focus on completing my novel. No one outside our home will know the sacrifices we made, but I always say and will forever believe that I have the best team! The five of you are a gift and an inspiration that words fail to do justice.

A special thank-you to Carmen Ho, Jen Hale, Catharine Chen, and Rebecca Sands for their editorial attention to detail. Love and appreciation for my beloved friend Kelly who always reminds me to take a break and be human, rather than reducing myself to just a writer.

Last but not least, I want to shout out the original band of Wattpad readers who were with me from the very beginning of *Lead Me Astray,* with special mention to Sandcat-, NoppityNope666, FMM2310, ClarityNMercy, DomiSotto, Maeve Shawler, and the QF Book Club. Thank you for believing in me.

ABOUT THE AUTHOR

—

Sondi Warner is the author of *Lead Me Astray*, a supernatural polyamorous romance with more than 130 thousand reads on Wattpad. When not writing, Sondi loves studying astrology, trying her hand at gardening, and painting. She lives in Baton Rouge, Louisiana, with her life partner, their four children, and their cat, Se7en.

If you liked *Lead Me Astray*, you'll love

DIRTY LYING FAERIES

by Sabrina Blackburry

When her best friend drags her to an art gala (definitely not her thing), Thea Kanelos doesn't expect a chance encounter with a handsome stranger to change her life forever. That stranger isn't just anyone—he's Devin Grayson, a powerful fae, charged with bringing Thea into his world.

Thea doesn't even believe in faeries. So there's no way she can make sense of becoming one. And her attraction to Devin has an underlying current that sparks, and then flames, into something undeniable—something neither of them can ignore.

Thea soon discovers that she is powerful in her own right and, as cracks in the fae world begin to surface, she may be the only one who can end the conflict that plagues her newfound love and the community they both share.

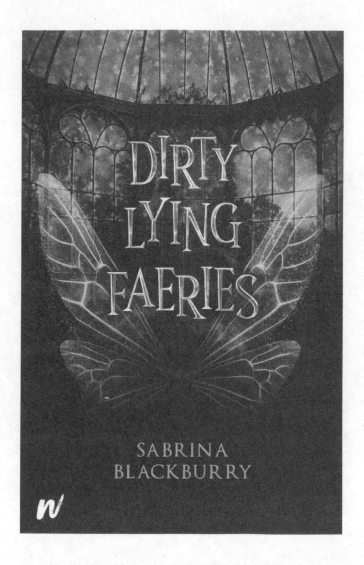

Available Summer 2022 in print and
ebook, wherever books are sold.